*With the Five of the Star separated
from each other and from their allies,
they must find the strength to carry out their
mission, despite their enfeebled states.
Mirauk's phantoms are hunting them,
and as Bahvley strives to remember his forgotten
past, they all face the might of Mirauk's magic
unlike they've ever encountered before.*

<u>Also by Celinka Serre</u>

Stardust Destinies I Variate Facing
Stardust Destinies II The Drought
(https://binkyproductions.com/stardustdestinies)

The Hidden Cove: Pirate's Misadventure
(https://binkyproductions.com/shortstories)

Stardust Destinies Short Stories
(found at https://medium.com/stardust-destinies)

You will find more books
published by Binky Ink at:
https://binkyproductions.com/books

Stardust Destinies

III

A SUBLIME SEARCH

by

CELINKA SERRE

Edited by Cleo Miele

Cover by Binky Ink

Binky Ink
A division of Binky Productions

www.binkyproductions.com/stardustdestinies

Published by Binky Ink
Edited by Cleo Miele
Cover by Binky Ink

ISBN: 978-1-998701-02-5

Dedicated to Vampy,
my dragon counterpart across the ocean.

ACKNOWLEDGEMENTS

I'd like to take a moment to highlight several people who helped make the publication of this book possible.

First off, I would like to thank my team of helpers on the fundraiser who helped plan, provided feedback, and spread the word: Vampy, Robin Wilding, Christine Graves, and Delaney Patterson. Thank you to you lovely ladies, your encouraging words and assistance motivated me while keeping me focused.

Through the fundraiser, I amassed a sizable army of dragons to fight with the Five of the Star for the Freedom of Life, as each contributor became a *Dragon Contributor*. With Green Dragons, Golden Dragons and Wizard Dragons providing much needed support.

Then the Elite Dragons swooped in, showing Mirauk he doesn't stand a chance.

Thank you to *all* my Dragon Contributors. Your donations brought me that much closer to my goals.

<u>Elite Dragons:</u>

Annie Blanchette
Jean-Pierre Bellot
Martin Bourdages
Michael Blatherwick
Miss T. Coyne
Robert Ralph

Last but not least, I must thank my editor, Cleo Miele, who once again did a stellar job at finding errors and providing any necessary adjustments to help make my narrative the best it can be.

And of course, I'd like to thank friends and family, and all my readers, who have enjoyed the two first books thus far and have encouraged me through their feedback and enthusiasm.

Thank you so much to everyone!
May the stars shine upon you!

Table of Contents

Recap On What Happened Last

When last we met our heroes, Tharguen and his team had travelled to Dûnelor. Due to the Dûnelorians' deal with Mork, some Telorians were captured while the others returned home to seek help. As the original plan for the Five had been to travel to the Twisted Forest, the Firlanians, who had come to visit, decided to go in their stead.

In Dûnelor, the Five discovered the deal and eventually reconciled with the Dûnelorians, who then changed their allegiance. However, Morkans were already on their way to capture Tharguen. The battle in Dûnelor served to bolster Niome's power, and upon looking into the Morkan Dukes' eyes, she discovered the existence of secret Morkan tunnels.

Due to everything Niome saw, the plans for the Five changed once again – no longer would they meet the Firlanians at the appointed spot with the others, but they would go their separate way and infiltrate the secret tunnels. This change of plan, however, was a secret. When it came time to part, the Five went into the river – dried up from the drought Niome had created – and left the others to wake to the sound of rushing water filling back in.

Inside the tunnels beneath the river, the Five discovered that the Morkans had been digging their way to Darakön, by order of Kàtchah. Disguising themselves as Morkans, they halted all digging for a time – until Kàtchah arrived.

Jimmy and Meysah left through a secret passage they prepared while undercover, but the others were intercepted before they could escape. They decided to try another way out, but Kàtchah was there waiting for them, accompanied by the Dukes, and recognised who they truly were.

Niome managed to escape on her own and hurried to catch up to Jimmy and Meysah, who were on their way to warn the dragons. Vigh and Boreth remained underground, captured. As Kàtchah sent Morkans after the other three, the two lords quickly sent a warning message to the others. Niome, who had slowed down in the face of a fierce blizzard, decided to make for Firlan. The Five had planned to regroup in the Twisted Forest anyway in the event they were separated.

As for Bahvley, Tharguen and the others, when they saw that the Firlanians were not at the designated meeting place, that the Five had disappeared, and that fire was afar, they too travelled to the Twisted Forest. There, they met the Tellens and found their Firlanian friends – as well as phantoms that sucked on people's blood and took their memories with it. These creatures, brutally strong, were linked spiritually to Mirauk.

The Telorians had seen these same phantoms when travelling to Dûnelor. Many had died due to these beasts. Bahvley grew worried, especially after Mellavøn's death, and became shocked upon remembering that *he* had been attacked by such a phantom long ago. He prayed to Gorthan's star to protect them, protect the Five, and help him remember how to destroy these creatures.

Timeline Review

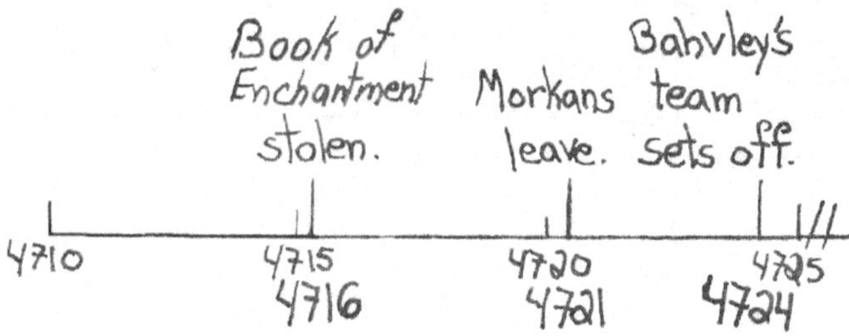

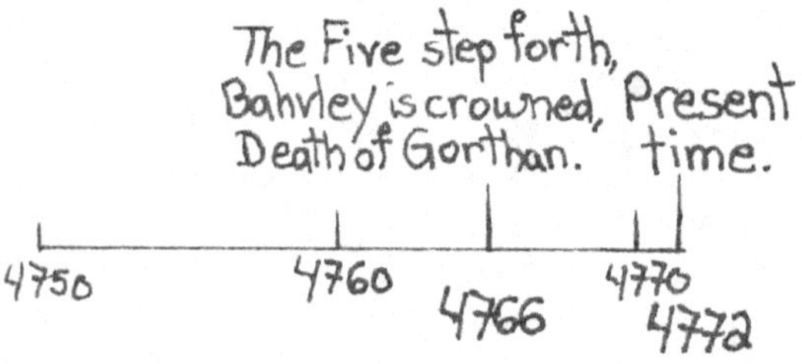

CHAPTER ONE:
Memory Evoked

*A*s the first snow fell, many of the Telorians wished to go out and search for their friends, perhaps even spend some time in the nice fluffy, fresh snow as a change of pace. However, whenever they stepped foot outside, they felt the frigid air, far colder than usual. Like the Tellens had said, this would be the harshest Winter in Kaulchèc history. Even the inner court gardens were closed off due to the cold. In any case, whether day or night, everyone was, in their own way, afraid to go outside – and the reason was clear.

As the days passed, the Telorians prayed for the safety of their vanished friends. As Winter elapsed, time seemed long, dreadfully long to every single one of them, as all they could do was wait, and apprehension set in.

Tharguen's nightmares had stopped; Bahvley was the one having abstract dreams now. He dreamt of the past, of times before the Big War. He dreamt about his fears for Niome and the others. But most importantly, he dreamt, at times, about Gorthan.

One night, Bahvley thought he was having a vision, so real felt his dream, at first. He felt as though he were fully awake, yet how could that be?

He sat up abruptly, making sure he was awake this time, and looked around the small room. *Nothing.* Had someone called his name? He had clearly heard someone calling his name. He lay back down. *Again!* There it was, not as a whisper or a shout, but someone speaking directly to him – someone right next to him.

'Bahvley! Look at me.'

'Who are you?' demanded Bahvley as he sat up, feeling terrified.

'Look at me and you'll know,' said the voice.

'You're hiding! Show yourself! I can't see you!'

'Do not search with your eyes,' the voice said soothingly, 'search with your feelings.'

Bahvley took a deep breath, somehow trusting the voice, then lifted his head. In a moment, he saw.

'No! This is some trick, some spell. How can this be! Gorthan?'

Gorthan stood in the room as solid as a normal polc, just as he had stood for many years before.

'But you're dead!'

Gorthan nodded. 'Yes. When the Morkans tortured me, I took a vow to Teloria,' he explained. 'I would not let them kill me and prevent me from helping my kingdom from the stars. I knew it was my time, that it was either their blade or mine, and I did what had to be done.' He paused. 'Listen to me, Bahvley. I've come to help you, to answer your call.'

'My call?'

'Yes. When you looked up at the stars many, many weeks ago. I've come to reassure you that your wishes have been answered.'

Bahvley merely gaped at him.Gorthan laughed. 'Do not be afraid. I am sure I'm not the first spectacle you've seen.'

'How can I be certain you're Gorthan's spirit?' demanded Bahvley.

'Because when the Moon is new, it is not there to watch over the stars.' Bahvley observed him quizzically as he spoke. 'The Moon protects the stars and ensures they don't fall or fade. It is the master of the stars, but sometimes, it takes a rest of its own and sleeps like every other living creature in this world. At times, when the Moon is hid, the stars shoot across the sky and come down before those who need their aid, and then return to the sky when they are done. I have come to you this night to help you find peace in sleep again.'

'I can hardly believe it,' Bahvley awed.

'You must trust that life has a way of working itself out. Things have happened as they should have, for your safety and for everyone else's. Yes, at times it takes a turn and there are losses – that will always be inevitable – but I am talking about now, about those who matter in the fight against the one polc who needs to be defeated.' A magical shimmer passed through Gorthan's eyes, and it seemed to Bahvley as though he was pondering the deeper meaning of his words.

'As for no one being outside the fortress to greet the Five,' Gorthan went on, 'there is no need. It's been taken care of. They will find elsewhere to spend this Winter, and in safety.'

'Are they safe? Where are they? They are alive, yes?' Bahvley clutched his hands over his heart and bowed his head. 'I wish I could contact them somehow . . .'

'I can only tell you so much. You know the truth in your heart,' said Gorthan. 'You can communicate with them through your feelings.'

'They're safe, or at least they will be.' Bahvley reached into himself, into the magic that ran in his family. 'I sense confusion, but I don't think they're in grave danger.'

'You see? You already knew.'

'Unless the confusion is my own,' admitted Bahvley.

Garthan's features grew sad. 'Tell Tharguen something for me.'

'Of course – anything.'

'Tell him . . . it wasn't his fault.'

'What wasn't his fault?' asked Bahvley, though he already suspected the answer.

'He'll know.'

Bahvley hesitated. 'Can I ask you something? Mellavøn . . . is she a star?'

'Yes, and you can pray to her whenever you need.' Bahvley smiled at his words. 'You've been through a lot. You've suffered severe trauma, Bahvley. Not ever having known or remembered those facts that so suddenly came back to you, having to deal with those memories for the rest of your life now.'

Gorthan sat down on the edge of the bed. 'I want you to think back. I know you're afraid, but this is the only way; avoidance doesn't help anyone. I know you've been through it before, but now, do it and feel it. I want you to think back. Remember it with the knowledge and wisdom you have today, and feel. The boat, the water, the air.'

'It was windy, but not cold. It smelled . . .' began Bahvley. 'Another boat was behind us. Liffwai and I were alone . . .'

* * *

Suddenly, scenes from the past flashed before him until his surroundings were stable and Bahvley was there. It was as though he was reliving the moment, floating beside himself, seeing it as an observer.

He and Liffwai were struggling to steer faster. The wind was on their side, but the other ship had caught up to them anyway. Cahti was with them, as were a few other survivors.

The vision skipped ahead.

A raspy, whispery voice slowly pronounced Bahvley's name.

Bahvley felt cold in the pit of his stomach, just as he had back then. He turned, as did the others, to face eight beings clad in black hooded armour. Sickly white skin and glinting eyes glared at them from beneath their hoods. The beings bore no weapons.

With surprising speed, the beings rushed the Telorians, grabbing them with strong arms, and agilely evaded when the polcs attempted to strike them.

Bahvley lifted his sword and stabbed one in the throat. It placed a hand on the blade and pulled it out.

Unmoving, Bahvley stared at the place where a wound should have been, where blood should have been gushing freely.

'That's not normal,' he muttered. His blood ran cold.

They fought the beings a while longer, and then the phantoms disappeared at the first sign of light.

The vision skipped ahead once more. The Telorians fended off the creatures during the night. The beings were strong and never tired out, and one of them sank its teeth into the shoulder of one of the soldiers who had escaped with them. He screamed agonisingly before going limp, his blood dripping from the creature's canines.

'Stars! These creatures are bloodsuckers,' Bahvley whimpered.

Bahvley grabbed one of the creatures, attempting to pin it down. Liffwai and Cahti joined Bahvley, and together they managed to get the creature down on its back on the deck.

The first light came. The other bloodsuckers vanished, but this one remained.

'Why isn't it disappearing?' cried Liffwai.

'Maybe they can't while they're being pinned down,' suggested Bahvley. 'If we can't enter their realm, then they can't enter it accompanied by us.'

More light came.

The creature stiffened.

'Stab it, now!' cried Bahvley.

Liffwai raised his sword and stabbed down into the creature, then into the wooden deck beneath it as the being turned to ash, leaving only its hooded armour behind.

'We did it!' laughed Liffwai. 'We killed one of them.'

Bahvley marvelled in trepidation. 'What manner of beast is this?! It cannot be this easy. They must be testing our strength. Tonight they'll attack us again surely, harder this time, more fiercely. They know our fighting capacities.'

The vision shifted to a night where only Bahley and Liffwai remained.

'Remember,' said Bahvley, 'they have one weakness, one sensibility: light.'

One of the creatures jumped towards Bahlvey, teeth bared, and Liffwai came between them, blocking its attack. Moving faster than Bahvley's mind could process, the creature tore the chest plate off Liffwai before pulling him close and going at his stomach.

Bahlvey cried out his name as the polc fell onto his back. The creature tore into Liffwai's gut. Liffwai screamed in agony.

Another phantom tore off Bahvley's helmet, and he ducked out of its way.

The vision blurred as it sped through the struggle between Bahvley and the phantoms. At last, he pinned one down.

The creature beneath him twisted its head in an unnatural way, biting into Bahvley's arm.

Bahvley screamed long and hard as he was pinned down heavily by the other creatures. The phantom sank its teeth deeper into his flesh, and he felt it drain him of his blood.

Then Bahvley remembered waking up, being tended to by the Kikies. Liffwai was dead, and Celor had wrapped his comforting arms around Bahvley as he wept for his lost friends.

* * *

Bahvley woke with a jolt. He was dripping with sweat and trembling.

'What . . . what was that?!'

He looked around. It was day – the sun was shining and he was back in his room in the Tellens's Fortress, in his bed, and alone. Still, he knew that Gorthan had come to him. He looked in the direction of the window.

'Thank you, Gorthan. Thank you!'

He dashed out of the room, still in his pyjamas, to find everyone else, for they had some destroying to do.

He ran through the hall shouting joyously, 'Tharguen! Stëinbøk! Hey, everyone! I've got great news!'

Tharguen stopped him in the hall as he ran after him.

'What's all this good news about? I haven't heard you laugh like this since last time we were home.'

'Tharguen, he came to me! Last night.'

'Who?'

'Gorthan! I had a vision.' He shook his head a bit, then steadied himself by putting his hands on Tharguen's shoulders. 'Gorthan appeared to me and spoke to me. He said that Niome was all right, that the Five were safe. And then I had a memory – I saw everything that happened during my journey escaping Mork in the boat.'

Bahvley took a breath. 'I only remembered feelings before, but now I remember every single detail. I remember how the phantoms got me. And I remember how we destroyed them! Come, I have to tell everyone about this!'

'Slow down,' said Tharguen, tugging on his arm. 'You know we can't kill the phantoms this Winter.'

'Of course not – we won't last the long cold night. We need to go till morning, but we should start planning as soon as we can. I tell you, this is the best gift ever!'

'Gift?' asked Tharguen. 'But your birthday was—'

'Last week, I know. Belated gift from the stars! The gift of memory! And a gift it truly is!' Bahvley beamed with hope.

'By the way, you lost me at *"We won't last the long cold night. We need to go till morning."*'

'I'll explain later!'

Tharguen laughed to see his friend so joyous. Since Mellavøn had died, Bahvley had been sorrowful, mostly keeping to himself. Rare was it that anyone saw a bit of a smile at the corner of his mouth. Now, he was full-blown laughing, out of relief.

Bahvley moved to continue down the hall but stopped suddenly, sobering. He met Tharguen's ponderous gaze. 'Gorthan asked me to convey a message to you.' Tharguen's eyes widened in earnest. 'It wasn't your fault,' Bahvley said gently. 'None of it was.'

Tharguen's eyes brimmed with tears as he bowed his head.

'You did what you had to whcn you trained Kàtchah. Gorthan does not blame you for his death.'

'It was a test for him, an opportunity for me,' whispered Tharguen. 'In the end, the training I gave him allocated him the mission to Teloria and permitted him to capture and torture Gorthan.'

'In Gorthan's words, it wasn't your fault,' Bahvley repeated soothingly.

Tharguen's mouth twisted in sorrow and he let out a sob. He pulled Bahvley into a hug. Bahvley returned the embrace comfortingly, and Tharguen wept for a few moments like that.

He pulled away and wiped his eyes. 'Thank you, Bahvley. It means more than I can convey.' He looked up towards the sky, knowing Gorthan would receive his intent. 'Thank you, Gorthan.'

A group soon gathered to discuss Bahvley's newfound memories, some of whom would then convey to the others what had been discovered. Present were Tharguen, Stëinbøk, Hunbøk and Derfbøk, Celor, Tithil, Mië and Dessimë, and Kchalami as well, all huddled in a room near the lounge area.

'I fear their skills have changed,' said Tharguen once Bahvley explained all he had seen and felt. 'Perhaps improved, if they've existed for that long a time. Mirauk must keep them in hiding in order to keep them hungry and lusting for blood and then unleash them when necessary.' There was a long pause. 'It might explain how Mirauk knew about you and knew of your power. How he knew you had escaped. I sometimes wonder if he truly had a vision or if he'd heard rumour of you through the phantoms instead.'

Bahvley rubbed his chin. 'Might explain him not recognising me, unless that truly was due to my inner magic. And then I escaped him.'

'Precisely,' Tharguen agreed, 'you escaped and survived. That's why you were such a threat to him.'

'But why not kill Bahvley off?' asked Hunbøk. 'Why didn't they suck more memory out of him? They were close to doing so in the first place.'

'Daylight was approaching when they got me,' said Bahvely.

'They could have come back,' voiced Stëinbøk.

'They were too close to our land,' concluded Celor. 'Our magic created a protective perimeter; Bahvley must've entered that bubble before the following night. If the phantoms are afraid of us, it would explain why they didn't heed you when we saw them on our way to Dûnelor.'

'How can they be so frightened of us?' inquired Tithil. 'We can't read their minds, they are blank to us – they're almost invincible.'

'It may be the medicine,' pondered Dessimë. 'For one thing, we shrink; we're almost invincible ourselves. I mean, have you ever met another being who shrinks, flies fast, floats in midair, and can stay in a magical jar and rematerialise or unshrink at any moment we choose? Furthermore, our medicine has a different kind of power than any I've seen on this continent so far. Our medicine helps those struck by the phantoms a lot better than any other.'

'It's not the *medicine*,' said Mië, 'it's our *magic*. You said it yourself, Dessimë, we shrink. We have abilities no polc has. Certain powers or spells, we have not yet used here or showed the polcs. We are too happy a folk for the evildoers – our hearts are too pure for them. Our goodness and love for life, nature, and people is so strong that if we fight them, we will overpower them, these creatures that are evil.'

She leaned forward in her seat. 'I remember Niome telling me her theory that there may be a chance Kikies are not affected by Mirauk's curse the same way polcs are or at all. That for us – being so, well, Kiki – looking into his eyes may not curse us, or perhaps only make us a little ill.' She studied the polcs. 'Do you understand what I'm trying to say?'

'I do,' said Kchalami with a nod. 'And if that is so, when we fight them you must not appear until later on, for if they know you're there, they won't approach you.'

'That's why when you entered the forest, they never went after you,' Derfbøk mused. 'You were full-fledged targets, yet they did not give chase. When we arrived at the fortress together, the phantom near the gates left. But when you travelled to retrieve the injured, the Kikies were not with you, and so the phantoms could attack.'

'I'll need all me best polcs out there,' sighed Stëinbøk, worry on his face, 'when time comes that we must fight.'

'My team will be with you,' said Tharguen. 'Some may be afraid or not yet ready. I'll give them the choice, for this will be their second real battle in their lives, but many, I know, will want to join the fight.'

'The Firlanians are all with you. That, I can tell you now,' said Kchalami. 'I know my friends well, and I believe none will want to miss this opportunity. It's a risk I'm willing to take.'

'By now the phantoms must have evolved, as Tharguen suggested. They must have become more sophisticated and advanced, both mentally and physically, these . . . monsters.' Bahvley shuddered. 'They were young then and satisfied with the little blood they got. It's obvious now they need a lot more; they're hungrier. They will be vicious, more aggressive, stronger. They know more than they did before when they were newly formed. But we, too, know more, and we are stronger also. We must work out a good strategy for this to work. Otherwise, we risk putting ourselves and everyone else in great peril.'

Out in the hall, Pete and Jeremy stood right outside the room, ears to the door, anxious and curious. Both were eager to know it all right away. As they listened to every word being said, they reacted silently.

Suddenly, someone pulled them away from the door. The two young polcs fell and looked up at the two somebodies: Neyith and Mimulus.

'Feeling a little impatient, are we?' asked Neyith.

'It's quite rude, you know,' chided Mimulus.

'We're allowed to find out,' protested Jeremy, not fond of being treated as though he were a child.

'Yes, but all in due time, my dear Telorian friend,' said Neyith.

'I don't see anything wrong with eavesdropping,' stated Pete.

'Eavesdropping,' began Mimulus, 'the word you use when overhearing while passing by and minding your own business. I believe you were spying.'

'And you two need to work on your spying skills,' said Neyith. The Telorians frowned.

'Perhaps next time you should try hiding in the room instead of plunking yourselves down in plain view,' suggested Mimulus.

'That's right,' said Neyith. 'For if you need to spy on enemy grounds, if you do it the way you're doing it now, you'll get caught. Here, well, some people may simply take offence.'

'But who has taken offence?' asked Pete. 'You?'

'Well, no, not exactly,' said Neyith.

'Uhuh-aha-ah-ah-uh!' exclaimed Jeremy in triumph.

'Who says we weren't passing by and heard something that caught our attention and decided to hear the details?' said Pete. 'Hm.'

'But there's a reason you weren't called to that meeting,' Mimulus pointed out.

'But we were only going to be told what was discussed afterwards anyway,' said Pete.

'Maybe not *everything*,' said Neyith.

'Well, we've missed too much of it now to know more of what's going on,' complained Jeremy.

'I bet you spy often,' Pete accused, 'you Kiki tele-paths. You probably wanted to spy yourselves but couldn't 'cause *we* were here.'

'Telorians,' muttered Mimulus, 'they're impossible! They love arguments. Simple things, said and done and understood in an instant, are taken and analysed and debated about and turned into arguments. How do they do it without driving each other mad?'

'We have mind battles,' said Neyith. 'It's the same thing.'

'Huh?' voiced Pete.

'We just wanted a little fun,' Jeremy sighed as the two walked away.

'What did I tell you?' said Mimulus.

'I think all polcs are like that,' reflected Neyith.

'No wonder Morkans love to quarrel with each other. I tell you, Neyith, we need to learn more about polc behaviour.'

'They're a complicated race.'

'Well, someone's got to do it,' insisted Mimulus.

'Good luck. I think I'll just stick with what I know now.'

'Sometimes I wonder if they like to hear themselves speak.'

'I know I do at times,' admitted Neyith.

'Oh my goodness, we're turning into polcs! We're arguing out loud!'

'That's a first! Mimulus, you do have a point . . . let's try to understand why arguing is like a sport to them.'

'And so?' demanded Lóim.

'We missed most of it because the Kikies told us it wasn't proper to "spy",' complained Jeremy.

'I wanted to know how to kill those monsters,' Huck said with disdain.

'Well, we heard that much,' said Pete.

'You hold them down until daylight!' asserted someone from behind the lads.

Pete and Jeremy turned their heads to see who it was and swallowed hard.

'Captain,' said Pete.

'Perhaps you'd like to join us?' said Tharguen.

'Uh, no – well . . .' stumbled Pete and Jeremy simultaneously.

Tharguen chuckled. 'Well don't look so worried. I'll tell you everything later.'

Indeed, everyone found out everything they needed to.

Slowly, a plan was devised, a strategy perfected. Anyone who had any ideas was free to share. Many of the polcs were eager for Spring to arrive so that they could get out there and destroy the phantoms once and for all, but others were frightened. Many from Tharguen's team preferred to remain inside to heal those who were sure to come back injured. It was necessary to keep many indoors and alive, and thus all had their role.

When the snow had almost completely melted, many Tellens returned to their posts at the shelters, mostly in case the five Telorians would arrive. No one spoke of the attack plan outside the fortress walls, aiming to catch the phantoms completely by surprise. No one truly knew if the phantoms understood the common tongue – they only knew they spoke the Morkan speech – but they preferred to play it safe.

When it was warm enough to stand a fight for a whole night, but still cool enough that the sun was not punishing or the heat not exhausting, Bahvley and Stëinbøk agreed that it was time.

On the third day of the fifth week of Spring, they stepped out. They were heading for the small clearing southeast of the fortress, two days away. They weren't going to let the phantoms hide from them in the forest; they wanted clear sunlight on them for when morning came, and for that, they had to begin the fight there at the clearing and wrestle until morning.

As they walked, they spoke of a celebration – that they had newly invented – for the founding of the Tellens' place in the forest. They also spoke of how they 'thought the phantoms were gone' so the creatures would think they could attack without any polc knowing of their presence. But they all knew the phantoms were lurking close at hand.

Stëinbøk had brought with him his best polcs for sprinting and fighting as well as those who wished to avenge themselves or a lost friend. Hunbøk, Derfbøk, Lernarbøk, Vessibøk, Merilenk, Nastafin, Dublenk, Corivøn and Attëgon were the brave Tellens to venture out with their King.

All the Firlanians had come as well as all the Kikies, who were in their jar at the moment – no one wanted the phantoms to sense their presence.

The Telorians who joined the fighters had been divided into two groups: those who would fight from the start, and those who would join in later or replace a recovering fellow knight. Some of the Firlanians would do the same, hiding up in the trees with the Telorians.

The small army walked briskly, resting at night at a shelter before continuing the next day. They reached the clearing before nightfall. Those of the second group of fighters quickly climbed to the safety of the trees near the shelter with some of the Firlanians who guarded the Kiki jar. The others prepared a bonfire below and sang a bit as the sun slowly set.

As soon as the last ray of light vanished, the five phantoms appeared before the polcs.

CHAPTER TWO:
Enduring the Night

As the polcs all watched the beastly creatures approach, pretending to be shocked, they each thought about what Bahvley had told them before leaving the fortress.

Arrows will be of no use – they won't damage them. A thrust of the sword will cause them to stagger back. A hit on the head may weaken them. A hit anywhere else may or may not injure them. The best way to battle them and defend yourselves is hand-to-hand combat.

Tharguen had coached the Firlanians and Tellens on some tricks he'd learned in Mork; his team was well-prepared for such combat already.

We must fool them into fighting us, Tharguen had instructed. _If we wait until morning to fight them, they will not engage. It's either all night or no fight._

One of the phantoms intoned in a hoarse voice, loud and clear despite its hazy form, _'Fekhisar bodokhlogat!'_

'Oh, you're not going to get any of mine,' Tharguen growled under his breath.

Bahvley unsheathed his sword. 'It's time to pay, you murderers!' he shouted.

Everyone hefted their weapons. The fight had begun.

The phantoms pounced at the polcs, receiving stabs and kicks in return. These Morkan beings were quick, for they had indeed evolved. So many polcs against so few enemies, yet they still had a hard time fighting them.

One phantom backed away from the fray before running back with such force, it pushed so many of the polcs to the ground. The creature then grabbed whoever still stood and hurled them onto the dirt.

In its fury, it grabbed Elmezni by the neck from behind. Struggling to pull himself out of the chokehold, Elmezni slashed with his sword, but the phantom yanked the blade out of his grasp and tossed it to the ground.

Elmezni felt the cold breath on his neck and heard the glee and satisfaction as its breath caught. He felt teeth sliding on his neck, searching for a vein.

Then he was pulled back and pushed forward, freed of its grasp. He spun around to see the phantom on the ground, a Tellen trying to strangle it with her sword.

'Are you okay?' she asked the Firlanian. He recognised her – it was Nastafin.

'I'm fine. Thank you,' Elmezni replied quickly as he picked up his sword.

Elmezni rushed to her side and bashed the phantom on its head with the hilt of his sword. The phantom ceased pushing against Nastafin's sword and rolled away, darting towards other fighters.

'These sure are difficult,' sighed Nastafin. 'Superb strength and magic combined.'

'We'll get them. I thank you again, Nastafin.'

'No problem.'

With one last glance, each ran in a different direction to help elsewhere.

Merilenk and Akchmassiel fought side by side along with Attëgon. Together, they had staggered away from the group for just a moment.

'You okay?' asked Attëgon.

'Yes, I'm only a little . . . how could I say it?' began Merilenk.

'Overwhelmed?' suggested Akchmassiel. 'Considering what happened to us.'

'Oh, but it's time for vengeance!' declared Merilenk.

Akchmassiel sensed a presence behind them. Glancing at the closest bundle of fighters, he recognised four of the figures. Attëgon and Merilenk exchanged a glance of suspicion while he clasped his sword hilt tightly.

Akchmassiel gave a signal that only the other two could understand: a count to three corresponding to three long blinks. They then spun around and pounced at the phantom, sending it to the ground. Akchmassiel slashed its leg while Merilenk impaled it through the stomach, but the phantom was so in need of blood, it had none to bleed out.

The creature stood, looking weakened, and breathed deeply. Then it clutched all three polcs in its muscular arms and lifted them with little effort, carrying them somewhere they knew not.

Kchalami, Bahvley, Saviel, and Eerzin soon came running to their aid, freeing their friends from the wretched beast's grasp. Bahvley glared at the phantom as the others held it back. Eerzin unhooded it to reveal a sickly pale face with dark rings under its eyes, gleaming dark eyes paired with pointy teeth crying out for blood.

'Long time no see,' seethed Bahvley. 'Here, take this!'

He punched the creature in the face, though the phantom fought back. It felt good, even if it didn't seem to hurt it.

Kchalami took his shield and banged the phantom's head. The phantom paused but a beat before it recovered all too quickly.

To think that we have to keep on like this all night . . . Bahvley looked up for a quick glance at the stars. 'Some inspiration for some fighting tricks would be great just about now!'

At the other end of the clearing fought Mittah and Jeremy along with Aterel, Mishcal, and Laurelmi. They had just rid themselves of one phantom that they then tossed to some Tellens, making for yet another slightly weakened phantom that would be a little easier for them to pin to the ground. Mittah bent over and took a deep breath.

'What's the matter?' asked Jeremy. 'Feeling tired?'

'Are you joking?' said Mittah. 'I'm just getting warmed up here! Trust me, if I was tired, I'd be lying on the ground.'

'Well, you gave me a fright there,' admitted Jeremy.

'*That's* a fright!' gasped Mittah, pointing at an incoming phantom.

Laurelmi delivered a high-angled roundhouse kick to its neck, but the creature grabbed his leg. Mishcal grabbed the phantom's arms and pulled them back as the others tugged their friend towards them, successfully freeing him.

The phantom came at them once more. It grabbed Mittah by the throat, choking her, and pushed the others to the ground. Stëinbøk came running seemingly out of nowhere and kicked the phantom's hands, causing them to loosen their grip on Mittah. The others shoved the phantom a ways off to fight it, leaving Mittah to recover.

'Thanks,' Mittah rasped with a cough.

'No problem. Are you okay?' Stëinbøk gently touched his fingers to her throat. 'You've got a bruise,' he said, concerned.

'Nothing I can't handle,' replied Mittah. 'It's going to take a lot more than that to put me out of the fight. Come on, let's go help the others.'

The battle raged on like this for quite some time. Tharguen was quite the match up against the phantoms, for he knew all their techniques, their tricks, and their language. At the very least, he was glad to have been in Mork for that one reason. He overheard the phantoms whispering about a backup plan, but he was on top of them before they could take their next breath.

Some of the fighters were beginning to show signs of fatigue. Some Telorians wanted to rest, as did a few of the Tellens. The Firlanians were still going strong, however, and the others up in the trees had adrenaline coursing inside them. As fighters climbed up, the phantoms moved towards the trees, looking suspicious.

Many of the other knights let themselves fall from the branches. Krystal and Malcom landed right on a phantom, and it lost its balance and fell onto its stomach. Krystal sat on its shoulders, Malcolm on its lower back as the phantom struggled, moving frantically.

'Pass me your shield,' said Krystal. 'Let's teach this Morkan a lesson.' Malcolm handed her his shield, and she banged the phantom on the head. It went limp. 'There we go,' she said smugly, handing back the shield. They both stood. 'I think I knocked it unconscious.'

'It doesn't seem so . . .' quavered Malcolm.

They still turned to leave the premises, though Malcolm remained wary and held his sword at the ready. After a few steps, he turned around with a great cry and jabbed his sword into the body of the phantom who now stood just half a step away from them, ready to pounce.

When Malcolm retrieved his sword, the phantom's face paled as it fell to its knees. Its eyes went blacker and blacker, a crimson ring forming around the pupils, and moments later it was up again, running after them.

Bahvley stood back a moment and thought to himself, *Only until morning.* Though in truth, this seemed like the longest night of his life. Kchalami, Derfbøk, Lenarbøk, and Dublenk stood by his side.

'This is worse than any army of Morkans,' Dublenk said gravely.

'It is,' agreed Lenarbøk. 'I don't know what could be worse than this.'

'Mork,' said Bahvley.

'I guess I had forgotten about that,' admitted Lenarbøk.

'I suppose there are much worse creatures than this in Mork,' mused Derfbøk. 'Still, these are bad enough. They've been destroyin' me friends, but they won't destroy me!'

He charged, and the others followed.

From up above, the others had a good vantage point. Tom observed that the phantoms were staying away from the not-so-big bonfire. He turned to the others, smirking as he devised his plan.

'How many of you have arrows to spend?' he asked.

'Arrows won't do anything,' objected Hunbøk.

'Oh, yes, they will,' asserted Tom, 'if thrown in a circle and lit by fire. With a spell, I'll have those phantoms in a controlled ring of fire. They'll have no choice but to stop and answer Captain Tharguen's questions.'

'I've got a few arrows,' said Corivøn.

'So do I,' said Vessibøk.

'I have some, too,' said Fimrel. 'We will need to coordinate so we can effectively form that ring and leave no gaps.'

'Great.' Tom nodded. 'Do you think you can make that ring of arrows without harming anyone?'

'If we do this quickly,' answered Corivøn. 'And effectively, indeed,' she added, nodding towards Fimrel.

Positioning themselves, they readied their bows.

On the ground, the phantoms had begun to move more chaotically. The Firlanians stuck together while the Telorians had moved away a bit, thinking they could escape for a short rest, but it had proven useless. The phantoms were fast and could easily jump over the polcs to reach other polcs.

One of the creatures pounced onto Gahli. She kicked forth and back, striking it on the head and on the knees, and shoved to get past it but fell flat on her back. Ihal and Huck rushed over, grabbing the phantom. Huck was pushed to the ground, but Ihal pulled herself back up and swung her sword so hard, the phantom fell.

Gahli got to her feet and the two girls hurried to Huck's side, still on the ground.

'I hit my head,' Huck groaned. 'Everything's spinning. When I move I feel nauseous.'

'We'll help you up,' said Gahli.

'Better to be sick than badly injured,' said Ihal.

Lóim and Pete rushed over as Gahli held Huck's hand and gently pressed her other hand to his forehead to ease the ache. Pete knelt behind and slowly lifted Huck's back as the other two supported him.

A dark booted foot abruptly landed on Huck's chest, pushing him back down. Everyone looked up – the phantom. Lóim and Ihal pushed and punched at it while Gahli and Pete helped Huck to his feet as quickly as they could, but the phantom shoved everyone away, grabbing Huck and digging its teeth into the polc's stomach.

The others came at the monster from all sides and pulled it away, forcing it to stagger away from the group. Huck stood, a little shaky, forgetting his nausea.

Tharguen rushed over to them, fear on his face.

'I'm fine,' said Huck. 'It didn't have time to get a taste of my blood.'

'No, but it had time to dig its teeth into you all the same,' said Lóim, noticing the bloodstain on Huck's leathers. It was growing bigger, and rapidly.

'We have to take care of that,' said Tharguen.

Tom had since crawled down and informed a few people of his plan, instructing them to force the phantoms together. When Tharguen got wind of Tom's deduction that the phantoms detested fire, he carried Huck to the bonfire and set him down gently.

'I think I'm beginning to feel the effects of blood loss,' admitted Huck.

'Just hang in there, Huck.'

So brutal, thought Tharguen as he wrapped the wound up with some cloth. Truthfully, he didn't know how much longer Huck would last. Where were Lenarbøk and Vessibøk? They could carry him away to safety. There was no time to lose.

As Tharguen rose, the phantoms gathered, Tellens and Firlanians forcing them closer to the fire. He knew it was now or never for Tom's plan.

Arrows shot down in a flash as Tom uttered the spell.

Eriëf daresap!
Itahlogim ereiëf!
Morilf aginer!

Fire formed a blistering boundary all around the phantoms, and Tharguen found himself in the middle of it. Huck, thankfully, was on the outside.

Tom frowned, feeling he should have been more prudent. Several Tellens and Firlanians were caught within the ring as well.

Tharguen looked about, turning around in a circle on himself. It was like in his dream – a ring of fire – and he was drenched in blood, stained on the side and in the front, though it wasn't his own.

The phantoms circled slowly around the ring, watching Tharguen as he walked in the same way, watching them, he and the five phantoms each at a different extremity. Tharguen tightly held his sword by his side in one hand.

'*Wakhik hakhev kuyokh echom hakereth?*' Tharguen quavered.

He was bound to find out sooner or later why they were here and what they wanted. Some of the phantoms showed surprise when he spoke their language, but the others, inexplicably, seemed to know him.

He went on, '*Wokh dikhed Mirauk colmakh nekedh kuyotho kitgok retakhif?*'

'Fairhaven!'

'I'm right here!' Bahvley taunted, glaring at them from across the tall flames. They did not respond.

'Bahvley?' Tharguen asked the phantoms.

'*Ewekhewer deskirpakh chussaro kiteskë mikh akvelrig,*' said another one of the phantoms, '*tukheb ekhsi tokhan wokhew tanwakh.*'

'*Wokh nekedh!*' Tharguen demanded with more authority.

'Niome Fairhaven!' said a third.

'What are they saying about Niome?' asked Tom, deeply concerned.

'They want her,' said Tharguen, his blood running cold amidst the scorching heat. 'That's what they came here for. They're looking for Niome.'

'They'll never have that satisfaction!' declared Bahvley. 'They may try to harm my sister, but they'll have to deal with me first.'

'Oh, they'll have to deal with me, too,' seethed Tharguen. 'Perhaps they ought to know she's not here. You got that, phantoms? *Niome si tokhan hakereth!*'

There was some grumbling among the shadowy forms.

'Tharguen,' said Bahvley, 'tell them we won't let them kill Niome.'

'*Ew wokhnit khetel kuyoth khikli kerkh.*'

'*Mirauk odkez tokhan tanwakh kerkh adekhed.*'

'*Takhwodkez ekh tanwakh?*' asked Tharguen, not understanding what the phantoms meant.

'What did it say about Mirauk?' asked Bahvley.

'I don't understand,' replied Tharguen. 'They claim he doesn't want her dead.'

'*Okit konowë wok hokit yirotesdeth kefiv!* . . . *Achnad kuyokh.*'

'You may try to kill me . . . but you'll never destroy the Five!' growled Tharguen. 'I will never let you hurt Niome!' he yelled out as he charged.

'No, don't!' shouted Bahvley.

As the flames extinguished, everyone rushed towards the phantoms, pouncing on them. The beasts, already on top of Tharguen, could have killed him had Tom not undone the fire spell.

'Die!' shouted Tharguen, hacking away angrily, albeit uselessly. 'Why can't you just die and leave us alone?! You bloodsuckers!'

'It's time!' yelled Bahvley, looking to the trees. 'Release them!'

Jeremy unstoppered the Kiki jar and all the Kikies flew down, taking on their larger forms, many of them on top of the phantoms already.

When the polcs touched the phantoms with fire, it weakened them substantially – not to mention their apparent panic at the presence of the Kikies.

The dark sky was no longer at its twilight. Day was perhaps a ray of light away.

At times the ghostly forms broke free, trying to flee, but the Kikies caught them again and again. The phantoms, now trapped, finally understood the polcs' plans.

'Just a final push!' cried Bahvley as flashes of Liffwai came to mind, scenes of their struggles on the stolen Morkan ship. 'We're almost there, we've almost won! We're doing it – we're destroying them!' He held on more fiercely as the haze of near-light touched the horizon. 'This is for Cahti, and Liffwai,' he seethed at the phantom beneath him.

Another slight ray came in to lift the darkness from the clearing. Still they waited for daylight.

One of the phantoms began to move more vigorously, biting and gnawing its way out the polcs' grasp, injuring those who held it. This phantom was more strongly built than the others – the same one that had bitten Bahvley all those years ago. It had also spoken to Tharguen more than its comrades during the fight.

'Hold it down! Don't let it escape!' cried Tharguen. 'This one must be the first of the phantoms, their leader – the most powerful one.'

Though everyone gave it their all, after thrashing about enough times, the phantom managed to crawl away from the grip of those who held it. It glanced back one last time at Tharguen, sneering, and before all of their eyes, it vanished.

Tharguen wanted to yell, *No!* but the protest got stuck in his throat.

A ray of bright light shone onto the clearing – at last, day had arrived.

The four remaining phantoms turned to four large piles of ash. Some of the Telorians fell through the air and collapsed on the ground, their grip had been so strong when the dust was formed from the enemy bodies.

'It is the dust Mirauk created them from,' voiced Celor. 'Trying to be a better creator than the Mighty Spirit herself, creating these phantoms indeed in his own image, and now, they are no more.'

Tharguen stood still, horrified.

'It's not over. One is still out there.' He pointed towards the north. 'And . . . and it's going to try to find Niome.' His voice shook, and his eyes stung with tears. 'After all our struggle . . .'

He put his head in his hands and wept, from fear, from pain, from exhaustion.

Bahvley put a hand on his shoulder. He too felt dismayed.

'It's not fair,' Bahvley despaired in almost a whisper.

In the aftermath of the fight, many of the injured returned to the fortress. Huck was still conscious, and the wound had stopped bleeding. He was carried off by the Tellens. Some lingered at the clearing with Tharguen and Bahvley, who ate, slept, and waited for the next night, but the remaining phantom did not return. Dejected, they travelled back to the fortress. All were instructed to report any sightings of the phantom by sounding the Horns of Earnestness. Stëinbøk sent out several messengers to give the new order.

However, days and weeks later, there was still no sign of it. It had almost certainly left the Twisted Forest, looking for Niome.

CHAPTER THREE:
Interrupted Hibernation

Temperatures dropped, but that didn't stop Jimmy or Meysah. They pushed on, knowing much relied on them, and especially knowing the enemy was in pursuit. As the wind picked up and brought in clouds, it rained ice pellets and soaked the two Telorians to the bone, even if they used Meysah's shield for shelter.

Still they went on, wet or dry, taking any means they could think of to stay warm and alive: fire, food, movement. Niome had previously taught Meysah a couple of spells to keep warm, but the cold of evil snuffed them out quickly. Only every few attempts did he succeed in casting the spells properly, but they helped all the same, and tremendously at that.

The Kiki medicine given to them proved most effective and perhaps even saved them from death, for it kept their bodies feeling warm and boosted their energy.

When the rain stopped, there was a thick layer of ice on the snow. The two no longer sunk into it, but skidded atop it. It was a good thing they weren't on the Hills, but they were coming close to the mountains, and the ground began to slope upwards. They had to use their swords as walking sticks, picking them into the ice so as not to slide down in the opposite direction, nearer the army following them.

Wind picked up again, bringing in more clouds. The lads feared more rain – or worse still, a blizzard, and indeed there was, but only when Darakön was less than a day away.

When they arrived at last, in the early light of Colouring the eighty-third, Jimmy and Meysah were just about ready to collapse. They walked now in the slightly warmer tunnels. They took the left tunnel, for they knew where it led – the dip.

At the dip, they walked into one of the lower tunnels and into an alcove before coming upon a sleeping dragon. They stood in awe, shivering from the cold, while watching it breathe and marvelling at their magical survival.

'Speak to it,' whispered Jimmy.

'*You* speak to it! I don't want to be thrown across the room.'

Jimmy got slightly closer to the dragon.

'Uh, excuse me. Excuse me!'

The dragon opened a single great eye, and Jimmy backed away. It stared at the Telorians for a tense moment before snorting out and rising to its feet, both eyes now fixed on the knights.

'We would've knocked, but you were asleep, so we thought we'd wake you quietly,' explained Meysah. 'We came to warn you—'

'First,' interrupted Jimmy, 'do you remember us?' He looked at Meysah. 'Need to be sure.'

The dragon nodded and gently touched Jimmy with its paw on the spot of his chest where his scar remained, as though it knew he had experienced severe wounds at the doorstep of their home many years ago.

Meysah continued, 'We got separated from the others. We came to warn you that Morkans plan to attack you.'

The dragon stood on its many legs, now alert, and walked passed the lads to the dip – the two followed. The dragon called out to its kin, shrieking, and then many other dragons entered the area. Some even appeared out of nowhere, for they had been stone-sleeping and now moved away from the walls. The knights awed at the sight as all the dragons turned to them.

'I think they want to hear the story in full,' said Jimmy.

'We discovered secret tunnels,' Meysah stated, projecting clearly through the cavern, 'made by Morkans.' He began to summarise the situation, explaining what had happened to the Five to bring Meysah and Jimmy to Darakön and how Kàtchah believed the books to be intact and hidden here.

'That's why we came to warn you,' said Jimmy. 'So that you can fight the Morkans off and protect your home.'

The dragons seemed to be agreeing. One of them approached the young knights and presented them its claw before taking hold of them and flying upward. It brought the Telorians to a hidden room and placed them at its entrance, blew a jet of fire into the room, and flew off.

It was a polc-sized room found at the top of the tall, steep broken stairway, high above all else, a platform before it serving as a makeshift balcony. It was moderately furnished with chairs and hay for a bed. A fireplace was now lit. A cord line near the fire indicated where the Telorians could put their wet clothes to dry. The room also housed a small kitchen set and a stocked pantry, and a cauldron sat over the fire as well. On the far wall stood a tall bookcase. Inside, they sensed the very strong presence of enchantment.

'Someone must've stayed here long ago,' mused Meysah as he and Jimmy donned warm robes that had been conveniently lying on the bed.

'Perhaps the polc who wrote the Dragon Prophecies,' suggested Jimmy, passing his fingers along the books on the shelves. His hand stopped at one of them. 'Look, a diary.' He pulled the book out and opened it as Meysah prepared some herbal tea.

Jimmy sat on the rocking chair, reading aloud. *"Summer the twenty-third, three ten. I have come to write the Dragon Prophecies."* I knew it! Told you so.'

Meysah turned to Jimmy, his curiosity piqued, as Jimmy continued.

"'I have established myself here. The dragons are caring well for me. As I see their visions, they see mine own. That is why they have chosen me. I visited them in my youth with my visions, and they listened after looking into my soul. That is how I knew they could see what I saw, and in turn I could see what they saw. I have now returned to them, after living in Teloria all these years.'"

Meysah poured the tea into two cups and then leaned against the wall, folding his arms and listening quietly.

"The visions never stopped, and I have written everything down. Now, there are even more than ever before coming to my mind and the dragons are helping me decipher it all.

"'I don't have much time left. I need peace and quiet and full concentration to write these prophecies. I am certain anyone else who will stay here will find it as hospitably warm as I do. I need to complete this before my time is up. Then, I wish to write about the apparitions and dreams that come to me – flashes of the future, as opposed to in meditation with the dragons." Oh, so not only was he a Dragon Prophet, but he had his own visions too.'

Jimmy continued. *"I want to return to Teloria, however. I know it will change drastically over the centuries to come. Thankfully, I will not be around when the dark times come. I will not go through the Portal, either, but become a simple star. Anyone who reads this will understand why, because they know now why they are in this room.*" He knew we would be here today – he knew we'd be reading this. And he left us some robes. How about it!'

Jimmy paused, his eyebrows raising. 'Wait . . . if this was written in 310 of Kaulchèc History, how am I able to understand it and read it as though it were written today?'

'Let me see.' Meysah took the book and read in his head. 'I understand it too. Isn't it in one of the ancient forms of the Common Tongue?'

'Maybe a spell was put on it?' Jimmy suggested, putting his finger on the book. 'Or on this room?'

'Or on us! Maybe suddenly we know the old language.'

Both knights walked out onto the balcony and studied the book. It seemed like a jumble of gibberish to them, and they could no longer decipher any words. It was in the ancient tongue, which they could not understand, let alone read. When they re-entered the room, however, the text appeared to them as though written in the modern Common Tongue.

'Very strange indeed.' Jimmy pointed at some biscuits. 'Don't take those snacks out there – I'd rather not know I'm eating food that might have rotted millenia ago.'

Meysah shrugged away the comment. 'Well, we know the dragons are letting us rest and recover here, so let's take advantage of their hospitality.'

'Maybe by reading more, we'll find the answers to our questions.'

'Maybe.'

'But first,' said Jimmy, 'hot tea and some sleep.'

Indeed, the dragons allowed the lads to rest and recover. Many times, the massive creatures came to check on them.

There seemed to be an enormous amount of provisions: nuts, dried fruit, pickled vegetables, dried and seasoned meats, cheese, crackers, biscuits. It all seemed to have never spoiled. They even opened the jars and tasted the contents to check, though they never took the food out of the room to test Jimmy's theory. They also observed that stepping out of the room after eating did not affect them, so with that they concluded the food was safe for consumption.

Jimmy and Meysah continued reading the diary to learn more about the Dragon Prophet and about this room. The polc had documented all of his thoughts and experiences. Indeed, there *was* a spell on the room – everything in it was seemingly untouched by time, as though it were still new. Hence the fresh-tasting food, the overall cleanliness, and the furniture smelling freshly done, like when they would walk into the shop of Lestomil the carpenter. The wood by the fireplace looked freshly cut, and the books on the shelf appeared to have been written that very same year.

Perhaps the preservation spell was also a renewal spell, renewing the room's contents to match the polcs inside and the time in which they lived. Perhaps someone would enter centuries later and it would match *their* time. Jimmy and Meysah were only glad that there existed such a spell, for surely they could keep their rations for when they travelled.

'I wonder,' expressed Meysah as the two lads sat on the edge of the bed, 'if we stay here long enough, will we age? Perhaps this polc came to write here to pause his ageing. He obviously set all these spells.'

"And if you're reading this now, then you know what you must do. I will reveal a secret to you: the dragons knew you would come." What?' gasped Jimmy. 'But they were asleep! *"Don't be fooled now, they were sleeping lightly."'* Jimmy made a face, rolling his eyes, as Meysah laughed internally. *"And the one who awoke first was awaiting your presence. It takes a lot more than a simple 'excuse me' to wake a dragon."* How did he know that?'

'He was a prophet,' said Meysah. '*Hellooo,*' he mocked. 'Or maybe he tried it himself. Read on.'

"A lot relies on the two of you. Yes, I regret to say that the other three of your party will not be joining you this New Year."'

'He really did know a lot. I guess those dreams connecting with the dragons were quite useful.'

'Oh, how he communicated with the dragons is still a mystery to me,' said Jimmy. 'Each strange sound is perhaps a word or expression. What they say beats me, and how they understand each other is *really* beyond me.'

'Jimmy, they're dragons – they understand each other because they all speak the same language. It's not that different from the Kikies.'

'Whatever.'

Yet, in their own way, the Telorians learnt to communicate with the dragons, who seemed to already understand the polken tongue. Together, they formed a plan.

Jimmy and Meysah lost count of time. They simply knew that days went by, but whether the time they slept was actually night or not, they had no way of knowing; they slept when they were tired and ate when they were hungry.

One day – which was actually the third day of the twelfth week of Winter, the eightieth of the season and of the year – while the two polcs were taking a stroll in the dip, they heard a pickaxe from right under their feet. Then it stopped. They bent down, pressing their ears to the ground.

'We're almost there,' they heard a voice say. 'We'll be through very shortly.'

'Good work.' Both knew that was Kàtchah's voice – it was so distinct, even someone who'd never met him before would recognise him. 'All armies are prepared.' Then he called out, 'Once we're in, search everywhere for the books! If you see, smell, or hear a dragon, avoid it. If it attacks you, kill it. You know what your objectives are and—'

Jimmy and Meysah lifted their heads, backing away slowly.

'If we speak,' whispered Meysah, 'they may hear us.'

The dragon standing nearby saw the look on their faces and understood it was time. It informed its mates and quickly brought Jimmy and Meysah to the room up high.

'But we want to fight also!' insisted Jimmy. The dragon gave him a sideways nod, closing its eyes. 'Not right away, eh? Well, then, we'll join later.'

The dragon nodded and turned to stone at the edge of the platform. Jimmy prepared his bow and his arrows whilst Meysah prepared his sword and shield. They blew out the torch and candles in the room and sat down. Then they waited.

A while passed before the sound of feet echoed through the caves.

Jimmy and Meysah crawled to the edge of the platform and peered over. From way up above, they saw Kàtchah ordering his people, pointing and waving his arms about and glittering – Jimmy deduced those were likely his jewels. Many Morkans crawled out from a grotto-like hole and one came to stand next to Kàtchah – Gohtek, they presumed, though from such a high place it was hard to tell for certain.

'They really were close by under us,' muttered Jimmy.

'Perhaps no less than a few feet,' deduced Meysah.

They heard Kàtchah shout, 'Come on, get moving! What are you waiting for?'

'Why doesn't *he* go,' muttered Meysah.

The Morkans began reluctantly but were soon stopped by a dragon who appeared in their way. They started to fire their arrows, and as it shrieked, many other dragons emerged, prepared to battle. Then Kàtchah yelled into the tunnel, 'Bring out the reinforcements!'

Many Morkans suddenly began to spill out from the hole. It was like watching a colony of ants crawl out and empty their hill.

Jimmy and Meysah slunk further back into the room. Dragon shrieks of anger or pain and Morkan shouts echoed through the lair as bellows of fire lit up the caves.

The dragon at the balcony stirred.

'It's our turn,' declared Jimmy.

'Look up there!' a Morkan called out. 'A secret chamber! I bet the books are hidden up there.'

'Good work!'

'Whoops,' said Meysah. 'Looks like our friend brought attention to itself.'

'They can't touch the diaries! They're sacred!'

Wasting no time, the Telorians hopped onto the dragon's scaled back and it flew down into the fray. Jimmy shot his bow at many Morkans headed for the pass and the stairs leading to the chamber. Even though it was half crumbled, they knew the Morkans would be able to make their way up somehow. The dragon swirled down through the air, then stopped and lingered right above Kàtchah.

'I suppose you think yourself clever, Kàtchah,' declared Meysah.

'What? I recognise that voice.'

'Indeed!' Meysah jumped down, landing on his feet and bending his knees low to cushion the fall before he rose to his full height. He was glad to see he was taller than the Morkan Captain. 'Surprise!'

'The Fairhaven brother. I should have known.'

'I'm surprised you even recognise me, let alone recognise my voice.'

'I'm good with faces and voices – I only need to hear or see them once. It's something I learnt from my Lord. Besides, you resemble your brother, and the King of Teloria's face is well embedded in my mind.'

'How impressive,' the Telorian mocked.

'I'll strike you down with one swipe.'

'Okay. Go ahead.'

Kàtchah readied his sword, but instead of striking he lunged away so that when Jimmy shot his bow, he got Gohtek instead. A good shot, too, even if just in the arm. Meysah scaled the dragon's back once more.

'Doesn't that polc ever die?!' he complained.

'Maybe only at the end,' said Jimmy. 'When all of this is over.'

'This fight, or this war?' Meysah sighed. 'Even so, either one, when will that be?' Jimmy shrugged. 'I don't want this fight to last longer than necessary.'

Jimmy shot more invaders as the dragon flew the knights back up to guard the room. The Morkans were faster than they had anticipated. The dragons, able to use their magic to heal themselves, killed as many Morkans as they could, squashing them, knocking them down, roasting them, or freezing them, but even at that, many had started up the long stairway.

Jimmy rained fire down on them, stopping many Morkans, but he was quickly running out of arrows.

Once all the arrows had been spent, Jimmy and Meysah started down the steps, wielding their swords tightly. Meysah bashed a Morkan back with his shield, and the Morkan fell into the open maw of a dragon. Jimmy swiped high and kicked another Morkan off the stairs, then Meysah jabbed one as Jimmy ducked to trip another.

They continued to fight on the stairs until all the Morkans who had dared to climb were dead, Jimmy and Meysah sustaining only minor injuries, shallow scratches on their arms and legs.

With a slight limp, Jimmy and Meysah marched boldly to Kàtchah.

'What do you want?' demanded Meysah.

'There are no books here,' asserted Jimmy. 'They were destroyed. Otherwise, Niome *would* have gone through the Portal. What did you expect?'

'I'll be back for you,' Kàtchah seethed as he ran back to the tunnels.

'You're obsessed!' shouted Meysah, exasperated.

In an instant, the passage was patched up, sealed by magic. No matter how much hacking and hammering the Telorians did, it was hard as a rock.

Meanwhile, the dragons dispatched any remaining Morkans.

'Someone's going to have to keep an eye on that passage,' said Jimmy before falling to his knees, exhausted. Moments later, Meysah and Jimmy passed out on the spot.

The dragons piled the Morkan bodies where the tunnel had opened and burned the corpses. Seeing them asleep on the floor, one dragon flew the Telorians up to the room and laid them gently on the balcony.

The dragons and the Telorians heard no more of the Morkans after that. Not that Winter. Although a few days later, water spilled in from where the passage had been, creating a little pool.

'How strange!' murmured Meysah.

'Will it flood?' asked Jimmy.

The guarding dragon shook its head and then drank from it.

'Oh, what the heck,' said Meysah. He dipped his flask into the large puddle and drank.

'Where is it coming from, though?' asked Jimmy.

'The river?'

'I can assume that much. But how? Who would flood the tunnels? Kàtchah? Destroying any remainder of his failure?'

'If so,' began Meysah, 'I hope the others weren't in the tunnels when they flooded.' Jimmy shifted uneasily, looking worried. Meysah felt a pang as he thought of his sister and master. 'That's one thing I forgot to ask Kàtchah . . . what became of the other three. If anyone would know, it would be him.' He began to speak more frantically. 'I hope they escaped before this flood. Maybe *they* caused it. Maybe for once, Kàtchah is dead. I hope he drowned. He sure deserved it. It would be gratifying for Mirauk to find out that Kàtchah—'

'Forget about Kàtchah! Let's think of how soon we'll be with the others and with the Kikies, and how they'll tell us of their adventure. We can only assume and hope, but soon enough, we'll know for sure.'

'That's reassuring,' said Meysah, nodding.

The water level steadied after a time before the new pool drained. Spring arrived, and the warmth of the Sun filled the lair. The time had come for Jimmy and Meysah to say their goodbyes to the dragons. They left the room just as they had found it.

In a token of friendship and thanks, the dragons offered to fly them to the Twisted Forest. On Spring the forty-eighth, a dragon soared high and fast with Meysah and Jimmy atop it – it was frighteningly exciting. Jimmy and Meysah had a few laughs as they mapped out their previous travels from atop the dragon's back. 'A dragon's-eye view,' Jimmy called it.

Before they knew it, they were landing near the Twisted Forest, though many trees seemed to have been burnt sometime in the last year. The two lads exchanged a sideways glance, worry etched on their faces.

Chapter Four:
A Good Trick

For many long days and nights, Vigh and Boreth remained in their cell, unbothered. Kàtchah visited a few times to remind them that this was no inn and that they were prisoners.

'As if we've forgotten.'

Sure, they got food and water and were perhaps a little taken care of, but they certainly didn't need someone to tell them that they were in a prison, let alone remind them that the Dukes had left to gather an army specifically to escort them to Mork and before Mirauk.

The two Lords did notice, however, that certain Morkans considered them special – perhaps in awe at how they had magically fooled the Morkans. For indeed they were special, important and valuable enough to bring before Mirauk, in any case.

As the Morkans gathered in the tunnels closer to Darakön, concentrated beneath the lair, the section where Vigh and Boreth were held captive grew sparse.

Eventually, few Morkans remained, only those who guarded the two imposters.

'They will have their fight on the dragons soon,' Boreth observed. 'I hope Jimmy, Meysah, and Niome have made it to the lair.'

'If they hadn't, we would've felt it,' said Vigh. 'I doubt that army reached them. Yet I feel so much anxiety already, perhaps I would not have recognised it.'

'The Morkans have gathered up north,' said Boreth.

'Their voices still echo in the halls, though,' said Vigh.

'Especially Kàtchah's!'

'Yes,' Vigh laughed. 'He travels often from one end of the tunnels to the other.' Then he paused. 'When all is quiet . . .' He paused again. 'Our chance, Boreth. You remember when Niome mentioned destroying these tunnels with the river water? I had been considering that back then myself.'

'Yes, but how are *we* supposed to—'

'I have a plan,' interrupted Vigh. 'When all is quiet.'

It was difficult to tell how much time passed, for the two warriors had not kept count for a long time now and there was no Sun or Moon to aid them either. All they knew was that one day, the echoes could no longer be heard. Either the fight was about to begin or it was already underway.

The two Lords got into position. First, Boreth curled up on the floor, moaning as if in pain – softly at first, then he let it grow louder as he began to rock. One of the oldest tricks in the book, but these Morkan guards were not the brightest of their kind, so the Lords crossed their fingers and hoped for the best.

Vigh pounded on the door. 'Pease! Help us! Something's wrong!'

The door opened and three guards walked in.

'Yesterday he was complaining that his stomach and head hurt,' Vigh explained, acting deeply worried. 'I thought it might be indigestion, but it's worse – perhaps it is an illness.'

Vigh thanked the Mighty Spirit in his mind for those few years he and Boreth had taken lessons with the players of the stage.

'What's wrong, you!' one of the guards demanded, slightly prodding Boreth with his boot.

'Aah, my head . . . I can't breathe!'

Boreth pressed his hand on his chest, the other clutching his head as he rolled and swayed.

'It's a trick,' deduced the guard. 'He's not really in pain.'

To his surprise, Boreth's face turned purple. He began croaking out intelligible words. Although Vigh knew Boreth had always been one to swim deep underwater and hold his breath the longest, part of Vigh grew genuinely worried. Still, he knew his friend well and trusted his act.

Vigh rushed to Boreth's side, kneeling and holding him. 'Please, I beg you! Help him, will you not?'

'Mirauk wants his prisoners alive,' another guard cautioned. 'It would be wrong of us not to help them.

Imagine if Mirauk found out we had let one of the Five die. Imagine his rage! It would cost us our heads.'

'Very well,' said the first guard with some reluctance.

'We have nothing, though,' protested the third guard.

'I have medicine in my bag,' said Vigh.

'I'll go fetch the bag,' the third guard conceded.

Vigh steadied Boreth a little. From where the guards stood, it seemed Boreth was no longer breathing – and he nearly wasn't.

The guard returned a moment later and tossed Vigh's bag to him. Vigh hurriedly shuffled through his things. Everything was still there, just as he had suspected – the Morkans had been too frightened of magical items to go rummaging inside the bag.

Vigh took out a bottle of herbal tea and had Boreth drink it. His other hand still in his bag, he gripped his knife.

The two Telorian Lords were being closely watched by the Morkans. Every move had to be calculated.

Boreth drank up and then sat up tall, catching his breath. But before the Morkans could react, he threw the empty vial at one guard's face. The glass shattered and the guard staggered back out of the room, bringing his hands to his face. Vigh handed one knife to Boreth, and the two quickly thrust their knives at the two other guards.

The guards jumped back in shock, giving Boreth and Vigh the opening they needed to stab them dead.

Vigh scooped up his bag. 'Where did the other one go?'

'That doesn't matter. We need to hurry – we may have little time.' Boreth glanced down the tunnel. 'When he went to get your bag, he went that way. Come.'

They strode along in haste before Boreth stopped.

'In here!' He tried the door handle – it was locked. 'Your special knife is required.'

Vigh slashed the lock and kicked the door open. Lo and behold, there were their weapons and satchels.

Vigh turned his head to Boreth. 'How did you know?'

Boreth shrugged. 'A feeling I get sometimes.'

They retrieved all their things, re-equipped themselves, and then proceeded to run down the south tunnel. They stopped at another door they knew led to a storage room and took what they needed.

They ran a long while before reaching the southmost secret room they had created – a room from which they had not completed digging an exit, one they had not included on their map. They had already been situated quite south to begin with, kept far from Darakön or their secret ways out, so they hadn't been able to escape through there.

It was quiet. Vigh bolted the door with axes while Boreth began digging upwards with a spade. A moment later Vigh joined him and started digging in the side wall, towards the river, with the pickaxe.

They dug for a long while. Boreth was done before Vigh.

The soil was soft going up but strong leading to the river. Once they broke through, they knew its waters would quickly fill up this room.

Perhaps a whole day and night passed while they dug. At last, they were almost there, as they began to see dampness in the soil.

'Open up in there!'

'Morkans!' Boreth turned to the door. 'I'll make sure they don't get in.'

He bolted it up more securely, pushing against it. The Morkans banged and pushed, and the door bounced.

'Hurry!' cried Boreth.

Vigh carried on as fast as he could. After the dampness came the mud. He gave one last big thrust with the spade and pickaxe, and river water came flowing in. At first it trickled, then surged with more force, and a fountainlike stream quickly became a gushing jet.

Vigh lunged to the side, pushed by the water.

'Quick!' he cried. 'Let's go! The room will be flooded within moments.'

Boreth went through the new exit first, grabbing a hold of the cold ground outside and lifting himself out.

The Morkans banged on the door, nearly breaking the axes bolting it.

Vigh hurled himself up, helped by Boreth. The two were now out in the freezing cold, partially wet.

The Morkans broke into the room, but the rushing water pushed them back as it gained momentum and surged more rapidly.

'We must inform the others and save our treasures!' cried a Morkan.

Vigh and Boreth listened as they bundled up.

'Fool! We lost our most valuable treasures – those two Telorains! We're dead.'

'Not if we inform the others of the flood.'

'Perhaps not. Nothing is stopping it – it's too strong. The hole is getting bigger. There's no use trying to patch it up – the water's already pouring into the hall. Come, hurry!' The Morkans then ran up the tunnel, heading north.

Boreth sighed in relief. 'So, it seems you have quite a few good tricks up your sleeves, don't you?'

'I save them for cold Winter days,' laughed Vigh. 'And now, we make for the Twisted Forest.'

They walked on the road that had been made by Firlanians long ago. It was a clear day, but with the bitter cold, it was unbearable. Even with the insulating spell Niome had cast on their garments, the cold seeped through.

They created a fire to keep warm and dry up better that night. The next morning, they began to walk for many days. When they arrived at the end of the road, they looked very much forward to reaching the Tweedle Woods and being reminded of their ghostly friend.

They built themselves a raft with the wood of the forest. It was so cold now that no fire could be started; they tried many times to no avail. They slept little and kept moving in order to never lose their body warmth.

'Does the river look lower to you?' asked Boreth.

'There's a lot of water in this river.'

'Yes, but it takes a lot of water to flood tunnels.'

'It could just be your perception,' said Vigh. 'Then again, your observation skills are better than mine. *We* know of the flooding, so maybe we *think* we see the river lower.'

After crossing the half-frozen river, they travelled southwards.

'To think the other three walked all the way to Darakön in this bitter cold,' said Vigh. 'It's too much to bear.'

'They know more spells than we do.'

'That's true.'

'I say we stop at the Old Grey House,' suggested Boreth.

'I agree.' At once, they changed course and made for the house. 'I thank the Mighty Spirit that house exists, and I thank Her that we're friends with those who dwell there.'

'Well, me too.'

'Well, that's a given,' said Vigh, 'considering.'

'Look at you, teasing me.'

'Well, the others aren't here, nor are the Kikies. Who else is going to make silly remarks to liven our spirits!' They both chuckled.

Two days later, they arrived at their destination. They needn't have knocked but once and the door was opened by Tlúnëe, who right away gave them blankets.

'It is the coldest Winter yet,' he said to them. 'Even for the Ghost Rider. We've not seen him since Summer.

He may be investigating the source of this foul weather, but I believe he is hiding from it.'

Tlúnëe looked at the wailing snow and shut the door.

'We know the source is Mirauk,' said Vigh. 'The Ghost Rider must be frightened of him and his magic if he's hiding.'

'We are all afraid of him and his magic,' sighed Tlúnëe, 'and a ghost of the Ghost Rider's nature can be used for evil purposes if discovered. Although I know our ghost friend will return to us in the Spring. As such, our letters will be delayed.'

'Letters?' inquired Vigh as he removed his hat and towelled his hair.

'Long has it been since I saw my parents or my brother, and it's been too risky to write letters for a while, but now we want to write to them anyway. It is news that is due. The Ghost Rider will bring this news in the Summertime – it is safer to rely on *him* than on any other messenger. But enough of that! I'm glad to see you, Vigh. Boreth left in such a hurry last time. I was worried about the rest of you. Speaking of which, where are the others?'

'Darakön!' said Boreth. 'It's a long story that should be told later.'

'I did not foresee this separation,' Tlúnëe admitted, frowning.

'Perhaps the cold is causing many unforeseen events, cloaking or shielding them from perception?' suggested Vigh.

'Perhaps, but it is most unfortunate that the other three are not with you.'

'We're anxious to know the story, though,' said Clahria as she entered the hallway. She held two mugs of hot tea for the travellers, offering them the tea before she embraced Boreth. 'Stars, you're so cold.' She placed her hands on his cheeks to warm them.

'I know. It's that weather.' Boreth gently placed a hand over Clahria's, leaning into her touch. 'I'm telling you, this is the doing of evil magic.'

'There isn't much we can do about that,' said Clahria. 'But we can certainly help you warm up.'

Vigh nudged Boreth teasingly, causing him to blush.

'Come, come,' said Tlúnëe.

Drúgan awoke from a nap and joined the group to greet the travellers. Boreth and Vigh shivered still. They set their things down in two rooms upstairs, washed up, and then sat down to some more hot tea.

After a good meal, cooked by Tlúnëe himself, everyone sat by the fire and the travellers, now markedly warmer and more comfortable, gave an account of their story. When they mentioned the phantoms, Tlúnëe shuddered.

'Well, I'm certainly glad to hear that the others are safe with the dragons,' said Drúgan.

'They'll be fine,' said Tlúnëe. 'Or they should be, anyway.'

'What about the three of you?' asked Boreth, sitting cuddled up with Clahria.

'We haven't had any travellers yet,' said Tlúnëe, 'but we know eventually many will be stopping by, as before.'

'The Ghost Rider has withdrawn,' said Clahria. 'We haven't seen him all Winter. He'll be back, I know he will – this is not the first time he's gone during a terribly cold Winter. Perhaps he does still have some sensation left when it comes to the cold, I wonder. Or perhaps, like Tlúnëe believes, he is investigating the source of the cold evil.'

'Perhaps he is sensitive to evil magic and hides away,' Boreth mused.

'Tlúnëe mentioned the Rider bringing letters?' Vigh prompted.

'Ah,' said Drúgan. 'He usually brings letters we write, and oftentimes returns with a bundle of letters from my daughter. During these times, though, it is too dangerous to write. Our friend may be a ghost, but if the enemy found him, with just a spell they could overpower him. If they got hold of our letters, they would learn secrets about us and Teloria.'

'Mirauk does not know of our houses' existence,' explained Tlúnëe, 'and how we can protect and hide all the people of Teloria within them. It must stay that way. Indeed, our ghostly friend is hiding from the cold of evil.'

'He has the power to not be seduced by evil,' Drúgan continued. 'This, he has explained to us. Mirauk cannot touch him with his magic so long as he steers clear of Mork. But he can still be intercepted, and if evil gets its hands on important letters, our houses will no longer be secret and the enemy might very well destroy our homes.'

'However,' said Clahria, 'it's been since the Big War that we've written. A lot has happened since then, and a lot more keeps happening every day, new discoveries, new developments. My parents don't know any of it. Nor do we know what's been going on at Zaccher Lake. Writing letters, even now, is a necessary risk we must take.'

'Communication within a family must not stay silent for too long,' Drúgan said grimly. 'There is much I am anxious to know from Maria and Tobias.'

'Tlúnëe,' said Vigh, 'you spoke of a brother.'

'You didn't know about their brother?' asked Boreth.

'No, but I assume you did.'

'We have a brother, Olúryn,' said Tlúnëe. 'He's a decade and three years younger than I am. If my visions are correct, we also now have a sister. She is perhaps twenty in polken years, just on the cusp between childhood and adolescence. I have not seen what her name is. That's also why we want to write to my parents. They don't know of my prophecies and improvements in healing magic, and they could be living many changes as well.'

Tlúnëe scratched his chin. 'Since the Big War, we've kept silent out of fear, but so much has happened here – so much hope and courage from you, Niome, Bahvley, Tharguen, and the others – and I know much has happened with my parents as well. We'd like to know.' He glanced at Clahria, his expression inscrutable. 'Maybe improvements . . . in healing.' He seemed concerned, the same concerned look on his face that Drúgan had but a moment ago.

Tlúnëe abruptly changed tones and became cheerful once more. 'And such, you know.'

'Well, I hope for everyone's sake that once the Rider sets off, the letters reach Zaccher safely,' expressed Boreth.

'They will,' said Tlúnëe.

As the conversation ended, Vigh watched how Boreth and Clahria were happy sitting huddled close together. It reminded him of himself and Tallelah. His memories were vague now, but his feelings, he remembered. For the very first time, he realised he no longer missed Tallelah. Perhaps his conversation with Meysah had helped him. *The learner teaches the master.*

However, he missed the emotions that came with being in love. And also for the first time since his loss, Vigh missed loving and being loved. He was happy for his friend, though, and that warmed his heart.

Chapter Five:
A New Year's Battle

Niome made for the Gate of Firlan at a brisk pace, arriving in the middle of the night on the second of the twelfth of Winter. Her presence had not gone unnoticed. Keeping a diligent watch due to the Morkan troops seen from afar, the Firlanians had quickly spotted her. The gate was already open when she reached it.

'Niome,' said a confused-looking Firnamel, 'what are you doing here? How come—'

'It's a long and complicated story,' she replied.

'But how come . . . where are . . . ? My apologies – welcome, please, come in. You look exhausted. My guards came and woke me when they saw you were near.'

'I know it's late in the night,' began Niome. 'I know you must be eager to learn news, but I must admit, I need sleep.'

'Certainly, you may rest,' said Firnamel, 'but I must ask, why are you here all alone? It troubles me.'

'Everyone is safe, as far as I know, so be comforted,' replied Niome. 'I will answer all your questions tomorrow.'

'Very well.'

Niome was then led to a room where she installed herself.

'If there is anything you need, my lady,' said the guard, 'you can find me down the hall. I watch at night and keep informed of what the watchers from the tower see.'

'Thank you,' said Niome. 'And you can just call me Niome. It makes me feel too sophisticated to be called Lady.'

'As you wish, then, Niome.' The guard smiled. 'Good night.'

Niome looked around the room, comforted to be indoors and warm. When she awoke the following morning, breakfast awaited her, a tray that someone had brought and placed on the table in the room.

As she ate alone, Niome realised just how dearly she cared for her Firlanian friends, for here she was, in their home, and they were not here – she missed them. She stood and went to find Firnamel.

Niome found the King sitting by the fire, where an empty chair awaited along with a table between the two chairs.

'Have a seat,' said Firnamel. 'I have here some tea and some biscuits.'

'Thank you,' said Niome as she sat down.

'You are a very honoured guest, Niome.' Firnamel furrowed his brows. 'It's unusual for one Point of the

Star to travel alone. The Star is an entity – it needs to be whole. All its polcs are its pieces, remember, and all of your souls are connected. You do recall what I said if you were to be apart? Everyone here is troubled. Come now, tell me your story – my son travelled to Teloria, and . . . has something happened?'

'No, Teloria is well. We were very happy to see Kchalami and the others. We meant to go to the Twisted Forest and they were going to accompany us, but Tharguen's team, well . . .'

Niome filled Firnamel in on all that had happened, omitting the part about the drought being her doing and their capture in the caves being an infiltration planned out long before it happened.

'We must prepare to fight,' said Firnamel, 'to defend the forest. If the Morkans troops fail to capture Jimmy and Meysah, they'll have nowhere else to turn but here. They won't go into Darakön – I'd be surprised if they dared. And they won't face Captain Kàtchah! For punishment?'

Niome nodded, understanding what Firnamel was getting at.

'So instead, they'll attack Firlan,' the King went on, 'and return to Mork with proof that they fought on Firlanian grounds. Then, they can go back to their Captain and claim *we* attacked *them*. Their Captain will be infuriated and put the blame on *us*, and then many more will come and declare open war in an endeavour to destroy Firlan. Mirauk has powerful ways beyond simple polcs and weapons.'

Firnamel downcast his eyes, and his expression grew sombre. 'It's happened before. That's why we must fight them and not let any escape, not one. We must kill all of them.'

'I feel partly responsible for this,' Niome said, feeling apologetic.

'Why?'

'Because I've caused this! The Morkans who'll come here, everyone being separated . . .'

'Perhaps, though I doubt it is so,' said Firnamel. 'It was not your doing that caused the five of you to be separated from Bahvley and the others. Why should the rest be your fault?'

Niome winced internally, wishing she could tell him the truth, the weight of it suddenly feeling heavier than before. But she only nodded, taking a sip of tea. Firnamel also seemed weary with some unknown worry, but the expression quickly passed, and Niome dismissed it as her own projecting.

Firnamel in turn informed Niome of the goings-on in Firlan. As Kchalami had previously confirmed, the Firlanians no longer kept their doors shut to travellers who did not have a spell to enter. In this way, the Firlanians had welcomed Dalvaran travellers, who in turn shared many discovered secrets regarding the Morkans.

'That's when I realised the time had come to change that rule created in fear and ignorance,' Firnamel explained.

Long ago, the King who ruled Firlan had chosen to isolate his people to protect them. Travellers allied with other folk, but never did the Firlanians let any enter their borders. A deal had been struck with Bob Tweedle, and only the Mighty Spirit knew how long ago *that* was.

'Times are different now. The prophecies are realities. We know who we can trust, we know who our allies truly are. We may fear Mirauk, but his power is working against him, for that is what we all have in common – whatever our beliefs or culture, our fear of him and desire to save the world has brought us all together against our one common enemy, whom we will no longer hide in fear from. A magical reconnection.

'I regret not helping Bahvley and Tharguen and the Team of Twelve. I can't help but feel partly responsible for their failure in Mork. I want to make amends for all the lost lives and all the lost years. The doors of Firlan are open to anyone, even if it risks that a spy may enter.'

'I believe you are wise enough to recognise the look of a spy,' said Niome. 'I don't doubt that Firlan will remain as safe a place as it always has been. But you have naught to feel guilty about. Bahvely and Tharguen needed to *not* get the wand, for they under-stood little of magic then. They've learned over the years how to tap into their inner magic, and they needed to travel to Mork in order to help *us* later on. But I do agree with you, and I'm glad you're going to help anyone in need.'

'What kind of an ally would I be otherwise?'

Niome smiled and took another sip of tea.

Every day the Firlanians remained alert, watching for Morkans. Niome hoped the Morkans would come, for that would mean Jimmy and Meysah were safe. She wondered about Boreth and Vigh. She was anxious about much and felt very responsible for much more.

It was during the celebration on New Year's Day when one of the Firlanian watchers sped to the Dining Hall.

'Your Majesty,' he panted, 'the Morkans have just entered the forest by the Northwest. They will be at our gate by nightfall tomorrow.'

'Captain, get your archers ready on the battlements.'

'Yes, my Lord.' He turned to go.

'Laribel!'

The Captain turned back to Firnamel.

'Thank you, and good luck.'

'You too.'

Firnamel rose. 'It is time. They will be upon us tomorrow.'

While the Firlanians took the time to pray, many readied themselves immediately. Niome admired how they all faced this threat bravely, though she heard whispers of how nothing could be worse than something that had already happened – something none were openly talking about – and how they had nothing left to lose.

Captain Laribel's archers stood on the battlements, spread out all around the fortress. A large team snuck out and hid among the trees and between the wall and tree wall.

Ready, Niome was on her way out when Firnamel stopped her in the hall.

'Are you certain you wish to fight with us?' Firnamel asked. 'You don't have to.'

'I know, but I choose to.'

Firnamel nodded, his white beard following the movement. Niome followed the army out and hid between the wall and tree wall near the gate. A soldier stood not far from her.

'Are you nervous?' he asked.

'Are you?'

'I almost always am.'

'Me too,' replied Niome. 'Every time I have to face a Morkan. Sometimes it's fear, other times it's excitement. Sometimes it's anticipation.'

'What is it today?'

'Relief. Relief that my brother and my friend are safe.'

'I wish I could feel relieved,' the Firlanian admitted.

'Everything will be fine,' Niome reassured. 'What's your name?'

'Meltissel.'

'Meltissel, nice to meet you.'

'Nice to meet *you*, Niome. It's an honour to fight with you.'

'And I'll be honoured to joke about this day with you when it's all over.'

'If we survive,' muttered Meltissel.

'Just follow my lead,' said Niome. 'You'll be all right.'

'Okay.' Still, Meltissel chewed his lip nervously.

'When I met Mirauk,' began Niome, 'he felt fear. If Mirauk can feel fear, so will these Morkans. You'll be fine.' Meltissel smiled, nodding.

Soon, they heard the Morkans approach. Niome emerged from her hiding spot, facing the intruders.

'How can I help you?' she asked. 'Let's see, Kàtchah sent you, didn't he? Did you find the lads?'

'No, we did not,' a Morkan growled. 'How did you get here?'

'We may have been fooled at first, but you see, your spells won't work on us now,' declared another Morkan.

As the Morkans sneered at Niome, Firlanians crept up behind them.

'I didn't cast any spell.' Niome lifted her hands in surrender. 'You're early – we weren't expecting you until sundown.'

'We?'

'Yes, me and my faithful Firlanian friends standing right behind you.'

Before the Morkans could turn around, the Firlanians were on top of them. Only a few got away. Meltissel emerged from behind the trees.

'That was very clever!'

'Yes, but not clever enough,' murmured Niome.

Though the Firlanians made short work of this smaller group of Morkans, it wasn't without injury.

Niome and Meltissel ran towards another group as the fight began in earnest. A fallen Morkan grabbed Niome by the ankle, sending her flat on her face.

'You won't get away that easily!' The Morkan readied his knife. 'If I defeat you, it'll be a shame Mirauk won't have a chance to finish you off himself.'

'He doesn't believe he can defeat me himself,' declared Niome. 'No one can.'

'You're wrong!'

The Morkan lifted his arm. Meltissel dove to the ground, sliding in between the two.

'I'm sorry, *you're* wrong,' he said as he deftly disarmed the Morkan and drove his sword into him.

'Thanks. That was very smooth,' said Niome, rather impressed.

'Oh, it was a fluke,' Meltissel said, waving a hand dismissively.

'Humble.'

They shared a smile before rushing along the tree wall after more Morkans. After dispatching several more, Captain Laribel and his archers from up on the wall spotted yet another few and brought them down.

'We should get back to the gate,' said Meltissel.

However, the area had been deserted. Everyone had scattered.

'This isn't going to work,' said Niome. 'This is what the Morkans want – for us to separate. They're stronger that way.'

'What are we to do, then?' asked Meltissel.

'Stand back!' Niome spread out her arms. 'Step away for a moment. I need space.'

Niome closed her eyes and spoke in a singsong, her voice deep and orotund. The sound resonated throughout the entire forest.

Rednë lerus!
Ehelt senscarid elotës üio.
Üio lilui ogë ileref,
Ot tahalt rehot denal.
Fi üio rednë lerus!

And then she repeated the last words, louder and louder.

Rednë lerus. Rednë lerus! Rednë lerus!!! REDNË LERUS!

Meltissel backed away with fearful eyes as the wind picked up around Niome, a whirlwind blowing out from where she stood and travelling around the fortress before returning to her. Archers and watchers felt the wind on their faces as it passed them.

Niome met Meltissel's gaze. 'Be ready, they'll be here right about . . . *now*!'

Any remaining foes and all the Firlanian knights had been carried by the wind, all together, the Firlanians overwhelming the scant Morkans.

Meltissel cast a puzzled look Niome's way, mouth agape.

'It's called a spell, my friend,' said Niome.

'I see.'

Together, Niome, Meltissel, and the Firlanians finished off the Morkans. All were now slain. Morning was on its way, and calmness filled Firlan Forest.

Firnamel stood by a window, praying for the safety of his people. Once finished he walked to the parapet, where he met with Captain Laribel.

'The forest of King Firlan Mittèlor has once again become safe and secure as always. Thank you.'

'It pleases me to hear it,' said Laribel. He turned to his team. 'It's done! We've won the battle. Time for bed,' he laughed.

Firnamel returned to the main hall and thanked Niome.

'Don't thank me,' said Niome, 'thank your polcs. I barely lifted a finger.' She winked at Meltissel.

As Firnamel congratulated his people, Meltissel whispered to Niome.

'Why are you not taking credit for the spell that saved us?'

'Boastfulness is not necessarily honour. It's an attribute I have trouble with,' admitted Niome. She let out a laugh. 'There *are* Telorians who take pride in boasting, though.'

She thought of Lóim, of the rivalry between many in Tharguen's team. She'd give anything to hear their bickering and have them here with her.

'Thank me when I destroy Mirauk. You, on the other hand,' – Niome clapped Meltissel on the back – 'should be proud for all *you* did. For all your agitation, you are a very skilled warrior.'

In the season that passed, Niome enjoyed the time she spent with her new friends, those with whom she'd fought the Morkans. She and Firnamel counselled each other and discussed many matters, including the rift in the Firlan line of the Mittèlor family. In this matter, Firnamel wondered if those left behind had indeed settled in the Twisted Forest. Nevertheless, he was comforted by Niome's wise advice.

Winter was unusually long; Spring was a warm and colourful one. At last, on Spring the forty-sixth, the time came for Niome to leave for the Twisted Forest. Though she was reluctant to travel alone, she was eager to reunite with the others.

'You've earned much gratitude in Firlan,' said Firnamel. 'I wish you a safe trip.'

'Thank you,' replied Niome. 'I've always felt comfortable here. Firlan has earned my gratitude as well.'

'Do come again soon,' said Meltissel. 'Or perhaps I shall visit you in Teloria. Perhaps at the wedding?'

Niome blushed. 'You'll certainly be invited.'

'I hope so,' laughed Meltissel. 'After all the raving I've heard from you! Where was I the last time you were here that I didn't meet Tharguen?' He shrugged. 'I *was* present at the banquet with the gifts.'

'You know, in a way, you're very much like Meysah. I hope you two meet some day – in person, that is. You'd really get along, you and Meysah *and* Jimmy.'

'Elmezni told me the same thing. I must be destined to meet them, then, perhaps at the wedding. Sounds promising.'

'Perhaps.' Niome smiled. 'Or perhaps you could come with me to the Twisted Forest and meet everyone. Then I wouldn't have to travel alone.'

'Thank you, but my place right now is here,' said Meltissel. 'Some other time.'

'Definitely.'

'Fare you well, and be careful out there,' Meltissel said as he embraced Niome.

'Farewell,' Firnamel echoed. 'May the stars watch over you.'

'Farewell!'

Niome left with her spirits high. By the end of the day, she had reached the Hills. It was a clear night and all the stars shone brightly. Niome lay on her back, looking up and smiling at the stars, and thanked the Mighty Spirit for her help and protection.

The next day, Niome saw a dragon flying overhead. It was quite high in the sky and moving fast. She watched it soar from Darakön towards the Southeast.

Niome continued, spurred by the thought that soon, she would be with everyone else and in Tharguen's arms once again.

Chapter Six:
Letters In the Wind

*I*mpatience filled the hearts of the Telorians. Too much time had now passed for the Five to arrive. At the same time, Bahvley had Teloria to think about. He couldn't leave his people waiting forever; it was already the thirty-second of Spring the thirty-second. It was time to return home.

'Why?!' objected Tharguen when Bahvley consulted him.

'We can't stay here forever! I am King. I have responsibilities! This isn't like the time when we left for fifty years – I need to be home for my people. The King of Teloria cannot be gone for too long. We have to go back home.'

'But we can't leave now!'

'We can't leave everyone at home waiting, Tharguen. It won't do.'

'Then just please wait a week or two more,' Tharguen pleaded. 'The Five just might arrive between now and then. I don't want to go home yet. I want to see Niome.'

'You may have to go home without seeing her,' Bahvley said with sympathy, 'but we'll wait, for I, too, long to see them.'

Tharguen nodded, leaning a hand on the fireplace mantel. He sighed. 'Being separated from the polc I love . . . I am anguished.'

'I know the feeling,' admitted Bahvley.

Tharguen looked up, curious. 'Is this one of the stories you've said you'd recount later?'

Bahvley nodded, standing beside his friend. 'There was a Kiki in Kikiland . . . she was so beautiful. She was quite older than me, in terms of how Kikies age, but I was mad about her and she about me.' Bahvley's eyes grew distant. 'For many years, we loved each other and were together. For a time I thought I could have a family in Kikiland with her, but that is not how things turned out.'

'What happened?'

'Eventually, I began to explore more of the ocean. I'd be gone a long time while the Kikies and I devised our plans and chartered the waters, even if it would be some time still – we were actively working to counter Mirauk's magic.' Bahvley placed his hand on the wood of the mantel. 'Reinia grew older, even looked it, but still I loved her.'

Bahvley bowed his head. 'We drifted apart, despite continuing to share moments together, and she fell in love with another man, a Kiki. As I grew more focused on my return home, I chose to let her go so she could have happiness and a family.'

Tharguen placed his hand on Bahvley's and squeezed gently. The two turned to face each other.

'We parted on good terms,' said Bahvley, 'with fond memories of each other. She is living with her new love, and we will both always care for each other. I will always love her, same as I will always love Mellavon, even if I know I will also love another again. Because that is the kind of polc I am – able to love one and dedicate myself to her for the time I am with her, but also able to continue to love all the others.'

Tharguen pursed his lips. 'See, that's where we differ. There has only ever been one for me.'

Bahvley smiled. 'I know.'

'Capult tried to match me up with Morkans. I always turned them down.' Tharguen let out a small quiet laugh. 'He was the sort to go on all sorts of intimate adventures. He even once made sure to know my type, down to the description. Always found me polcs who matched it.' Tharguen chuckled. 'You can't imagine the number of Morkans he found who fit that description. And I was reputed to be the best-looking Morkan in all of Mork, save one other, so all those "matches" were *very* interested in me.'

Bahvley quirked a brow. 'Who was your rival?'

Tharguen let the question hang before answering. 'Merlik.' Bahvley let out a low whistle, and Tharguen chuckled. 'I know.' He sobered. 'But amidst all that, there truly was but one who had my heart.'

'He was persistent, this Capult,' said Bahvley.

'Perhaps. And it's not that I didn't fancy any of them, for many were beautiful, or that I didn't have any needs or urges.' Tharguen brought a hand to his heart. 'But I knew in my heart how I felt, who I truly was, and the thought and promise to myself to see Niome and tell her how I felt quelled any other feeling.'

'Your dedication to my sister has been second to none. You are truly devoted to her.'

Tharguen's eyes brimmed with tears. He bowed his head and spoke softly. 'And then I found her again. I was able to tell her how I felt.'

'It took you long enough after finding her, though,' Bahvley teased gently.

Tharguen let out a sob brightened by a laugh. He looked up at Bahvley. 'I love her so much, Bahvley. She will always be the only one for me.'

'I know.' Bahvley paused, feeling a pang in his chest even as he knew his duty to his kingdom. 'But we have to go home.'

'I know.' Tharguen bowed his head again. 'I have to hope that I'll see her again. I have to hope that she is safe, wherever she is. I have to hope that she will return to me, and then we can bind our love through magic.'

'Your love is already bound through magic,' Bahvley reminded him, 'and always has been, for it is a pure and true love. And when the Five return, you will be able to celebrate that love officially.'

Tharguen nodded, weeping. 'The magic of marriage is different. It would allow me to know she is safe as though I were with her . . . I wish I knew now.'

'Me too.' Bahvley hugged Tharguen, doing his best to comfort him, all while weeping too.

Tharguen was not the only one who felt the need to stay. Far too many from his team were too concerned for them to leave now.

'I'm sure they've escaped by now,' said Tom as many of his friends paced to and fro.

'How can you be so sure?' demanded Gahli. 'We were all asleep when the river swept them up.'

'We have no evidence that they escaped or went through a secret tunnel, as you claim you dreamt,' Pete said, eyeing Tom with scrutiny. 'As far as we know, they could've been washed away by the tide.' He paused. 'The tide of doom.'

'Now you're sounding like Lóim. Captain Tharguen said—'

'It doesn't matter what Captain Tharguen said, Tom,' Lóim interrupted, giving him a sceptical look.

'If they had been swept away,' began Tom, 'there would've been debris, knives and such, left floating or on the shore. All their things were gone.'

'As though the Morkans came out of a secret tunnel and took them, and then the river refilled once they were in,' said Huck, backing up Tom's 'theories'. He'd spoken of it to some, merely mentioning it was a deduction, never revealing what he already knew to be true and *all* the details he'd seen in his meditations.

'Wherever they are,' said Ihal, 'the Morkans have got them in their grasp.'

'We can still be optimistic,' said Gahli. 'Perhaps they escaped.'

'And where would they go once escaped?' Lóim demanded conclusively.

'Somewhere close and safe?' suggested Mittah. 'It was too cold to travel *this* far this Winter. They could've gone to Firlan.'

'What if they tried to travel all the way back and the cold took them?'

'Lóim!' shouted Gahli. 'Please! I don't like insinuations that our friends are dead.'

'Sorry, but we have to look at all possibilities, and one is that your Jimmy may not be coming back anytime soon.' Gahli glared at him with revolt. Lóim averted his eyes. 'That . . . Meysah may not be coming back.'

'Why would you be so worried anyway, Lóim?' asked Jeremy. 'Mere seasons ago, you despised the polc.'

'Hmph.' Lóim turned his head to the side, crossing his arms.

'I refuse to think that any harm has come to them,' declared Ihal. 'Just the thought is too unbearable. The thought of not being able to be held in Meysah's arms . . .' She trailed off.

'At least Meysah knows how you feel about him, Ihal,' said Gahli. 'I didn't even get the chance to tell Jimmy . . . to tell him how I've admired him from afar for so many years since his return from Mork.' She smiled wistfully. 'How I find him so dreamy, even more so in person. How in the time I got to know him in Dûnelor . . . how I've . . .' Her shoulders slumped. 'Fallen in love with him.'

'I can imagine being unable to express such strong emotions can be tormenting,' expressed Lóim. 'I just can't shake off the feeling that something terrible has happened. I keep seeing it in my mind. *That's* tormenting!'

'Except you don't have to instil those visions into *our* minds!' retorted Ihal.

Lóim narrowed his eyes. 'Oh, so I can't express myself now?'

'That's not what Ihal means!' cried Gahli. 'We just want to be able to reassure each other instead of discouraging each other.'

'No reassurance will come if we keep on yelling like this,' stated Mittah.

'Who's yelling?' shouted Lóim, Ihal, and Gahli all at once.

'Maybe they travelled another way,' suggested Tom. 'Perhaps a mission led them away from here.'

'A mission? A . . . *mission?!*' cried Ihal. 'What mission is more important than—' She stopped herself. 'It's true, they have priorities, considering their power.'

'Maybe they won't come back,' began Lóim in a lighter tone, 'maybe—'

'Again! Insinuating that they're dead!' shouted Gahli.

'I wasn't insinuating that!' insisted Lóim.

'Oh, really?'

'Don't jump to conclusions before I'm done speaking! All I was saying was that it's possible they won't come *here*. Maybe they thought it was too late to travel here.

Maybe, thinking that we already left, they went home. To Teloria. *Not dead.* Te-lo-ri-a!'

'Then maybe they'll just come here after they see we're not there,' Ihal concluded.

'Or wait until we go home,' argued Lóim.

'Or maybe they're on their way!' shouted Tom at the top of his lungs. Everyone stopped, and there was silence. 'Maybe they're on their way here now,' he repeated quietly.

'Then all the more reason for us to stay and wait,' said Gahli.

'Especially if Captain Tharguen wants our opinions as well,' Mittah agreed.

'But King Bahvley might make a decision on his own,' Jeremy cautioned, 'and then we'll *have* to go home. He's right when he says it's been too long for them to come now. There are too many duties at home for him, for us. We cannot neglect our kingdom. *He* cannot neglect his kingdom. If the Five are elsewhere, whether on a mission or held captive, they have their things to do and we've got ours. Personally, I think we might have to return home. We can't stay here forever, putting our lives on hold.'

'I have to agree,' admitted Lóim.

'What if they're about to arrive?' Tom said calmly.

'That's why we're still here,' said Pete.

'But we've been saying that for the past weeks,' sighed Lóim. 'What if they're not coming?'

'You know, you've repeated that a lot,' seethed Gahli. 'I'd say you were impatient, not to mention *pessimistic.*' She put her hands on her hips.

'He's eager to go home,' said Ihal.

'We do have important things to do there,' Lóim protested in defence. 'It's high time we went home.'

'You know, for someone who always looks for a good reason to boast, seems to me you're acting quite cowardly,' Ihal condescended.

'Yeah, what are you afraid of? The remaining phantom?' asked Gahli.

Tom, Huck, Jeremy, Pete, and Mittah looked at each other and sighed.

'That is so like you, Lóim,' said Ihal. 'Self-centred! Conceited. Always thinking of yourself, what *you* want, what's best for *you*.'

'That's not true.' Lóim frowned. 'You misunderstood me. And what about you, staying so you can see Meysah again? You're thinking of your needs, too. Well, sorry if I think of my own. Besides, doesn't everyone look for something worthy to do that they can be remembered by? Isn't that why we're all out here? Don't we all want to be worthy of honour? Or the prestige we earn when we help with simpler tasks at home?'

'We all want to fight,' Ihal said in a low and steady voice, though she continued to glower. 'We all want to be remembered in the history books and for all to know that we fought for the Freedom of Life. That's why Meysah is out there right now.' Lóim swallowed but did not avert his gaze this time. 'That's why the Five were formed. That's why Bahvley is our King and Tharguen our Captain. You . . . *you* want honour and prestige. All *I* want is the Freedom of Life.'

She stalked out of the room. Lóim started after her.

'Let her be,' said Mittah. 'She obviously misunderstood. Let her vent.'

Lóim stopped and nodded, feeling dismayed.

At last, Bahvley could wait no longer. He had made his decision. They *had* waited a while more, yet still the Five never arrived. It was time to go home now. Bahvley had promised Selemil he wouldn't be gone longer than a year.

He spoke to Tharguen, who at last agreed it was time. They both then took the matter up with the Firlanians, who decided to stay and wait some more. Before their departure, Bahvley wrote a letter to the Five.

Dear Niome, Meysah, Vigh, Jimmy, Boreth,

I apologise for not staying for your arrival, but duties were calling us at home. You'll find that the Tellens are very hospitable people.

We have been worried about you and can't wait to hear your story. We ran into some trouble ourselves. I'm sure the Firlanians have already recounted the story.

We miss you greatly, all of you. I won't tell our people of your misadventure – I'll pretend that you chose to stay here. I don't want to worry Teloria, though I myself am extremely worried about you. Please, come home soon.

With love,

Bahvley

P.S.: I, too, emphasise on 'come home soon'. I agree with Bahvley and cannot wait to see you. Or hold you in my arms, Niome. The Kikies and certain people miss you very much, Meysah and Jimmy. I love you, Niome.
Tharguen

Bahvley entrusted the letter to Kchalami so he could deliver it to the Five once they'd arrived. Tharguen approached Kchalami, a weight on his heart, as the Firlanian Prince placed the letter in a safe place.

'You love her, don't you?' Kchalami averted his eyes. 'Kchalami,' Tharguen said firmly, taking a step forward. 'This does not change the friendship you and I have.'

Kchalami met his gaze. 'I would never . . . I respect that she loves you.'

'I know. That is why I trust you. Why I trust you to remain here while I return to Teloria. Why I trust you with our letter more than anyone else. Why I know that you of all people understand how I feel and wish to see Niome return to us safe.'

'You are an honourable polc, Tharguen, and a better friend than I would be were I in your shoes.' The two exchanged a wan smile. 'I appreciate you, and I promise to be true to our friendship and to my friendship with Niome.'

Tharguen placed a hand on Kchalami's shoulder before embracing him fondly. 'You are a better friend than you realise. Thank you.'

Kchalami pulled away. 'Stay safe in Teloria . . .and alive.'

'You, too, stay safe and alive.'

And so it was, on the forty-ninth of Spring, that the Telorians left for home, set to arrive there twelve days later. Stëinbøk had embraced them all and bade them all safe travels.

'I have grown very fond of you,' he had said.

Tharguen had scanned his team with his eyes to find the one Stëinbøk referred to, having seen the young Tellen King blush when he said this. There was something in the way he had said it.

Tharguen remembered watching Niome in the Morkan caves as Gowtch, his heart making him yearn to hold her in his arms, unable to say anything at the time. When he held her now, there was magic that surged through his entire body. True love was incomparable, without description.

His heart grew heavier with each step he took towards Teloria as he yearned for his one true love and hoped for her safety.

On that very same day, in an old grey house, many other letters were being written. Drúgan had already written his letter to Maria and Tobias and now wrote to the unknown people of the far-off lands. No one knew who dwelt there, or if the Kaulchèc still existed.

'Someone ought to tell them what they caused,' Drúgan had stated, 'for after all, Mirauk's power and desire to rule the world came from one simple spell at the beginning of Kaulchèc History. If those people, or any people, exist in that faraway region, they have a right to know what is happening.'

Drúgan cast a spell on the letter so the people could read the Common Tongue whether or not it was not their native tongue.

Soon after, the Ghost Rider took both letters with him. He would ride on for weeks and years, all around the world and back if he had to, in order to find someone to give the letter to.

The Ghost Rider paused at the door and turned his helmeted head to Vigh and Boreth. 'Good luck. May the stars protect you.'

Boreth and Vigh exchanged a surprised look before thanking him – it was the first time either of them had heard him speak.

Tlúnëe clasped hands with their ghostly friend. 'Be careful out there. We need you back safe.' Something passed between them, and the two nodded solemnly.

'I will,' the Ghost Rider assured.

Drúgan smiled. 'I will see you upon your return, my friend.'

The Ghost Rider tapped the place where he kept the letters. Then he turned, mounted his ghostly horse, and galloped away at wind's speed, vanishing before he could disappear in the distance.

'Surely you know the polc who hides behind the Ghost Rider's armour,' said Boreth, looking into the distance.

Drúgan shrugged, shutting the door as he shuffled away, chuckling.

'Tlúnëe?' asked Vigh. 'You're the prophet.'

'I see the future.' Tlúnëe shrugged, waving a hand in dismissal, and followed his grandfather.

Boreth turned to Clahria, who only shook her head. 'I honestly don't know. What I *do* know is that he's been helping my family since before I was born.'

Twelve days later, Boreth and Vigh were ready to leave.

'Be careful,' said Clahria. 'Many creatures roam out there, and even if they don't intend to harm you, they may be used for evil's benefit.'

'Don't you worry, my love,' Boreth reassured her, 'we'll be safe. Of course we will.' He chuckled. 'I'll miss you.'

Vigh turned his back to them to give them some privacy, not understanding the strange feeling that filled his heart. Perhaps it was time to forget the past and fall in love again, though he said nothing of the matter as the two Lords set off.

Somewhere a little north of them walked Niome. She had travelled through the Hills almost straight ahead and crossed where the Ortim River split towards the Twisted Rapids. She found a nice spot with many rocks to help her jump to the other side, then she turned southwards.

Niome was not far now from the Twisted Forest. It was the second of the tenth of Spring. Once she found a place to rest, she sat down to write Tharguen a letter and alleviate her longing.

The wind picked up as night fell, causing the pages in her notebook to flip. The wind whistled like a warning.

Night fell completely. Niome had not yet completed her letter.

Before she could close her book, a dark armoured hand slapped down on the page and ripped it out. Yelping in shock, Niome backed away, clutching her book close to her bosom.

As her letter blew away with the gusting wind, the figure stepped forward.

'Who are you, phantom?' demanded Niome, remembering the figures they'd seen on their way to Dûnelor. 'What do you want?'

Niome worried why she hadn't sensed its approach. What magic was this, that she had not felt its presence until its hand gripped her book?

'*Fekhisar bodokhlogat!*'

'What are you saying? Who are you looking for? What do you want?'

'*Niome Fairhaven!*'

Niome's stomach knotted in fear. Her blood ran cold. She backed away, fumbling for the Tweedle Spell Book.

'Tweedle wrote me a spell for this, I'm sure of it,' she said to herself, keeping her gaze on the phantom. 'Where is it?'

The phantom ripped another page out as it tried to grab the book. Niome unsheathed her sword and slashed the phantom, but it did it no harm. She fumbled around for the *Dragon's Wind*.

The phantom unhooded itself, revealing its pale face. Then it pounced, giving her no time to fight back. As it bit her in the thigh, Niome cried out loudly. She tried to fight back, kicking, punching, and swinging her sword.

The phantom struck her head with such strength that darkness took her.

It sucked on her blood all night. Then, before the first light of day, it vanished.

Chapter Seven:
Absences

It was just around evening when Jimmy and Meysah entered the forest on that late Spring day, quite some time before Niome would approach the forest herself. As they waved the dragon goodbye, it soared into the air and back towards its lair. They then turned back to that which worried them – all the dead trees and burnt underbrush.

'Look at all this!' gasped Jimmy. 'A quick flight to bring us to this?'

'Look over there,' said Meysah. 'The trees are still intact.'

'D'you think Em took advantage of the drought to create a forest fire?'

'Possibly,' said Meysah. 'He *is* capable of a lot, unfortunately. Though we shan't say a word of it to the others.'

'The drought? Why not?' said Jimmy. 'It's over now.'

'I have a feeling that it isn't. And anyway, Niome said she'd let us know when it would be okay to tell the others. Remember? She's in charge of this. So until then, not a word.'

Soon, they entered the deep trees. It was the middle of the night now. They heard voices nearby.

'There it is,' said the first.

'Who?' Jimmy whispered into Meysah's ear.

'Shh!'

'We can hold out till morning,' said another voice.

'We jump down and attack,' said the first.

'Attack who?' whispered Jimmy.

'*Sshhhh!*'

Then there were no more voices.

'They heard you, Jimmy. You scared them away.'

'*I* scared them away? Your shushes are louder than my whispers!'

There was a sudden strange grumbling noise. It was close.

'What's that?' Jimmy quavered, speaking slowly.

A dark figure approached them.

'Uh, it's one of the invincible ghosts,' Meysah trembled.

The lads slowly backed away and started to run backward before they bumped into someone. They turned around to find themselves facing a polc clad in forest colours. Startled, they yelped and ran off.

'Wait!' shouted the polc.

There were many '*waits*' called out by many different voices. At last, they stopped, but then there was another sound – the sound of people struggling or in pain.

Jimmy and Meysah exchanged a look and nodded. They drew their weapons and returned to see the phantom attacking the polcs. They pounced on the phantom and held it back, but it quickly pushed them off and stared at them.

'Who are you, and what do you want?' demanded Meysah.

'Fairhaven!'

'That's my name!' Meysah gasped.

'Niome Fairhaven!'

'Oh, Niome's not with us.'

'We won't let you hurt her!' declared Jimmy. The phantom began grumbling to itself.

'Jimmy! What do you remember of the Morkan tongue that Tharguen taught us? I think it only speaks Morkan.'

'I think "you" is *kuyoth* or something. *Kuyoth, kuyokh . . .*'

'Thanks,' Meysah said sarcastically. '*Kuyokh,* go!' Meysah commanded, pointing away. 'Niome's . . . not . . . here.'

Seemingly deterred, the phantom began drifting off.

'No!' cried Jimmy. 'Do you realise what you just did?! She could be on her way!'

'Oh no,' Meysah realised. 'I've sent a phantom after Niome. No!' Meysah dropped his shoulders, hanging his head.

The forest dwellers approached them. 'I take it you're friends of King Bahvley.'

'Bahvley! He's my brother.'

The two polcs bowed, and others approached.

'He is our friend. We are Tellens, the people who live here and serve our King, Stëinbøk.'

'Nice to meet you,' said Meysah. 'I fear I just made a mistake in sending that . . . creature away.'

'You saved us,' said the Tellen. 'I'm Lirogon. These are me friends: Estemlenk, Gardëvøn, Kelnabøk, and Passtëgon.'

'I'm Meysah.'

'And I'm Jimmy. We were supposed to come here with Bahvley, but we got delayed.'

'We know the story. They told us,' said Lirogon.

Meysah perked up. 'Ah, then you must know that the other three should be coming here, too. We got separated. Have they arrived?'

'Not so far as we know. You'll find out once you join your friends at the fortress.'

'Is the fortress far?' inquired Jimmy. 'I don't want to run into another one of those creatures.'

'The others of its kind have been destroyed,' said Kelnabøk.

'Me King and yours, and our friends and yours, fought them and held them down until mornin',' said Estemlenk. 'You see, they lose their ability to vanish when being held by a mortal, and with the Sun, they turn to dust.'

'How did you know how to destroy them?' asked Meysah.

"Tis a long story, one that I'm sure King Fairhaven can't wait to tell you himself,' said Lirogon.

'King Fairhaven,' Jimmy said, grinning. 'Sounds sophisticated. Not like the Bahvley we know.'

'No,' replied Meysah, 'the Bahvley I know can be quite annoying from time to time. I'll sure be glad to see him again, though.' Jimmy agreed.

'Come and rest yourselves at our shelter,' continued Lirogon. 'Night is a dangerous time to travel, phantom or no phantom. Animals hunt, too.'

They followed the Tellens to the shelter, where they spent the night. The next day, they travelled with the guidance of Passtëgon, who had duties awaiting him at the fortress, while the others remained at their posts.

The eight days it took them to reach the fortress were pleasant. Passtëgon told them about his culture, his people, and of their names – Jimmy had found them quite peculiar.

They arrived in the night. Jimmy and Meysah couldn't wait to see Bahvley and Tharguen again, let alone Gahli and Ihal. After all they had been through, it was such a relief to know they'd be with the others again. Not to mention, they wanted to boast about how they had made Kàtchah and his forces retreat.

They were led to the main floor where the Firlanians had gathered. Elmezni pounced at them right away, pulling both polcs into a hug.

'What took you so long?! Where were you? What happened?! We've been worried sick!'

'We could ask you the same,' replied Jimmy, chuckling.

'Elmezni forgets our absence at the Ortim River,' said Krystal. 'Some of us were injured from the phantoms, and then there was that fire.'

'Oh,' said Meysah. 'Well, we ran into some trouble as well.'

'Tell me about it!' sighed Jimmy.

'Well, it sure is good to see you,' smiled Elmezni, his sister nodding beside him.

'Where's Bahvley?' asked Meysah. 'We're dying to see the others.' The Firlanians fidgeted uneasily, unheeded by the two lads. 'And we all know who *Jimmy's* dying to see.'

'Meysah, come on!' Jimmy blushed.

'Uhm, we, uh . . . well . . .' started Elmezni.

Kchalami stood and strode over to them, handing them Bahvley's letter.

'What's this?' asked Jimmy.

'Just read it,' said Kchalami, his expression solemn.

Meysah creased his brows in confusion, unfolding the letter. The two Telorians read intently.

'So, what, they're not here?' Meysah sighed. 'What a disappointment!'

'I know,' Kchalami sympathised. 'They left last week.'

'Great,' Jimmy said sarcastically. 'That's when we arrived at this forest.' He shook his head. 'We can't go try to stop them now. It's too late – they're probably almost home. And we have to wait for Niome, Boreth, and Vigh.'

'I'm sorry you only got here now,' expressed Elmezni. 'But *we're* here, you know.'

'That's true,' said Meysah, offering his friend a wan smile, though deep inside, he was upset at this development.

'Even had we seen them, it would have been only us,' offered Jimmy. 'Niome, Vigh, and Boreth have yet to arrive, and the five of us being separated from each other might have worried Bahvley and Tharguen more.'

'I suppose,' sighed Meysah as Jimmy rubbed his back. 'I really wanted to see my brother again.'

'Speaking of the other three,' began Akchmassiel, 'do you know where they are?'

'No,' replied Meysah.

'Nor what's happened to them,' said Jimmy.

'That's why our meeting point is here, and why we were asking the Tellens if they had arrived,' explained Meysah. 'We got separated from them.'

'I'm sorry to hear, then,' said Akchmassiel. 'This Winter has indeed been harder on you than on any of us. Even those of us who were wounded by the bite of a phantom.'

'You were bitten, too?' gasped Jimmy.

'Yes. I woke up thinking I was still in Firlan, planning the trip to visit you lot in Teloria.'

'Let's not allow our thoughts to linger on those dreadful creatures,' said Kchalami, his expression inscrutable. 'Come meet the Tellen King. I believe he's somewhere taking care of business and has yet to hear of your arrival.'

They followed Kchalami and found Stëinbøk in the garden, sitting quietly. Stëinbøk was quite pleased to meet the two Telorians and told them it was an honour, expressing his eagerness to meet the other three. Meysah and Jimmy told him of the phantom they encountered that was now out of the forest. Stëinbøk was glad it had left the territory.

Within the fortress, Jimmy and Meysah made themselves comfortable. There was much news to share in the days to come. However, Jimmy and Meysah grew more and more worried about the others. They still had not arrived.

'Now that Tharguen and the others have returned to Teloria, this makes it longer till we see Gahli and Ihal again,' said Jimmy as he and Meysah sat around the hearth. 'Are you worried about Lóim?'

Meysah shrugged. 'I don't think he'd do anything like what you're implying.'

'He was all over Ihal in Dûnelor.'

Meysah rolled his eyes. 'That was before she and I started a romantic relationship.'

'And he was jealous.' Jimmy made a face, placing his hand out as though presenting something.

Meysah shook his head. 'I know how Lóim feels about Ihal, but I also know that he has principles. Yes, part of me is worried – how can I *not* be – but I cannot believe that he would take advantage of her like that. He cares too much about her for that.' Meysah shifted. 'Besides, he's changed from how he once was, and . . . I've rather grown fond of him. I'd like to think he and I have a bond now, a mutual respect.'

'I wouldn't worry about Lóim,' said Elmezni as he entered the room and joined the two lads. 'The whole time they were here, Lóim reassured Ihal, made sure she was safe, and gave her hope that you'd arrive here soon.'

'Really?' Meysah raised his brows.

Elmezni nodded. 'That's when he himself wasn't worrying about you. He genuinely wished to know you were safe.'

'That's actually . . . a lot kinder than I thought he'd be,' admitted Jimmy.

'He's not heartless, Jimmy,' Meysah argued.

'You're defending him now?'

'Well . . . yes, I suppose I am,' replied Meysah.

'You do remember him making fun of you and putting you down all those years, don't you?'

'I thought you were getting along with him.' Meysah recalled their debate on the relationship between magic and the Mighty Spirit.

'Well, yes, but . . .' Jimmy shrugged.

'He's changed,' repeated Meysah. 'He was on my team in Dûnelor, and . . . I guess I discovered a different side of him, that's all.'

'He has more respect for you both *and* for your relationship with Ihal, Meysah, than you give him credit for,' said Elmezni.

'I suppose that makes him my friend.' Meysah smiled to himself.

'He's certainly mine,' said Elmezni.

Jimmy rolled his eyes, bobbing his head from side to side. 'I suppose I did enjoy conversing with him . . .' He rolled his head dramatically. 'Fine, he's *our* friend. I'll try not to taunt you about him.'

'Appreciated,' said Meysah. 'Don't worry, you'll find someone else to complain about.' The three of them chuckled.

On the second day of the tenth week of Spring, Meysah woke up in the night in a fright, though he had not been dreaming. He felt cold but hot in the face, and he shivered from fear. An extreme panic filled his body as a piercing pain shot up his leg. Shivers ran through his spine.

He bounced out of bed and went to wake Jimmy.

'You always wake me up way too early in the morning, don't you,' Jimmy said groggily.

'It's not morning.'

Jimmy sat up and noticed the expression on his friend's face. 'What's wrong?'

'Something's happened.' Meysah was trembling. The sight worried Jimmy. 'I don't know what, though, or to whom, but I sensed something just now when I woke up. Something bad, *really* bad, has happened to someone we love dearly.'

'I'm sure whoever it is will be fine,' Jimmy tried to reassure him, 'but why didn't *I* sense it?'

'Maybe it's a connection I have with this person.' Meysah took a deep breath to calm his shaking body.

'You don't think something's happened to Bahvley, do you? I hope they'll be all right, whoever it is you sensed. I suddenly feel scared, though, more than when I'm in the presence of Morkans – it's as though I can sense through you what you felt.'

'I wish it were only a case of a weird stomachache,' admitted Meysah. 'Strangely enough, I wish it were one of those, but it's more than that.' His breath quavered.

'You're scaring me, Meysah. I don't know what to do. Your face says it all.'

'How do you think *I* feel?' snapped Meysah as a surge of the shakes overtook him.

'It's okay. It'll be okay,' Jimmy reassured, rubbing Meysah's back. 'We may soon find out, and everything might be all right like it always is.' Jimmy hugged his friend tightly.

'What if Niome, or Vigh, or Boreth, or Bahvley, or Ihal, or . . .' Meysah brought a hand to his forehead. 'How are we supposed to know who I sensed?'

'We're not.'

Jimmy was right; they were not meant to know. They sat on the bed next to each other, frightened, confused, and unable to sleep.

CHAPTER EIGHT:
The Undefeatable Few

Vigh and Boreth were just a day or two away from the Twisted Forest now and walking steadily when something caught Boreth's eye. He stopped, staring at the ground.

'What is it?' asked Vigh.

'There are marks on the ground. As though someone was struggling, fighting. Look here and there – the grass is flattened.' Boreth crouched. 'I only see one set of prints.'

'What could someone have been fighting?' Vigh inquired eerily.

'Or *who* did that . . . thing . . . fight?' Boreth noticed something else. 'What's this?' He plucked some grass and studied it. 'Blood! Dried!'

'How long?'

'From this night – less than a full day's cycle, I believe. We can still catch the person or thing. The prints continue that way.'

The two followed the trail at a run, but the prints stopped very abruptly and turned into horse prints. They followed the sporadic trail for more than a day before stopping.

'It leads to those woods,' said Vigh.

'No,' said Boreth, 'I don't think so. But wherever it leads, it's too far and out of our reach. We've delayed long enough – the others will be waiting for us. If we need to, we'll return to investigate further.'

'Very well,' said Vigh. 'I don't even know what we were going after. But we may find out in due time.'

They turned back and travelled to the Twisted Forest, reaching it at last four days later. They took in the sight of burnt trees and, for a while, they walked through the ashes.

'I don't understand,' voiced Vigh.

'It's . . . you know what it is,' Boreth said with disdain. '*He* took advantage of the drought. That's what he did.'

'That might explain our friends not showing up. Yet, something tells me there's more to it than just a forest fire.'

'Do you think there was an attack?' asked Boreth.

'I don't know, but I do know something tragic happened for them not to arrive at the appointed time.'

'This reminds me of the camp imprisonments,' said Boreth as he stepped over a fallen tree.

'You're right,' said Vigh. 'There was a fire then, too.'

'And when we were travelling . . .'

'The team never showed up.'

'Because they were ambushed. Except' – Boreth recalled that time of turmoil, his eyes going distant for a moment – 'I was the one not to arrive because I was on that team.'

'It was the first and last time we fought in separate teams,' said Vigh. He ducked to pass under some low branches. 'Never again did we split up and not fight as partners. We had thought it would help to have each expert with a different Captain.'

'See, even then, we were destined to work together or perish otherwise,' said Boreth. The two lifted broken branches to swipe them aside as they walked towards the lusher part of the forest. 'For even then we were, well, practically invincible when we fought together.'

'Like Gorthan always said, "Life has strange ways of working itself out."'

'Gorthan,' said Boreth, pausing only long enough to hack away a thorny branch. 'I miss him. He once told me that the Mighty Spirit gives us the desires and passions that coincide with the plans of the stars. We wished to be Masters because it was the way of the stars. And look it, we're even Lords now.'

'Only sometimes can we alter destiny,' mused Vigh. 'I wonder what Gorthan's plan was. Could he have altered his fate, or did he choose to die?'

'I think he chose to die,' said Boreth. 'We, on the other hand, choose to live.' He looked up at the sky. 'And I believe the stars will protect us.' He tripped on a fallen branch then, staggering forward before catching himself. 'But we should probably still watch our step.'

Vigh smiled as they walked on in silence.

The Lords reached the lush part of the forest by the next day.

'Hey you, down there!' a voice called out. 'Please wait a moment!'

The forest dweller climbed down from a ladder that gave access to a makeshift shelter. Vigh and Boreth exchanged a look as the polc smiled at them.

'I'm goin' to need your names, even if I suspect who you are.'

'Oh, I'm Vigh and this is Boreth. We're here to join our King and friends, King Bahvley and Captain Tharguen and his team.'

'Then I can give you me help. I am Devnolenk. Welcome to the land of the Tellens. I have been told quite a bit about you.'

'Would you happen to know if the others have arrived?' inquired Boreth as the polc led the Lords through the dense greenery of the burgeoning trees.

'Sorry, I don't, but you'll know soon enough.'

Soon enough indeed, for after a week's travel through the forest, guided by Devnolenk, they arrived at the fortress.

As soon as they stepped in, Jimmy and Meysah pounced at them, arms wide open. They excitedly recounted their encounter with the phantom and informed them Bahvley and the others had had to leave, showing them the letter.

'But where's Niome?' asked Boreth.

'She hasn't arrived yet, I guess,' replied Meysah.

'What do you mean? I thought she was with you,' Vigh said with a scowl.

'No. *We* thought she was with *you*,' Meysah said slowly. 'Remember? We left and she stayed with you.'

'But she escaped while we stayed trapped,' said Boreth.

The four of them exchanged wary glances. Meysah chewed his lip as Vigh put a hand to his brow.

'She could've gone to Firlan,' suggested Jimmy. 'She could simply be late. We know how it is in Firlan – you want to stay.'

'Maybe.' Vigh and Boreth exchanged a worried look.

Though the lads were hopeful, it brought little comfort to the two Lords, especially after Meysah recounted his panic episode. The lads remained cheery, however, especially after hearing about how the Lords escaped, now understanding the pool of water that had formed in Darakön.

The Lords said nothing of the blood they had found. Blood they both feared belonged to Niome.

Time passed, and still Niome had not arrived. It was far into Summer now and everyone had grown worried. Boreth and Vigh took it upon themselves to go investigate, considering one phantom remained. They insisted they go alone. Jimmy and Meysah insisted otherwise, but Vigh argued that if something had indeed happened, it was easier for the Lords to go by unseen.

Thus, Boreth and Vigh travelled for two and a half weeks through the forest and to the plains towards the forest north of Zaccher Lake.

'Remind me what day we are,' said Boreth as they entered the northmost Zaccher wood. He shivered, tightening his scarf.

'The fifth day of the eleventh week.'

'Colouring is on its way, though it feels far frostier than it should be. We waited too long before coming here . . . the evidence is gone, yet we *know* we need to investigate. Although I don't quite understand why th—' Abruptly, he stopped.

'What don't you understand, Boreth?'

Boreth lifted his hand up in a sign to wait. 'I hear people,' he whispered.

Over the wind, two voices could be heard. The Lords slunk behind some trees and peered over the sides. There were indeed two polcs who appeared to be hunting. Both were covered up with scarves; only their eyes could be seen.

The hunters were clad in leathers that blended with the foliage. The two masters could not identify the polcs from this distance. They crept closer.

One of the polcs was now out of view. The other stood with a sword in one hand, creeping close to where a rabbit munched away. She crouched, poised to strike her prey.

A twig snapped beneath Vigh's foot. The bunny hopped away, and the crouching polc rose and began looking about. The Lords took a few cautious steps back. The polc spun around, surprised.

'Who are you? What do you want?' She pointed her sword at them, though her grip was somewhat relaxed. Her voice was harsh, yet muffled by the scarf.

'We mean you no harm,' Vigh answered quickly, raising his hands in surrender. 'We apologise for surprising you.'

'We're looking for someone – a friend. We believe she travelled this way,' said Boreth.

'I saw no one. How can I believe you are truly' – the polc glanced at their sheathed swords – 'harmless?' She had a strange air.

'Because we're Telorians,' said Vigh. 'And we're looking for another one of our kind. Her name is Niome.'

'I've heard no one with that name.' The woman seemed familiar, yet her demeanour was unrecognisable. 'How do I know you're telling the truth?'

'We *are* being truthful,' said Boreth.

The polc took a step closer, her sword still pointed at them. She studied them more carefully.

'You know what,' Vigh said dryly, feeling more confused than anything, 'you're right. She's not here. We'll go now.'

'Yes, please do.'

The Lords backed away before running the way they'd come, stopping only once they were out of the woods.

Vigh bent to catch his breath. 'Tell me that wasn't Niome.'

'It didn't look like her, not in that hunter's gear. She did not wield her usual sword, and we didn't see her face, but her voice . . .' Boreth took in a deep breath, still panting from the run.

'Niome doesn't act like that. She would've recognised us.'

'It could be someone who sounds like her,' suggested Boreth, 'but I feel like . . . it was her. If that was Niome, it's not the one *we* know.'

'Are you suggesting . . . ?' Vigh swiped his hand through the air with a shake of his head. 'No. It can't be. The fate of the world depends on her – it can't be.'

'No, it can't. It could just be a wary polc who reminds us of her. We could be so worried that we attribute . . .' Boreth stared into the distance of the wood. 'I think it best we kept this to ourselves.'

'I think so too,' agreed Vigh.

A few days later, Boreth spied a large group of polcs from afar. He quickly grabbed Vigh and pulled him down with him, lunging behind some rocks. Boreth peered above their makeshift hiding spot before he crouched back down, leaning his back against the rocks.

'There's a good number of Morkans coming this way. I think they may be headed for the Twisted Forest.'

'How far are they?'

'Perhaps a day.'

'Your farsight really has improved.'

'Yes,' said Boreth, turning his head to look at Vigh, his expression grave. 'And if I can see them, there's at least one of them who's bound to see us.

We'll have to hurry and get back to the forest in time to warn Stëinbøk.'

'Do you think it's the Dukes?'

'No. They would have already come and seen us gone. But I can tell you who I do think it is.'

'Oh, please don't.' Vigh laughed mirthlessly. 'I'd rather not have the surprise spoiled.'

The Lords dashed across the plains as fast as their legs would carry them, trying to gain another day or two ahead of the army. They took only a short rest in the night once they hit the forest. They arrived at the fortress ten days after they had seen the army, bounding up the stairs to find the others.

Jimmy and Meysah quickly found Stëinbøk, who was joined by Hunbøk and Derfbøk.

'What's this I hear about Morkans?' the Tellen King asked.

'There's an army of Morkans on its way here,' explained Boreth. 'Or at least, I believe they're coming here. They were perhaps a day away when I first spotted them. Now, they could be two or three days away, hopefully. But they're in these woods.'

'I don't appreciate Mirauk sending his troops here,' said Derfbøk.

'It was bound to happen,' said Stëinbøk. 'Did you think he would ignore our existence forever? I've been expecting this for the past few decades.' He paused. 'No horn has been sounded. It's impossible to go through unnoticed in the Twisted Forest at this time of year.'

'What if they're pretending to be friendly?' asked Jimmy.

'You think?' Vigh pondered.

'In that case, an ambush could do,' said Stëinbøk.

'Like in Dûnelor?' suggested Meysah. 'We should be careful that they don't pull the same trick on us here.'

'Who could have possibly been sent here?' wondered Jimmy.

'They won't leave without putting up a fight first,' Hunbøk surmised.

'That might not be necessary, if we play our cards right,' said Stëinbøk.

'What about Niome?' asked Meysah. 'If she runs into them—'

'Your Majesty,' Dublenk called out, arriving in a hurry. 'There is a large number of polcs at our door. They claim they're from Teloria.'

'Or maybe not,' said Meysah, narrowing his eyes.

'They *seem* friendly enough, if you don't mind me sayin',' said Dublenk. 'They have horses with them, dark horses.'

'Horses?' exclaimed Boreth. 'My farsight is not good enough yet – I didn't see that they were riders. This means they were right behind us the whole time!'

'Meysah,' said Vigh, 'we didn't find Niome. We don't know what to make of it, but we should wait for her here until she sends a message or arrives.' Meysah nodded, dismayed. Vigh patted his shoulder in sympathy.

'Dublenk,' said Stëinbøk. 'Gather up as many as you can. We'll welcome these so-called Telorians and ambush them.' He gave out instructions as he hatched out his plan, then turned to the four Telorians. 'I suggest the four of you lie low.' Jimmy scowled. 'For now,' the Tellen King added, nodding towards Jimmy, 'and once we've confiscated their weapons, you can do what you want.' Jimmy smiled. 'Derfbøk, with me.'

Displeased, Stëinbøk made his way to the gates with Derfbøk. Dublenk had gathered Lenarbøk, Vessibøk, Attëgon, Corivøn, Nastafin, Merilenk, and many others, all of whom plastered diplomatic smiles on their faces to greet the imposters also wearing fake smiles.

'Welcome to me fortress,' said Stëinbøk. 'Long has it been since we've had visitors, let alone contact with Teloria.'

The Morkans entered the antichambre.

'Thank you. I am Captain Oldomil. This is my team.'

'I see you have horses,' said Stëinbøk. 'Guards, lead the horses to the stables and feed them. They've travelled long.'

Several guards led the dark horses away.

'Let us make you feel more comfortable,' said Stëinbøk. 'If it pleases you, I can even have your weapons polished and sharpened for you,' he offered as his polcs started retrieving weapons from the Morkans, though many insisted on keeping them. 'As is our custom for guests,' he added, assessing his enemies mentally – there were twenty of them.

After more 'polite' exchanges, the Tellens insisted they serve their guests honourably, taking more weapons from the Morkans before any of them could protest. The Tellens were then joined by the Firlanians as all trained their weapons on their 'guests.' The Morkans were surrounded and outnumbered.

'Tough luck!' said Kchalami. 'We Firlanians arrived quite some time before you did.'

'And so did we,' declared Boreth from behind a door.

'And for your information,' began Vigh as the four of them emerged, entering the hall, 'Oldomil is an old name that has not been used in a long time. I think I'd recognise' – they stepped closer to the Captain – 'the real Oldomil . . . Kàtchah! Who, by the way, is grey with old age and spends his time knitting for his children's shop. You might want to do some research next time, Kàtchah.'

Kàtchah shifted uneasily.

'But see, I *am* confused, because you were destroyed.'

'My *tunnels* were flooded and destroyed, not *me*,' snarled Kàtchah. 'Them being destroyed does not mean *I* was. Once I saw what was happening, many of us were able to dig ourselves out. We retreated to the caves, near Dalvar, before deciding to come here.'

'Talk about invincibility,' Boreth muttered to himself, clocking Gohtek and Sikhlah among the Morkans.

'I hope that Mm-mm – that you will be punished by your superiors for your failures!' sneered Jimmy. 'Doesn't he ever die?' he complained to Meysah.

'As a member of the Inner Circle, I have only one superior: Mirauk.'

'I told you you wouldn't succeed,' declared Meysah. 'The dragons are far too powerful for that.'

'So where's your Wizardess sister? Where is she hiding?' Kàtchah tried to look past Meysah and the others.

'If you don't comply,' began Boreth, 'she'll cast an awful spell on you. She is just waiting for our cue.'

'You know that I won't surrender without a fight,' said Kàtchah, narrowing his gaze.

'Niome!' Boreth called out. There was no hint of her absence present on any of their faces.

'You're bluffing.' Kàtchah folded his arms.

'Oh, no he's not,' said Vigh.

'I don't believe it,' said Kàtchah.

'*Eimai stöihugat . . .*' started Boreth.

Maybe this was just the spell to send thoughts to another, but none of the Morkans knew that or could understand it.

'What's he saying?' demanded Kàtchah.

'It's called Ancient Telorian,' Jimmy condescended.

'He's instructing Niome,' said Vigh, hoping Kàtchah would call their bluff.

'I'm not worried,' said Kàtchah as he deftly produced a knife from his boot. 'She's probably not even here.'

'*Dan eimai siginelef,*' continued Boreth.

'He's just rattling out words, sounds,' claimed Kàtchah. 'This is gibberish. There won't be anything to—'

'*Idenas!*' yelled Boreth. Kàtchah instantly shut up, looking worried. '*Mehetot Niome!*'

Boreth entered a brief trance, but his message never reached Niome. Instead, it bounced to all four of them, forcing them all into a magical trance, heads jolting up, arms outstretched, bodies aglow.

Kàtchah backed away, dropping his knife.

'Give up your weapons! NOW!' shouted Stëinbøk.

The Morkans surrendered all of their weapons and the Tellens bound their hands and legs. A few Firlanians, including Kchalami, lowered their weapons.

'So, at last I meet the famous Captain Kàtchah,' said Kchalami. 'You're lucky you came *here* and not to Firlan. You would've been completely destroyed there.'

'The thought did cross my mind,' admitted Kàtchah. 'But if a few dozen of my polcs passed near there going after *those* two' – he pointed his bound hands at Jimmy and Meysah – 'and were never seen again, I wasn't going to go there myself.'

'My father probably ensured your troops didn't reach our friends,' said Kchalami.

'I recognise some of these Morkans,' Jimmy said smugly. 'Yes, remember me? You thought I was a Morkan Captain while you were all under a spell. Even you, Kàtchah, believed it for a moment as well. Gohtek gave me the title. Blame him.'

'I didn't think it possible for a Telorian to trespass in such a secret place.'

'Oh . . . and you're still alive,' Jimmy mocked Kàtchah. 'What a pity.'

'Jimmy!' snapped Boreth, giving him a warning look.

'I'm just saying, it's funny how it all happened,' Jimmy justified.

'I knew there was something wrong! I knew you weren't who you seemed to be, but no one listened to me!' complained Sikhlah from among the Morkans.

'Take them away!' said Stëinbøk, annoyed.

Tellens and Firlanians led the Morkans to prison cells.

'Kchalami,' said Stëinbøk, 'I want you and the others to accompany me when I escort them out of the forest.'

'I want that too,' Kchalami confirmed.

'We're coming too,' said Meysah.

'For once, these Morkans will learn not to mess with the Tellens,' said Stëinbøk.

'Apparently, they haven't understood yet that some polcs may be more powerful than them,' said Vigh. 'Why do we have to gather up all the people of the world to fight them so they can understand that all we want is for things to be simple again, the way it was before? No complicated spells, no Portal, no prejudice, no greed for power. They are destroying our world!'

'Sometimes I feel like I'm the brutal one,' admitted Boreth.

'Right now, we have to act,' said Stëinbøk. 'They surrendered – that's good enough for me. As long as they don't attack, I will not either. I have a message I want Kàtchah to deliver to Mirauk. Tomorrow, we lead them out.'

Stëinbøk and many other Tellens, Kchalami and the other Firlanians, and the four Telorians escorted the Morkans and their steeds away from the forest. The

Morkans grumbled as they trudged along, whining about this humiliation.

'Niome has not yet joined you, has she?' Kàtchah observed.

'What?' the four Telorians voiced all at once.

Kàtchah chuckled, feeling smug. 'Otherwise, she'd be here. I thought her voice ringing useless lessons in my ear was missing. You actually managed to fool me, once again. Congratulations.'

'She may not be here now,' Meysah began defiantly, 'but she's on her way.'

Kàtchah chuckled sinisterly.

'Oh, and when you return to Mork,' said Elmezni, 'you can tell Mirauk that we destroyed his phantoms.'

'That's impossible!' exclaimed Gohtek.

'It isn't,' Krystal said pointedly. 'We held them down when the Sun rose and they turned to ash.'

'Well, I never . . .' breathed Kàtchah. 'I never thought the secret would be discovered. Mirauk never thought, after all the information he received from your King, that Bahvley would ever remember his encounter with them.'

'Thought, or hoped?' asked Meysah, menace in his tone. Kàtchah glowered at him but remained silent the rest of the way.

By evening of the tenth day of travel, they were out of the forest. Stëinbøk strode to stand before Kàtchah.

'Tell Mirauk that his phantoms are destroyed, that the books you sought no longer exist, and that you were outsmarted by the Five and your tunnels, flooded. Those are the messages from the Telorians and Firlanians.'

Stëinbøk's face remained impassive.

'As for me and me people, tell him the Tellens will not easily forget being disturbed by conniving Morkans, and that Mirauk will have to deal with us before we let him destroy Teloria. I did not appreciate having those phantoms on my land!' A sad expression shadowed his face briefly.

'Oh, don't worry,' Kàtchah sneered, 'I'll tell him.'

'I'm going to let you go now,' said Stëinbøk. 'You're going to have your horses and your weapons, but if you attack, you will be killed.' He leaned forward and got into Kàtchah's face, putting steel in his voice as he spoke through his teeth. 'If you dare come back, make no mistake, you will be killed on sight. Pray to your Lord that you do not have to return. Do you understand?'

Kàtchah nodded without argument – he glared, but he knew when he was at a disadvantage. Stëinbøk gave his people the signal. All present trained their weapons on the Morkans as the Tellens unbound them and returned their weapons. Once freed, the Morkans mounted their horses.

'Now go!' Stëinbøk commanded.

'Come!' shouted Kàtchah. '*Sikht iliw ebekh rikhet keyatshim,* for Mirauk will fight back even more wrathfully!'

The Morkans galloped away. The Tellens, Telorians, and Firlanians watched them fade into the distance.

'Are you certain this was the wise thing to do?' asked Vigh.

'What else could I have done at this point?' asked Stëinbøk. 'I showed the enemy compassion and respect—'

'But they don't *deserve* compassion or respect!' interrupted Jimmy.

'And that proves me better than them. It means we have more strength. I'm surprised they left fearfully. I *was* prepared to fight them, but I didn't want to be the one to initiate the attack.'

'I think Kàtchah has some form of admiration for you,' said Meysah, nodding to the Tellen King. 'He is smart enough to recognise a worthy opponent, I'll give him that. But just that, nothing else.'

'In case they do return,' began Stëinbøk, 'we're going to have to endure the Winter this year and watch. At least it will be less cold than the last.'

'I'm prepared to stay out here,' said Kchalami.

'So are we,' said the four.

'Let us return to the fortress before making any further decisions,' said Stëinbøk.

Many Tellens set off to inform the watchers at the nearby shelters while the others returned to the fortress.

CHAPTER NINE:
Starting From Scratch

Over green plains and meadows rode Tobias upon his white steed. The Sun shone brightly, and magic called to him. He had left his Zaccher home some days prior, following the magic that tugged at his mind and took him south of the woods near Zaccher Lake.

As this morning passed, a strange feeling came over him. His horse neighed nervously.

'What's the matter, Wassta? What do you sense?' The horse pawed at the ground. 'I feel it too. Take me there!'

Wassta galloped a while more, following her nose as well as her magical sense. Tobias espied something on the ground from afar. As he got closer, he saw it was a polc.

Wassta came to a stop near the polc, and Tobias dismounted. He crouched beside the figure. The young woman was very pale and cold, yet her heart still beat, albeit at a slow rate, and she was breathing. Bite marks were on her leg, her pant leg torn, and droplets of blood speckled the ground around her.

Tobias produced a potion from his satchel and poured it down the polc's throat. He picked her up gently and draped her over Wassta before mounting the horse.

'Let's bring her home.'

They rode for three days, wherein Tobias tended to the girl as best he could, for he had not the proper medicine with him. He arrived home in the night and woke everyone up. His son, Olúryn, prepared a bed for the young woman, while his wife, Maria, and daughter, Gabriella, prepared medicine.

'What could have done this to such a vulnerable polc?' Olúryn asked, concern in his voice. 'It's as though her very blood has been sucked out of her.'

'I don't know,' replied Tobias. 'Many dark creatures roam from Mork, hunting anyone who refuses to join Mirauk. Fell, indeed, was her fate.'

They placed her onto a bed. Maria soon came in with the medicinal concoction and herbs for the bite. When she was done tending to the woman, she went back downstairs. Tobias and Olúryn removed the polc's cloak and folded it.

'Who is she?' inquired Olúryn.

'I don't know. Certainly not an evil polc.' They studied her gentle face.

'She's very beautiful.'

'You don't know her past, Olúryn,' warned Tobias. 'Keep your feelings in check. You could be sensing some power or magic. You know your emotions are

heightened, and you must be careful. You still have . . .
be careful what you say, because the last time you—'

'She won't die. Look, she's made stronger. I can
tell. She's not from the Twisted Forest – her garments
are different. Do you think she's Telorian?'

'Telorian! I haven't heard of anyone leaving Teloria
in ages,' said Tobias. 'Then again, it has been a long
time since we've had word from Clahria or Tlúnëe.'

Tobias covered the woman with a bundle of
blankets. Now, all that was left to do was wait and
check up on her later to see how she responded to
the medicine.

'I know it's too dangerous to send word out,' said
Olúryn. 'We could be discovered by the enemy.'

'Perhaps we may yet find clues of who she is,'
suggested Tobias.

Olúryn rummaged through the young woman's bag.
'I say she's Telorian and about ninety-five, a hundred
years old? She could be another one of those explorers
ready to try anything in the name of their kingdom.'
Olúryn paused. 'Interesting. Father, look! Potions, herbs,
books . . . a wand? A . . . cylinder? I won't touch that. But
we could sift through the books.'

Tobias took the books in his hands, one by one,
reading the titles.

'*New Book of Spells.*' He looked inside. 'No information.' He opened the next one. '*Tweedle Book of
Spells.* The first page has been ripped – only a few
portions of it remain.' He read the letters out loud. 'N-
A-V-E.'

'We can put the letters together and give her a name,' suggested Olúryn. 'It'll be a while until she wakes, and we can't refer to her as *the young woman* all the time. So: Navë. It's original.'

'Navë, it is,' confirmed Tobias. 'She has a book of personal notes.'

'Should we read it?'

'No, not without her consent. It's personal. At least now we know she knows magic. Two spell books? Think about it – this is no mere explorer. We'll learn all we need to know about her and how she got into this state when she regains consciousness.'

Tobias began returning the books to Navë's bag. Olúryn noticed Navë's hand sticking out from the blankets. He tucked it back in and paused, seeing the ring she wore on her left ring finger. He felt a pang of unease.

The four who lived at the Zaccher Grey House continued to care for 'Navë' while she slept. For days and weeks Niome remained unconscious, having disturbing dreams and visions, even becoming delirious at times. But when she awoke ten weeks later, those dreams and memories no longer mattered, for she could not re-member them. All she knew was that she was opening her eyes to a stranger's home and someone sat on the bed, watching her.

At first her vision was blurred. As it cleared, she saw a handsome polc not much younger than herself.

'I knew you'd wake today; I foresaw it,' he said, smiling warmly.

'What *is* today?'

'It's the forty-second of Summer, the seventh day of the sixth week.'

'And the year?'

'Forty-seven-seventy-three.' He studied her face. 'Do you not remember what happened to you?'

'No.'

'My father found you and brought you here. You were injured and unconscious. I'm Olúryn.'

'I . . . don't remember who I am. I can't remember.' She frowned, disheartened.

Olúryn sobered. 'That's what I feared.' He took a beat. 'You were out a long time. Your attacker was likely Morkan and sucked on your blood, as we gather from your wounds – it appears your memories were extracted, too. Do you remember anything or anyone?'

'No . . . I can't.' Niome propped herself up. 'Where am I? *Who* am I? Where do I come from?'

'Well, we found a book with perhaps your name, but most of it was ripped out. We call you Navë.' He paused. 'I understand this is difficult for you. There was a diary amongst your things. We didn't look inside; that is personal and yours. You can read it and find out what you may.' He offered Niome a sympathetic smile as her face creased with worry. 'What we do know is, you're a student of magic lore.'

'Then why can't I remember a darn spell to cast upon myself to heal myself?'

'Because you've lost your memory.'

Niome sighed, feeling depressed.

'Come, you could use some fresh air. Let me show you around the house, and you can wash up and eat a good meal.' Olúryn gave her an encouraging nod. 'It will help you remember things. Trust me. And it will heal you better.'

'Okay.'

Niome slowly sat up, her numb limbs tingling. After wiggling her extremities a bit, she got out of bed. Her head didn't hurt, and she felt alert.

Olúryn introduced her to everyone else in the household, and Maria showed her the lavatory and lent her some clothes to wear. When Niome was done washing up, the others gave her a tour around the house and yard.

Olúryn recounted how Tobias had found her and how long she was out, telling her of his family's magic works. And for days to come, she was retaught about magic and history.

Niome experienced a few dreams about her childhood, but nothing more. She clutched her ring often, wondering about it. She knew nothing, yet somehow she felt attached to this item, comforted by it, felt longing as she gazed at it.

Niome was very curious about magic, wanting to know more about this unknown force she sensed. She had not yet dared to read the diary, for she was inexplicably afraid to. There was a heaviness on her shoulders that, as Navë, she could not identify. Recurring faces appeared to her in her dreams at times, yet never told her much, with only brief glimpses.

Niome accompanied Tobias when he went out hunting several times. On one such occasion, she came across two travellers claiming they were searching for a friend. The strange encounter left her wondering about her identity even more.

Colouring arrived, and Niome had still had no dreams that told her who she was. Her memory was still a complete blank, and the distinct lack of progress worried her greatly.

'Maybe you were a simple knight,' suggested Maria as she and Niome prepared supper one afternoon. 'You were, after all, dressed for it, though I don't think the magical items you carry belong to someone else.'

'I looked over various spells, but I doubt I could ever make them work.'

'That's because you don't believe, Navë. Once you find out who you truly are and you believe in whatever power's within you, the spells will work.'

'Have you read the diary?' inquired Olúryn, joining them and setting to work cutting vegetables straight-away.

'No.'

'You should,' he said. 'It could be the answer to everything.'

'Or perhaps a burden, or a disappointment,' said Niome. She paused. 'Will Mirauk become a star?'

'He will,' Maria answered gravely, 'unless he is destroyed. Then, because he is so deeply evil and has threatened so much of what the Mighty Spirit created, he will not be reborn, and all of the world will be rid of him forever. The Mighty Spirit works that way. He will become a part of her, a part of the overcoming goodness.'

'There is a chance he may be reborn,' Olúryn countered, 'though he would be a different polc, tested by magic to become a benevolent being, his soul cleansed of evil. Still, if destroyed, he won't become a star able to instill his evil in the hearts of innocent polcs . . . for eternity.'

'Someone should go to Mork and kill him, then,' Niome stated matter-of-factly.

'It's not that simple,' said Olúryn.

'I know. His eyes. The curse.' Niome sighed. 'What are the names of the five Great Wizards of Teloria?'

'There is no fifth,' said Maria. 'There are only four.'

'But I remember five,' protested Niome. 'There are five, like the Five of the Star.'

'What star?' asked Olúryn, his curiosity piqued.

'I don't know, but there is a fifth. What's her name?'

'Navë, listen,' began Olúin, 'I know you're mixed up about everything, and it's true we've had no news from my grandfather since I was a baby, but do understand—'

'I don't have to understand anything! Don't talk to me as if I am a child.'

'That's not what I intended,' Olúryn said apologetically, his heart sinking. 'I'm sorry.'

'Look, I remember the number five! I clearly saw it.' There was a beat of silence. 'I dreamt that Teloria had a King,' continued Niome, changing the subject.

'Then I hope for Teloria's sake that it is true,' said Maria.

Niome stood and wiped her hands before leaving the room. Olúryn went to follow.

'Olúryn, no!' his mother cautioned. 'She needs her time alone. It's difficult for her. Her entire life has been stripped from her mind. How would you feel if you lost all your memory and had to start all over?'

'I wouldn't struggle so much or resist those who wished to help me,' muttered Olúryn. 'I'd start a new life and let the memories come when the time was right. It's when you *don't* think about it that a lost thought comes back to mind. And if my memories never came, I'd be all right because I'd have new ones, in my new life.'

'That's what you say now,' said Maria, 'but is that what you'd say were you in Navë's shoes?'

Olúryn looked away, hesitating. 'I wish I could give Navë all the answers she's looking for.' He turned to leave. 'This isn't difficult just for her, mother. Like it or not, she's part of our family now, and I . . .'

As he left, Maria sighed. Olúryn stepped outside and kicked some rocks to release his pent-up emotions.

Niome sat on the edge of her bed, weeping. She wished she could miss someone, feel worry for others she knew. She wished she could see a face when she yearned for the polc who gave her this ring, wished for him to hold her in his arms, but she could not remember or cling to any images of the past.

'I think you read a story about the five Great Wizards,' a small voice suggested.

'Gabriella, how is that possible? Then again, I can't remember what books I've read or not. Do you think there are five?'

'I don't know.' Gabriella entered and sat down beside Niome. 'You could be an important polc. It would be fine if you were.'

'I feel like a child,' said Niome.

'So do I.' They both laughed. Aged forty-eight, Gabriella was a very young adolescent. 'I think I'd be scared, too. Everyone wants to be special and important, but everyone who's special and important has big responsibilities. At least, that's how it is in stories I've read. If you were exploring near here, and no one explores anymore, it might mean you are somewhat important. *Or* that you know an important polc.'

'In your stories, do the heroes or their friends run away from their missions?'

'I don't think so.'

'No, I suppose not,' said Niome.

'Navë?' Niome looked up to find Olúryn in the doorway.

'Come in,' said Niome.

'Why don't you go help Mom, Gabby?'

'Okay.'

Gabriella stood and skipped out of the room as Olúryn sat down on the bed beside Niome.

'She's very wise. I suppose that's what growing up in a magical family does.' He paused. 'I'm sorry for the way I spoke to you earlier. I don't know how difficult this is for you, but I do know that you can't live in the past.'

'But what past?' asked Niome. 'I can't remember my past. I fear the responsibilities of I don't even know what! That's why I haven't read the diary yet.'

'Maybe just read one page today, and then wait before reading more. You don't have to read the whole thing now.' Olúryn fidgeted with his fingers. 'I'm worried about you. What if you never remember? You could start a new life for yourself, Navë. It's been a long while.' He turned his head to her before averting his gaze again. 'I'm not saying to rush anything,' he added quickly. 'Just consider the possibility of starting a new life . . . if you understand what I'm trying to say.'

'What if terrible things happen because I don't remember?'

'What if they don't?' Olúryn stared at Niome a moment longer. 'Just think about it.'

Olúryn stood and left, leaving Niome to ponder his words. She did as Olúryn suggested, picking up the book and reading just a page. All it said was '*Notes from the Pleessies,*' with a spell in a strange tongue below it. Wondering how she knew the Pleessies, she turned to another page that left her wondering who had shared secrets from Mork with her. *Am I Morkan?* was among the questions she asked herself.

Her dreams grew dark, yet somehow the visions reassured her that she was not Morkan, though they frightened her terribly.

There came a knock at the door during the fourth week of Colouring. Tobias answered to see the Ghost Rider atop his horse.

'Ghost Rider!'

He dismounted and walked to Tobias. 'I bring letters, though I am mightily delayed from hiding from Morkans – Morkans who know enough magic that they may sense me.'

He handed Tobias the letters, then took Tobias's hand and squeezed gently. Though he wore gauntlets, kindness and warmth passed through his touch, as it always had, which was appreciated and reciprocated. Tobias had had many good chats with the strange ghost in the past. Though the Ghost Rider was secretive, Tobias considered him a comrade. Tobias smiled at him, and they nodded to each other.

The Ghost Rider made to mount his horse but paused. He turned back to Tobias. 'I don't know what awaits me where I am to ride. May the stars shine upon you and keep you safe, Tobias.' There was sincerity in his voice.

'You too.'

The Ghost Rider mounted and left hurriedly. Tobias took the letter addressed to him from Drúgan and walked to the living room, where sat his wife. Gabriella and Olúryn were with Niome.

'A letter from Drúgan!' said Tobias, fanning the letter.

Tobias read the many pages aloud as Maria listened intently. Then they pondered about all that was shared with them.

'Then who is Navë?' Tobias wondered. 'They mention the Five of the Star, the new King, all of which Navë recalled. Could she be one of their friends?'

'Navë remembered five Great Wizards,' said Maria. 'When speaking of them, it almost sounded like . . . the Five of the Star were supposed to meet at the Twisted Forest, as mentioned by the two Lords. What if . . . ? No.' She shook her head.

'It's a shame Tlúnëe didn't share his new prophecy,' said Tobias. 'Your father only mentioned that our son had a new disturbing prophecy about the Five but didn't tell them for their own good. Do you think Navë is—'

'No,' Maria cut him off quickly.

'But she's a Wizardess!'

'Tobias, we can't jump to such conclusions,' said Maria. 'Especially not if we're to tell our children about the letter. Do you know how that would affect Olúryn – hope that might be false? Ever since his curse . . .' She sighed. 'And Gabriella is young. We don't want to cause her any despair.'

Tobias agreed.

'Assuming Navë *is* the Great Wizardess of Teloria,' Maria went on, 'well, that would imply that the world may perish because of this tragedy. We have to think positively – we have that kind of power. We can't suggest anything to Navë, because then she may start to think she's remembering when, in fact, they could be events she never lived. We cannot influence her progress.' Tobias interlaced his hands with Maria's, nodding his understanding. Maria squeezed gently. 'We mustn't hope, nor must we despair.'

CHAPTER TEN:
Lies for Truth

As soon as the Telorians arrived home, they were bombarded with questions. *Where are the Firlanians now? Where are the Five? How did it go in Dûnelor? Did you find allies at the Twisted Forest?* They answered all these and more as best they could. As to the Five, Bahvley and Tharguen told them the others had chosen to stay in the Twisted Forest a while longer.

Being home once again brought minimal comfort. When Bahvley and Tharguen arrived at the Royal Halls, they were greeted by the King's advisors.

'Good morning, Selemil, Henker. Nsarmön, nice to see you,' said Bahvley, doing his best to put on a smile.

'Welcome back,' said Selemil.

'What is the matter?' asked Henker, concern in his voice.

'Nothing,' Bahvley replied quickly, trying to sound casual.

'I am not easily fooled,' the elder polc replied.

'Nothing's wrong,' Tharguen said nonchalantly, though he would have liked to add, *Other than just about every-thing.* He felt on the verge of tears.

'Niome is not with you?' asked Selemil.

'The Five and the Firlanians decided to stay in the Twisted Forest,' replied Bahvley. 'They wanted to investigate some things. Niome says it has to do with helping the strength of the Star grow.'

'Then what could be the matter,' Nsarmön said as a statement, looking at Henker. 'I mean, everyone's safe.'

'Everything's fine, but we've been through a lot,' admitted Tharguen.

Bahvley and Tharguen recounted their adventures, excluding many details and instead pretending the Five had been with them the whole time. The phantoms were a good enough excuse for their weariness.

'Niome's concerned for our kingdom's safety,' explained Bahvley. 'She suggested I mention to you her request that all Wizards of Teloria create a common spell that could help protect our kingdom.'

'That is a wise decision,' agreed Henker. 'I was going to suggest that, myself. Niome certainly knows where to put her focus at which time.'

Bahvley sighed in relief at his fib being believed – it was a good thing he knew his sister well enough for the ruse to be trusted.

'I'll talk to the Wizards about it,' said Selemil, nodding Henker's way. 'Bahvley, you don't have to worry about travelling around the kingdom.'

'Thank you,' said Bahvley.

'I would like your opinion regarding where to focus our armies next,' began Nsarmön.

'They can stand by,' Bahvley replied quickly and dryly. 'We won't be attacked any time soon; it would be an unwise move for Mirauk. Don't you know that?'

'I was only verifying—' Nsarmön answered hesitantly before being interrupted again.

'Gorthan never needed to verify. He always knew by instinct.'

Bahvley left the room.

'—since you were gone, in case you had spotted any armies,' Nsarmön completed to Tharguen.

'I apologise,' said Tharguen. 'Bahvley's been feeling on edge lately. We all have. The phantoms . . . the memories of him being bitten will linger a while. Magic knows when the remaining phantom will return. I understand your asking, Nsarmön, and appreciate your role to this kingdom. We do miss Gorthan, though.'

'I know. I do, too.'

'Excuse me.' Tharguen left the three and went after Bahvley. Finding him in the corridor near the King's study, he turned him around by the shoulder.

'What's wrong with you?! Gorthan would've asked the same question, were he here. I know you're feeling awkward, but so am I. Believe me – this is a true nightmare. It's not easy. We're *lying* to them in order to protect them.'

'I'm having a hard time with this. I can't seem to . . . I don't know anymore. Perhaps it's easier for you to pretend and lie than it is for me.'

'What's that supposed to mean?' demanded Tharguen. 'It was difficult in Mork, and it's no less difficult now.' He paused. 'Bahvley, they'll come back. Sooner or later.'

Once they returned to Selemil, Henker, and Nsarmön, the group continued their discussions. Though the atmosphere was uneasy at first, Henker's jovial manner soon rubbed off on the others and alleviated some of the tension.

Two nights later, Bahvley awoke in distress. His entire body was shaking and he was terribly frightened. A sharp pain tore through his leg, and he cried out in agony before the sensation passed. A cold sweat dripped down his back, for it felt like he was being struck by a phantom all over again. It took many deep breaths to calm himself enough to go back to sleep.

When Bahvley awoke the next morning, he informed Tharguen. He would have felt more comforted had Meysah been there too.

As children, whenever Bahvley had a stomachache, he sought out Meysah. Meysah often had such ailments and was used to them, and he would say: *'Don't worry. I always get weird stomachaches, and it always passes. I'm sure it's nothing. You're just anxious. You get used to them.'* Bahvley would remind Meysah of his own wise words when it was his turn to say, *'I don't feel too well. I have a weird stomachache.'*

Bahvley needed Meysah to tell him it was nothing now. Yet, he could not ignore what he'd experienced. A deep fear gripped him.

Later that day, Tharguen encountered Henker. The elder Telorian observed him with a dubious expression upon his face.

'Are you feeling all right?' asked Tharguen, genuinely concerned.

'I think I'm the one who ought to ask *you* that,' replied Henker. 'I can read eyes.'

'We're just tired, that's all.' Lies had once rolled well off Tharguen's tongue. Now, they made him wince internally.

'I hope so,' said Henker. 'But when someone repeatedly says that things are all right, it almost sounds as though they're trying to convince themselves.' Henker's eyes softened. 'Is there something that you're hiding?'

Tharguen answered quickly, 'Not at all.'

Henker nodded, looking disappointed. Tharguen wondered if he suspected the truth, being able to foresee at times. As he strolled home that day, he wondered if he should just tell Henker the truth about what happened.

Tharguen made plans to train with his team in even more elite techniques he'd learnt in Mork. While small in number, he at times desired to call them his army, for they had grown strong and overcome so much together. They had matured and gained much experience since departing for Dûnelor. He was so proud of them, for above all else, they all had survived.

The wind picked up one day, wind coming from the north, as Tharguen stepped outside his door. A strong gust blew in his face and a piece of parchment fell before Tharguen.

He watched as it slowly settled, then caught it with one hand. He noticed it was addressed to him. His heart skipped a beat – it was from Niome. Her delicate handwriting, always would he recognise – that and the repeated instances of *I love you*s and *I miss you*s gave it away.

Once again, he was separated from her and held a letter she'd written for him, just like so many years ago.

She spoke of what happened in the tunnels and of her longing in travelling alone, that writing this letter had made her feel better. The letter gave him hope, and yet – why had it been ripped out? If the wind had brought it here to him, perhaps it had been magically sent to him by Niome, he reasoned.

Tharguen read the letter again and again, for it brought him comfort. He showed it to Bahvley, who also felt heartened at this first morsel of news from the Five in what felt like ages. At last, there was something they could hold on to when sorrow threatened to overwhelm them.

Bahvley wished to clear his mind of all that had happened. He had chosen to travel the kingdom and bring comfort and aid to his people where he was needed. Thus, when he felt fear, he gave hope to others. When he wished he could express his woes, he listened to the concerns of others.

He rode from town to town, meeting with the wisest, the masters, and the locals, while remaining on the lookout for imposters. A strange feeling had taken root inside him. If Tharguen had been able to infiltrate Mork, of all places, then a Morkan could perhaps do the same in Teloria. How else could Mirauk have known so much about their plans to go to the Twisted Forest? Something just didn't add up.

Yet despite his best efforts, he found nothing out of the ordinary on his travels. Concluding the kingdom was safe, he returned shortly before the New Year.

Chapter Eleven:
Remembering the Past

'Come with me, Navë,' Tobias said with a smile.

'Where to?'

'I am going to enlighten you!' He grinned wider. 'We are going to discover who you are by seeing what you're capable of doing. Come outside with me.'

It was the thirtieth of Colouring, and Tobias's hope was contagious. He was set on helping Niome remember her fighting skills, Maria wished to help her connect with her meditations and songs, and Gabriella wished to taunt her magical memories back, while Olúryn desired to help her remember the people in her life.

Tobias led Niome outside to the yard, where he held out her sword.

'When it comes to swords, hunting for food is completely different than fighting for your life.'

'Like fighting an army for the Freedom of Life?'

'The Freedom of Life,' mused Tobias as she took the blade from him. 'I wonder who first said that.' He thought of the letter from Drúgan.

Niome tested her sword, swinging it about in salute. 'So, what's the plan? Are you going to show me—'

Tobias swung his blade without warning, taking her by surprise, but Niome blocked with her sword as quickly as the cut came. This surprised Niome even more.

'If I tell you what I'm about to do,' explained Tobias, 'we won't know what kind of reflexes you have. Besides, I don't need to teach you how to fight – you already know how.'

He slashed again and again, and she parried and blocked. Then she sidestepped with a fancy flourish of the wrist in an effort to disarm Tobias. He raised his brows, appraising her.

'How did I know that?' Niome asked, astonished.

'You just did.'

They sparred a while longer and Niome kept surprising herself, as her muscle memory had her performing moves her mind could not have even conceived of. After some time, they switched to knife-throwing, and again Niome's skills were reflected in her instinctual techniques.

'Not bad!' Tobias complimented.

Olúryn returned from hunting just then and waved at the two as he walked towards the house.

'Suppertime already?' inquired Niome.

'I guess you two didn't see the day go by, huh?' said Olúryn.

'Navë is very skilled,' said Tobias.

'She must've learned from Gorthan, then,' said Olúryn.

'The Chief of Knights?' asked Niome. 'Gorthan . . . the name does sound familiar.'

Tobias and Olúryn smiled at each other. Though Tobias knew Gorthan had passed away, he also knew that if Navë had indeed learned from him, a part of him still lived on in her.

That evening, Niome meditated with Maria to help quell her nightmares. Maria lit a few candles and placed them on a small round table. Sitting on cushions, Niome and Maria sat across from each other. Maria then closed her eyes, guiding Niome to do the same.

'All there is, is magic and your understanding of it,' Maria guided. 'You can see life as though you were a star. You feel and live moments that come to you. They are clear. Focus on the first vision that comes to you. Now you stand as yourself, no longer looking from above. You are there. What is happening around you?'

Niome was surrounded by stacks of books, shelves upon shelves filling up a large room. Her back to the door, Niome held a book with golden lettering on its cover. Before she could read the title, she realised she wasn't alone and began trembling. She turned to face the other polc.

Niome screamed, terrified of the warrior from her vision.

'Stay focused, Navë! What does this polc look like?'

'His eyes are . . . ! He's too evil! I can't stand it, but I keep looking at him. I don't have any control over what I'm doing.'

'It is the past which you see,' said Maria.

The polc in the vision took several menacing steps towards Niome before she was transported to another memory.

Partly relieved, Niome focused on this new echo of her past, where a elderly woman lay in a bed, struggling to speak. Although Niome had no memory of this woman, she knew she was dying and it made her weep. A breath later, Niome found herself in a field. A ghastly figure hovered above her as it sank its teeth into her flesh.

Niome's eyes shot open with a gasp. Breathing heavily, she shook her head.

'There's no more. I've lost it. We need to start again – I need to find out what happened next!'

'Maybe that was when you lost your memory,' suggested Maria, opening her eyes. 'These were all past events. Let your mind rest. Give it time to process, to understand what you have seen and perceived.'

Once Niome had retreated to her room, Maria spoke with Tobias.

'She could have been Elina's student. It's very possible,' suggested Tobias. 'Elina had many students. The way she describes that woman, it's like the description your father made.'

'The bite marks on her leg . . . that's where she has a scar.'

'The evil polc, however,' breathed Tobias, 'it couldn't have been Mirauk, could it? Many have described him . . . but Navë could not describe him.' He leaned forward, resting his chin on his hands. 'What makes me wonder is the room you say she was in. There have been stories of Mirauk's study described as a library of sorts, but no polc has ever seen it for themselves, much less survived long enough to describe it in such explicit detail.'

Tobias locked gazes with his wife. 'Except one, so we hear. If Navë is that one, then I hope her memory returns before too late.'

Tobias and Maria chose not to share these thoughts with their children, worried it might perchance affect Niome's recovery. Maria was adamant that neutral magical energy was necessary to her healing.

Tobias continued to practice more combat techniques with Niome, noting where she excelled and where her technique left much to be desired.

'I don't know how to use a bow!' complained Niome.

'You don't know that. And neither do I. Here.'

He handed her the bow and gave her targets, observing her carefully.

'Seems to me you're quite familiar with the bow, but don't practice enough.'

'I wish I could say you were right and that it is one skill I've neglected perhaps more than I should have,' said Niome.

'Well, Navë, now's your chance to improve.'

Handing her more arrows and taking some himself, the two resumed their target practice.

As Niome sat sewing, Olúryn joined her, sitting down beside her. Aged 120 polken years, his features were well defined and smooth.

'Did you used to sew a lot?' he asked. Niome looked up at him. 'I know, silly question. But I noticed you pay a lot of attention to detail.'

'I think I can say I like things done right,' said Niome. 'I wish I could say I had my grandmother's touch, like Gabriella with tea. But I don't know who my grandmother is.'

Olúryn smiled sympathetically. 'Your fighting skills are remarkable. You must have trained with the best masters of Teloria.' He paused. 'I had a friend once in Teloria who liked to sew.' There was a touch of sadness in his tone.

'I probably sew as a pastime,' Niome surmised. 'I remember a few other girls like me, friends of mine, in a vague vision.'

'That's always good . . . uhm, sewing or fighting?'

'Both. You know, fighting with Tobias reminds me of the fun competitions I used to have with my brother.'

'Your brother?'

'My brother!' she answered, eyes wide.

'Was he older or younger?' Olúryn asked excitedly, leaning forward with interest.

'I can't remember. I think older, but I see younger.'

'Then you had two? What did they do?'

'Fight?' Niome guessed.

'Well, don't ask me – I don't know the answer. But somewhere deep inside, *you* do.'

Niome pondered that for a moment. 'I didn't know I had a brother.'

'Do you remember your parents?'

'My father was . . . a farmer, I believe. Though I also feel he may have had another proficiency before that.'

With Olúryn's help, Niome began to remember a few people over time. Memories were vague, but she could recall their personalities, functions, and on rare occasions, their descriptions. However, only with the meditations did some childhood events return to Niome in dreams, and never could she remember her relationship to the people in those dreams.

'I bet you this Tweedle polc was messy,' giggled Gabriella as she let pillows fall to the floor. 'He's got a spell called *Cleaning Up.*'

'What are you doing?' asked Niome.

'I want to try a spell,' said Gabriella as she moved a few objects around.

'You might need this,' said Niome, taking the wand out of her bag.

Gabriella took the bag and placed it under a pillow on the floor. 'Since you seem to know so much, Navë, why don't *you* try it?'

'I will,' declared Niome.

Niome took the book and waved the wand as she spoke the spell.

Find, I must,
This important item;
Crucial, it is,
For my security;
Into my hands
Must it appear!

Items placed themselves neatly in their place, and a white cylinder landed in the palm of Niome's hand.

'It worked!' Gabriella rejoiced.

'Perhaps we should try this outside,' Niome cautioned.

Trying to find how to activate it, Niome turned the cylinder over in her hands as she and the younger polc stood outside on the frosty grass.

She swung it, shouting out. Wind blew from the cylinder, and all the leaves scattered about. The squirrels that had been in range scurried away to safety.

'It's the—' Niome suddenly ran into the house, shouting, 'I know what this cylinder is! It's the *Dragon's Wind*!' She beamed as everyone paused what they were doing. Niome recognised the song Maria was singing, though she knew not where from. 'That song – it evokes in me the sense that I have to prepare for something.'

'Prepare for what?' asked Gabriella.

'I have absolutely no idea.'

As time went on, certain aspects of Niome's magical abilities returned. To test them further, one day Tobias took Niome to the Great Rock of Zaccher Lake. The rock was between the lake and the northern forest, where they both curved.

Tobias dismounted his horse. Niome observed the rock – it had greyish-blue streaks in the centre, and in certain spots they were more purple.

'I saw this rock in my dreams,' said Niome. 'Except the streaks were red.'

Tobias didn't answer but simply smiled and helped her dismount. Facing the rock, he pronounced a spell.

Nelassima po srodo felessekold,
Nelassima po srodo dlogesseh,
Etel notissima po folerëop,
Etel ntissima po foëlessifëi!

'I believe I've heard that spell before,' Niome recalled as the stone opened up.

'It's quite possible,' said Tobias, 'if you knew Maria's father and our two other children.'

Together, they descended into the magical apothecary.

'These are our various potions,' explained Tobias.

Niome took it all in – the place was enchanting. 'Is there one for bringing back memories?'

'Unfortunately not.'

'What does this one do?' asked Niome, pointing at a peach-coloured potion.

'It brings someone back to life.'

Niome wavered suddenly, crying out. Tobias hurried to her side to steady her.

'Flashes . . . in my head. Someone's lying on the ground, bleeding. No, wait – the blood is disappearing.'

Niome calmed as the vision faded.

'Another flashback, I believe,' Tobias said with a nod. 'I believe you've used this potion before.'

For the seasons to come, Niome slowly recalled her childhood and even some more recent events. Ultimately, however, they were insignificant, as they never told her who she was, though they were pieces of her life all the same.

Niome desperately wished to remember the people close to her, but she couldn't. In all this time, with all these memories, Niome never remembered anything about her mission, the Star, the other four, Bahvley, or even Tharguen. She desperately wanted to remember the people most crucial in her life – the people who, when they appeared in a few odd flashes, made her feel longing or comfort.

'Instead of focusing on people you don't even know exist,' said Olúryn, 'focus on yourself.'

'I know what I have to do,' sighed Niome as they stood in her room. 'I have to find out who I am, look deep inside of my soul, and rediscover myself. I thought it would help me if I knew about the people close to me, but I can't remember . . . it's already Summer again.'

'Summer the second only,' said Olúryn.

'Haven't they come looking for me?'

'They could be searching anywhere for you, Navë. What if you were meant to meet them somewhere? Maybe they're still waiting for you there.'

'I just want to know who I am, what my mission is, who I know and what our relationships are.'

Olúryn cast a glance at her ring before averting his eyes. Niome took hold of her ring, fiddling with it on her finger.

'I still can't even remember who gave me this ring,' she said, staring down at it.

Olúryn turned his back to Niome. 'I wish you'd remember,' he muttered.

'You wish I'd forget!'

'If it's better for you to know, then you should know,' he said , turning to face Niome again. 'All I want is for you to be happy. Obviously, not remembering is not making you happy, and frankly, I'd feel better too. Yes, I'd be relieved if you forgot, but I don't wish it upon you! Someone out there loves you very much, and he made a promise to you and you to him.'

'What if whoever gave me this thinks I'm dead? Then he'll move on, no?'

'No, not that easily or that quickly,' said Olúryn. 'Not for someone like you. I know I wouldn't. But it doesn't matter what I think.'

'Your opinion is important to me,' said Niome.

'And what about how I feel?' Olúryn asked gently. 'This is as difficult for me as it is for you, in a different way, yes, but . . .' He caught himself and blurted, 'I have to watch what I say. Never mind.'

'Why? Tell me, why do you have to watch what you say? Why is there secrecy in this family when it comes down to how you feel . . . how you feel about me?'

His jaw set, Olúryn met Niome's gaze. 'Because of a curse that was set upon me a long time ago.' He blinked back tears.

Niome felt a pang. 'What happened?'

'I was barely an infant when my family was attacked by Morkans. A Morkan Wizard duelled my uncle. In response to his taunts regarding the Wizard's magic, the Morkan claimed he would set a terrible curse . . . and there you go.' Olúryn bowed his head. 'Only later was the curse *determined*, but it was revealed when it was set.'

He fell silent.

'So what's the curse?' Niome asked gently.

'Every time I reveal any emotions of . . . love . . . towards anyone who is not related to me by blood, they die. Even mere friendship kills those I come to care for. That is why I have to be careful of how I express myself.' His brows creased in chagrin. 'Because if I love you, you will die. And there's nothing I can do.'

Olúryn walked to the open window, gazing out. 'The only way to cure it is to come face-to-face with the most powerful Wizard, but as you already know, that would set another curse on me.'

He laughed mirthlessly. 'Oh, that Wizard was proud of himself when he announced the antidote to lift this curse off me. Drúgan killed him. My uncle had trouble living with himself knowing he was meant to have protected us but failed. It was not his fault.' After a pause, he sighed. 'By now, I've seen what my curse can do.'

Gripping the window frame, Olúryn continued. 'My first few romances could have been flukes, for they were simply young infatuations and none of them died. Later, when I was older, I'd been quite taken by a young scout. She was so beautiful. That was when I knew love, real love, for the first time. And she loved me. I thought the curse had been merely a fear, a way for the Morkan Wizard to control us, and I let myself feel all the love I had for her.'

Olúryn paused, tightening his hold on the frame. Niome said nothing, only listened intently as he went on.

'She was killed. I tried to justify it as a death by sword, not the curse. It took me a long time to get over her. Then, there was a traveller from the Twisted Forest. She was weary and needed rest. I felt something for her, and I had hope again. I told her that I was interested in courting her, but I was careful not to mention my emotions. That same night, she died. We're not even sure what of.'

Olúryn inhaled shakily and wiped the side of his eye with his finger.

'Granted, my isolation hasn't allowed me to meet many new people too often, but the coincidence with how these polcs made me feel when I looked at them, spent time with them, held them, and their fate . . . it confirmed that the curse was real.'

Niome's eyes stung with tears of sorrow for Olúryn. He looked back at her, still gripping the window frame so hard, his knuckles had turned white.

'Now, all I have to do is say someone is pretty and it's a risk,' he spat. 'I shouldn't even let myself think or feel anything for anyone! My father worries that it's voicing it that kills them.' Olúryn bowed his head. 'As though silence will save them. I don't know if silence helps . . . but I felt what I felt, and that might have been enough to kill them.'

Olúryn stepped away from the window and turned to Niome. 'Now, you've been living here a year, and I've been very careful to not get attached to our friendship that I feel in . . . certain ways.' He sighed. 'I don't know what's worse: seeing a lover die, or living without love.'

Niome closed her eyes and shook her head. 'I'm sorry those you loved died.' She offered him a hopeful smile. 'Maybe Mirauk isn't the most powerful Wizard.'

'Then I wonder who is.'

There was a long pause.

'Well, now that that's cleared up, perhaps you can tell me what you wished to say before. I doubt it would hurt me now.'

Olúryn smiled wanly, stepping towards her. 'Ever since my father found you, ever since you came into our lives – you have changed us all. You have changed me. There's something about you. Everyone here senses that there is something special about you. I admit, I can't fully determine what it is I feel.' He looked away and breathed out angrily, 'But I do feel what I feel.'

'Well, it's not my fault!' Niome said defensively.

'I'm not blaming you!'

'You keep talking about how you feel. What about how *I* feel? Here I am, with some sort of attachment to this ring that I can't even identify. I know *you*'d want me to forget. Well, there are days I wish I'd forget, too.' Her tone was stern.

'I'm sorry.' Olúryn put his hand on her arm. 'I'm afraid of everything I might feel towards you, even if it does just end up being purely friendship. I wouldn't want to kill you by simply appreciating your presence in my life.' Olúryn pointed at the ring. 'And I wouldn't want *him* to lose you because your friend was cursed.'

Niome cupped his cheek and smiled. 'I know you're only trying to help. It *is* difficult.'

Olúryn took her hand in his, and she gave him a warm embrace.

'I don't understand how right now,' began Olúryn as they hugged, 'yet somehow I do – I am hopeful that time will help us both.'

CHAPTER TWELVE:
Message In a Beak

With Winter close at hand, Vigh, Boreth, Jimmy, and Meysah decided to travel to one of the shelters by the water whose magical currents flowed from Zaccher Lake. The two Lords hoped being near such magic might give them some answers, though they did voice their reasons to the others regarding their hunch that this was where Niome had been waylaid.

Accompanied by Nastafin, Attëgon, and Dublenk, the Telorians slowly grew accustomed to the straw beds in the wooden huts situated within the trees. Only a small fire could be lit. However, the shelter was well isolated from wind, and when the open kettle was placed above the fire, the steam spread to the other rooms and the larger area felt cosier.

'How long are we going to have to stay out here?' Jimmy whispered one night while they were keeping watch, sitting by the shelter's largest window.

'I don't know. Perhaps all Winter.'

'I sure hope not.'

'Well, I know we've got to stay out here until Niome arrives,' said Meysah.

'Then I hope she arrives soon.'

'Yes.' Meysah paused. 'I'm worried, more than ever. What if she doesn't come here anytime soon?'

'Nonsense!'

'This isn't normal, Jimmy. Something has gone terribly wrong that the stars have not planned, and I felt it.' He bounced his knee nervously. 'I keep feeling it every day, and as you saw, that message Boreth sent to her bounced right back to us.' A trembling wave passed through him from head to toe before his body calmed again. 'This nervousness is going to make me sick.'

'If you start sneezing, we'll know,' said Jimmy, smiling gingerly. 'I'm sorry. I'm afraid I've lost my touch.'

'No, you're just worried, too, and that's okay,' said Meysah.

'Hey, let's worry together!'

Meysah chuckled. 'There you go! Another silly comment successfully delivered.'

'I wish I had more of them in mind,' admitted Jimmy.

'You're still keeping watch?' Nastafin asked as she approached.

'Sorry, did we wake you?' asked Meysah.

'No, I couldn't sleep. I can take over.' The two lads nodded and stood. 'If it makes you feel any better, if something *has* gone terribly wrong, the stars did plan it.

That simply means Niome has something to discover from it.'

'Thanks,' said Jimmy.

'It does help, in a way,' said Meysah.

Nastafin often shared such wisdom with the Telorians. She had studied magic in her youth and had grown quite knowledgeable. And as her sagacity differed from that of the Lords, they often engaged in spirited debates, which sometimes led to disagreements amongst the group of watchers.

Every day that passed was another day of anxious waiting, hoping to find Niome striding in. The New Year came, yet still Niome had not arrived.

One evening, as Vigh, Dublenk, and Attëgon were watching outside, they heard Nastafin telling a story to Boreth, Jimmy, and Meysah. The others outside weren't quite listening, except for Vigh.

After a while, he stepped closer to the entrance and glanced inside through the crack in the door. He watched Nastafin as she told her tale. Then he glanced at his feet and walked back to the other two watchers, brushing away the emotion that had suddenly come over him.

Boreth followed him out discreetly. 'Are you okay?'

'Yes, I'm fine,' Vigh said casually. 'Why?'

'Because I thought I saw you – well, it looked like there was something you wanted to say.'

'No, no.' Vigh would not meet Boreth's gaze.

'You're certain you're fine?'

'Positively.'

'If you say so.' Boreth went back in. Vigh leaned on the ramp.

'It's true, you do look bothered,' said Dublenk. 'You shouldn't let your fears get to you like that, but of course, you already know that.'

Vigh nodded as he gazed out.

It was cold, and there was snow. Meysah was starting to *catch* a cold. Jimmy noticed him sneezing and saw he looked exhausted. Meysah decided to lie down for a nap – he was tired and cold, and he felt his nose stuffing up.

Meanwhile, Vigh and Boreth had ventured away from the shelter to go hunt.

'Vigh, you've been acting very strangely lately,' Boreth noted.

'I'm worried. That's all.'

'Is that why you have not yet spoken a word today?' inquired Boreth. 'Is that why you're so reserved of late? You haven't cracked a single joke since the New Year.'

'If I may correct you,' Vigh pointed a finger at Boreth, 'you're the joker of us two.'

'Oh, you are just as much a joker as I am, and you're trying to be funny *now*.'

'I don't like where this is going,' Vigh said dryly. 'Meysah is sick, you know. I think we should return to the fortress.'

'We?' asked Boreth. 'We can't all leave the shelter.'

'No, but the four of us could go,' said Vigh.

'Why not just Attëgon with Meysah while the rest of us stay here, as is what we should do? Attëgon said he'd gladly carry him if necessary.'

'No. We can send Nastafin with Meysah, or the four of us can leave, but we've got to stay together. We've already got one point of our Star lost and gone, separated from us.'

'And why send Nastafin away?' Boreth asked in suspicion. 'Or send *yourself* away?'

'It would do me good to go, anyway,' admitted Vigh. 'I feel rather . . .'

'You feel what?'

'Distracted!' Vigh said bitterly, slapping a low branch away.

'I think I understand,' said Boreth. 'Although I do agree about the Star sticking together.' He paused. 'I don't call Clahria a distraction. You can't avoid such—'

Vigh whirled on Boreth, stopping in his tracks. 'I'm not avoiding it, but ending it at the very beginning.'

'And what if something good were to come of it?'

'I doubt it,' said Vigh. 'Not for me, anyway.'

'All right, then. Suit yourself. But that's a very *wise mistake*,' Boreth emphasised.

'Oh, will you stop it,' snapped Vigh, resuming. 'Like you're one to talk. How many times have you had your head in the clouds thinking of Clahria? How many times were you away from Teloria? How many times did she come before your duties? How many times did you speak of her in the tunnels?'

Vigh laughed mirthlessly. 'You don't call Clahria a distraction. Then what is it? Do you worry too much about her? When you're fighting a Morkan, do you truly think of your kingdom and of saving your own life? Or do you think of Clahria and her songs?'

'Are you done?' asked Boreth, annoyed. 'Why criticise Clahria? Sounds to me like you're jealous.'

'You wish!'

'Why are you being so difficult? And childish!' Boreth jogged ahead of Vigh to stop him, hand on his shoulder. 'How many times has Clahria given me hope? When I heard about my dead relatives from the Dal-varans, the thought of her helped me through it. In the tunnels, I spoke about her because it kept me sane.'

Boreth sighed. 'Why do you refuse to love? It is a gift! And for your information, when I fight, sometimes the thought of her may come to me, for I fight for her, too, but never has she *distracted* me in any way. Yes, I think of her a lot, but when I do, it comforts me.'

'Look over there – a deer,' Vigh said conclusively, walking away.

'Nothing I say gets through to you,' Boreth sighed under his breath. 'Impossible polc.'

Finally, Boreth let the matter go and decided to let Vigh deal with it his own way, though they never did return to the fortress.

Meysah got better, and within a week, his cold was gone. The bitter days had passed and milder weather was on its way.

'What day are we today?' asked Meysah as he and the others stood outside, looking down from the rail.

'Isn't it supposed to be Spring?' asked Jimmy.

'Actually,' said Boreth, 'it's the ninetieth of Winter.'

'But there *is* no ninetieth of Winter!' insisted Jimmy. 'Not this year, I think.'

'This year, there is,' Nastafin confirmed. 'As there is every four years. Those years, there is an extra day before Spring.'

'That's so strange,' mused Meysah. 'I've always wondered why that was.'

'Some say that it's the mark of the dragons' New Year,' said Attëgon. 'The dragons may sleep in Winter, but every four years, on this day, they awaken.'

'Sometimes you can even hear their shrieks from here,' said Dublenk.

'It *is* written in the knowledge books that the dragons age differently,' added Vigh.

'It's also said that they live on forever,' said Nastafin. 'But that is more of a misconception. To us, it would seem so – that they live forever – but each year more to them is four years more to us.'

'But the knowledge books say otherwise,' argued Vigh, his tone condescending. 'That that theory could be flawed.'

'Do you have another theory to explain it?' Boreth taunted, catching Vigh's glance. 'Polcs don't know *every-thing*.'

'Maybe the dragons have grand celebrations,' suggested Meysah, bugging his eyes out at his master.

'Who knows?' said Attëgon. 'They don't come out of their lair, though. Not to date, they haven't.'

'Then how do you know that—' began Jimmy.

'The shrieks,' interrupted Meysah. 'And people have spent time with them, remember? The diary?'

'Oh, right,' said Jimmy. 'Yes, I do remember reading something about it. You're right, Meysah.' He looked at the Tellens, who seemed confused. Jimmy briefly explained about the diary they'd found written by the Dragon Prophet. 'I believe he mentioned something about this in passing. Now, if I could only remember the exact—'

A shrill shriek rang out from above, silencing them.

'Something tells me that wasn't a dragon,' said Dublenk as they all scanned the sky for the source.

'The shriek was too eerie for that,' agreed Attëgon.

A large black bird flew overhead in circles, hovering above the polcs. It resembled a giant crow.

The winged creature flew down slowly, its gleaming red eyes scrutinising the Telorians. It sniffed the air as it continued its descent.

'Prepare your bows,' instructed Boreth. 'Something tells me it's from Mork, that it's intelligent and has come after us.'

'So the Dark Lord realises his phantoms failed,' said Meysah, 'and he sends this creature. What is he hoping to accomplish?'

Its eyes flashed yellow. The polcs trained their bows at it, but too many branches obscured a clear shot.

'It could be a cousin of the water creature from the Ortim River,' voiced Jimmy. Meysah shivered at the memory.

'A spy?' inquired Attëgon. 'If it's come for you, there may be more of them.'

The crow got low enough for them to shoot but rose back up quickly. Their arrows barely nicked the avian as it disappeared into the horizon.

'We'll have to be a lot faster next time,' sighed Boreth, 'and shoot with a lot more force.'

Two weeks passed before there was another sighting of the giant Morkan crow. Assuming it had since reported back to Mirauk, the polcs remained vigilant.

It was early morning on the first day of the third week of Spring. The light of dawn had just appeared, and Jimmy and Dublenk were near the lake to fetch water. They passed through some thick foliage near the lake's edge.

Then they froze.

Perched by the water were the silhouettes of several large dark birds.

'Do you see what I see?' Jimmy whispered, his voice barely audible.

Dublenk nodded. The two slowly backed away to hide behind the underbrush and watched.

'Do you think they've seen us?' asked Jimmy.

'Even if they did,' Dublenk whispered back, 'they're not heeding us. We should warn the others.'

'Or maybe shoot the birds dead,' replied Jimmy.

'It would be unwise to do so. There are too many for our two bows alone. Furthermore, we do not know their strengths.'

They backed away again and darted back to the shelter.

'There are several giant crows by the water,' Dublenk announced, out of breath.

'How many?' asked Attëgon, looking as troubled as the other two felt.

'I don't know the exact amount.'

'Shall we ready our bows, then?' said Nastafin, already hefting her weapons. 'And go shoot them out of our territory?'

'No,' warned Boreth. 'They ought to have caught your scent. They're beasts, and beasts from Mork besides that. If we go now, they'll be expecting us. But they won't be expecting us to *not* show up. Let us wait for them to come to *us*.'

As the Sun slowly rose, the polcs waited with weapons poised. When they heard the flapping of wings, they bent their bows, but the birds never came into view.

A looming shadow from above alerted them of the birds on the shelter's roof, and not a moment too soon, for the Morkan crows dashed down at them.

Boreth shot his bow and pierced one's wing. The birds flew up, swirled upside down, and darted back down again, thrusting their beaks and clawing at the polcs. Though they shoved the defenders down, the polcs shot continuously as the birds soared up to rush them again.

Attëgon lost his footing, falling from the shelter's ledge and into the snow below. Dublenk quickly followed as he lunged away from a crow's talons. Another crow pushed on Nastafin, and her shot went wide. Balancing herself precariously on the edge of the ledge, she tried to shoot her attacher.

Vigh reflexively reached for her, putting an arm around her waist to steady her, but she slipped out of his grasp and landed atop her two comrades.

'Nastafin?' Vigh called out.

'I'm okay,' she called back.

Vigh peered over the edge before he was lifted up by the shoulders and shoved against the tree cabin's wall, the bird's sharp talons digging into him and pinning him in place.

That's when he realised Boreth, Jimmy, and Meysah had been similarly pinned by the giant crows, lined up beside him. Backs against the wall, they had nowhere else to go.

The Morkan birds finally released them, taking a step back. The largest of them sniffed at each of the Telorians before it shrilled, red eyes flashing yellow once more.

The four birds opened their beaks wide, and rolls of parchment dropped from each beak before each polc. Shrieking again, the apparent leader flapped its wings and the others followed suit, soaring up and heading back to Mork.

As the Telorians exchanged wary glances, the Tellens climbed back up the ladder, relieved the birds had left their friends unharmed.

'Messengers from Mork,' Boreth spat with disdain, picking up his parchment. The others bent to retrieve the messages left for them as well. 'And they'd be wise to never return.' He unrolled it. 'Ah, so Mister decided to give us each a message – a short and sweet one, on top of that.' He let out a throaty sigh.

'What does it say?' asked Attëgon, favouring his back where it was sore.

'"*I know where you are.*" That's good to know.' Boreth rolled his eyes.

That brought a chuckle out of Jimmy. 'Like we hadn't figured that out. Is he trying to be funny?'

'Kàtchah could've easily told him where we were,' said Boreth, shrugging.

'Mine says: "*Don't think I'm not ready*",' said Vigh. 'Is that supposed to be a threat?'

'Mine is: "*I'm waiting for the right moment. A word of advice – be prepared.*" Aw, how kind of him to advise us like that.' Jimmy sighed. 'He's trying to instil fear in our hearts. Although I don't see how *this* is supposed to scare us. There are only four, though – none for Niome. Do you think the birds found her and gave her hers?'

'I don't know,' said Meysah as he unrolled his parchment. He froze. His voice was low and grave as he read aloud, "*Niome has been taken care of.*" He swallowed hard.

'What's that supposed to mean?' asked Dublenk after a moment.

'I don't know, but then he writes in parentheses: "*I laugh merrily at this thought.*"' Meysah looked at the others. 'I'm worried. I already was before these notes arrived, and now even more so . . .'

'What's he playing at?' Jimmy shook his head. 'Does he *know* what's happened to Niome?'

Boreth and Vigh exchanged sideways glances.

Vigh turned away. 'I need to take a walk.' He hurried down the ladder.

'Vigh!' cried Boreth, going after him. He caught up with him a little ways from the shelter. 'Vigh, what are you concluding?'

'That polc we saw,' began Vigh, stopping to turn to Boreth, 'if she was Niome . . . what if she's gone evil?'

'That's ridiculous. It's Niome we're talking about.'

'Oh, yeah. These letters are ridiculous!' said Vigh, overlapping with Boreth's sentence. 'I can hardly believe them. I can hardly believe *him*! You say we're talking about Niome? No, it's *Em* we're talking about here. He sent a whole flock of giant crows just to give us this . . . ? While he sits on his bloody throne, laughing joyously at his evil little plans, scheming cunningly, manipulating his people like puppets? Proud that he succeeded in annoying the kurssus out of us? No, I won't take it! We need to find out what he means by all this and what truly happened to Niome.'

'Vigh, he wants us to worry.'

'By kurssus, he does!'

'He wants us to think terrible things. The only reason he's doing this is to distract us, because right now, he's pacing to and fro in his study trying to come up with a plan, panicking and fearing us because he knows his kingdom will fall.'

'I hope you're right,' sighed Vigh, 'but right now, I find it a little difficult to believe.'

'I understand.'

Together, they returned to the shelter. As the others sat down inside to eat, Vigh sat on the edge of the ledge, watching his feet as they dangled. A shadow approached him, though he couldn't tell whose it was.

'Go away. I want to be left alone.' The person turned and started off. 'Wait,' he said. Something told him he'd be comforted by this person's company. 'Come sit.' He turned his head as Nastafin sat down. 'Oh, it's you.'

'Yes, it's me. It isn't only your fellow Telorians who are concerned.' She paused. 'So, what about me?'

'Nothing. I just thought it was Meysah or someone.'

'I *am* someone. You know, today was the first excitin' day we've had in a long time.'

'Though it would've gone better if—' He stopped himself.

'If Niome were here? You can't escape the fact that it might've been the same had she been here, too. We don't know what's happening with her, but she doesn't know what's happening with you either. Wherever she is, she's discoverin' and understandin' something important – so important that she can't return yet. When it's time, she'll come back. There's no point in gettin' all riled up about something that's not in your control.'

'I see her as my own daughter sometimes, or a niece. I'm her master in the art of weaponry, as I am the master of both her brothers. They are all dear friends to me. It would've also gone better had the others been there – Bahvley and Tharguen, their whole team. I mean, where are the Kikies when you need them? I could sure use some Kiki jokes right now.'

'You've got Jimmy and Meysah.' Vigh laughed lightly. Nastafin continued, 'You seem to be taking this harder than the others.'

'Like I said, I was her master.' There was a pause. 'Meysah is having a hard time, too. He's a lot better at hiding it than I am.' He paused again. 'But he's got Jimmy.'

'And you, Boreth.'

'It's not the same. We're not as lighthearted anymore. We've seen too many dark days to . . .' He trailed off.

'Maybe it's time to forget those dark days,' suggested Nastafin. Vigh thought of Tallelah.

There was a long pause.

'By the way,' Nastafin said with a hint of a smile, 'thank you for trying to save me from falling, even though it was but a short fall.'

'It was nothing,' Vigh replied quickly. 'You would've done the same. I'd've done the same had it been Boreth or anyone else.'

Nastafin didn't reply; she only smiled and left Vigh to himself.

CHAPTER THIRTEEN:
Stealth and Spywork

Many weeks passed and Summer came. Jimmy and Meysah desired to return to the fortress, but Boreth and Vigh were determined to wait at the shelter. In truth, Meysah wanted to go home and be with his brother. However, the last thing the Telorians needed was to be even more scattered.

Yet, stubborn as they were, the young knights packed their bags on the morning of Summer the sixth, ready to make for the fortress.

'All right,' said Vigh. 'Go, then, if you think we'll come after you, but we won't.'

'I thought you wanted to leave this place' – Meyah poked Vigh as he voiced his title – 'Master.'

'I did, but I changed my mind.' He looked at Nasta-fin. 'I, uh . . . it's best if I stay for now, for Niome's sake. I no longer feel the way I did before.'

'I still think you'll join us,' declared Jimmy. 'By lunchtime, you'll say: _"Oh, shucks, let's go."_'

'No, we won't,' stated Boreth.

'We'll just see about that,' said Meysah.

The lads draped their satchels over their shoulders and exited the shelter. The two Lords watched them go down the ladder and walk off out of sight.

'Aren't you going to go after them?' asked Attëgon.

'Oh, just wait,' said Boreth. 'They'll come back. By lunchtime they'll be saying to each other, "*Oh, shucks, let's go back.*"' He and Vigh chuckled.

Jimmy and Meysah travelled all day towards the fortress. By nightfall, they had not yet come to the next shelter. They paused to take a look around.

'Are we lost?' Jimmy asked quickly. 'I think we're lost.'

'No, it's just a little further that way,' Meysah said, pointing noncommittally in an unclear direction before setting off again.

However, when they indeed walked a little further that way, still there was no shelter.

'I'm tired,' complained Jimmy. 'Maybe we should camp.'

'Wait, shh.'

'What?' Jimmy looked around.

Meysah brought a hand to his ear to signal that he heard something. They both snuck several steps towards the sounds and spied a small fire a little ways further. They crouched low, crawling closer, and peered through the underbrush to see what was going on.

There were many Morkans camping, several of them asleep, others still awake.

'How did they get here without being seen?' whispered Jimmy.

'I don't know. Sneaking through the forest, passing far from the shelters? Maybe the birds got an overhead look at the forest and relayed the information to them.'

'Maybe that's what they were actually here for,' said Jimmy, 'and the notes were a diversion.'

They watched a bit longer, hoping they would hear the Morkans' plan.

'I think we better go,' murmured Jimmy.

'You're right. We should warn the others.'

Before they could turn around, two big hands were on both their mouths. They both let out a muffled yelp. In no time, their feet were bound, their hands fastened in front of them, and they were brought into the camp.

'So, what do we have here?' asked a Morkan, standing up and walking towards the Telorians. By the intricate gems on his garments, Meysah surmised he was the Captain.

'Let us go!' growled Meysah.

'I'm afraid I can't do that,' said the Morkan. 'We need some . . . answers.'

'So do we!' Meysah defied. Jimmy kept his mouth shut.

'In case you're wondering how we got here, it's called sneaking.'

Meysah rolled his eyes.

'I'm sure you're familiar with the term. We're looking for Telorians. Perhaps you know them.'

Jimmy shook his head followed by Meysah, both realising that none of these Morkans had ever seen them before.

'I'm sure you've met a certain five Telorians?' the Morkan went on. Both lads again shook their heads. The Captain thrust a finger in their faces. 'Tell me, who are you two? Come on! Speak!'

There was a long pause – Meysah was wracking his brain to come up with a convincing lie, and he could tell Jimmy was doing the same.

'What, are you mute?'

'Uh . . .' Jimmy hesitated, uncertain how to respond.

'I'm not—' began Meysah.

'Then talk.' The Captain stared pointedly at Meysah, who stared back blankly for a brief moment.

When Meysah spoke again, he put on a Tellen accent, bringing it on gradually and keeping it mild.

'We're only Tellens travelling back from the lake. We've never met any Telorians before.'

'And you expect me to believe that?'

'It's the truth,' Jimmy added. The Captain kept his gaze on Meysah, ignoring Jimmy.

'Captain,' said another Morkan, 'perhaps we should ask about their King.'

'Yes,' the Captain said, smirking. 'Since you can't tell me what I know you know, you must tell me about your King.'

'That, I will not,' spat Meysah.

'Oh, you will defy me now, Chatty?' the Captain rebuked, leaning on his front foot.

Jimmy jerked forward as though to defend Meysah before stopping himself.

The Morkan Captain turned his attention to Jimmy. 'Got something to say to me, Mute?'

Jimmy opened his mouth to respond.

'Captain,' interrupted the other Morkan.

The two Morkans took a step away and whispered to each other for a while, arguing in their tongue.

Jimmy leaned slightly towards Meysah. 'Outsmart them,' he whispered without moving his lips.

'How?'

'Make them fear us – I mean the Five. You're the only one he's listening to. I'm mute, apparently, at least according to *him*. You, on the other hand, could do with some muting sometimes.'

Jimmy straightened, looking smug, and Meysah nudged him, resisting the urge to laugh or retaliate with a quip of his own.

The Morkans returned.

'Now you, Chatty, and your friend, Mute, will either take us to your King, or you—'

'No, please!' Meysah pleaded as he fell to his knees, grabbing the Captain's hands and holding on to him. Jimmy swallowed a snort in his throat. 'Anything but that. Don't involve our King! These matters concern none of us Tellens. I'll tell you about the Telorians, just don't involve our King.'

'I knew you'd come to your senses,' the Captain sneered. 'Okay, then. Stand up and speak.'

Meysah obliged. 'They are powerful. They can make people do things against their will. They wanted to fight Kàtchah, but we only escorted him out. They had our

King do other things – oh, they're terrible. You have to find them!'

'Kàtchah?'

'Uh, yes. Or at least, that's what they said his name was.'

'All right, then. Tell me more about them,' the Captain prompted.

'Two Lords, uhm . . . what were their names? Bigh and Voreth, I believe.'

Jimmy snorted in his throat for real this time, unable to contain himself. The mortified look on Meysah's face told him he hadn't intended to make the mistake.

'Well, *he* remembers names and can write them well,' finished Meysah.

The other Morkan produced some parchment and a feather. Jimmy blinked – this *had* to be a joke. It was like the scenario of a comedic play the players of Teloria were putting on to make fun of the Morkans. Maybe he'd write the script of this someday.

Taking the feather and dipping it into the ink, Jimmy considered transcribing the false names Meysah had shared but quickly decided not to push their luck. Instead, he wrote down the Lords' names as he voiced them, though the Captain gave no indication of hearing Jimmy at all. Despite his annoyance, the lad so wished to chide Meysah and boast about being better at lying to Morkans than he was.

'Ah, yes, *Vigh* and *Boreth*,' Meysah resumed. 'They can fight so many at once. They creep up on you, and next thing you know, you're dead. They're smart, they and the two lads can . . . can outsmart anyone at any time.' Jimmy wrote the names. 'Jimmy and Meysah.'

'What about the Wizardess?'

'She hasn't arrived yet. They got separated from her, but they told us about her. She can look into your eyes and read your thoughts.' Meysah sounded like a gossip. 'She can have you see her as who she *wants* you to see her as. Together, they have spells – all of them have spells, *terrible* spells. Oh, you must find them! Just leave us Tellens alone. Who knows what they're having some of me friends do now!'

'Clearly, they're in distress,' the Captain concluded, turning to the other Morkan. 'They tell the truth. For the Wizardess was . . .' He left the sentence unfinished and merely inclined his head knowingly.

'What . . . what happened to the Wizardess?' asked Meysah, barely loud enough for the Morkans to hear.

'Are you asking us?'

'Yes. We all wonder about Niome Fairhaven,' Meysah added, recovering quickly. 'Of course, not in the same manner as the Telorians. But if you tell us, we'll show you which way they went.'

'She was intercepted,' said the Captain. 'And that's all we'll tell you.'

'What? You should tell us. After all, we had to deal with those phantoms of yours.'

'Phantoms!' the Captain shouted angrily. 'What did you do to them? Speak. Or I will never let you go.' He unsheathed his sword.

Meysah leaned back cautiously, bringing his bound hands up in surrender in front of him. 'It was those Telorians, their King Bahvley's doing. I don't know what happened, but we hear they stayed up all night, and in the mornin', the phantoms were gone.' The Captain scowled. 'But many of our polcs died.'

'Well, listen – bring us to where the Telorians went, and we can work out a deal.'

'No, no deal,' said Meysah. 'Because next, you'll be asking for more. Besides, you didn't tell us what we desired to know.'

'You didn't tell us your names!'

Meysah hesitated, trying to come up with Tellen names.

'Come on, Chatty, don't go mute on me now.'

Jimmy sighed gutturally, resisting the urge to roll his eyes.

'Chattylenk,' Meysah said with a deadpan look, feeling bold. 'And that's Mute-lenk!' He chuckled as he pointed at himself and at Jimmy, trying to ease his nerves.

'Your *real* names.'

Meysah dropped his shoulders. 'Tucklenk and Sottilenk.'

'Now, you don't expect us to actually tell you what *truly* happened to Niome Fairhaven, hm?' said the Captain's guard.

'I demand it,' asserted Meysah, nearly losing his accent.

The Morkans laughed in condescension.

The guard pointed his sword at Jimmy. 'Do you demand it now?'

Jimmy grabbed the flat of the sword with his bound hands and pulled hard, sending both Morkan and sword to the ground.

Before Jimmy could do anything more, Meysah brought up his hands to stop him. 'Don't!'

'Don't!' the Captain told his guard as he raised his sword at Jimmy. 'We need them to comply. They are not stupid Tellens, and they *can* fight. *Ewekh tanwakh thmëo kit yolpakhmech!* The guard nodded. 'It's complicated. We don't know everything Mirauk knows.' He turned to the two knights. 'Sleep now. Tomorrow, you will bring us the way the Telorians went, and we will arrange some sort of agreement.'

'All right,' Meysah conceded.

The Telorians were led to an area where many Morkans stood guard. The Captain sat with his guard a little way closer to the fire.

When the Morkans around them were asleep, Jimmy whispered, 'Can you distract the Morkans? I'm going to send a message to our Masters.'

Meysah glanced around. 'Okay, pretend you're asleep. I'll cover for you.'

Meysah turned and rolled, stretched, yawned, and complained aloud to himself that the ground was too hard as Jimmy mumbled the spell. Unaware of the magic happening before them, the Morkans snorted and ignored them both.

'It's already suppertime,' observed Vigh. 'This is not normal for them. They would have otherwise come back.'

'Or,' said Dublenk, 'they actually are continuing on.'

The two Lords sighed. Boreth shook his head.

When night came, both were unsettled. That's when they received the message.

'Time to leave the shelter,' announced Vigh. 'We have to find the lads. They're relatively safe, as far as the feeling goes, but they've been captured by Morkans.'

'I wonder who sent these soldiers,' mused Boreth. 'Kàtchah or . . . Em.'

'Hurry!' Vigh urged.

They left with haste, running almost all night. Boreth took the lead, stopping from time to time to look around and listen carefully before continuing on, everyone else following close behind him.

Near twilight, Boreth stopped and pointed ahead. 'Over there,' he whispered. 'Follow me.'

'We should travel by tree,' suggested Attëgon.

As he started up a tree, the others followed. They slowly and discretely passed through the branches, going from tree to tree to finally arrive at the campsite where the knights were being held captive. From their vantage point, they could see the entire camp.

'Look, there they are,' whispered Boreth.

'They're bound,' noted Attëgon. 'I thought you said they were relatively safe!'

'We can't take on this many Morkans,' said Nastafin.

'Oh, yes, we can,' declared Vigh. 'We sure can. There are, what, fifteen of them, more or less? I have a plan:

We'll take down the watch guards first, then we'll work our way in to free the lads.' He sighed. 'I have been hard on Meysah lately. I wish I'd not chided him so much. If anything should happen . . .'

'We should wait to see what's been going on,' suggested Boreth. 'It's too close to morning to go by unnoticed.'

'Get up! Tucklenk and Mister Mute!' the Captain ordered. 'It's time for you to show us which way the Telorians went.'

'We'll need to have our legs unbound,' remarked Meysah.

'What?'

'Well, we'll have to walk, no?' Meysah had a partial smile. The Captain growled.

'Guards, unbind their legs. And surround them! They'll lead us, but not take the lead.'

The guards did as told and grabbed hold of the captives. Another guard was told to carry their bags and weapons. With that, they started on their journey.

The knights and the Morkans travelled all day. At night, they settled again.

'I need reassurance,' pleaded Meysah. 'I need to know what you plan on doing with the Telorians.'

'They need to be brought to Mork,' said the guard.

'Hold your tongue,' the Captain pointedly said to his guard.

Meysah laughed. 'Do you really think they can easily be captured?'

'Maybe not as easily as you, but yes,' the Captain replied.

Jimmy let out a guttural sigh of frustration. When captured, Jimmy knew from experience that they could escape their predicaments, but these Morkan didn't. He would not have a Morkan think he was an easy catch – but he said and did nothing, though he glared at the Captain.

The Captain shooed the others away, dismissing them. The guards led the lads away and surrounded them, binding their legs once more. The Morkans set up their camp.

Jimmy heard a rustling sound come from above, and a small stone fell to the ground beside him. He looked up and saw Boreth, who discreetly waved at him from above. Jimmy turned back, smiling and pressing his lips together in an attempt to hide the smile.

'Heh!' a shout came from a fair distance away.

Two guards went to investigate.

Vigh and Dublenk grabbed the Morkans, covering their mouths with their hands, weapons drawn on them.

'Who sent you?' Vigh demanded in a half whisper.

'You won't get a word out of me,' one of the guards sneered.

'Dublenk,' said Vigh.

Dublenk put his knife to the second guard's throat. Vigh did the same to his capture.

'Tell us,' Vigh pressed, 'or we'll kill you both. Who sent you?'

'Was it Kàtchah, or was it Mirauk?' demanded Dublenk.

'Nice try,' the second Morkan condescended.

'Are you after the Telorians, huh?' Vigh's whispers became more harsh.

'As a matter of fact . . .' said the first Morkan.

'What makes you think you'll catch them?' asked Dublenk.

'They must have a weakness,' said the second guard. 'They are only powerful in theory.'

'You think?' seethed Vigh. 'Then why am I holding you, cornered, knife at your throat, with you feeling threatened?' The Morkans didn't answer, though their eyes widened. 'Don't underestimate the strength of the Star. I, as much as the others, am not easily fooled. You, on the other hand, take the stories of my friends for facts. I've got to hand it to them, they're quite clever, leading you astray like that. So, tell me – what are you to do with us?'

'Bring you to Mork,' growled the first guard. 'By order of Mirauk.'

'We won't let that happen,' declared Vigh.

'Then you shall have to kill us,' the second guard taunted.

He kicked Dublenk in the stomach, freeing himself from the Tellen's grasp, but Dublenk recovered quickly and slashed the Morkan's throat.

The other Morkan didn't move. 'Go ahead, kill me. I will scream so loud, you'll go deaf.'

'Not so easily,' said Vigh. 'You will go back to the camp, with me in disguise, and if you try anything, my friends will shoot you. You are being watched.' Vigh pointed upwards at the tall treetops. 'When we return to your camp, you will give me the bag that contains the two prisoners' weapons. You will not utter a single word. Is that clear?'

Dublenk took hold of the Morkan while Vigh donned the dead one's cloak. He started off as Dublenk escorted the guard.

'And so?' asked the Captain.

'We saw nothing,' said Vigh. 'It was probably animals. We should still be wary.'

Meysah and Jimmy gaped at the cloaked Vigh, recognition on their faces, before schooling their expressions. The other Morkan took the bag of weapons and gave it to Vigh. Then he cast a meaningful glance at the Captain, the type of look that says it all.

The Captain signalled the other guards, who instantly surrounded Vigh and unhooded him.

'I knew it!' the Captain hissed.

'Oh, but you don't know who I am,' Vigh sneered.

Dublenk snuck over to the lads and untied them. Vigh tossed the bag their way.

The Captain swung his sword at Vigh, who ducked and lunged at him, grabbing him around the waist, and they both fell down.

From the treetops, Boreth, Attëgon, and Nastafin rained down arrows on the Morkans. Weapons in hand, Jimmy and Meysah joined the fray, jumping forward and slashing at their enemies. Once their numbers had thinned, Attëgon, Boreth, and Nastafin jumped down from their vantage point and landed on top of Morkans, moving into the midst of battle.

They made quick work of the soldiers. The knights were more skilled, but the Telorians had fought more adept Morkans in their time, including the Dukes.

Boreth grabbed an arrow and plunged it into a Morkan's face, spun around, and lifted his shield to block an incoming blow. Jimmy jumped and rolled over Boreth's shield, arcing his sword at the Morkans and slicing their armour where it was most vulnerable.

Meysah jabbed his sword backwards as Attëgon plunged his through another Morkan's abdomen. Nastafin shot arrows at a Morkan advancing on Vigh, stepping forward each time she nocked a new one. She knelt and shot higher, and the arrow plunged into the Morkan's shoulder from above. The Morkan grunted, jerking and plucking the arrow out, giving Vigh the opening he needed to impale him.

When few Morkans remained, the Captain turned to the Telorians, the four of them standing together now.

'You are fools,' he seethed.

'No, you are,' declared Jimmy, finally speaking more assertedly without any accents. The Captain's eyes widened. 'For until now, you were falling for our bluff.'

'He speaks,' the Morkan whispered.

'Of course I speak!' Jimmy remonstrated. '*You're* the one who decided I couldn't.'

'Tell us what happened to my sister,' Meysah demanded through gritted teeth.

'Never!' the Captain fumed.

He lunged forward at the Telorians, meeting Meysah's sword and his doom, as did the other Morkans.

In little time, it was all over – the Morkans had failed again.

Jimmy spat on the Morkan Captain's corpse. 'That's for mocking those who cannot speak.'

'Will they ever learn?' sighed Boreth.

'At least these didn't have to live knowing of their folly, unlike Kàtchah,' said Vigh. 'I don't know what's better: living as a failure without knowing it, or dying knowing it.'

'Thank the stars you came,' breathed Jimmy, smiling his appreciation to the masters.

'We better inform Stëinbøk,' said Nastafin. 'When enough time has passed, Mirauk will realise this army failed at capturing you and he'll send more troops. He's hunting for you, and he won't stop until he has you.'

'Then it is in vain that he hunts us,' declared Vigh.

'If he destroys us, he can't be destroyed. We're the only ones who can defeat him, or at least Niome is,' said Boreth, 'but we feed her power through ours, and there is a reason we are here – that there are five of us and not just one.' He rubbed his stubble. 'Perhaps other undefeatable Morkans await our blades. Nevertheless, if we're destroyed, Mirauk can die on his own terms and become a star, a very dark star.'

'Hang on,' said Meysah. 'If being slain prevents you from becoming a star, how come Gorthan became one? I mean, I know Elina was ill – that's different – but Gorthan was tortured. Wasn't he slain?'

'Perhaps not,' replied Boreth. 'They tortured him, yes. Then he died. Niome spoke of her theories, and his star is clearly seen in the sky. Henker presumes that he knew they'd kill him, and since he still wanted to be able to help us after his passing, he took his own life, knowing he'd be more powerful in this way. There is no way to know for certain, but perhaps someone has had contact with his spirit and heard his tale. Obviously, he was not slain.'

'That's true,' agreed Vigh.

'Let's not linger here,' said Attëgon. 'Me King awaits.'

Reunited, they left the premises and returned to the fortress. Now informed of the matter of the Morkans, Stëinbøk knew he would have to prepare and be vigilant. The Telorians, Attëgon, Dublenk, and Nastafin remained at the fortress, with Stëinbøk and others replacing them at the shelter. After all, they'd been gone very long and had earned a good break.

CHAPTER FOURTEEN:
A Crucial Moment

Niome could no longer ignore the tugging she felt that drew her outside one fine afternoon near the end of Summer.

'Keep in mind all the dangers out there,' Tobias cautioned.

'It may be too dangerous for travel,' agreed Maria.

'Whoever did this to you,' said Olúryn, 'whoever harmed you is still out there, and could very well do it again.'

Niome sighed. They meant well, she knew, but this was precisely why she needed to go.

'If you don't want me to go, that won't change a thing. I'll still go – in secret, if I have to – but I'm warning you now, for I don't want to go alone.' She frowned. 'Why do I get the sense I've gone somewhere in secret before? Wait . . . that's how it all started!'

'How what started?' said Tobias.

'I don't know, but that's how it started. And now, I'm going.'

'Then let *me* go with you,' said Olúryn.

Niome paused, staring at him. For a moment, a different face appeared to her, as if from a vision. It felt familiar, but she could not place it.

'I've been through this before,' she muttered, leaning forward on a chair, 'an argument about a trip. I don't know who with, but I know this polc came after me. *They* . . . how many were there?'

Her train of thought stopped abruptly. It was the same thing every time: she remembered someone or an event in a brief flicker, she followed the memory, and before it could reveal anything of significance to her, it dissipated.

'*I'll* accompany Navë,' said Tobias. 'That'll be best.'

Niome and Tobias set out the following day on horseback and rode through the forest and through the northern fields for many days, often stopping to observe and explore. Niome would touch the trees as though memories were within their grasp – memories from forest battles, memories of a ghost in a tree, memories of fortress walls behind trees – but only brief glimpses were they, and never enough to know for sure.

Tobias showed her the place in the fields where he had first found her.

'I remember a fence,' said Niome. 'It was night. And we were hurrying up to get through quickly.'

'Who's "we"?' asked Tobias. Niome shrugged. 'Do you suppose you were escaping Morkans?'

'Perhaps.'

Niome dismounted her horse and walked around.

Tobias cocked his brow, curious. He took Niome's horse and walked it beside his own, following Niome. She stopped and looked up into the sky – there was a dragon flying low.

'Uh, Navë? We should get back.'

'Why? It's just a dragon.'

'From what I recall, they don't appreciate us polcs because we've been using their Portal. There *was* a time long ago when dragons and polcs lived in harmony.' Tobias deliberately stated how things were before the Five allied with the dragons, hoping this would prompt Niome to correct him if she were one of them. 'Lately,' he went on, 'they attack all polcs. Perhaps someday we can be at peace with them again.'

The dragon flew down, landing before them. Tobias placed a hand on the hilt of his sword and steadied the horses with the other.

The winged creature walked to Niome and gently tapped its paw on her head. Niome smiled at it. Then it peered carefully at her and appeared to grow saddened, lowering its head.

The dragon snorted before it soared up into the air and away.

'What was that all about?' asked Niome.

'It appears the dragons have some sort of affinity towards you,' said Tobias. 'That behaviour . . . you are known to them.'

Niome nodded, walking back to the horse with a smile on her face. She stopped suddenly, swaying in place. She cried out and put a hand to her forehead.

'No. I don't understand. It can't be – these flashes that are coming to me . . . I can't take it!'

Tobias moved to Niome and steadied her by the shoulders. 'I suspected flashes might flood your mind.' He pressed his lips into a thin line. 'I look to you like a father looks to his daughter. All I want is the best for you, Navë. Tell me what you need from me to help you through this, and I will do it.'

'I want to go home.'

'Which home? Navë, you are someone else that I don't know. Please specify.'

'I don't yet know my original home . . . for now, I believe I wish to go to *your* home, for it is the only home I know.' She felt lost, like a little child.

Tobias guided Niome by the hand and helped her mount the horse. Together, they rode back home.

Niome was still seeing fragments of memories when they reached the Zaccher Grey House. These flashes were snippets of moments she lived, something someone said, or one action done out of many from a random day, all bombarding her mind in a dizzying onslaught of visions. They would quell after a time before beginning again, and after several days, the flashes were constant – Niome could no longer see the present.

Colouring came, and the flashes continued. Yet there were rare moments when they stopped for a short time.

One such day, Niome was sitting in the living room, sipping tea with Olúryn as she told him everything she saw whenever the flashes occurred – if her words could keep up with the visions.

Her face paled as she was plunged back into a series of memories.

'Navë, what is it?' Olúryn asked, worried. 'What do you see?'

'Too much. So many flashes . . . I feel nauseous, stuck here in the depths of my mind.'

'Are you able to describe what you see?' Olúryn took a step towards her. He put his cup on the small table and knelt down in front of her. 'Can you make sense of it, Navë?'

'There's too much for me to process what I see! It's too fast.'

Niome's eyes were wide. She dropped her cup.

Olúryn took her hand. 'Father!' he called out, ignoring the spilled tea. 'Father!'

He put his other hand to Niome's chest to feel her heart rate. 'Navë.'

'I see too much – I feel dizzy.' She began hyper-ventilating, her chest heaving. She grabbed at her hair, pressing down on her head, hoping it would quell the ache.

'It's okay, it'll be okay. Look at me, Navë. Focus.'

'But I can't see you!'

'Focus on me. Use magic to see, for you know what this room looks like, you know what I look like. Follow the sound of my voice.'

'I have a potion that might help,' said Tobias as he hurried to Niome's side.

'I feel afraid,' said Niome, her entire body shaking as sweat beaded on her face. 'I see faces, evil faces.'

'Navë,' said Tobias, 'I'm going to feed you a potion.'

Niome nodded. Olúryn let go of her hand as his father approached her, placing the rim of the vial to her lips so she could drink.

'It will take a while before it begins to take effect,' explained Tobias.

'Aah!' Niome pressed her hand over her heart. 'No, not the pounding!'

'Pounding?!' exclaimed Tobias and Olúryn both.

'You said it wouldn't return!' cried Niome.

'Who said it wouldn't return?' Tobias implored.

'You said it would stop now that I've . . .' Niome did not finish her sentence.

'Who is she talking to?' Olúryn asked Tobias.

For a moment, Niome became herself again – lost and scared, but still Niome Fairhaven, speaking to Elina.

'All that depends on me . . . where are . . .'

She fell to the ground and began to moan in pain, repeating what she said at first. Tobias and Olúryn propped her up, at a loss for what to do. Niome asked aloud who she'd been speaking to, but the pounding stopped, and her breathing calmed.

With tears streaking her face, she wrapped her arms around Olúryn as she fell into his embrace.

'You're all right, Navë,' Olúryn soothed, relieved.

'What's happening to me?'

'You've experienced the worst of it, I believe,' said Tobias. 'From here on, it should be uphill.'

'I hope so,' murmured Niome.

Olúryn held her tightly and instinctively kissed her brow in comfort. He gently rocked back and forth as he held her, soothingly leaning his cheek on her head and caressing her hair.

The flashes had truly stopped since then. Aside from a few sporadic inspiring thoughts, no new memories arose in Niome's mind. Now well into 4775, when the fourth day of the eleventh week of Winter came, she remembered her birthday and attributed the memory to magic.

'Well, then,' said Tobias, 'this calls for celebration!'

After a time, Niome remembered more details such as that. She also started to remember aspects of the other four of the Star, yet never who they were in relationship to her.

Spring arrived, though there was still a good deal of snow on the ground, which seemed familiar to Niome. She vaguely remembered two young lads playfully teasing each other.

'Olúryn,' said Niome, knocking on his open bedroom door. 'Could you give me some advice on something?'

'Anything I can do to help, Navë. Come on in.'

'Am I bothering you?'

'You never bother me. I mean, it's not in your habits.' Olúryn was folding clothes neatly on his bed, and he placed a folded shirt on top of a pile.

'Are you planning to go somewhere?'

'Just to investigate the region,' replied Olúryn. 'We do that sometimes to see if travellers are passing by or if the enemy is moving this way.'

'Oh, well, I had a dream that said – I believe – I should travel some more, while there's still snow on the ground. I know there's very little left, but I think I might remember more about my Winter travels that way.'

Niome stood close to the door still as Olúryn folded the clothes, walking from his drawers to his bed.

'You can come with me, if you like. I think it'll be good for you, too.' He paused. 'Though I believe that's not the advice you came here to ask me about. What's on your mind?'

'I'm stuck on something. I don't know whether I should altogether forget about it and move on, or stick to the unknown principles of . . .'

'Navë, I'm sure whatever you want to experience is okay, and whoever may be upset will forgive you.' Olúryn observed her, staying by his bed. 'You are not yet who you always were. If you want to try something out—'

'It's not about trying something out,' said Niome. 'It's about what I've been denying for a long time.' She took a step towards him.

'I've been trying to ignore it myself,' admitted Olúryn, turning to face her, 'for two years, since you've arrived. I thought you said you weren't ready to move on. Now that your memories are returning, are you sure you . . . ? I do wish . . . well, I wouldn't mind . . .'

Niome let out a laugh. 'I don't know when I'll remember. In how many years? But I want to be happy now, too. I don't know what to do.'

'I can't decide for you.'

'I know, I just . . . I don't know anymore what's best for me to do, that's all,' admitted Niome. 'I just long to be wrapped in affection.'

'Follow your heart,' said Olúryn, taking a few steps towards her.

Niome glanced at her ring and back at Olúryn. He, too, looked at the ring and back to her. He averted his eyes before turning and taking several steps away.

'If you feel you must stay loyal, I understand and I will not hold it against you, for my feelings for you help me to sympathise.' He stopped and stood still, bowing his head. 'Besides, I wouldn't want my curse to harm you, though by now, I doubt it will. I've dared to express more, and I've dared to feel more than I have in a long time. You're still alive, but I still fear that my curse may kill you, and *that* hurts me. It hurts me more than the thought of starting something with you and losing you if you were to remember who you are.'

'The curse doesn't scare me. I do feel the need to stay loyal, though.'

'I understand,' said Olúryn, his voice low.

'And I will keep the ring on, but . . .' She paused. 'While I am here with you and staying here with you, I wish to be here with you.'

Olúryn turned his head to the side.

'Do you mean that?' He smiled mildly. 'Are you saying . . . ?' Niome nodded slowly. Olúryn turned to face her again and walked back to her. 'You're certain you want this?'

'Right now, yes. I don't know about tomorrow, I don't know about next season, but right now, it is what I want.'

'Then I'm glad, for it is what I want too.'

Niome took his hand and held it tightly. Olúryn leaned his forehead against hers, both nervous. He began to close the distance, his lips grazing Niome's, but as he gently kissed her, magic surged between them. An empowering sensation reverberated, and the need for affection in the way either of them had wanted it a moment ago was replaced by the mere desire to care for each other as friends did. Somehow, the magic allowed them to know the other felt the same without the need for words.

'Did you feel that?' asked Olúryn.

'Yes. What could it mean?'

'I guess we'll learn it in due time.'

Olúryn held Niome in his arms, and they both felt content, as though being held was all they needed. As though what they needed most was comfort.

Olúryn and Niome rode to the plains in the north the next morning before making their way south to the Ortim River, always keeping their gaze to the west. When the river split into the Rapids, they travelled back east, not far from the Twisted Forest. Niome felt a strong presence of magic there, one that almost pulled her towards it. Yet, she could also sense a sinister energy about it that made her instinctively know that right now was not the time to travel there.

After riding for thirty-three days, Niome and Olúryn simply rode back to Zaccher Lake having nothing to report about enemy travellers, though Niome did have a few new memories to share.

CHAPTER FIFTEEN:
The Missing

For what seemed to be a long time, life in the forest was all right. However, slowly and almost imperceptibly, polcs started disappearing – Tellens from different shelters would vanish without a trace.

It began with one who had gone hunting and never returned. Many Tellens searched but could not find their friend. Gradually, more disappeared. As none found any bodies, they knew not if they were dead.

When Stëinbøk learnt of what was happening to his people, he and his close companions returned to the fortress – the Tellens could not afford to have their King disappear as well. Stëinbøk ensured word went out that the Firlanians were to return to the fortress posthaste, and he told the four Telorians it would be best for them to remain there.

'Someone is takin' me people,' Stëinbøk told the four, 'and I think we can assume that someone is Morkan.'

'They didn't appreciate our courteous ways,' Lenarbøk surmised with derision.

'I knew we should've fought them!' complained Meysah. 'Just like we did to the ones who captured Jimmy and me.'

'When in Kalteli,' Vigh told Meysah, 'do as the Kaltelians.'

'Do they even still exist?' Meysah muttered under his breath. 'Bahvley said the whole kingdom was deserted.'

'Vigh is right,' said Derfbøk. 'We appreciate you following our laws. Never kill when unprovoked.'

'Unprovoked!' exclaimed Jimmy. 'It's because of them there were Morkans to capture us.'

'Though this time, we could've followed Telorian standards,' conceded Stëinbøk. 'I admit that it would've been reasonable in this case, but it could have brought too many Morkans to our forest, and then, by our own fault, Teloria would be in grave danger. I do not wish to condone a course of action that will put Teloria, our true country, in greater jeopardy than it already finds itself in. Especially when its Great Wizardess is indisposed. However, more Morkans have come anyway.'

'We don't know if it's the same ones as before,' said Hunbøk.

'I doubt Kàtchah would come back,' voiced Boreth. 'He's afraid of us.'

'And only goes where he is bound to succeed,' Meysah reminded.

'Kàtchah sure didn't come with that little army that was sent here,' said Vigh. Meysah nodded exaggeratingly and bounced his hands in unison, following his nods, to emphasise what he had just said. Vigh smiled and nodded in return. 'They *must* know we destroyed them. They do, after all, know our whereabouts.'

'Perhaps this army's here to do what the other failed to do,' suggested Derfbøk.

'Me question is,' began Stëinbøk, 'how many are they? And where are they hiding?'

'That's two,' said Jimmy.

Stëinbøk laughed despite himself. 'I wish I still had me sense of humour.'

'Does age and wisdom, and experience on the battle-field, really take that away?' inquired Meysah.

'Not completely,' said Vigh, smiling.

'Or maybe almost not at all!' said Boreth, suppressing a laugh.

'Obviously, the Lords are laughing at some witticism we aren't privy to,' Meysah whispered to Jimmy. 'Maybe they asked themselves the same question when they were our age.'

'Well we' – Jimmy gestured between himself and Meysah – 'shall *never* lose our wit!'

Stëinbøk smiled fondly at the two lads, greatly wishing he could drift off into a merrier state. 'I appreciate your attempt at lightening the mood, lads, though now we need to figure out where the Morkans are hidin' and where they're keepin' me people.' He slumped his shoulders and sat down.

'The lake,' Jimmy said conclusively, breaking the silence.

'What?' said everyone else at once.

'If you think of where those who disappeared were before they disappeared,' started Jimmy, 'at first, it could've been anywhere, but then more and more got taken – all from closer and closer to the lake. Perhaps five shelters away one day, then three another, in whichever direction. This may be for convenience of proximity. It's a good thing you came back when you did.'

'Are there more reported missin'?' Stëinbøk asked Hunbøk.

'Let me verify.' He left the room.

'If Morkans can dig tunnels under the Gord Plains,' continued Jimmy, 'with an entrance smack in the middle of the river—'

Meysah nudged him. Jimmy caught himself in the revelation he probably shouldn't share at this time.

'Which is what they *claimed*,' Jimmy continued casually, hoping he hadn't revealed too much, 'then they can certainly dig tunnels under a lake. They could easily sneak into the forest again, too, if extremely careful and if a small number dig unnoticed. Then they capture one when the Tellen is alone and dig some more between captures. More Morkans join to help capture more, and then it's maybe a dozen or less against one Tellen. A very effective trick.'

'And perhaps the army that was there had come to start the job or join the first group,' mused Boreth.

'Quite the detective,' said Lenarbøk.

'Since there was no drought,' said Jimmy, 'the entrance could very well be a tree stump or in a bunch of hedges. If that's so and there are tunnels, this was Kàtchah's idea, and we can certainly expect to see Gohtek again.'

'I've trained him well, haven't I?' Boreth said boastfully.

'I *was* a Captain to those Morkans, for a time,' Jimmy muttered low to Meysah.

'Verily,' said Vigh. 'Selemil should be proud, of both of you.'

'I knew those crows were up to more than giving messages,' Jimmy added. He narrowed his eyes. 'Bird's-eye view of the forest.'

'Clever,' breathed Boreth. 'They probably scanned the area for their masters.'

'Your Majesty,' Hunbøk said in a panic as he returned, 'there's been another disappearance! *By the lake.* Reported in just now.'

Everyone looked at Jimmy. He himself was shocked to hear his theory was completely correct.

'I think it's time to get a team goin' and find out what these Morkans want from us. They're tryin' to say somethin', but I'll get me people back, that's for sure!'

The four Telorians prepared for travel and met with the Tellen King immediately. Stëinbøk was accompanied by Hunbøk, Derfbøk, Lenarbøk, Vessibøk, Merilenk, Nastafin, Dublenk, Corivøk, Attëgon, and the Firlanians.

While Spring was underway and the trees were budding, the air was bitter, as this Winter had lasted unnaturally long.

'I think it's best if we avoid splittin' up,' said Stëinbøk.

With every step they took, bringing them closer to the lake, the more reluctant they were to speak. They were ever wary and vigilant, lookin about constantly. At night, they slept not in shelters, but in the trees.

By the third day, they were close.

'We should finalise our plan now before we're too close to the lake,' Stëinbøk spoke quietly.

'"*The Morkans move by night.*" Remember what Tharguen told us on our way to Mork?' said Vigh. 'They prefer the night. Indeed, their eyesight is keener then, so dark Mork is. They may not emerge from their hideout during the day. Either may give us an advantage in the day, but them the advantage at night.'

'I agree,' said Kchalami.

'Some of us are ready to sacrifice ourselves,' said Krystal.

'We'll let ourselves be captured to find out where the entrance is,' said Elmezni.

'You can't!' exclaimed Jimmy. 'You're too important to us!'

'That's the point,' said Elmezni. 'Trust us. We know what we're doing.'

'My brother has skill,' said Krystal, 'and I have wit.'

'I've got wit, too!' Elmezni objected softly.

'I hear something,' Meysah warned. 'We're too loud.'

'We should travel by tree,' suggested Attëgon. 'A skill we have that Morkans do not.' His eyes landed on the Telorians. 'You are the only non-forest dwellers. We will show you how.' The Telorians gave their accord.

The polcs scaled the trees as they followed the Tellens' lead, a few to each tree.

'Are you sure the branches won't crack and break?' asked Vigh, a little unsure of himself.

'Just hold on firmly,' said Boreth, already getting the knack of it. 'I did it when we saved Jimmy and Meysah. It's actually quite thrilling. I'm surprised you don't quite feel secure doing it, a Lord of your stature,' he laughed.

'That's the point,' complained Vigh, 'I'm too tall.'

'You must climb on all fours,' said Nastafin. 'That's how the animals of our forest branch from tree to tree unnoticed.'

'I don't care for *your* opinion,' Vigh replied dryly.

'It seems there's a lot you don't care about.'

'I care about too much! I only *entirely* don't care about Morkans.'

'So you do care about my advice.' Nastafin gave him a pointed stare.

'Please, don't twist my words,' sighed Vigh. 'I would've wished for someone else to show me.'

'What are you avoiding?'

The question hit too close to home for Vigh. 'I don't like . . . being close to people.'

'You get close to other Telorians,' noted Nastafin.

'You have a lot of guts, asking me questions that don't concern you!' snapped Vigh, his whisper harsh.

'You have grown . . . bitter . . . towards me.' Nastafin looked hurt. 'I don't know what drives you to be like this, but if it continues, you'll push more people away.'

Nastafin hurried up ahead. Vigh paused in his movement and sighed.

After a time, Meysah was travelling beside his master. 'Harshness is not necessarily the answer, Master.'

'What do you mean?' asked Vigh.

'You told me that once. Seems you've forgotten. You can't linger in the past.'

Vigh looked at him blankly.

'Don't look at me like you don't know what I'm talking about! I heard you this afternoon. Nastafin was talking about the same thing as I am, and so were you.'

Vigh looked down at the ground below. 'The pain from the memories is too hard to bear. I somehow can't let go, Meysah. The emotions bring it all back. I wish I'd forget it all forever. I just . . . any reminder . . . well . . .'

'I understand, but don't lose your chance, Master Vigh. You've trained me to trust my instincts and be hopeful. Niome's taught me to believe in intuition and be mindful. Think about it.'

They resumed and soon heard Jimmy, who was a tree ahead of them.

'Urgh, why does it have to snow?! It's Spring!'

'Don't we go through this *every* year?' said Meysah. 'You'll reach old age and say the same thing still!'

'It's not the same this time.'

'How so?' demanded Meysah.

'The cold season's lasting too long,' complained Jimmy.

'How is that different?' argued Meysah. 'It always lasts too long.'

'This is going to go on forever,' muttered Boreth.

'I guess some things need to change,' said Vigh, 'and some things *never* change.'

'Tone it down!' said Dublenk, suppressing a smile. 'We don't want to be heard.'

The group continued on and reached the area the following night.

They scanned the large lake carefully – the entrance to the Morkan hideout could be anywhere. They remained in one area to silently spy. When enough time had elapsed, at times a night or two, with them hearing and seeing nothing, they moved on to another area to wait and observe as they had the previous sector, travelling along the lake to the south side. If they heard anything seemingly unusual, they stayed longer, but it always turned out to be merely an animal or a hunting Tellen. Still, they were not hasty, lest they miss their chance at finding the secret entrance.

The days became warmer while the nights remained cool. By the ninth week of Spring, they had reached the opening of the lake, where the stream flowed in.

Boreth, Laurelmi, and Corivøn 'shared' a tree. When night came, the three continued to chat in low whispers.

'I'm exhausted,' sighed Laurelmi, 'not physically, of course, but . . .'

'But your eyes and ears are tired,' said Corivøn. 'I feel the same. Me eyes are beginnin' to see blurry.'

'Rest your eyes,' said Boreth. 'Don't push your body to its utmost limits if you don't have to. There are many others watching the exact same thing.'

'Imagine, nice soft cosy beds,' said Laurelmi. 'I've never been out of a fairly decent bed for this long before. Hay is okay. These branches are hard for my back.'

'Try the floor,' said Boreth. 'Try the ground. Well, you have, and grass is okay. Sand, too. But those Morkan tunnels were the worst. I'm sure sleeping in Mork itself would be more comfortable than that.' The three of them chuckled. 'This isn't so bad, though it could be better. I'd like to put my feet on the ground again soon.'

Just then, something caught Boreth's eye. He leaned forward.

'I think I see something,' he whispered more quietly than before. 'A moving shape on the other side of the stream.'

'You *do* have excellent far-seeing vision,' whispered Laurelmi.

Boreth narrowed his eyes to observe the figure carefully. 'That's a Morkan, all right. Where's Stëinbøk?'

Corivøn pointed to a tree on the left.

'Time to move on to the next phase of our mission.'

At dawn, Boreth informed the others of what he had seen. Jimmy was uncertain whether he enjoyed the validation of having been right about all of this, but at least now they could rescue the missing Tellens.

They crossed the stream by tree until they reached the north side. They positioned themselves strategically, ready for nightfall.

Several Morkans emerged, though they could not tell from where. More movement caught Vigh's attention, who was perched with Nastafin, Aterel, and Kachmassiel. There was a Tellen below, and Aterel bit his lip to stop himself from shouting a warning.

The Morkans pounced on the Tellen from behind, immobilising him and seising his weapons.

Akchmassiel twitched, looking ready to jump down. Vigh put his hand on the Firlanian's arm to stop him and shook his head. The Firlanian Captain understood.

'Come on,' jeered a Morkan, 'are there more of you about?'

'You'll try to get us all,' the Tellen spat disdainfully, 'but you'll fail.'

'Your words are kurssus, just like you and all Tellens,' another Morkan snarled as they carried him off.

'Oh,' started Nastafin to herself, pressing her lips into a thin line. She opened her mouth and breathed in to shout, but Vigh clamped a hand to her mouth to stop her. Both widened their eyes before Vigh pulled away. The two remained silent.

The Morkans and their captive had disappeared from view. The group had missed their chance to follow their quarries.

'We're ready to sacrifice ourselves,' Elmezni announced the following morning as the Tellens, Firlanians, and Telorians conferred in a huddle close to the same tree.

'We'll leave marks at the entrance,' said Krystal. 'We'll try to find out what's going on inside, but there's no guarantee we'll be able to get back out.'

'I know of some who are willing to sneak in and investigate while others create a distraction,' said Stëinbøk.

'What will be your mark?' asked Hunbøk.

'We can leave my silver dragon necklace,' said Elmezni. 'Though I hate to have to leave it behind, it's the best way. It takes the colours of the surroundings and looks like what it's touching. That's why no one sees it around my neck, but it's always there – look.'

He held it out. Now they saw the shimmering silver, but as he let it fall back onto his chest, it turned peach again.

'I'm told it was made with dragon scales cooked into crystal before being mixed in with the silver,' explained Elmezni. 'It's ancient. I don't know who made it, but it's been passed down for generations. Perhaps it's as old as Kaulchèc History itself.'

'With this kind of magic,' said Krystal, 'only those with excellent visionary skills may find it.'

'Good,' said Boreth. 'Finally I'll get to be on the ground again, standing solidly on my two feet. I'll find it for sure. I may need help, though.'

'I wish you good luck, then,' Stëinbøk said to Elmezni and Krystal.

'Thank you,' said Elmezni. 'Tonight is when the Morkans get fooled, yet again.'

Elmezni and Krystal walked side by side, having received the warning that Morkans were tailing them.

'Are you ready?' Elmezni whispered.

'Are you nervous?' Krystal whispered back.

'So, uh, what should we talk about?'

'You know, I haven't seen any Morkans around lately.' Elemzni rolled his eyes at his sister. She shrugged. 'Perhaps they won't come back.'

The Morkans pounced at them from behind – there were six of them.

'You thought wrong!' said one.

At first, the Firlanians fought them off, kicking and punching fiercely.

'You've got impeccable timing,' Elmezni said sarcastically.

'Thanks,' said another Morkan. 'We should put this in the records. Mirauk'll be proud – a compliment from a Tellen.'

'Firlanian!' corrected Krystal. 'Perhaps you forgot we were still here. Perhaps you forgot that we destroyed your so-called bloodsuckers.'

'Plus one point for the boy's compliment, minus three for you.'

The Morkans pinned the two Firlanians on their stomachs and bound their hands and ankles. Then they flung them over their shoulders like luggage and carried them away.

'Let go!' shouted Elmezni.

'This is pure gold!' said a Morkan. 'We've captured two Firlanians – such a rare occurrence.'

'Rare occurrence?' asked Krystal.

'Oh, yes. It's rare that a Firlanian gets captured. In fact, it's been a long time – too long. *We* will be praised.'

'Urhg!' both Krystal and Elezni sighed.

The Morkans passed through the forest and went to the entrance of their caves. Elmezni realised he had forgotten to put the pendant in his hand; it was in his pocket still. He began to shake and twitch. The Morkan stumbled over and Elmezni fell right at the foot of the entrance, the pendant slipping right out.

'Don't think you can escape!' one of the more muscular Morkans snorted.

'Such a thought never crossed my mind,' replied the sly Firlanian, speaking truth.

Once the Morkans picked him back up, they all entered the cave. Elmezni and Krystal flashed each other a quick smile and nodded.

CHAPTER SIXTEEN:
The Rescue

Once the Sun was up, Boreth jumped down. 'Ah, that feels good.'

'Now there's no need to fear falling,' said Vigh from his branch.

'Aren't you coming down?'

'No, I think I'll stay here.'

'Your loss,' replied Boreth. 'The ground is a wonderful thing.'

'We're coming,' said Merilenk. Down he jumped, along with Attëgon, Corivøn, Kchalami, and Falmozni.

'Let's go!' said Boreth.

Wasting no time, they crouched and crawled along near the water's edge. They searched almost all day.

'I think I see something,' said Corivøn.

The others joined her near some weeds.

'I'm not sure. I need you to tell me if I'm hallucinatin' or if me eyes are as sharp as I think.'

Boreth crouched low, leaning his head as close as he could without touching the weeds.

'That's the pendant, all right.'

'But then where's the entrance?' asked Falmozni. 'I mean, how do they get through here without getting infected by the weed?'

'The entrance could be anywhere around here,' voiced Attëgon

'Boreth,' said Kchalami, 'we require your expertise.'

'Sometimes I wish there was someone better than me that *I* could rely on.'

'Interestin' way of boastin',' said Corivøn.

Boreth chuckled. Falmozni put his gloves on and reached for the pendant.

'I'll keep this safe for Elmezni.' He placed it around his neck.

'I don't understand,' said Boreth.

He looked about, trying to refocus, but his eyes were aimed at a large rock that stood right by the weeds.

'The rock!'

He bent down and the others helped him lift it. It was quite heavy, but they managed to move it aside, and indeed it was the entrance, for it revealed a hole – quite obvious, thought Boreth, once you understood how obvious it was.

Boreth popped his head in and out again. 'That's a tunnel down there.'

'How did they do all this, for all this time? Digging and camping out until they could camp inside, without being seen or heard?' said Merilenk. 'These Morkans . . .'

'We should make a mark,' said Kchalami. 'Some will be sneaking in.'

'Hang on!' said Boreth, signaling the others to wait.

'What are you doing?' objected Attëgon.

Boreth jumped into the tunnel and looked about. It was a closed room except for where the tunnel continued downward. It smelt like the tunnels from under the Gord Plains, like moist earth with a fallow smell added to it. He followed the path awhile, sneaking along the wall, and then the tunnel split into two.

Boreth returned and the others put the rock back.

'Do you realise how dangerous what you just did was?!' exclaimed Kchalami.

'I've done it for more than a season before,' stated Boreth.

'But not by choice.'

Boreth averted his friend's eyes. Quickly, briefly, before catching himself.

The others were a little ways further now, looking for a branch to plant by the entrance.

'Boreth? You snuck through the tunnels *not* by choice, right?'

Kchalami had caught Boreth's hesitation, and his tone was one of suspicion. Somehow the Lord was unable to lie to Kchalami's face, not entirely – he respected him too much. And the Prince caught the strange glint in his eyes.

'Of course not,' said Boreth. 'If I'd had it my way, no one would've been taken by Morkans that night.'

'But you were there by duty?'

'Duty, I guess, since Vigh and I destroyed the tunnels. Yet, why does Kàtchah not die?' Boreth shrugged, turning away.

'Boreth, what are you not telling me?' Kchalami manoeuvred in front of Boreth and placed a hand on his shoulder to stop him.

'How do you mean?'

'Were you not there by choice?'

'Of course!' Boreth realised his mistake and the verbal trap Kchalami had set. He sighed.

'You *were* there by choice! There were no Morkans at the river, were there?'

'I see there's no use hiding it from you anymore,' said Boreth. 'However, I can't tell you more than what you've deduced. We all vowed secrecy regarding the course of this duty or the reasons – or anything of it, for that matter – until it is all over with. In other words, until Niome lets us know it's safe to.'

'I understand,' replied Kchalami, 'or at least, I understand a bit.'

The others returned with a very leafy branch and stuck it in the bush in such a way that the Morkans wouldn't notice. Satisfied, they returned to their 'tree camp.'

'Any luck?' asked Stëinbøk.

'We found it,' Boreth confirmed.

'Good. I have a plan,' said Stëinbøk, 'but first I need to know that me people are still alive.' He paused. 'I wish me father were still alive. He could have certainly figured out what to do.'

'Your father's still with you,' said Meysah. 'He'll always be in your heart, and his star is looking down on you.'

'It is. Thank you.'

'We don't mind going,' offered Vigh.

'No,' said Stëinbøk. 'It's too risky! Perhaps you are skilled, but perhaps you'll be walkin' into a trap. It's best if you stay.'

'I agree,' said Jimmy. 'The last thing I want is to go into *more* Morkan tunnels.'

Lenarbøk, Dinankch, and Batel volunteered to investigate the tunnels. Meanwhile, Stëinbøk hatched a plan to draw the Morkans out.

Several days passed, and the Tellens who'd entered the tunnels had not returned. The company waiting in the trees concluded they had been captured. That left Stëinbøk with twenty polcs by his side, four of whom had to stay hidden – the Telorians.

When Stëinbøk reiterated his plan, he emphasised once more to the four Telorians, 'For now, your presence should remain unknown.'

Night fell. When the Morkans passed in the wood, they came upon Stëinbøk and his polcs.

'Why, hello there!' Stëinbøk condescended. 'I believe you have people of mine.'

'Well now, they belong to Mirauk,' retorted a Morkan.

'They never *belonged* to me,' the Tellen King snapped. 'They're free people. Nonetheless, it is me job to protect them. Do I have to trade me place for theirs?'

'No, but you may trade someone else's!' the same Morkan replied slyly.

'What do you want?' Stëinbøk asked through his teeth.

'The Telorians!' said many Morkans at different instances, sounding like an uproar of cacophony.

'What do you want the Telorians for?' insisted Stëinbøk.

'What do you think? Deliver us what we want or we'll start killing the Tellens we have.'

'Don't forget the Firlanians you have, too. I'll make sure you don't hurt them either. Bring me me people, and then perhaps I'll think of letting you have the Telorians.'

The Telorian Lords had been correct in deducing this was all to get at them, on top of exacting revenge at the same time. As they had suggested, Stëinbøk had used them as leverage, though he did not feel secure about it.

'That's not good enough!' the Morkan sneered.

'Are you the Captain?'

'No.'

'Tell your Captain,' Stëinbøk warned, 'to meet me here, at this very spot, with me people and the Firlanians, and I will give up the Telorians. They will be with me here. I will go fetch them meself. Meet me here in three days' time.'

Several Morkans were stirring, readying their weapons.

'I suggest you take up me offer and deliver me message to your Captain. You see up there?' Stëinbøk pointed, and the Morkans looked up. 'Every one of those archers has an arrow pointed at each of you, watching every one of your moves. If you try anything, they will unleash their arrows. If you do not bring me people with you next time, they will unleash them.'

'And if we don't return in three days' time?'

'You will! This is your last warning.'

The Morkans growled, but they backed away from Stëinbøk and eventually turned and walked away.

'Your Majesty, we can't possibly trust these Morkans,' protested Derfbøk.

'I didn't want to let them know that we can pursue them inside their hideout.'

'And if they don't come?'

'We'll go after them. We don't know how many of them there are, but if we have to pull them out one by one, we will. The Captain will be heavily protected if he comes. They may yet oblige. This plan has just yet begun.'

'May! It's an indefinite word,' muttered Derfbøk.

Derfbøk had been right. When the appointed night arrived, the Morkans never showed. Instead, Lenarbøk, Batel, and Dinankch returned.

'What, are these Morkans mocking us?' complained Stëinbøk.

'No,' said Batel, 'they didn't even know we were there.'

'We went by like ghosts.' Lanarbøk grinned.

'Did you find the others? Are they well?' Stëinbøk asked, somewhat heartened but urgently wanting to know how his captured people were faring.

'Alive and well,' Batel confirmed quite cheerfully.

'It's only a ruse to try to get the Telorians,' said Dinankch. 'They don't seem to want to kill anyone . . . yet. Perhaps Mirauk has something else planned for them, like using them as his slaves. As if he needs any more.'

'They like things complicated, Your Highness,' said Lenarbøk.

'How many were captured?' asked the Tellen King.

'Four dozen captured Tellens, including Elmezni and Krystal,' Batel reported, hands clasped behind his back.

'That's nearly all of Firlan,' sighed Kchalami, climbing down a tree.

'Guarded by two dozen Morkans, more or less,' continued Batel.

'They are bound. They get fed regularly, but conditions are poor,' said Lenarbøk. 'Some may begin to get ill. And me younger cousin is there – that worries me. She's always been in me care.'

'What about Elmezni and Krystal?' asked Kchalami. 'Any . . . signs of illness?'

'Same as the others,' said Lenarbøk.

'You were gone a long while. How did you do it?' asked Stëinbøk.

'The same way the Telorians did,' said Dinankch. 'Slow and quiet. Listening in on them.'

'And I quote,' said Batel, *"That King is mad out of his wits! I will not go out there. Not unless the Telorians themselves go mad, for that would be a very happy day for Mirauk's sake."* There was more, but it's unimportant, more or less.' Batel shrugged, looking like he wished he had more to report.

'Perhaps we should alter our plan, Your Highness,' suggested Lenarbøk.

An idea came to Stëinbøk. 'You're right, Lenarbøk. It's time to play mad.'

A smirk rose on the side of Lenarbøk's mouth in slight amusement.

'Ooh, yayee!' said Jimmy, popping out from behind a tree, the other three behind him. 'I acted mad in a play once, with some of the finest Telorian players, too!'

'They needed a young boy, and Jimmy was fit enough,' explained Meysah.

'Yes. Meysah, on the other hand, well, he's just naturally a mad polc.'

'Well,' said Meysah, 'I guess it takes one to recognise one. Eh?' He nudged Jimmy.

'One last thing,' began Dinankch. 'Jimmy was right. The Captain we're dealing with . . . is Gohtek.'

'I knew it,' Jimmy hissed.

'Somehow, I am not at all comforted,' sighed Stëinbøk. 'Come, let us rest. There is much effort to be put into this new instalment.'

Stëinbøk was going to give Gohtek one final chance at battling this fairly. The Tellen King had his principles, and although he had the upper hand, he wanted to let the Morkan Captain fight this with honour. However, Gohtek's cowardice was more than apparent.

Everyone set up in trees, several set adrift on the lake in a small boat. Stëinbøk rolled the rock off of the tunnel entrance.

'Is everyone ready?' he asked.

'Wait,' said Meysah, mussing his hair and tucking out his shirt. 'Do I look crazy enough?'

'Yes,' said Vigh, 'very nice.'

Merilenk, Aterel, Petruni, and Saviel, situated on the lake, began to sing rambunctiously like drunken polcs. The others endured their incessant repetitive singing all day long.

> *Isn't it nice,*
> *To be able to go,*
> *To comfort in ale*
> *And set worries adrift.*

> *Isn't it nice,*
> *To completely let go,*
> *The troubles with ale*
> *No longer exist, oh!*

Hopefully, this would be enough to annoy the Morkans and drive them out of their hole.

'How long will it take, you think?' asked Boreth where he waited in the forest with the others. 'How much more of this do we have to put up with? I admit, it was funny at first, though.'

'I'm going to have this song stuck in my head for days after this,' sighed Vigh.

Suddenly the singing stopped.

'It's working!' said Jimmy.

Down at the lake, four Morkans were seen exiting their hideout and walking towards the edge of the river, where the boat floated near the riverbank.

'What in the kurssus is all this ruckus?!'

'Everyone's gone mad,' said Merilenk as though it was just the way of things in life. 'The Telorians . . . I can't even speak of it.'

One of the Morkans waved his hand to dismiss them and turned to go.

Aterel shot an arrow. It landed in the trunk of a tree before the Morkan.

'Sorry,' he said, his tone nonchalant, 'you can't go back. It's the rule of the game.'

'They *have* gone mad,' said a Morkan.

Before the Morkans had any time to react, the rest of the company was on top of them. The Morkans fought back but were quickly bound and surrounded. Stëinbøk approached them.

'Make a move, make a sound, and you'll get shot. See up there? Every arrow is on you.'

'I hope you realise that my Captain will not send anyone out to investigate the noise!' The Morkan narrowed his eyes. 'Not after he realises we're never going to return.'

'Then we'll get them another way. I just wanted to play his game for a while,' said Stëinbøk. 'He wanted us to go mad – we've gone mad!' Stëinbøk spread out his arms wide and held them there a moment. Then, pointing towards the tunnel, he added, 'It's his turn to play our game now.'

'At least four of you will have been dealt with,' said Attëgon.

The Morkan reached for his knife, his hands unbound. Stëinbøk cursed he hadn't noticed the sly move. A knife came at Stëinbøk, who turned sideways to take it in the arm instead of his chest. He groaned as the knife lodged into him.

Arrows whistled down from the trees and shot the Morkan down. Before the other Morkans could pull the same trick, they met the same fate.

'These are skilled Morkans,' said Stëinbøk, plucking the knife out of his arm, voice a little shaky at first.

Hunbøk immediately started dressing the wound. The King looked at the older polc who once had so meticulously cared for his father. He had watched Hunbøk do the same for his father so many times. Stëinbøk had not just donned his father's crown a few years earlier – he had taken up the mantle.

A heaviness came over him, as though realising, after all this time, that he was King and what that truly meant. 'This is so complicated!'

'It doesn't have to be,' said Vigh, walking to him. 'You could deliver us now and—'

'And what?' Stëinbøk cut in. 'Let you be captured and beaten?! No, no more risks.'

'Risks *will* have to be taken,' insisted Vigh. 'We need to go in there. You tried everything else – you tried doing it the Morkans' way. Your people need to be saved.' He pointed at the tunnels. 'No, we need to go inside, and we need to go now.'

'Then *we'll* take the risk and go,' declared Lenarbøk. 'Dinankch, Batel, and I. Let *us* be the bait, Your Majesty. We'll go back inside the tunnels and let the Morkans know of our presence, then we'll run out with them after us. There are too many traps for us all to go; it would give them the upper hand if we all went inside. We need to drive them out, just not with noise.'

Stëinbøk pressed his lips together, reluctant to relent. 'If you get caught . . .'

'We won't,' asserted Batel. Thus, the decision was made.

That night, the company burned the four Morkan carcasses. In the morning, they readied themselves for yet more fighting. The three volunteers tossed the rock aside and slipped inside the tunnel. They crept along, listening. It was the same old story with the Morkans, repeatedly saying that Stëinbøk had gone mad.

'These Tellens, they don't know how to reason,' Gohtek complained to Sikhlah.

'Let me out!' cried a voice. The polc banged on the door.

'That's minus four points now,' said Gohtek. 'You better be careful, Firlanian. Soon you'll have no more points to credit you for lunch.'

Batel clenched his teeth. 'These Morkans and their points,' he whispered harshly. 'Is that how it is in a Morkan school?'

When the corridor was empty, the three stealthers walked to the scrap pile and took many long pieces of metal. Each moving to a door, they broke the locks, and on the other side of one of those doors were Elmezni and Krystal.

'The halls are empty?' asked Krystal, eyes wide. Dinankch nodded. 'Another meeting. As I can see, you found the pendant.'

'And it's not the first time we've snuck in here,' admitted Dinankch. 'We're going to drive the Morkans out, as many as possible. Here, take these. There's a scrap pile down the hall. Open as many doors as you can, try to find your weapons, and then run straight up – it'll bring you to the exit. We're going to get the Morkans' attention. We were going to do this ourselves,' he explained, a small smirk creeping up the side of his mouth, 'but since the halls are empty, we figured we might as well take advantage of the opportunity to free you and create more havoc for the Morkans.'

'Thanks,' said Elmezni. 'You sure picked the right time to come.'

Right away, the freed prisoners set to work. The other three went to the pass that led to the meeting area.

'You could use an extra polc!' The three turned their heads. There stood a Tellen, around one hundred years of age, with her bow and a hand on her hip. 'We found our weapons.'

'Hessildu!' exclaimed Lenarbøk, embracing her. 'Little cousin! I'm so glad to see you're okay.'

'Well, cousin, I am able to take good care of meself. Since I'm not *little* anymore.'

'You're still and always will be me baby cousin,' Lenarbøk said with a smile. 'I always took care of you like you were me own sister.'

'And I've always been grateful for it.'

'Morkans!' shouted Dinankch.

The Tellens shot from their bows, injuring several Morkans, killing a few, and disrupting the rest.

'What's going on?!' shouted a Morkan.

'You want us?' shouted Batel. 'You'll have to come after us!'

Many Morkans started pouring out of the room, too many to shoot at now. Larnarbøk, Batel, Dinankch, and Hessildu turned to run the other way.

'Wait!' Gohtek told some of his best. 'It could be a trap. We won't fall into it.'

The other Morkans pursued the Tellens, who dashed out of the tunnels. Not one prisoner was left. If a Morkan tried to stop them, he was killed.

Only the last few remained chasing now, and they were behind the four acting as bait. Hessildu paused, turning, and shot a few arrows as the others ran on, then sprinted ahead to catch up.

The two Tellens and two Firlanians ran out and plopped onto the grass, out of breath, where stood everyone else with weapons at the ready. The escaped Tellens rested a ways further while the Morkans who ran out after them were shot down and dragged away.

Everyone sighed in relief.

'Let us wait for Captain Gohtek,' Stëinbøk advised. 'He's bound to come out sooner or later. He cannot dig his way to Mork, and his food rations won't last forever. Unless he's so barbarian, he'll eat the corpses of his people.'

'It will be more difficult to catch the rest,' said Derfbøk.

'We're goin' to have to get close to them,' said Hunbøk, 'real close.'

'This is unbelievable!' yelled Gohtek. 'All the prisoners are gone! The others are dead! They out-number us. We have a better chance of escaping if we get out than if we dig our way to another exit. They can pursue us at any moment. I am no coward – I would rather face them. Stay ready with your weapons!'

Reluctantly, the Morkans followed their Captain out. Three days had gone by since everyone had fled. Some Morkans had started to dig toward the other side of the lake, but that would take them deeper into the forest, and to Gohtek, doing so was a greater risk than anything else.

The remaining Morkans exited their hideout and were immediately surrounded. Weapons were drawn but not trained on the Morkans yet.

'I knew you'd come out sooner or later,' said Stëinbøk.

'You caused this!' Gohtek accused. 'The death of my army!'

'I'm afraid you're causing your own downfall, Gohtek,' declared Boreth, who then recognised Sikhlah standing beside his Captain. The younger Morkan glowered at the Telorians as they glared back with equal disdain. 'Remember what Stëinbøk said? That you'd get killed if you returned?' The four Telorians walked closer to him. They had no visible weapons on them and were barefoot.

'You *are* mad!' breathed Gohtek. 'You've got no weapons, and still you dare to approach me.'

'You can walk away alive, Captain,' Jimmy warned, 'if you do as you're told.'

Gohtek backhanded Jimmy across the face with his hand full of jewels. Jimmy bounced back, grunting in disdain. The Morkans pounced at the Telorians and grabbed hold of each of them. The Tellens did nothing.

'And I took orders from you,' seethed Gohtek. He got in Jimmy's face. 'I've been waiting to beat you since the day Kàtchah told me who you are. You are so lucky you're valuable to Mirauk, or I would disembowel you here and now.'

There was a long pause after that.

'It's easy, eh?' said Meysah, 'I guess the Tellens don't want to waste time fighting you.'

'They've brought enough trouble to this forest,' said Derfbøk.

'I said I'd deliver the Telorians if you returned me people to me,' said Stëinbøk.

Nastafin fidgeted, uneasy.

'Steady yourself,' Attëgon whispered to her.

'Leave this forest,' Stëinbøk commanded. 'Bring your luggage to Mirauk!'

The Morkans approached the Telorians with rope to bind them. Before they could, the Telorians pulled out knives hidden in their sleeves and stabbed the Morkans dead.

The remaining Morkans came at the Telorians but were kicked away. Immediately, the Tellens aimed and shot all the Morkans down. Only Gohtek and Sikhlah remained – and not by coincidence.

'Clever and quick!' disdained Sikhlah. 'But where's your most powerful Wizard of all, huh? Most powerful? I think not! You want to know where she is?' He taunted at Meysah. 'Dead!'

He laughed as Meysah swallowed, his breathing beginning to quaver. 'He-heh. That's right. The last *sarikh-pekamav* is to thank for that.' Sikhlah stared deep into Meysah's eyes as he smirked, tilting his head low, and spoke in a deep hoarse whisper with all the disdain and loathing pride he possessed, 'The phantom got her!'

Vigh and Boreth looked at each other, remembering the strangely familiar scarved polc.

'That's not true!' shouted Meysah, shaking with anger.

He pounced at Sikhlah and killed him in one blow, digging his knife into his throat.

Gohtek sprang forward, ready to strike. Jimmy was in the way. Gohtek met his gaze, sneering, and lifted his gleaming sword.

'Go ahead!' Jimmy taunted angrily. 'I'll come right back to life! Lift it higher!'

And he did.

A single arrow landed straight at Gohtek's chest. He dropped his sword before Jimmy; it fell at his feet.

'I knew it would come to this, but I did it for my superiors in Mork.' He coughed. 'Kàtchah will avenge himself!' Gohtek fell to his knees and onto his side, looking up at Jimmy.

'So will Niome,' declared Jimmy. 'Kàtchah isn't here because he knew it would come to this – he sent you to your death. He will see his own soon enough. I'll see to it myself if I have to.'

'Kàtchah will never die, but become a star when he is ready and help Mirauk! Like the others of the Inner Circle!'

Gohtek died there. But the Telorians wanted to hear more.

'So now we have to ensure *more* evil polcs get slain!' sighed Meysah. He lifted his arms up in defeat, discouragement and frustration seeping into his voice. 'Who else is so powerful that they must be killed in order to keep peace in the world once Mirauk is destroyed? Who is in his Inner Circle?!'

'The responsibility is not as fun as it once seemed,' admitted Jimmy, 'at the beginning.' His sober and mature voice took away any hint of a joke.

For the first time, he was not trying to make a joke to his friend. The two knights who had been but lads at the start of this whole journey, who now were maturing into men, suddenly saw each other as much older as the gravity of their destinies settled onto them more heavily.

The four looked at the dead Morkans and back at each other. Nastafin walked over to Vigh.

'Are you okay?'

'I'll be fine.' He put his hand on her arm. He held in his tears. 'I could use your logical reasoning, though. Regarding what was said about Niome.'

Meysah looked at Jimmy. 'Do you think she's dead?'

'I don't know. It's hard to believe. Then again, she won't receive our messages.' Jimmy pressed his lips together in a straight line. 'And . . . I somehow can't bring myself to make a joke for us to stop worrying.'

'She's not dead,' declared Boreth, giving in. 'She's alive and well. We saw a polc who looked like her when we went to investigate near Zaccher.'

'Why didn't you say so before!' Meysah shouted tearfully as he turned to the master, upset. 'Boreth, why?!' He pushed the Lord aggressively with one hand.

'Because the person we saw was not *our* Niome!' shouted Vigh.

'Then it *is* true,' Jimmy said, his voice thick with grief. 'She got struck by the phantom.'

'Then she *is* dead,' wept Meysah. 'For she must've forgotten all about us.'

'She could be slowly recovering!' said Nastafin, hope in her voice. 'If she had lost all of her memory or died, Mirauk would've come instead of trying all these methods to make you lose hope. Keep faith. Stay strong. Niome said she'd give you your cue. Wait for it.'

'Well, I've done all the waiting I can handle,' Vigh snapped in a low tone. 'My patience has run out!'

Nastafin shook her head. 'So has mine.'

'I'm sorry,' said Vigh, uncharacteristically apologetic, his tone genuine.

'I'll ensure our freed friends have everything they need.' Nastafin left the scene.

'Come,' said Stëinbøk to his people. 'Let's clean this mess and go home. It's time we returned.' He looked at Gohtek's dead body with dismay.

'By following Kàtchah's rules,' began Boreth, 'well, it brought him to his doom.'

The Tellens gathered the Morkan corpses and burned them.

'Next time,' said Hunbøk, 'the Morkans will make sure many of us die.'

'Then so be it,' declared Stëinbøk. 'But they won't succeed.'

'They won't come back after this,' Derbøk surmised. 'They'll wait and figure out a plan, a new one that most likely will not work any better than this one. But they'll wait. It's the only logical move.'

'Good,' said Stëinbøk, 'because I, too, am at me wit's end.'

'Elmezni!' shouted Falmozni. Elmezni glanced up at his friend as he took off what he had around his neck. 'Here!'

'Oh, my pendant. Thank you!' Elmezni put it around his neck.

'I kept it safe,' said Falmozni. 'I know it's very special to you.'

The two walked off to help the others.

'Vigh.' Kchalami approached the Lord. 'Mirauk *wants* you to be grieving.'

'I know . . . I know it too well. But he won't get our power!'

'No, he won't. Because whatever has happened to Niome, the Star remains strong. We've seen proof of that today. And your friends are ever here for you – always.' He paused, bowing his head. 'I must believe – *we* must believe that Niome is safe.'

Exchanging a smile of sympathy with Vigh, Kchalami left to continue helping everyone get ready to travel back to the fortress.

Before they left, Vigh approached Nastafin.

'I want to apologise for the way I've been acting. I know I'm not the easiest polc to endure.'

'Definitely not!'

'I'm sorry if your patience has been worn thin, Nastafin. It's difficult, with everything that's going on, to . . . to put my past behind me.'

'What do you mean?'

'I–I don't want you to be angry at me . . .'

'I'm not.'

'I don't want to be angry at you, either.'

'I'm not angry,' Nastafin assured. Vigh smiled. 'I know it mustn't be easy with Niome gone. But you have had proof that she's doing fine. Trust that she'll contact you once the time is right.'

'She will recover, whatever happens,' said Vigh, truly believing it. 'I know that now, thanks to you.'

'Try not to be so stubborn sometimes?' Nastafin suggested. Vigh nodded in response and she put her hand on his shoulder, smiling in return.

'Then we are on good terms, yes?' asked Vigh. Nastafin nodded. Vigh hugged her, briefly, then turned to leave.

'Vigh.' He looked back at Nastafin. 'What guarantee do I have that you won't snap at me again? I am merely asking.'

'Well, that's the beauty of it all – I can't give you one. My mood jumps when it does. Though I don't think it'll jump as often anymore.'

Nastafin let out a small laugh and returned towards the others. Boreth, who stood nearby, walked by Nastafin.

'He's warming up,' said Boreth. 'His shell is slowly peeling off. Give him time.'

'I'm encouraged,' she replied. 'He surprised me with his apology. I thought we'd never get along.'

'Oh, Nastafin, he's not just getting along,' said Boreth. 'But he sure is slow about it.'

Nastafin smiled, comforted, then laughed a little at the situation.

Boreth went to tease Vigh. He had to; it was the duty of a good friend. 'You sure are slow about everything.'

'And you're fast. I mean, you and Clahria, what, fell in love instantly?'

'Perhaps, but I didn't have a past that kept haunting me, Vigh. I'm only saying it because I'm proud and happy you're moving on. I know it's difficult.'

'Yes, but I'm not in love, and I'm not—'

'Fine. Be like Meysah.'

'Boreth!'

'What?!'

'Don't give me that look.'

'Look, Meysah, our masters are goofier than we! You take after him . . . the Ihal thing.'

Meysah laughed. Then he sighed.

'It's true, we argue a lot. I miss her, but all in all, I'm dealing with it pretty well, I think. I only wish Niome were here.'

'It's not meant to be,' said Nastafin as she passed by.

'I worry, though,' said Jimmy, 'if a phantom got her, if that's true, then Em knows about all the secrets and . . . the Old Grey House . . .'

'Jimmy,' Nastafin began in a soothing voice, 'if he did, he would've done many awful things and destroyed a lot. Yet, the world still is. Why would he be wasting his time trying to ruin your hope? I don't know Niome, so I can reason logically without emotions getting in the way. Trust me – Niome is powerful. There's more to her than even you give her credit for. Let her fulfil her current destiny. There's a lot Mirauk will never know. She has too much in her for one phantom to be able to extract – or if it had, there's too much of it to fit inside its mind.'

'I guess you're right,' admitted Jimmy.

The host of polcs circled the lake and travelled until they reached the fortress, on the fifth of the twelfth week of Spring.

Chapter Seventeen:
A Hidden Threat

fair year was 4774 for many in Teloria, as was 4775. For some, however, the past years had been the most cruel of all. Bahvley was worried and growing annoyed with time and himself. The Kikies were beginning to fear, even if they knew what had happened. For Tharguen, the time that passed was heartbreaking. He had had enough!

'Bahvley!' yelled Tharguen as he barged into the Royal Halls. He gave no hello to Dex, though the doorguard took no offence. Into the office Tharguen strode and shut the door. 'This is as far as my patience goes! I cannot take it anymore!'

Bahvley was sitting at his desk. Maps and papers and books were strewn across its surface and on the floor – calculations, drawings, personal notes. The room looked more scattered than usual. Bahvley said nothing but put aside his things. He looked tired.

'It's already the end of the second week of Colouring, of 4775, Bahvley. What are we to do?'

'Well,' Bahvley calmly replied, 'Niome or no Niome, I have to do this. I have a kingdom to protect. We are going to plan our attacks with or without the Five.'

'Plan attacks?!' Tharguen exclaimed in disbelief.

Bahvley stood. 'We need to prepare for when Mork attacks us. We know Mirauk is powerful, but what if we were to eliminate some of his troops? I mean, how powerful can Mirauk truly be when he stands alone? Think about it.'

'So that's what you've been up to – acting like a Wizard gone mad, obsessive, a hermit in your office. Come on. Everyone knows that ten thousand soldiers wouldn't destroy Mirauk if they gave one giant blow together. You know that. Admit you feel as crazy as I do right now.'

'He'll be less powerful than if he has all those armies to back him up,' insisted Bahvley. 'We can have the Dalvarans attack from the Northeast, the Dûnelorians from the South.' Bahvley showed Tharguen his plan on a map, placing peons in specific locations. 'Hopefully, by then the Kikies will have returned from the Ocean by boat. We can come in through here' – Bahvley's finger traced the map, following the Ortim River to the Malgar River – 'and the Firlanians can enter from the Dakodol River, and the Tellens can come and guard these areas over here.'

Tharguen blinked at him with even more disbelief.

'Kurssus, Bahvley! Since when did we become like this – like Mirauk, needing armies and armies to gain power to restore the no-power way of things? It's ironic, really. Since when did we become children of violence and revenge? Since when did we become traitors to what we believe in and murderers of life? These wars destroy nature as well. The Kikies have made me understand that better than ever. You should know this, too – you lived among them for fifty polken years! I can swear I hear the stars, the Moon, and even the Mighty Spirit cry at times.'

A fantastical image intruded in Tharguen's mind of Bahvley laughing and turning into an evil being. The sight was monstrous and frightening – it was fear, *his* fear.

'Don't turn into some evil creature!' he commanded the thought away. 'I'm scared.' This, Tharguen said under his breath, mostly to himself, his subconscious.

'You know what, Tharguen, you're right. The problem is, this is the only way I can deal with the pain of the fact that they might not come back – that they might be dead.' Bahvley began to weep. 'I've suppressed it all this time. Tharguen, all the hope I had in me has gone. I don't know what to do anymore. I don't even want to be King anymore.'

'Bahvley, that's not you talking!'

'It's over.'

'No, it's not,' said Tharguen comfortingly. 'Snap out of it. This is exactly what Mirauk wants – for us to lose hope and give up because he thinks it's the only way he can regain what he lost, but there is no way he can ever get what he wants from us.' Tharguen implored, 'We cannot let him.'

'What if something terrible has befallen them? Now I know how they must've felt when they thought me dead . . . it's terrible. I caused them such pain, and now I'm being punished.'

'You are not,' asserted Tharguen, hands on Bahvley's arms. 'Everything will turn out as it should be, as it was written in the Prophecy Books. Remember, we're in the Dragon Prophecies. Just get a hold of yourself.'

'Are you not fazed by this at all? I don't know. You're Niome's husband-to-be and . . . now . . .'

'Bahvley, I came in angry. I'm as worried as you, yet . . .' He sighed seeing his friend in a state he had been in just a moment before. 'Maybe the ring I wear has a special connection with the ring Niome wears – I fumble at it all the time. Somehow, despite my fear, I know it deep in my heart that they, the Five, are fine. There's a reason they haven't returned yet. Though, we need to keep giving orders "on behalf of" them.'

Tharguen's expression softened. 'You're my best friend in the world and soon-to-be brother, and *nothing* is going to change that. They *will* return. I have to believe that.' Bahvley nodded to him. 'The only thing that frustrates me is *our* attitudes, the war preparations.'

'You know what? Forget the preparations. When the Five come back, that's when it'll be time to start preparing. Until then, I'll just do my duty as King as best I can.'

'And I'll stand by you, and we'll get through this together.' Tharguen placed a hand at the back of Bahvley's neck in show of support and comfort. 'You're my brother in magic, Bahvley. Nothing will ever change that. I'll always stand by your side.'

Bahvley's lip quavered as he stared at him for a moment, mustering the courage to face his past wrong-doings and the emotions it would lead him to feel.

'I'm sorry I told you to fall in line.'

Tharguen's eyes were instantly filled with sorrow. He knew what Bahvley was referring to – their quarrel of so many years ago, in Mork.

Bahvley's eyes filled with tears. 'I was so scared you'd die,' he whispered.

'I was scared *you'd* die.'

'Tharguen, I thought he'd killed you! I thought Mirauk had killed you. Whoever leapt at him wielded your sword . . .' His voice cracked, and tears pricked his eyes.

'Oh, Bahvley.' Tharguen's vision blurred with tears of his own.

Bahvley whispered again. 'I'm sorry I said I didn't need your death on my hands.'

'I'm sorry I told you I didn't need you as my King.'

'I do need you,' they both said. A meagre smile tugged at Tharguen's mouth. The ache in Tharguen's heart at the memory eased.

His voice wet with chagrin, Bahvley whispered, 'We lost everyone.'

'I know,' replied Tharguen, voice cracking, 'but at least we didn't lose each other.'

Bahvley pulled Tharguen into a tight embrace, and they held each other for a long moment.

Those details from their past quarrel that they had never voiced had always tugged at them. But now all had been said, all had been reconciled – truly reconciled – at the moment when they both needed it most.

At last, they pulled away. Tharguen wiped his eyes, letting out a self-conscious laugh. Though tears still flowed from his eyes, Bahvley smiled at him – a genuine smile for the first time in seasons.

'I just don't know what to say at the Grand Meeting next week,' he said at last. 'What am I supposed to tell my people?'

'Speak from the heart, Bahvley.'

The grand meeting took place on the second day of the fourth week of Colouring at the Royal Halls, where any voice travelled far. The Halls were magical in that way. Many from the far sides of the kingdom attended as well as Tharguen's team, including the Kikies.

As part of his preparations, Bahvley had prayed to Gorthan for inspiration, knowing his spirit had helped him before. Yet if no inspiration came, he was at least comforted knowing Tharguen was by his side, as were Selemil, Henker, and Nsarmön.

Tharguen leaned towards Bahvley and whispered, 'Remember what we discussed.'

Bahvley stood, and the crowd quieted. He appreciated that kind of respect. The King welcomed his people.

'I'm still not used to these sorts of reunions,' he admitted. 'Selemil always had the best introductions, so pardon me if there is a lack of extravagance.' The people laughed. An honest King was always appreciated.

He sighed. *Honest.* He wished he could be honest about that one crucial detail as well.

Bahvley spoke of the Morkans, dissuading the people from feeling discouraged, despite his own dismay. He spoke of what Niome might be planning for her return with no hint of despair in his voice.

'I am certain they're quite busy, the Five, as are we. You know how they can get carried away,' he said as he smiled fondly, 'especially Meysah and Jimmy with their antics.'

'You and Tharguen, too!' shouted one of the Telorians from Tharguen's small team. Bahvley chuckled.

He then heartened his people with talk of the strength of the Telorian armies. In the midst of their unpredictable journey, Bahvley had often forgotten how esteemed their people were, Nsarmön chief among them. He was greatly skilled, Gorthan's perfect match. Bahvley did not give him the credit he deserved, but today he would change that.

'Ever since Gorthan left us, some of us may have lingered in our grief. In his sacrifice, he saved more than just five lives. Nsarmön has taken up the mantle well. In fact, he is perhaps Gorthan's only equal. They were like brothers in spirit and still are. Two of a kind. Thank you, Nsarmön.'

The Chief of Knights smiled.

'We also have our unique team of Telorians and Kikis – Tharguen's army.'

The army cheered.

'Yeah, that's us!' shouted Lóim.

'Do the mighty Captains wish to say a word or two?' Bahvley invited.

Tharguen stood. 'I can assure you, my team is one of the finest. Much more skilled than those Morkan armies.'

'And my Captain can decode the Morkan language!' boasted Mittah.

'Ah, but the real master's Nsarmön, I think,' said Tharguen.

'I believe Bahvley's the true hearty knight,' declared Nsarmön. 'That is why we chose him as our King.'

'But you see,' Tharguen rebutted, 'Nsarmön stays quiet in his chair now, but when those Morkans come along, they won't get past him alive.' The two smiled at each other. Nsarmön acknowledged the appreciation.

'I have a question!' someone in the back called out, an old lady with a high-pitched nasal voice. She had a peculiar air about her, or so Bahvley felt. He bid her to ask her query. 'What about attacks? Do you plan on ambushing Mork before Mirauk attacks you? Wouldn't that be the better thing to do for Teloria?'

'Perhaps unwise for now,' Bahvley replied with tact.

'But what are your plans for later? I think as citizens of Teloria, we have the right to know.'

'I cannot reveal any details of that sort for the present,' said Bahvley.

He glanced towards the Kikies. They caught his thoughts, shrank, and flew to the back. In the blink of an eye, the old lady was gone.

'Let us continue,' he said distractedly, 'with the knowledge that Selemil has certain magical powers that can protect us until the Five return.' Bahvley proceeded to list all their allies who were willing to help in the war against Mirauk. 'We are greatly blessed.'

'Do you know when the Five will return?' someone in the audience asked.

'Unfortunately, they never specified,' answered Bahvley. 'So, no, I do not.' And that was the truth.

'Do you know if they're safe?' asked someone else.

'They are in the hands of the Tellens,' said Bahvley, swallowing hard. 'If they weren't safe, we would've felt it.'

Yet indeed he had.

When all his people had gone, Bahvley took Tharguen, Selemil, Henker, Nsarmön, and the Kikies to his office to discuss more crucial matters, for he was unsettled.

'Where has that old woman gone? I know evil when I see it! I could almost sense it like it was right next to me, and it wasn't a trick of the eye.' Bahvley was breathing heavily.

'It is indeed an odd sort of sorcery,' agreed Henker, 'if the lady had disappeared by the time the Kikies reached her.'

'Ran away, more like,' said Tharguen.

'She'll report to Mirauk – it's inevitable. That might explain how he knew of certain things.' Bahvley rubbed his chin anxiously, certain of this theory.

'Bahvley,' began Selemil, 'is it possible you're being a bit paranoid?'

'Did you not hear her? The question she asked, so early in the meeting? Usually no one dares to ask such a question until the subject is opened by the speakers.' He took a breath. 'It's the way she said it. Besides, she said *"you"* . . . *"before Mirauk attacks you"!* I think that's clue enough.'

'*You* instead of *us*,' Henker whispered to himself.

'A trespasser? An imposter!' mused Tharguen. 'But you checked the entire kingdom. You had a feeling before she made her presence known to us. And you investigated everywhere!'

'Obviously not well enough,' Bahvley bit back. 'Obviously I missed something. I had a hunch then, yes, and now I have a feeling. I want to know who this person is, how she got here, why, where she's staying, what her disguise or craft is. There aren't two old ladies with that distinct voice, lean yet wealthily supplied with still dark hair, as far as grey hair goes, and spectacles on the tip of her round nose. There's only one way we can find her, and there are only ten folks who can do it.'

'I can put my team on the lookout,' said Nsarmön, 'for any suspicious polcs. They're a good judge of character.'

'That works. Thank you.'

'You' – Celor pointed at Bahvley – 'must stay here for there to be no suspicions on her behalf. We'll fly fast, we'll fly everywhere. We will find this lady one way or another!'

Bahvley nodded, imploring his friend to be cautious.

'We will be,' Celor reassured upon reading his thoughts.

'Dismissed,' Bahvley said with a meagre smile.

CHAPTER EIGHTEEN:
Adherence and Fealty

The Telorians of Tharguen's team gathered to reflect on what had been discussed at the meeting. As Eerzin's home was the most spacious, that was where they convened.

'There was something odd in King Bahvley's attitude,' observed Mittah. 'Did any of you notice? It was almost as though he noticed something in the crowd.'

'Everything's gone wrong!' sighed Huck.

'If you ask me, I don't think they'll be coming home anytime soon,' declared Lóim.

'Who?' demanded Ihal. 'The Five?'

'That's rather pessimistic of you,' Tom said dryly.

'It's realistic,' replied Lóim. 'Let's face it, they're gone. They could be gone for years more. They could be in Mork right now, as far as we know. We can't let our lives be ruled by that. Yes, I – we need hope that they'll come back, but we can't wait for them. They may be in peril or they may be conquering. Let's let them do what they must while we do what _we_ must.

My point is, we need to take action before it's too late. It's useless to wait.'

Lóim knew he was right. They couldn't depend on the Five. They had to be independent.

'So, what? That's it?!' snapped Ihal. 'We give up on them, go attack, conquer or fail, and be awarded? That's just great! You always wanted something to be awarded for, something to be able to boast about. Go fight this war yourself.'

'Ihal,' Gahli said gently, 'I don't think he meant it that way.'

'You know what?' said Lóim. 'I will, and first, I'll go find them.' He stood and made for the door.

'What are you doing?' sighed Jackley.

'I'm going to the Twisted Forest.'

'You can't go alone!' protested Pete.

'Anyone who wishes to join me may do so,' said Lóim.

'This is ridiculous,' said Eerzin, moving to block Lóim's way. 'You don't have to prove anything to us.'

Lóim looked at him, then at Ihal. 'It appears I do.' He walked around Eerzin to the door before the older polc could stop him.

'Then I'll go with you, if no one else will,' said Malcolm. 'I won't let any harm come to you, my friend.'

'Thanks.' Lóim and Malcolm left.

'We can't let them go alone,' insisted Gahli. 'Teams stick together!'

'Gahli, you can't go!' protested Ihal.

'Why not?! Don't you want to find out as much as anyone else?'

'Come, then,' said Jackley, 'let's go help them, before they regret it or encounter the enemy. I don't want any harm to come to them.'

More from the group left to join Lóim and Malcolm, comprised of Gahli, Jackley, Huck, and Calireth.

'You can't ask me to choose between you and Lóim, Ihal,' said Mittah, 'but you sure can ask me to stay with you and not break our team up more than it already is. We can try to stop them, though I'm not sure how.'

'Where are the Five?' muttered Tom. 'Niome's like a sister to me. I wish she were – I want to learn more magic from her. If I only knew of a spell to keep the others from going, but such a thing probably doesn't exist. They're free to choose what they want to do, right? I think it's a mistake, though. We all want to know what's happened to the Five, but . . .'

'There's only one thing we *can* do,' declared Eerzin. 'Go inform the Captain. He can command them to stay.'

'That's right,' agreed Mittah.

'All right,' said Eerzin as the rest of them stepped out. 'We're a team, and we're sticking together. Come, let's go.'

The others were already out of sight.

There were a lot of people out in the streets and alleys, polcs from all the four corners of the kingdom returning home or heading to inns. When Tharguen's small army reached the Royal Halls, it was evening. Dex admitted them into the Royal Halls.

'What's happened?' he asked.

'Some are acting on an impulse that they don't understand!' cried Jeremy.

'We need to see Captain Tharguen right away,' explained Ihal.

'He's with Bahvley in the lounging area. Follow me.'

Dex hurried and the team followed. When they entered the room, they heard Bahvley shout, 'I know that lady was evil!'

'An emergency!' Dex interjected.

'Evil lady!' exclaimed Tom. 'That's why you were acting so strange.'

'Who cares about the evil lady?' shrilled Ihal. 'She's not more important than the rest of our team.'

'What do you mean?' asked Bahvley.

'Lóim and the others left to go back to the Twisted Forest to find the Five!' blurted Mittah.

'What?!' exclaimed Tharguen, rising from his seat.

'We were discussing things,' began Pete, 'and then Lóim and Ihal started arguing. It wasn't her fault, nor his. He just said he'd fight the war himself and go find the Five.'

'It *is* my fault,' admitted Ihal. 'I'm the one who said he should fight it himself.'

'You have to go find them!' Mittah and Jeremy implored together.

'Where are they?' asked Tharguen, already securing his belt and ensuring he had most of what he needed.

'Gone!' they all exclaimed.

'When did they leave?' asked Dex.

'This afternoon,' replied Ihal.

'We were stuck trying to get through the crowds and thought you were home,' said Jeremy. 'We're sorry we couldn't reach the Royal Halls earlier.'

Tharguen sighed, bringing a hand to his forehead. 'No, that's understandable, Jeremy. Can you get my horse, Dex? It's in the Royal Halls stable.'

Dex acknowledged and left the room.

Dex knew their secrets – Bahvley trusted him, and he in turn told them his. Bahvley was even thinking of promoting him from Doorward to Commander, for Dex always protected him. Perhaps a better title would be fitting, though the decision had not yet been made for the young polc who had more skill than he showed. Tharguen regarded him highly as well.

'Who has gone?' Tharguen asked solemnly. 'Who is with Lóim?'

Everyone started naming those who left all at once, and Tharguen understood none of it.

'Can one person speak?!' Bahvley shouted to be heard over the discord.

'Lóim left,' started Jeremy, 'and Gahli, Malcolm, Jackley, Calireth, and Huck.'

Tharguen studied those who were present and realised it was everyone except those six.

'Stay with Bahvley,' Tharguen requested.

'You can order them to come back!' insisted Tom.

'That's what I plan on doing,' asserted Tharguen. With that, he left at great speed.

Tharguen rode to the gates and out of the kingdom. He ate while he rode and continued on all night. It was midmorning when he found Lóim and the others. They were in the field, just a little past the northeast corner of the wall of Teloria. They were on foot, to Tharguen's relief.

Tharguen rode past them and turned his horse around to halt before them.

'You sure run fast,' he said, staring down at the polcs.

'C-Captain,' Gahli stammered. 'Uh . . .'

Everyone stopped and faced their Captain, surprise and uncertainty etched on their faces.

Tharguen furrowed his brows as he studied them. 'What do you think you're doing?'

'We're going to the Twisted Forest,' declared Lóim.

'What good is that going to do?' asked Tharguen.

'We're going to find the Five,' said Malcolm.

'We're going to find out what happened to them,' said Calireth.

'What about Morkans?' demanded Tharguen. 'Can *six* of you fight an entire army? Dozens of us could barely fight five phantoms! We are not as powerful as the Five – we can't fight so many alone. How many times do I have to tell you for you to understand that we are mortal beings?' He let his sorrow seep into his tone. 'I don't want you to die! Perhaps we all want to know what happened to the Five, but perhaps we're just not meant to. And six of you decide to depart on such a perilous journey? What about me? What about the others?!'

'Captain,' began Lóim, looking down and kicking the earth gently before meeting Tharguen's gaze once more, 'we're doing this for the benefit of everyone else.'

'You do not have my permission!' Tharguen growled angrily. 'An army obeys their Captain.'

'Sorry,' said Huck. Others echoed the feeble apology.

'Yet, I somehow cannot . . .' Tharguen paused. 'I find myself unable to order you to return.' He sighed, then spoke sadly, 'Do what you will. I . . . if you find Niome, tell her . . . nevermind.'

Tharguen held back his tears as he rode off past them, headed for home. When he returned, he would not tell the others what happened. He did not want to discuss it – not at first. He couldn't understand why he had not been able to give the six knights the order to come home. Bahvley suspected why, but respected Tharguen's need to leave it be.

Two days passed. Tharguen was alone at home, pondering, worrying, and obsessing. There was a knock on his door. When he opened it, he was surprised to see the six who had left.

'What!' said Tharguen as a statement of command to hide his surprise.

'We know you would've liked to go yourself,' began Lóim, 'but that no one could go, that we have to wait until they come back. Upon seeing you and speaking to you, we came to understand that, and we decided to return.'

Tharguen said nothing.

'We understand that it wasn't fair to you,' said Gahli, 'nor to the others. We realised that the Kikies have their rights, too. Bahvley told us about their trip to find the old lady.'

Still, Tharguen was silent.

'We also realised that a team should conjoin and look out for each other, no matter what,' resumed Lóim. 'Tom made me realise that when we got back. We . . . we're not meant to know, we're not meant to be there right now. Our fate lies at home, with you.' Tharguen was at a loss for words. 'We're sorry, Captain. It won't happen again.'

'Well, I sure hope not!'

'We did you wrong,' continued Lóim. 'I started it all. I don't know what I can do to make it up to you. You must be disappointed in me.'

'My punishments are severe,' said Tharguen, again masking his emotions.

'Just don't dismiss me from the team, nor the others, please?' Lóim's eyes were pleading.

'Why would I dismiss you from the team, Lóim?' said Tharguen. 'I don't want to do that. You're a good fighter. I can't lose you – any of you. I'm just glad you came back, that's all. So, forget about my punishments. I can't think of any.'

'No?'

'No.' Tharguen smiled. 'I wasn't angry at you. I was simply . . . confused.'

'We understand,' said Malcolm, relieved.

'Thank you for understanding. Thank you for coming back.'

Tharguen knew they had meant well when they left – he couldn't fault them for that – and he was glad they had respected his wishes once he expressed them.

'You are forgiven, but don't don't test me like that again.'

'Yes, Captain!' they asserted.

They left, and Tharguen went to inform Bahvley of what had transpired.

Colouring lasted long and Winter started warmly. Nsarmön left for Telor with his army, while the others remained in Teloria City. The Kikies returned from their investigations at the turn of Winter to Spring of 4776. They had not found the old lady. The Five still had not yet returned.

Several more weeks passed where impatience grew. Tharguen and Bahvley were arguing in the Royal Halls, as they always did nowadays, when Dex came knocking at the door of the King's study.

'What?' snapped Bahvley.

'There is someone here to see Captain Sumperale,' said Dex. Though his tone remained calm, his face betrayed the hurt he sometimes felt when Bahvley snapped at him.

'Let them in,' replied Bahvley, his voice calmer. 'And . . . thank you for everything. You do not deserve my ire.'

Dex smiled. 'As long as you are aware of it when you let your anger out my way.'

'Have I told you recently how much I appreciate you and all that you do here at the Royal Halls?' asked Bahvley, a sheepish smile on his face.

'You can remind me with a pint of ale, Your Majesty.'

Bahvley chuckled. Dex knew how to diffuse his anger. The Doorward was more than just a ward now; he was a confidant, a friend, perhaps even at times an advisor to both Bahvey and Tharguen.

With his usual pristine posture, Dex left.

In no time, a young polc entered. He had pale brown hair and seemed shy at first.

'I was told I would find you here,' he said, addressing Tharguen.

'How can I help you?' asked Tharguen.

'I, uh, I'd like to join your army.'

'All right. Stand tall,' instructed Tharguen, measuring up the knight, guessing he was about Jimmy's age. 'Let us see if you have the qualifications. I need to know your age and training, and of course, your name.'

Tharguen noticed that the polc had copper shimmers in his hair, giving him a familiar air.

'Eighty-seven in polken years, sir. I trained with Gorthan for a while, but never had my own master. After that, I was a guard on the wall, in Telor, in Lani, and in Dulma, all for very short times. They suggested I go to Bassett, where they need more polcs, but I want to do more than that.'

He spoke now with full confidence and determination. 'I've been a guard and archer since I started in Telor, shortly before the Morkan attacks of 4776. I must apologise for not coming to any general meetings or celebrations. I never came forth before, as grief was still with me. I was afraid to face you and too young still.'

His honesty was bold. That, too, was familiar.

'Do I know you?' asked Tharguen.

'Yes. Somewhat – we never met. Uh . . . well, you might have seen me much, much younger. But . . . well . . .'

'What is it?' asked Bahvley. 'It's okay, there's no need to be shy around us.'

'Yes, I'm maybe too timid today,' the young polc admitted, glancing uneasily at them.

'That's all right,' Tharguen reassured.

'Obviously, you've suffered a trauma that has stayed with you a long time,' said Bahvley, recognising yet more traits.

'Yes, it will always be there,' stated the polc. 'So will yours.'

Tharguen studied him carefully. He wasn't as shy as he looked, but more cautious in how he showed his wisdom and boldness.

'What is your name, lad?' asked Tharguen.

'Uhm . . .' He took a deep breath and stood tall, rolling his shoulders back. 'Ray Pumpernickle.'

'Pumpernickle!' exclaimed Bahvley and Tharguen simultaneously.

'Are you related to Liffwai Pumpernickle?' asked Bahvley, seeking confirmation though he already knew the answer.

'I'm his younger brother.'

Memories flashed through both Bahvley's and Tharguen's minds of their journey to Mork, when Liffwai, alongside Queevsil, had pledged to protect Bahvley with their lives. Bahvley remembered how he and Liffwai had fought off the phantoms, fought for their lives, how Liffwai had stepped in front of Bahvley to save his life against the phantoms on that ship. His pale face when Bahvley awoke and Liffwai lay dead in the bed next to his.

'Liffwai spoke seldom of you, Ray,' said Tharguen, 'but he spoke fondly of you when he did.'

'My brother and I never got along much. No one in our family wanted any of us to be fighters. My parents were strict when it came to our protection. Liffwai rebelled. Before he left, we resolved our differences, so at least he died knowing we were reconciled . . .' Ray bowed his head. 'And Queevsil was as much a brother to me before our quarrels had begun. The two of them were inseparable.'

Those two had indeed had a fiery quarrel during the trip to Mork; Bahvley remembered their devotion to each other well. Queevsil had pledged to Bahvley first, being the perfect polc to be his decoy. He had stood against Mirauk with courage before the evil Lord had struck him down.

'I don't want to be a farmer, or a teacher,' Ray continued, 'but a knight, and avenge myself on those who killed my brother. Because that's the very reason why my parents didn't want us to be warriors. They feared death.'

The fire in Ray's eyes was akin to the fire they had seen in Liffwai's.

'I understand how you feel,' said Bahvley, 'but revenge is not a good attitude to have. You want to follow in your brother's footsteps, but are you not afraid of getting hurt?'

'I'm not afraid of death,' declared Ray. 'Nor of pain. It's a vicious cycle. Morkans killed Liffwai's friend, so he completed his training to be a knight. Morkans killed him, and now it's my turn. I want to do this.'

'Seems to me you're not so timid anymore,' said Tharguen, smiling.

'I've warmed up,' admitted Ray, a small familiar smile tugging at the side of his mouth.

'Why have you never come before?' asked Tharguen.

'I was afraid. Liffwai died, and I was scared to hear the story from you. I wondered if he had died a valiant death like he always said he would. Also, despite our reconciliation, I was worried his complaints of me might have sullied your perception.'

'Ray, Liffwai never spoke ill of you,' said Bahvley. 'He felt bad for always quarrelling with you. He spoke of you more highly than you think. He actually wished you wouldn't follow in his footsteps, for he knew the life it would give you.'

'He didn't think of that when he left,' retorted Ray.

'You're still upset about it, aren't you?' Tharguen deduced. Ray nodded.

'Your brother was one of the bravest,' said Bahvley. 'If it weren't for him, I may not have survived, on many occasions. We were the only ones left, or so we thought.' He stole a glance towards Tharguen. 'Liffwai almost made it to the shores of the Kiki land. Perhaps had I not been bitten and passed out, I may have been able to do more to help him.'

The memory, now that it had returned, still felt fresh and raw – trying to save Liffwai, collapsing beside him on the deck of the ship.

'I myself have grieved. I blamed myself for not being able to stay conscious long enough, but those phantoms got me in the end as well. I could have very well died, too, and not lived to tell the tale or be King, or to tell you how brave your brother was and how much he loved you in his own way. Those phantoms are destroyed now.'

Bahvley took a beat. 'If you have any doubt about joining the war, don't do this for the wrong reasons.'

'I choose to fight,' Ray said with conviction. 'I want to fight alongside those who fought with my brother, Liffwai. I want to fight for the Freedom of Life.'

'I see your will and determination are strong,' said Tharguen, 'just like Liffwai. They complement your shyness.' He smiled, standing tall as well. 'Ray, you can certainly be part of my team.'

'Thank you.'

'You truly do resemble your brother, now that I look at you properly,' said Bahvley

'I miss him, and I feel bad . . . about many things.'

'He knew you didn't mean to argue,' Tharguen reassured.

The three chatted a while longer, reminiscing about those lost.

The next day, Tharguen called a meeting with his team. They met around the hearth in the Royal Halls, the Kikies present as well.

Tharguen and Ray stood as the rest settled into seats.

'Do you think they'll accept me into the group?' Ray asked Tharguen nervously.

'Why wouldn't they? Ray, you are a brave polc. Being part of a team will help you put the past behind you.'

'I know.'

'Who's this?' inquired Tom.

'That's what we're here to talk about,' said Tharguen. 'We have a new team member. He has good training; he trained with Gorthan.'

'Gorthan!' exclaimed Mittah. 'A lot of us did part of our training with him. That's a sign of potential,' she said, laughing. Ihal looked at her. 'What? It's true!' Mittah argued. 'All the best trained with Gorthan, because Gorthan was the best.'

'Why don't you introduce yourself, Ray?' said Tharguen.

'Uh, hi, I'm Ray Pumpernickle. I'm from Telor. I wasn't expecting such a warm welcome.'

'Why not?' asked Lóim.

Ray shrugged his shoulders.

'Sort of reminds me of when I first approached Gorthan, asking him to appoint me a master, and the first time I met Vigh,' said Bahvley. 'Almost too shy to ask. Next thing I know, I'm King.' The others chuckled.

'A down-to-earth King is always good,' replied Tharguen, nudging Bahvley with his elbow.

'So what made you want to join *our* team?' asked Gahli.

'You could've joined anyone else,' said Mittah. 'It makes us feel special.'

'I wanted to fight with Tharguen,' said Ray, 'because I wanted to fight with the two people who fought with my brother, Liffwai.'

'The one the phantoms killed,' said Ihal. 'I'm sorry.'

'Thanks . . . it's okay. He fought in Mork with Tharguen and Bahvley, so they saw him before he died – Bahvley did at least – and Eerzin, who stayed in Teloria because he was injured, also fought with my brother and was his friend, as was Fimrel. I'm with those who knew him best, and those who fight with them: you. So now, I'm part of the team.'

'Well, then,' said Lóim. 'Come on over and sit. We need to introduce ourselves. I'm Lóim. You may have heard of me as an arrogant polc, which I used to be. If we ever met in the past and I mocked you, I apologise. I'm nice now.'

'Ni*cer*,' teased Jeremy.

'Still arrogant, though,' said Tom.

'Not as much!' insisted Lóim. Ray laughed. 'I'm trying to make a good impression here, for once.' He turned to Ray. 'Oh, and don't be surprised if the Kikies read your mind every day.'

'We only do that from time to time,' insisted Celor. 'We don't intrude on a person's privacy. Well, we're *training* to respect a polc's privacy. It's so second-nature for us to automatically read minds, it is a challenge to hold back. But like you, Lóim, we're making efforts.' He winked and Lóim shook his head, though he chuckled along with Celor.

'You make it sound as though we spy on you, the way you say it,' Tithil joked. 'All the time?' he added incredulously, accompanied by Forthil in unison.

Ray joined the group, leaving Bahvley and Tharguen standing on the sidelines.

'He'll get along well with the others,' Bahvley told Tharguen with a small smile, observing how the others were already accepting and integrating him into the team.

'Yes, he will.'

'They're a good team.'

'He's been without a brother for so long. I feel I want to take care of him like he were my own.'

'That's true, you're a single child. Sibling rivalry is the worst, trust me. Though, with Meysah and Niome gone, I miss it. And now, especially without Meysah around, I, too, want to take care of Ray.'

'It's a shame we never knew him when he was young. We could've comforted him.'

'He wasn't ready to face us,' said Bahvley.

'That's true,' said Tharguen. 'I see Liffwai in him. The way Liffwai was when we last saw him. Like I saw you in Meysah.'

'I see it as well,' said Bahvley. 'He's going to be a great asset to this team. Though he still needs guidance, he's strong – physically and emotionally. Magically, he may need some guidance too.'

In no time, Ray became good friends with all the rest of them. Slowly, he began to heal from the woe he had carried for so long.

The Kikies left again in a new attempt to find the strange old lady. They were gone almost a full year this time, informing trusted masters and Wizards of Teloria of an imposter.

Bahvley and Tharguen had many private meetings between them. Their concerns for the Five grew more with each passing day. Still, they had not returned.

It was that morning of the twelfth week of Summer of 4777 when Bahvley and Tharguen took the day to discuss in secret the best path forward now for the kingdom. Together, they came to one definite decision.

They were no longer going to wait for the return of the Five.

CHAPTER NINETEEN:
Home

Since her last trip, Niome had been in a complete state of tranquility. The flashes had long since stopped, her dreams of distant memories had also stopped, and with them, somehow, so had all her worries. Niome had let go and simply surrendered to magic. The others of the Zaccher Grey House, on the other hand, grew concerned.

Tobias had spied Morkans in the distance, thus putting any travel or exploratory plans on hold for the better part of the year. Unbeknownst to anyone, this group of Morkans had snuck in and out of the Twisted Forest to learn what had become of Captain Gohtek and had returned to Mork unheeded.

On the fourth day of the ninth week of Spring, the fifty-ninth of the season, the house was calm. Olúryn had gone investigating for Morkans, and Gabriella and Maria had left for the Zaccher Lake Great Rock for medicine and supplies.

Only Tobias and Niome were home. Tobias sat in the living room, reading again the letter Drúgan had written them. He studied the letter and all it contained, wanting to solve the mysteries that muddled his mind.

Niome slept late, awaking near noon. She woke slowly. She could somehow sense that this was no ordinary day.

She stood from the bed and strode to the window with careful steps, feeling dazed as if straying in a dream. As she got dressed, a heavy weight formed in her stomach. She ran down the stairs.

'Good morning, Navë,' said Tobias.

'Navë,' whispered Niome to herself. She stepped outside, taking in lungfuls of air to calm her quickening nerves.

'Navë!' Tobias hurried to join her at the door. 'Is something wrong?'

Niome turned to him, marching back into the house. 'Greatly wrong.'

'Tell me,' Tobias urged, 'what's greatly wrong?'

'It's too complicated to explain, too complicated to understand,' Niome blurted, looking about, trying to gather and process her thoughts. She paused. 'What are you reading?'

'Drúgan's letter.'

'Drúgan's letter,' she whispered, trying to still her racing mind as she became overwhelmed. She began to pace. 'Someone must've stopped by to mention the meeting place.'

'What meeting place? Navë, what's troubling you? Does this have to do with Mirauk?'

'With Mirauk and everyone else!' Niome slumped down and began to weep.

'Navë,' Tobias said gently, 'whatever is the matter? You've been so calm lately – what has gotten you so distressed? I can't help you if you don't tell me—'

'No one can help now! It's too late. It feels as if it's the end of the world. Before, I didn't know what I know now.' Niome collected herself as Tobias put a hand on her back, sitting beside her.

Niome calmed and wiped her eyes. 'I can't tell you how bad things are for sure, but I can tell you that now, my secrets are no longer my own. How powerful has Mirauk grown? I don't know. But my responsibilities are greater now than they've ever been, for he knows. Do you understand what I'm trying to say?'

'I think so.'

'How can the only ones do their duty if they are separated from each other, from reality and from truth, from . . . themselves? I thought it was fun at first, the mission, and suddenly the weight of the world is greater than it was before we had to leave the others and . . . Tharguen.' She looked at her ring and brought it to her bosom.

'Who's "we"? Is it the other four? . . . Niome?'

Niome nodded to Tobias. 'It was one of Mirauk's phantoms that he let loose to hunt us. That is what got me.'

Relieved, Tobias hugged Niome, exhaling.

'Things will be all right now. Obviously Mirauk doesn't know *everything*, for this hidden house still stands. The others will be back soon.'

'*I* want to tell them about this,' said Niome, pulling away. 'This happened because I finally let go and discovered *myself*, through meditation, instead of trying to remember everything about my life and the people around me. I guess it's better late than never.'

'At least you were not destroyed, so there is much hope yet of defeating Mirauk.' Tobias smiled fondly. 'I'd like to hear your story, Niome.'

'First, I'd like to send a magical message to the other four to come meet me here.'

'You may. I'd love to meet them.'

Niome closed her eyes and took a deep breath. She recited the words clearly. As she spoke, her face and her body changed as she rebecame herself again – completely and powerfully. Tobias leaned away to regard Niome with this new perspective and saw, for the first time in his life, the serenity and power of magic come together as Niome sent out her thoughts and knew the others were receiving them.

Eimai stoïhughat,
Dan aimai siginelef,
Idenas mehetot Meysah, Boreth, Jimmy, dan Vigh.

What would have frightened Morkans bewildered Tobias. Niome opened her eyes. Now she truly was herself again, as though nothing had ever taken her memories or her life away.

'I'll tell you about that, too – the incantation.'

'I'll get us some lunch!'

Tobias got them sandwiches and some juice. He and Niome sat down in the living room. Although her worry was eating her up inside, Niome smiled and pleasantly started her story.

'It all began when Elina passed away. She whispered something to me . . .'

Over the afternoon and into the evening, Niome told all. Tobias listened intently to her adventures, including the secrets she had kept prior to her unfortunate encounter with the phantom. Every last detail, or almost every one, Tobias knew.

'It ripped the page right out. My sword was of no use! I pushed and kicked it, but it bit my leg and I struggled so much. It knocked me unconscious, I think. Obviously, it sucked on my blood, and my memories were taken along with it. I just don't understand why it was alone. I'm worried Mirauk knows every one of my secrets, including the few things I omitted while telling *you*.'

'You have so much magical information within you, I doubt a phantom had capacity enough to extract it all.'

'I don't know – I have to go back out there. I have to see if Teloria's okay, if everyone at home is okay, if Tharguen's okay. He had these nightmares, you know – I think he dreamt of what would happen to me if a phantom were to get me, for he woke me up one night, the night he gave me this ring, and asked me to promise him I'd never forget him.' Niome furrowed her brows in chagrin and bowed her head. 'I fear I broke that promise.'

'No, you didn't,' Tobias assured her. 'Remember all those times you clutched it and stared at it? I saw it in your eyes. And Olúryn does tell me a lot of things, between father and son. It was perhaps the only emotion in you from your past that remained – even when you awoke, it was there. Somehow, you remembered Tharguen.'

'I guess I did.' Niome yawned.

'It's late.'

'I've been talking all day.'

'Get your rest. After all, the Great Wizardess needs to build up her strength! She has a lot of catching up to do.'

They both smiled.

'When the other four arrive, they won't stay *that* long; I'm eager to go home to everyone. To Tharguen, yes, I see your look,' Niome added as Tobias chuckled. 'But while I'm here, alone with you, I want to take the time to thank you. You found me the very next day after my dreadful life-turning night. You saved my life, Tobias, and in doing so, you saved Teloria and the Great Ocean Valley and have made a great contribution in restoring the Freedom of Life.'

'*I* didn't save your life. *You* did. You called upon me. Your powers drew me towards you. Days before it happened, I left the house to ride in your direction. I sensed the magic, magic I could not understand days before I found you. It was your magic that brought me to you.' Tobias's determined eyes grew soft and he smiled teasingly, adding, 'But if you like, I'll take credit for it.'

Niome's sleep that night was disturbed with worries of *How much does Mirauk know?* as she tossed and turned in bed.

Maria and Gabriella returned that same week, at that end of ninth week. Niome told them her story and what worried her now. Maria agreed to meditate with Niome, but it did not seem to matter. Niome's fears were not quelled.

Niome prayed to Elina's star that night, hoping for her guidance. It was a few nights later, when the Moon was hid, that Niome got her answers.

'What?' Niome called out, waking up with a bounce. It was dark out. She was wondering what had woken her up, realising she had actually fallen asleep. She looked towards the sky.

'What time of night is it?' she asked herself aloud, searching for the Moon's position as she sat up. 'Where's the Moon?'

'There is no Moon. Not tonight.'

Niome turned around. The shimmering ghostly spirit figure of Elina was standing near her bed.

'Elina?'

'You asked for my help. Right now, the only way I can help you is to tell you in person.'

'Help me now?' Niome sighed in defeat. 'Why didn't you come sooner?'

'I did. I sent you Tobias. I couldn't come sooner – you weren't ready. You had to stop thinking with your mind and let your soul reconnect to magic. You had trials to live in order to grow in your power. You weren't going to learn anything if I aided you. That would've made it too easy. Nothing's easy when you're a wizard, but it doesn't get much more difficult than this.'

Niome pondered for a short while. 'So that *is* why I could never remember before.'

'That, and Mirauk sending you energy imbued with his malice didn't help.'

'I've really missed you,' admitted Niome.

'I know. But I'm always with you,' Elina comforted.

'I know. Just . . . the responsibilities. There's no one to ask for help from, no one to rely on, no one who knows better than me because I'm the one everyone seeks help from, 'cause I'm supposed to know everything. Then again, there's Bahvley, and the others, too.' She paused.

'To answer your question,' began Elina, 'yes, Mirauk knows much, but not everything. Your magic is strong. Even *I* can't understand how you did it, but . . . somehow, while you were unconscious, you were aware that your memories were leaving you and you were able to protect or block certain secrets.'

'Like what? What did I block?'

'Search within your soul, Niome. You know what was kept to you alone. Remember your first assumptions or the first memories that returned to you.'

'The magical shield? So Mirauk doesn't know about that completely, only so vaguely, it isn't enough for him to know that I can create one around Teloria. He knows of the Pleessies, though, and of their shield, but not of them telling me how to create one, so he can't imitate it. I must start on it as soon as I get home.'

'Is there anything else the phantom wasn't able to collect?' probed Elina.

'The phantom had gotten other people before me. He got a Firlanian – I don't know who – and from them perceived how to destroy Firlan.'

'If that information has trickled into your blood,' said Elina, 'then the phantom lost it while collecting your memories. Otherwise, you wouldn't know this.'

'The Old Grey House! He missed that! Thank goodness. But he knows all about my experience with his nephews. He knows too much. He knows how to destroy Teloria as it is now.'

'Yet he's done nothing to Teloria.'

'Perhaps he's waiting for something. For me to die? I have a strange predicament, as though there is a spy lurking.' She looked at Elina, waiting for confirmation.

'These are your instincts,' explained Elina. 'They are telling you things you must discover. *I* cannot help you with that.'

'You know, a lot more matters to me now than it did before,' admitted Niome. 'Before I got bitten, I mean. Every day matters. Little things I took for granted. I went about my daily life, but what I didn't realise was how every choice I made affected me and everyone else. I went to Firlan . . . maybe I should've continued on to Darakön.'

'Niome, what you don't understand is that many things happen for a reason. This had to happen to you. You've grown ever stronger, and soon, you'll start discovering the new powers that you gained from this. It threw Mirauk off; he has no knowledge that you lived. He may have doubts, but what does he know for sure? What proof does he have that what he did get from your memories is *really* how things are? He thinks he can take his time. Let him.'

Niome nodded. Elina hugged her.

'I have faith in you,' said Elina, backing away.

'Don't go yet!' cried Niome. 'Elina, don't leave me yet, wait!'

But Elina was already gone, vanished. Her star shot back up into the sky.

Niome walked to the window and looked out. 'Thank you,' she whispered.

Several days passed before Olúryn returned home. Niome was holed up in what had been her room for several years now, writing notes for the magical shield. She heard Olúryn's horse – it almost sounded like Greyer. Niome had been waiting impatiently for the other four to arrive.

She watched Olúryn enter the house from her window. He acknowledged his parents, who informed him Niome was upstairs and had something to tell him, and headed straight to her room.

Niome continued to look out the window.

'Hi,' said Olúryn. 'I'm back, from a very *boring* expedition.'

'Did you see anyone out there?' asked Niome, looking afar.

'No.'

'No group of four?'

'No, why?' Olúryn took several steps towards her.

'It's time to go home,' said Niome, smiling.

'But you *are* home,' said Olúryn. He put his hand on her back and extended the other arm to indicate he wanted a hug.

Unheeding him for now, Niome replied, 'No. *My* home. It's time, or soon it will be, for me to go to my real home, Teloria – Teloria City, on a little street not that far from the Royal Halls.'

'I don't understand.' Olúryn took a step back. There was silence. 'Navë?'

'Niome.'

'What?'

Niome turned to face him. 'Niome Fairhaven. That's my name.'

Olúryn took a moment. On his face dawned the realisation of what Niome had said. He muttered slowly, 'Navë . . . Niome Fairhaven, the letters on the page.' He paused. 'Niome,' he said carefully. 'You were wondering if I saw your friends out there. Are you expecting them to join you here?'

'I called on them with our magical verses.'

'Niome,' Olúryn repeated to himself. Then, 'It'll take some getting used to after calling you Navë all these years.'

Niome laughed. 'Don't look so troubled, Olúryn. It's still me, just my normal self now.' She walked up to him and granted him that hug, which he returned warmly.

Olúryn pulled away, hands on her arms, and hesitated. 'So . . . what's his name?'

'Tharguen.'

'He must love you very much.'

'After having a premonitory dream, he made me promise I'd never forget him.'

'And you never did!' asserted Olúryn.

'You know,' said Niome, putting her hand on his cheek, 'I still love you in my own way, and always will.'

'I know.'

They embraced tenderly again. Olúryn held her tightly. This was the embrace he'd longed to give her since his trip, and somehow, he felt better than he thought he would after that revelation.

'I'm relieved for you,' said Olúryn.

'And I for you. You can find someone now. The person with whom you are meant to be.'

'No, I can't,' he replied, shaking his head. 'I'm cursed, remember?'

Niome merely smiled. 'You're not cursed. Not anymore.'

Olúryn blinked back tears, wishing her words to be true. 'How? I don't understand. I've never met the most powerful Wizard—'

'You have. You're standing right in front of her.'

Olúryn took a moment, leaning back as though hit with another realisation.

'I don't mean to boast,' continued Niome, 'but we were meant to meet. I was meant to grow through this trial and conquer over death, which should've been the outcome, and to cure you. Which, if I'm not mistaken, I did cure you when we first met, or at least when you first saw me.'

'But how are you . . . ?' He paused.

'When I looked into Mirauk's eyes, he cowered.' She mulled that over. 'After he tested me and caused me one kurssus of a magical headache, that is.' She exhaled a laugh. 'That, and it's in the prophecy books.'

'You met Mirauk!' exclaimed Olúryn. 'Right, of course – you're the Great Wizardess of Teloria, Niome, who went to Mork and stayed at my grandfather's house. I forgot that in his letter, it's *you* he talks about. You have got to tell me, Na – Niome, how all this started. When did your adventures begin? Because if I am truly cured, I understand now how I actually felt about you. I sensed your magic right from the beginning. This hope I had that I misunderstood . . . my first assumptions . . . I knew there was something about you.'

Olúryn laughed. 'I admit, I feel a little embarrassed after what we expressed, although . . . you *are* beautiful, and the affection I feel for you is still there. But I understand it now. I feel close to you, despite the fact that we never acted on what I felt, and you will remain close to my heart forever – but I am not in love with you. The love I have for you is not the same I felt for my first real love. And it is filled with a gratitude I cannot put into words.'

Olúryn's eyes sparkled with tears. 'I am cured. I can love again – love for real. I can find my one true love.' He wiped his eyes and took Niome's hands in his. 'You've just made me feel so happy, Niome.' He laughed again. 'I guess you're not a student of magical lore after all, but a master.'

'Things have their way of working out,' said Niome, quickly glancing back towards the window again. 'The other four . . . are the others of the Star.' Niome turned back to Olúryn. 'You *will* come visit us in Teloria, I hope.'

'Of course! Maybe I'll meet someone there. Now, I want to hear your story, and what happened to you that you forgot your entire life!'

'Sit down,' advised Niome. 'It's a *long* story.'

'You do realise you're going to be telling this story *many* times?' Olúryn said a couple of days later. 'Even to the other four, the part we already know. That actually makes your full story longer!'

'You should write a book,' suggested Tobias. They were all sitting in the living room.

'Maybe I will,' mused Niome.

'I expect to get a wedding invitation soon,' said Olúryn.

'I'll send Tlúnëe,' said Niome. 'He'll already know from his prophecies, and he'll come inform you. Besides, I'm sure Boreth will be spending a lot of time there, especially after this. He'll inform them.'

'Niome,' said Gabriella, 'that cylinder that blew the wind – what is it called again?'

'The *Dragon's Wind*. Very effective in battle. Although, sometimes I just need to be present in the field and the Morkans scurry away like mice.' Everyone laughed.

Niome was going to miss this second home – *her* second home. Nevertheless, she knew she needed to return. She longed to see everyone, to discuss wisdom with Henker and Selemil, to reconcile with Bahvley from when she kept her secrets from him.

She wanted him to know how much she greatly loved him. Her older brother was such an influence on her, she admired even his faults. It was no wonder to her why he had been chosen as King, long before his departure, by the people of Teloria. She missed him terribly, as she did the other four.

She longed to be in Tharguen's arms and gaze into his handsome eyes, to hear him say over and over again how he would protect her as he promised when they were younger.

Niome drew in a deep breath as she watched Maria, Tobias, Olúryn, and Gabriella chatting away. It was time to continue the mission to save the world. It was time to go home.

CHAPTER TWENTY:
Message Received

That Colouring, Stëinbøk ordered many of his people to do a thorough search of the entire forest for Morkans. He didn't want to be caught off guard by them again. The forest was vast, and unprotected by walls as Teloria proper was, for it *was* part of Teloria. The kingdom spanned from Telor Lake to Zaccher Lake, south of the Ortim River.

'If Mirauk wants to destroy Teloria, he's goin' to have to destroy a lot more than just a wall,' Stëinbøk had declared, 'and deal with a lot more people than who *he* knows as Telorians!'

The Tellens found no Morkans, however. No trails, no weapons, not even tracks in the mud. Jimmy and Meysah only wished Kàtchah would've come to die by their swords. They had almost killed him at Darakön; the dragons had nearly made toast of him. Vigh and Boreth wanted to see him dead as well, if only because he had caused much torment for Telorians and Firlanians and was said to be part of Mirauk's Inner Circle.

Despite this, the four had renewed hope upon learning no new Morkan army had come to the forest. They sensed the arrival of good news.

Time passed until it was Spring of 4776, the fifty-ninth of the season, the fourth of the ninth. The four were going over strategies. Vigh and Boreth were with Stëinbøk, Jimmy was with the Firlanians, and Meysah was keeping a watch in the tower with some Tellens. Meysah had grown impatient to the point of wanting to keep a lookout for Niome himself. At the same time, the Tellens were teaching him to see into the distance better than he currently could.

It was close to noon when it happened. All of the four simultaneously went into a trance. Immediately after . . .

Meysah started bounding down the stairs, eyes wide. Vigh and Boreth looked at each other, stunned. Hunbøk thought they had gotten bad news, for they left in a flash. Jimmy looked at Elmezni, surprised.

Elmezni guessed it. 'Is it Niome?'

'Yes!' Jimmy ran off.

The four of them ran right into each other in the halls, literally bumping into one another.

'Did you get a message?' Boreth asked quickly. 'Because we did!'

'I did!' Jimmy answered excitedly.

'Me too!' Meysah confirmed.

'Finally! I can't believe it,' sighed Vigh, his relief apparent.

'We have to go to Zaccher Lake right away,' said Meysah. 'Niome's there! She's fine, she's all right! She's alive!'

The four hugged each other tearfully, so relieved were they. Then Meysah and Jimmy held each other's arms and bounced up and down with joy – it was a Kiki sight. Others approached.

'We're going to Zaccher Lake!' rejoiced Meysah. 'We just received a message from Niome. We don't know what happened to her, though, or why we haven't heard from her in so long.'

'We wish to leave tomorrow,' Vigh informed their friends.

'Tomorrow!' exclaimed Meysah, scowling. 'Why not now?'

'Because we need to say our goodbyes,' explained Vigh. 'In order not to be rude, of course,' he added quickly. 'But we'll be back.'

'*Your* goodbyes,' Boreth said teasingly. 'If I recall correctly . . .' He paused deliberately. 'You need to come back anyway. You'll see, spending some time away from . . .' He purposely cleared his throat.

'Boreth!' warned Vigh, speaking through his teeth. 'Not here! You're as bad as Meysah and Jimmy.'

'I've trained him well,' grinned Jimmy, laughing and nodding.

With purpose, the four started off in their separate directions.

'Meysah!' Kchalami caught his arm. 'Will you be stopping by here before going to Teloria?'

'Niome has to meet the Tellens, right?' Meysah surmised. 'Like Vigh said, we'll be back.'

'We'll be waiting.'

'I hope so,' said Meysah. 'I know Niome missed you.'

'She means a lot to us, to Firlan, to me,' said Kchalami. 'I need to see her before I go home, know that she's alive and well.'

The Firlanian Prince led Meysah aside and took a deep breath. Then he spoke, his voice grave, 'My father's weakening, Meysah. He hides it well. He has secret powers no one else has. Niome can read his thoughts and teach them to us. If the Kikies read his mind, they would not know how to relate it. It's family secrets, from Telorian blood. Niome is the only reason why my father's still alive. He wants to fight and protect Firlan, but he . . . he might not make it.'

'Kchalami, why have you not told anyone of this before?'

'We kept it secret. We did not wish to worry anyone. He even kept it from me – I had to deduce it. But it's more complicated than even that.'

'Then how are you sure?' asked Meysah.

'He had a . . . fitful episode. And then others had them, too. When the Morkans came last, they shot poison into the air that infected many. Mirauk sent us an illness. It evaporated, but those who breathed the air while it lingered were infected. We don't know who has it, but that attack my father had, it wasn't something nature caused him.'

'I'm sorry.' Meysah didn't know what to say. 'It worries me, too.'

'We don't want Mirauk knowing his trick worked,' continued Kchalami. 'Some of us continue to deny that it might be an illness brought on us as a vapour. We tested our plants and animal life, and only us polcs seem to have inhaled something changing our bodies in some way, affecting . . . our minds, I believe. I'm ready to discuss it with someone of greater power like your sister. I would've already done so, had she come earlier, but things didn't turn out the way anyone planned.'

'They never do, unfortunately. Yet fortunately, if something doesn't work out for—'

'For Mirauk,' said Kchalami, overlapping and concluding. 'You know, Meysah, in Teloria, with Tharguen's capture in Dûnelor and all that, an appropriate moment never arose. And I wasn't going to burden your brother with it when he has enough on his plate as it is. I figured we'd wait. With Niome gone, there wasn't much else we could do anyway.'

'I understand. Kchalami, my sister will find a cure. I promise.'

Vigh was in his room packing his things and making a list of foods he wanted to bring. There were some interesting fruits in the Twisted Forest that he just *had* to bring along to snack on. He left his door open for the others to join him if they were ready before him.

'I'm told Niome sent you a message,' said Nastafin.

Vigh looked up, startled. The Tellen woman was standing by the open door.

'Yes,' answered Vigh. 'I was going to talk to you about it after I had gathered my things and my thoughts.'

'You must be very relieved.'

'Am I ever!' admitted Vigh. 'I have my assumptions of what happened to Niome. I believe, if what Sikhlah said was true, that she forgot much and it has taken her all this time to remember.'

'Well, whatever it was, it's over now,' said Nastafin.

'She's at Zaccher Lake, but I thought no one lived there.'

'Magic dwells there, *we're* told,' said Nastafin. Vigh smiled. 'So I suppose you're goin' to go home after this, huh?'

'Well, not just yet,' said Vigh. 'First we'll see how Niome's doing. We'll be back here for sure. Niome needs to meet you and you need to meet her, everyone here. Besides, she can help protect the Twisted Forest by sharing advice wiser than we could ever tell you. Magical secrets, potions, spells – you know, that kind of thing. So, we're definitely coming back, and we'll be staying a while before we go back home.'

'I'm glad to hear it,' said Nastafin, her expression inscrutable. 'You . . . the four of you will be missed greatly here at the Twisted Forest. By many.' Again, Vigh smiled but said nothing. 'Well, I better leave you to your packing. You must have a lot to consider, especially now. Perhaps I'll see you before you leave tomorrow.' Nastafin started out.

'Nastafin!' Vigh called out. She paused, turning back to Vigh. 'You were right – about Niome being relatively all right. I'm sorry I was . . .' He smiled sheepishly.

'It's fine.' Nastafin smiled back and left.

When Jimmy, Meysah, Boreth, and Vigh were ready to leave, they supped and went to bed. They awoke early, before the Sun was up, and parted with their friends, who were already eager for them to return. When the four reached the forest's lake, into which poured the stream flowing from Zaccher Lake, they followed the stream up towards their destination.

As they approached Zaccher Lake, it was eventide of the seventy-fourth of Spring. That's when they realised they were on the wrong side of the lake.

'Look over there,' observed Boreth. 'I think I see a house in the distance.'

'Maybe we should've gone walking on the northern side instead,' sighed Jimmy.

'Well, we're not going to go back around and back up again,' said Meysah, his eyes bugging out as he nudged Jimmy teasingly.

'I know that. I'm not stupid, you know.'

'The stream's not very wide, nor very deep,' said Vigh. 'If we watch where we step, with our trousers rolled up, we can easily get across.'

'Well, what if we step where it's deeper?' muttered Meysah.

'That's why we're going to *watch* where we step,' replied Jimmy, a playful grin on his lips as he nudged Meysah with his elbow.

'Do you believe it's another Old Grey house?' asked Vigh, suppressing a laugh.

'Drúgan's daughter's,' said Boreth. 'We knew of it before. Why didn't we see it?'

'When the two of you came and saw the different Niome?' inquired Jimmy. Boreth nodded.

'It wasn't time,' said Meysah. 'It was only time once Niome had sent us the message. That's why you didn't see it before.'

'That's true. You're right,' said Vigh.

'Do we want to cross this stream and then rest?' asked Boreth. 'Or rest and then cross it?'

'Cross it!' said the knights.

'Cross it now,' said Vigh with the others' words.

'Then we all agree.' Boreth smiled.

'Let's find sticks, so we *know* where to step,' Vigh said with a boyish grin, teasing Meysah.

'Why not use our swords?' suggested Jimmy.

'Well, if you want to slip,' said Boreth, 'you can use a smooth sword on a slippery, slimy rock.'

Chuckling and teasing each other, the four found long and thin sticks, rolled up their trouser legs, and dove in, taking small and indeed cautious steps. As it got darker, it became harder to see. Meysah slipped and got wet, partially falling into the water, but Jimmy caught him before he fell in completely.

'Why is it always *me* who has to fall into the water and get all wet?!'

'Because you're prone to that?' replied Jimmy, bugging him.

Once they reached the other side, they rested that night and Meysah dried his clothes. The next morning, they headed towards the house.

'We're finally going to meet Clahria's other siblings and her parents,' said Boreth as they walked.

'Are you nervous?' asked Vigh. 'They say meeting the parents can be nerve-wracking.' He laughed.

'*I* was saying that, Vigh, for your information, because Clahria spoke highly of them to me. These people are as special and esteemed as Drúgan, Clahria, and Tlúnëe.'

'I was only teasing,' Vigh defended himself, suppressing a chuckle, 'though it seems you might be a little nervous, by the looks of it.'

Boreth rolled his eyes as the other three laughed.

In the early afternoon, they reached the Zaccher Old Grey House. At last, the Star would be whole again.

Niome was in her room when she sensed Meysah, Vigh, Jimmy, and Boreth approaching the house. A quick glance out the window confirmed what her magic had told her, and she smiled as the four came upon the door and knocked.

Maria answered. 'You must be the other four.' She smiled, looking at each of them.

'We are,' Vigh confirmed.

'Come in,' said Maria, 'you are greatly welcome.'

Niome dashed downstairs, skipping stairs in her hurry. It had been so long since she had last seen them that they seemed changed. Niome perceived the growth and wisdom in each of their faces; even Meysah, whom she had always considered childlike, appeared to be a grown polc, handsome and wise, just like Bahvley.

Relief washed over them, and as one, the Five heaved tearfully.

'Niome!' they all exclaimed. Meysah had a trickle of tears running down his cheeks and Niome blurted out a sobbed laugh of joy as the five of them embraced, finally reunited.

Meysah squeezed his sister tightly before pulling away to stare her in the eyes. 'By the stars! Whatever happened to you?'

'It's such a complicated story,' admitted Niome.

The others heard the excitement at the door from inside the house and came to join the group.

'They've arrived!' Gabriella squealed excitedly.

The four introduced themselves, as did the Zaccher Grey House dwellers.

'Drúgan spoke very highly of you in his letter,' said Tobias. 'Especially of you, Boreth, for I hear you have my daughter's heart, and now you have our blessings.'

'Thank you,' said Boreth, his cheeks reddening.

Vigh nudged him playfully, suppressing a laugh.

Maria offered some snacks to the arrived travellers as they settled in the living area with Niome for a proper catch-up. Jimmy's stomach growled as he eyed the appetisers.

Then Maria, Tobias, Olúryn, and Gabrielle left them to speak in private.

As soon as the Five were alone, they bombarded each other with questions.

'What happened to you?' asked Boreth. 'We sent you magical messages, but you never received them – they bounced back to us. We even thought, for a time, that you were dead.'

'Perhaps I was,' replied Niome, 'in a way.'

'How? What happened?!' Meysah's eyes were pleading for answers, reflecting the worry he'd felt all these years.

'What happened to *you*?' Niome countered. 'How did you Lords escape?'

'You first,' said Jimmy, pointing a finger at Niome.

'Okay.' First, Niome recounted how the cold and fatigue had led her to Firlan and the battle that ensued. 'I made myself a new friend that day, Meltissel. He's quite eager to meet you. He and a few others would've travelled with me, but they had to stay in Firlan.'

'You mean you travelled alone after that?' asked Meysah, his tone a little indignant. Niome was glad that some things about her younger brother hadn't changed.

'Yes,' said Niome. 'I chose to travel alone, since I was off to meet you at the Twisted Forest.'

Meysah folded his arms. 'I wouldn't have let you travel alone, and I'm sure neither would Mom and Dad.'

Niome smiled. Meysah always brought up their parents when he was trying to hide his worry. 'Meysah, we're not children anymore. We can take care of ourselves, *remember*?'

'Yeah, well, we have parents who worry, okay?'

'Because *you've* never done anything rash before,' muttered Jimmy.

'Oh, I miss arguing with you,' Meysah finally admitted. 'I also missed you so much, I got sick with worry. Don't worry me like that ever again, okay?!'

Niome laughed and put her hand on his cheek. 'Okay. I promise. I've missed you . . . *and* arguing with you, too.' They all chuckled. 'It's been a long time. But you still have Jimmy to argue with!'

'Oh, don't worry, we did,' said Jimmy.

'When you travelled alone,' began Boreth, steering the conversation back to their misadventures, 'is that when the phantom got you?'

'How did you know?'

'Morkans told us. Specifically Sikhlah.' Boreth waved his hand. 'We'll explain later.'

'Yes, that's when it happened,' confirmed Niome. 'I did wonder why it was on its own, though.'

'The others destroyed them,' said Vigh, explaining what the Five had learnt about Bahvley's restored memories and the night they had all fought the phantoms. 'But only one escaped and . . . evidently completed its task.'

'Em must know every secret you know by now,' said Jimmy, his slumped shoulders conveying his dismay.

'Not quite,' said Niome. 'Mirauk thinks I'm dead – or at least the true me.'

Meysah gasped. 'You said his name!'

'We can scream it if we want now,' said Niome. 'And we can tell the others about our change of plans. Tobias, Maria, Olúryn, and Gabiella already know.'

Meysah accepted this answer. He and Jimmy both looked relieved by it.

After retelling some of the events of the past years, Niome added, 'The day I sent you my message is the day I remembered.'

'We may have seen you,' said Boreth, who sat closest to Niome, opposite Meysah. 'But you did not recognise us.'

'I remember, yes,' said Niome. 'I apologise. I was not myself.'

Boreth nodded, though he was still troubled. 'But the secrets that Mirauk does know?'

'He doesn't know everything,' said Niome, putting her hand on the Lord's knee. 'Elina's spirit came to me to confirm this.'

'Gorthan's spirit came to Bahvley,' Meysah piped up. 'That's how he remembered how to destroy the phantoms. By seeing them, he remembered that they had gotten him, but—'

'The phantoms got Bahvley?!' exclaimed Niome. Her gaze shot to Vigh, who had omitted that detail earlier.

'Long ago. He and you both are all right now,' Vigh reassured.

Appeased, Niome explained how her magic had protected certain details and secrets, like the Old Grey Houses, the location of the Dalvara secret caves, or the Pressies' magical shield.

'What about the Kikies?' asked Jimmy.

'I am uncertain,' admitted Niome. 'Mirauk knows of their existence, but much about them, he is likely not to know.'

'He surely knows the phantoms were afraid of them,' said Vigh.

'That's because such purity is a threat to such evil,' asserted Niome. 'Yet if that is so, such evil is a threat to such good also. What Mirauk does *not* know is that the Kikies' willpower is stronger than that of any other being. More than any polc, especially. They can never turn to malice – not unless they choose to give up completely all love that lives inside of them.'

The Five halted their storytelling for the moment to sup with the others of the house. After the meal, the travellers freshened up before gathering in Niome's room. The setting was similar to when they had met in secret in Dûnelor, except this time, there was no need for dimmed lights or shut windows.

They installed themselves comfortably. It was Niome's turn to listen to their story. After hearing of their travels before arriving at the Twisted Forest, Niome's eagerness to know about her other friends had her asking, 'So how's Tharguen? And Bahvley?'

The other four hesitated. It was Meysah who answered. 'Uhm, we don't know.'

'What do you mean you don't know?' Niome scowled. 'You spoke of them just earlier, that Bahvley remembered about the phantoms and that they destroyed four of the five phantoms.'

'We knew that because the Firlanians told us,' explained Jimmy.

'I don't understand.'

'They weren't there when we arrived,' said Vigh. 'They had already gone home. Otherwise, I'm certain they would have travelled here with us to see you.'

'That means they must be worried sick about us.' Niome clutched her ring, feeling the longing. 'I miss Tharguen so much.'

'I kept this,' said Meysah. He produced the letter Bahvley had written. 'Bahvley wrote us this.'

Niome read the letter, hugging it closely to her chest before returning it to Meysah.

'I still don't understand why Merlik let you go,' mused Vigh.

'There was something strange in his gaze,' Niome assessed, 'something I have not been able to determine.'

Their musings went to the magical room in Darakön where Jimmy and Meysah had found the diary of the Dragon Prophet.

'I still marvel at how that room is enchanted,' Meysah said in awe, 'because we could understand the polc's diary, even if it was written before Kaulchèc History.'

'I always thought the Dragon Prophecies were written after the Kaulchèc arrived,' said Boreth.

'They were, by him,' replied Meysah, 'whoever he was, but before that, there was another scripture of the dragons' thoughts. The one with the diary was only completing the work of the other before it was too late, and he began before the Kaulchèc arrived and completed it after.'

'This is very insightful to our people's history,' Niome said thoughtfully. She opened her mouth to speak again, pausing but a moment as a thought occurred to her. Her eyes met Meysah's and Jimmy's. 'Did you travel to the Twisted Forest by means of a dragon?'

'We did,' replied Jimmy. 'After defeating all those Morkans.' He sighed, slumping his shoulders. 'That Kàtchah . . . he just doesn't die!'

'I saw it,' said Niome, 'and I sensed your presence with it. Even if the dragon was very high.'

As the night wore on, the Five continued to recount their adventures and muse about their discoveries.

'There was another army of Morkans,' said Niome. 'Tobias saw them. I suppose they snuck in and out undetected.'

'Kàtchah must've sent them to find out what happened to the others,' concluded Jimmy.

'I sure am sorry I wasn't there,' said Niome.

'It was meant to be that you were away,' said Vigh. 'Had you been with us, the phantoms might have harmed more Tellens.'

'Many things that happened were meant to be,' said Niome. 'Mirauk thinks I'm dead, or as good as, and I cured Olúryn from his curse. You, Vigh, met someone.'

'Stop it!' Vigh tried to hide his face behind his hand as he rubbed his forehead.

'I sure am relieved to hear Gohtek is dead,' admitted Niome.

'If Kàtchah had been there,' said Meysah, folding his arms, 'I'm sure he would've escaped. Again, we wouldn't have been able to kill him.'

'No,' declared Niome. 'That's false. Kàtchah didn't go because he knew of the peril he would be putting himself in if he went. Kàtchah can only make decisions to keep himself out of harm's reach, not caring what happens to others. That's because he needs to die on his own to keep Mirauk's power growing. He knows a form of magic and is intuitive through it. We're going to have to find a way to lure him into the trap he never falls into to be able to destroy him.'

Niome grew serious as she narrowed her eyes at the other four. 'One of *you* will be fighting him. There are others that must be destroyed so they cannot become stars: Mirauk, Kàtchah, Merlik and Garkhktak. There will be a fourth, and there will be a fifth.'

'But are Merlik and Garkhktak not two?' inquired Boreth.

'The twins form one entity of evil power in magic. I fear each of us will fight one of the mightiest and evilest five. I know I'll be battling Mirauk. One of you will fight his nephews, another Kàtchah.'

Niome's expression turned thoughtful. 'Yûrk might be a distracting vassal, like Beshrig was, an asset to Mirauk. Tharguen killed Beshrig. If Yûrk is a vassal, I predict that Bahvley is fated to kill him, and if so, there are two more polcs we have not yet met.'

The other four exchanged glances, but remained silent.

'Our match – that's who they are,' Niome continued. 'If there was a way to find out who was whose match, we could prepare ourselves better. I only know that Mirauk is mine, and we don't even know who the two remaining Morkans are. As for the others, when the time comes to destroy them, you will find yourselves alone with them where none of you, or none of them, can escape. It will be a duel to the death.

'Perhaps we may only know who our match is at the very end, when we are alone with them. And . . . only when we have destroyed them will we be powerful enough to become stars to *spread* the good, and not just stars to *inspire* good.' Niome sighed. 'There is no way out of this. It is our stardust destiny.'

'You really did discover much throughout your time here,' noted Meysah. 'More will come to you. You have developed knowledge and skills that are *in* you now but that you may not consciously be aware of until later, since it all came to you while you did not remember yourself.'

'You understand much more about magic than you used to, Meysah,' Niome voiced with a grin. 'I'm glad of it, for you have magic in you which you will one day learn to use as I have.'

'I wonder who among us is Kàtchah's match,' mused Jimmy. 'While I'm not eager to find out who that is, I am eager to see him slain.'

'We have an advantage right now,' said Vigh, rubbing the stubble on his chin. 'If the Morkans think Niome dead and we encounter any, they'll be petrified. To see that you survived, Niome, with all that you've suffered, all that Mirauk's thrown at you . . .'

'Mirauk's confused,' said Niome. 'He knew I was alive after the beast got me. He sent his malicious energies to me, but Elina countered them with her protection, and Gorthan as well. The day I remembered myself again, Navë died. The weak, lost, vulnerable, and confused Navë, scared about too much to explain, was defeated. I vanquished her and took over my own life again.'

Niome allowed herself an air of boasting. 'Mirauk doesn't know that, or at least I don't think he does. He thinks I finally died. Hopes it.' She inclined her head. 'Another possibility is, he thinks that Niome the Great Wizardess has died yet Navë survives, that Niome will never return and Navë is the new me and therefore not a Wizardess – not capable of destroying him, not a threat.'

Clasping her hands together, she went on. 'The day I became me again, Mirauk sensed something, so perhaps he is aware I've been alive all this time and sensed a part of me die. Now, we can't be too sure of it, but he likely has suspicions and wants to make sure I really *am* dead. I am certain he wants to learn which part of me actually died.' Niome caught herself. 'I can't be too proud or too arrogant about my recovery, though. It was far too slow for my liking.'

'You can't be too hard on yourself, either,' said Boreth, arching a brow.

'Better that than to lose myself in pride and greed like Bortah Mittèlor did long ago.'

Boreth leaned forward. 'Niome, that phantom took nearly all your blood and memories. Anyone would have either died or never remembered ever again, which is what Mirauk expected and assumed. And you defied that.'

'Boreth's right,' agreed Vigh. 'That is an incredible feat, Niome.'

'You *have* grown wiser,' said Jimmy.

'Not enough,' insisted Niome, smiling nonetheless. She shrugged. 'Unless it'll come slowly in order not to bombard me with all the new wisdom. I do know that I'm far wiser than any of you,' she continued mockingly.

'If there's one thing that hasn't changed about you, my dear sister, it's . . . well, your Kikiness.'

Niome offered Meysah a silly smile. 'Really?'

'Of course,' replied Meysah. 'I analysed Jimmy – I'll analyse you.' The three of them laughed loudly.

'Settle down,' Boreth chided. 'We don't want to wake the others.'

'I guess not,' said Vigh. 'You do want Clahria's parents to know you're a perfectly respectful gentleman with manners, after all.'

'Har-har-har,' Boreth said sarcastically, rolling his eyes.

A bit reluctantly but with joy in their hearts, the Five concluded their exchange and readied for bed. They finally knew all that could be said openly to the others.

A week more did the Five stay at the Zaccher Grey House. Niome, while eager to meet the Tellens and return home, was reluctant to leave this cosy home, for it had been her home as well all these years. She would miss those who dwelled here greatly, and she told them so as she prepared to leave on Spring the eighty-fourth at dawn.

'I promise to visit you,' said Niome.

'Promise from the bottom of your heart?' asked Olúryn.

Niome walked up to Olúryn and spoke so low that only he would hear. 'I won't forget you. You taught me a lot.' They embraced amiably.

'Come to Teloria,' Niome said to the others, 'and soon, for I don't know when I'll be able to come and visit. This was my home for what seemed too long. Now, it seems as though my time here was not long enough.'

'The future frightens you,' deduced Tobias, 'doesn't it?'

'It does,' admitted Niome.

'It frightens the enemy more,' said Maria. 'There are many things one can guess, but too often, there are things better left unknown. Don't focus on what you do not know. Focus on what you *do* know.'

'I will, then,' Niome said, smiling.

'Take these.' Tobias handed Niome a stack of letters. 'They are letters from us to Drúgan. Please deliver them for us.'

'I will do so,' said Boreth. 'I will deliver these myself.'

'May the stars protect the five of you,' said Tobias, 'as they have been all this time.'

'Thank you,' said the others, and together at last, they left.

Niome dared not look back yet, for she knew if she did, she would want to return. Only when they were at a fair distance did she chance a glance back. She closed her eyes to take in all that had just happened to her, all that she had lived in that house one more time.

'*I* think we should go by the fields,' said Niome. They had already crossed the river and were redirecting themselves towards the Twisted Forest. 'I sense . . . that is the way, if we want no more trouble in the Twisted Forest.'

'Then by the fields, it is,' said Vigh.

They heard the sweet chirping of the birds as they went, as though they were rejoicing that the Five were reunited.

'Something tells me you didn't tell us everything, Niome,' mused Boreth as they all walked merrily. 'Something happened between you and Olúryn.'

'I cured his curse. But if you must know, for a brief moment, there was something there, only emotionally. But we both felt a change and knew it was something else unawarely. That's how I never forgot Tharguen.'

'Well, we won't say a word to Tharguen about it, even if he's not the jealous type,' assured Meysah. 'And even if it was something, both you and Olúryn needed to experience it. I shall not tell. Even if Bahvley comes and commands me! Anyway, he knows how stubborn I am.'

'Believe me,' said Niome, 'we all know how stubborn you are.' She let out a small laugh. 'But I won't keep it a secret from Tharguen. I'm just not sure of the best way to broach the subject, that's all. It's important to me to keep the honesty between us. The magic of our love requires it.'

'But even then, you somehow knew and remembered him,' said Vigh after a pause. 'That's amazing.'

Soon after, the Five settled down for a quick rest.

They were three days into their journey when they saw horses in the distance. Vigh and Boreth reached for their swords and Jimmy his bow.

'Don't draw your weapons,' said Niome. The others reluctantly put their weapons away. 'There's no need to fight them.'

The horses approached. The Morkans halted before the Five as the Telorians stood waiting.

'Well, what do we have here?' said the Captain as he and his polcs unsheathed their swords.

'We're Telorians,' said Vigh, estimating twenty Morkans.

'Maybe now, but soon you'll be corpses.' The Captain smirked wickedly.

'Why are you trying to sneak into the Twisted Forest through the back?' inquired Niome. 'Don't you know you'll be found and killed?'

'Who are you to assume our plans?' demanded the Captain. 'Who sent you?'

'No one sent me,' replied Niome. 'I am merely defending my friends. We'll block your path! You won't get past us!'

The Morkans laughed.

'I realise none of you have seen me before, but perhaps you know me by name: Niome Fairhaven!'

Again the Morkans laughed, even harder this time, and louder.

'Hah!' guffawed the Captain so loudly and strongly, the Five could have sworn he stopped breathing. 'That's the most ridiculous thing I've ever heard. Don't you know? Niome's dead.'

'Look at us. We are five!' said Niome placidly.

'Good cover-up,' said the Morkan. 'However, you cannot change facts. Niome no longer is!'

'Look into my eyes and tell me that,' Niome commanded firmly.

All the Morkans looked upon Niome mockingly. But then the horses began to fidget and neigh nervously, and the ground began to quiver. As the Morkans realised the truth, they were afraid.

'Mirauk knew you'd meet us. He fed you a pretext. Mirauk didn't send you here to sneak into the forest,' asserted Niome. 'Mirauk sent you here to confirm his suspicion that I was not dead. So, go now, back to your Lord in Mork, and tell him he knows less than half of what's in me. That phantom didn't get everything. Never will anything be able to get all of my memories or secrets, and never will anything or anyone destroy me.'

'Let's go!' shouted the Captain in a fury.

The Morkans veered from the path atop their horses and galloped away in haste and fear.

'So now, Mirauk will know,' said Vigh, concerned.

'That doesn't mean he has the advantage,' Niome reassured.

They continued on for four more days before reaching the forest. Jimmy and Meysah were pleased to see some of their Tellen friends when they arrived at a shelter that night, most notably Lirogon, Estemlenk, Gardëvøn, Passtëgon, and Devnolenk, who had greeted them upon their first arrival at the forest.

'You mean to scare you.' Niome playfully nudged her brother.

'Did they mention they saved us from the remaining phantom?' asked Estemlenk with a wink.

'All I did was tell the phantom you weren't here,' Meysah explained to Niome, 'and it went after you, so I sent it after you.'

'Mirauk sent it. You saved yourself and others, Meysah. It was meant to get me.'

'What an adventure, though,' said Boreth.

'And Niome,' Meysah teased, 'you started all this.'

'You're the one who continued it,' Jimmy reminded him.

'Strictly speaking, Elina started it,' said Vigh.

The Telorians installed themselves for the night and fell fast asleep except for Niome, whose mind wandered to Tharguen. Her worries were consuming her. When meditation did not calm her nerves, Niome began to sing softly to herself in an attempt to lull herself to sleep.

Niome stopped when she heard a voice. It was low. She glanced about – no one was awake. The Tellens keeping watch out on the shelter's balcony were silent. There was absolutely no noise around her, and Niome noted that the voice did not belong to anyone near, yet she could still hear a distinct voice. It was almost as though the speaker were muttering to himself. It was morbid, elusive.

Niome stopped all movement to listen more carefully.

'*No . . . that can't be. I have to find out, once that's done . . . wait. Oh, I understand now.*'

Niome knew this voice. She'd heard it long ago. Yet, she could not determine who it belonged to. All she knew was that the voice belonged to a man.

As the Tellens outside began to chat amongst themselves, Niome could no longer hear the voice.

Niome was ever wary the following day, pre-occupied by the mysterious voice. For fear they were being followed, Niome mentioned nothing of it to the others but remained on her guard the whole day.

That night, Niome heard the voice again.

'*We can't do that.*' There was some noise around this polc, whoever he was. '*To attack the Telorians without . . .*' More noise. '*. . . that won't work . . .*'

That's when Niome realised the voice belonged to a Morkan, and she could only hear it in absolute silence. She began to suspect she recognised its speaker.

When morning came, Niome voiced her suspicions to the others.

'I think we're being followed,' she whispered.

'How so?' asked Boreth, glancing about up, down, and all around.

'I've been hearing a voice, two nights in a row,' Niome informed them. 'It sounds familiar. I can only hear it in absolute silence, though.' She paused. 'I fear it's Kàtchah.'

'What trick does he have up his sleeve this time?' sighed Vigh.

'We must remain vigilant,' said Meysah.

'This is unfortunate,' voiced Jimmy. 'Unfortunate for him, because we'll kill him before he does anything.'

When night came, the five Telorians made camp in an abandoned shelter, ready to listen to the voice.

Boreth scratched his head. He turned to Niome. 'Did you hear anyone reply to this voice you heard last night? It seems odd to me that one Morkan would speak out loud in the Common Tongue and not the Morkan tongue.'

Niome shrugged. 'Have Kàtchah's actions ever made sense before?' Meysah snorted a laugh in his throat.

Boreth considered this. 'You say you only hear the voice when you're fully focused, in absolute silence? Perhaps—'

There was movement below the shelter – the sound of weapons and the patter of feet scaling the ladder.

Vigh stood abruptly, unsheathing his sword. The Telorians carefully peered over the edge to find Tellens carrying a slain deer.

'Tellens!' Niome exclaimed in relief.

'Of course!' said one of the Tellen. 'Telorians, I see. Me brother and I are here to rest and caught ourselves a deer.' The Telorians helped the Tellens with their hunting catch. 'I remember chattin' away with the army's Captain, Tharguen. He spoke a lot of Niome Fairhaven. Said she was the most beautiful and powerful Wizardess of all time.'

'I am she,' said Niome. 'These are the other four of the Star.'

'Well met. Tharguen was right! Very beautiful indeed. My compliments to your survival of whatever kept you away this long.'

'Thank you,' Niome said with a smile.

The group chatted jovially as the Tellens prepared their meat. When the Tellens retreated for sleep, the Telorians settled back down in the adjacent chamber.

'I suppose there aren't enough Tellens anymore to fill in at all the shelters,' mused Meysah. 'Especially after the fire and the incident with the phantoms.'

'The fire,' muttered Niome. 'Mirauk took advantage of my drought. We must be careful how we use our magic. But if he's able to use my magic for his advantage, I can certainly use his for mine.'

The Five grew quiet.

'I don't hear any voices,' said Meysah.

'That's because we're making too much noise,' said Niome. 'We have to be silent, so not a word.'

Without argument, the Telorians grew even quieter.

'*What do the Telorians have in mind?*'

Niome widened her eyes. 'There. Did you hear?'

The others shook their heads.

'I hear nothing,' said Vigh.

'Listen more carefully,' insisted Niome.

'*If I can find a way to . . .*'

'Again!'

'*Oh, what a brilliant idea. There's only one concern about it now . . .*'

'Still nothing,' said Jimmy.

'But didn't you hear it?' Niome asked, her voice pleading. 'Something about a brilliant idea?'

'Not at all,' said Meysah.

'Perhaps we can't,' suggested Boreth. 'Perhaps only Niome can hear it. And perhaps it's not a voice, but a thought.'

'A thought?' asked Vigh.

'That *would* make sense,' Niome said thoughtfully. 'Then maybe there's no one following us after all, and that would explain why I only hear it in silence.'

'If you only hear bits and pieces of it now, perhaps if you meditate to focus on it more, you'd hear the full thoughts,' suggested Boreth.

'You're right. And perhaps when I meditate,' said Niome, 'I'll gain control over *when* I hear it.'

'This must be one of your new abilities,' Meysah pointed out.

'One I am ready for now,' Niome agreed.

'How can you tell between *thinking* you're ready and *being* ready for something?' asked Jimmy.

'You don't,' said Vigh.

'Magic will tell you,' offered Niome. 'When it's time, the will of magic will overcome you and you'll feel it flow within you, and like instinct, you'll just know. You'll be able to tell the difference then. You experienced it when you left with Meysah to find me and Boreth took you on as his pupil. You were only ready then, not before.'

With that, forgetting the voice for the moment, the Telorians lay down for some much-needed sleep.

In the days and nights that followed, wanting to focus on travel and having no time to meditate, Niome occupied herself in order not to hear the voice. She busied her mind with future magical plans, polcs she intended to have magical discussions with, places that required investigating, and other things that had come to mind since fully regaining her memory.

Passing by the lake, the Five travelled on to the fortress, reaching it in the early morning of the eighth day of Summer. It was warm and beautiful.

The Telorians surmised the watch guards had informed Stëinbøk of their arrival, for the Tellen King and Kchalami, along with several other Tellens and Firlanians, were present at the gate to greet them.

Kchalami pounced to embrace Niome, laughing in relief. 'You had us so worried!' he exclaimed. 'What in the world happened to you?!'

'It's a long story,' replied Niome, returning the embrace warmly, 'which will take many days to explain and many more to understand.'

'Niome Fairhaven,' said Stëinbøk. 'You are greatly honoured and respected among polcs, and a very welcome guest at the Twisted Forest. I am Stëinbøk, King of the Tellens. But to me, your brother Bahvley is *me* King.'

He clasped Niome's hand in his. 'Long have we awaited your arrival and worried about you with your friends! Now that you are here, I understand what they meant when they said you were the most powerful, for it shows in your eyes. I can sense your magic. Long have I waited to seek counsel with the most wise. This is why I now kneel before you.' Stëinbøk crouched onto one knee and bowed. 'Fairest and wisest of all polcs, we Tellens are ready to receive your guidance.'

'You may rise,' said Niome, smiling. 'I don't need you to bow before me – your friendship will do. We're all in this together. You need my help, and I need yours. I require no more than that which I mentioned.'

Stëinbøk looked up at Niome before he rose.

'You have still your part to play in this great tale, Stëinbøk,' she continued. 'I may be powerful, but I have an equal, and only once he is destroyed will I be worthy of such appraisal.'

'Then welcome, Niome. It is a pleasure to meet you.'

'An honour.' Niome bowed politely. 'The others spoke much of you, and very highly too.'

With introductions made, the Telorians were led inside.

Once settled in, Vigh went to see Nastafin. Night had fallen. She hadn't been at the door to greet them, and his heart yearned to see her.

Vigh steadied himself before knocking on the door of Nastafin's room. As Nastafin let him in, it seemed to Vigh she had been sleeping. It was true he had put off seeing her, for it meant telling her things difficult to admit.

'Am I bothering you?' he asked.

'Not at all. You're back.' Nastafin paused. 'Which I knew before, but I didn't want to crowd you when you arrived.'

'You wouldn't have.' Vigh paused. 'You're sure I'm not disturbing you?'

'No, really.' There was another uncomfortable silence. 'I met Niome. I was right about her – she knows how to make one feel special about themselves.'

'Yes,' agreed Vigh. 'Niome's special herself.' He hesitated. 'If you want, I can come back tomorrow.'

'Nonsense! You're here now. Anyway, I can't sleep much these days.'

'I'm sorry.' Vigh paused. He gathered his courage and gathered his thoughts, trying to say what he had trouble admitting to even himself. 'Well, uh, can I reassure you about something?'

Nastafin nodded.

'I'm not entirely sure how to say it. But it's important that I tell you now . . . no matter how it comes out.' Vigh sighed, scowling. 'It's funny how even at my age, with my experience and wisdom, I still have difficulty with certain matters.'

'Well, tell me what they are,' said Nastafin, sitting on her bed. 'And don't worry about how it comes out.'

Vigh sat down beside her, feeling foolish.

'While I was away,' began Vigh, 'my thoughts turned to you. I . . . missed you. I can't deny it to myself, nor to you – not anymore.'

Vigh stared at Nastafin with tenderness in his eyes.

'I think I'm in love with you. I have been from the very moment I met you.' He bowed his head. 'I know I wasn't always pleasant towards you. I was stuck in the past with my woe and projected it onto you. I hope you can forgive me for that. For the fact is' – Vigh met Nastafin's gaze once more – 'I love you, and no matter how much I try to understand it, I can't. I told myself I'd never love again, so hurt was I. And I never did, for fear of losing again the polc I loved. Until now.'

His heart hammering and his chest tight, Vigh waited for Nastafin's reply, but she remained silent. He continued.

'Gorthan once told me that I might find love again in another life. He told me this shortly after the Big War. That was before my fate was discovered. Now, if all goes well, this will be my last life. I won't have another chance at love – to be reborn, forget my woes, and start anew to find happiness in love. This is the last chance I have.'

Vigh reached for Nastafin's hand. 'I'm ready to move on, and to forget my past and start again. I won't lie to you anymore, nor to myself. I just want to be with you . . . if you'll have me.'

This time, Vigh did not look away as he waited for Nastafin's reply with earnestness.

Nastafin squeezed Vigh's hand and smiled. 'I will have you.'

Vigh let out a relieved laugh, unable to stop himself from grinning boyishly. He cupped Nastafin's face and leaned in tentatively. Nastafin closed the distance, and the two kissed tenderly.

Vigh wrapped his arms around her, breathing deeply in contentment. For the first time since losing Tallelah, Vigh felt light, untroubled. Long had it been since he felt the sweet touch of love.

Smiling and feeling young again, Vigh and Nastafin continued to kiss and hold each other as Vigh made more promises to the new woman he loved.

After but a few days with the Tellens, Niome felt at home. The Five finally revealed to their friends their secret mission and the drought Niome had created, which Mirauk had then used to cause the fire.

In all the excitement of sharing and counselling each other, after a few weeks, Niome still had not taken the time to meditate to focus solely on the voice she heard in the silence, for with a fortress full of polcs, there was little silence to begin with.

Niome one day discovered the garden in a quiet area of the Fortress where Stëinbøk often went to clear his thoughts. So that night, she returned and sat on a bench in the back of the garden. It truly was peaceful – absolute silence filled the air.

Niome heard the voice, loud and clear as though the polc stood next to her. It made her heart drum – it frightened her. Yet she knew with her magic channelled through meditation, no longer would it give her reason for anxiety.

Closing her eyes and taking a deep breath, Niome began her meditation. Now, she could perceive the full thoughts from the voice.

We must wait and find out more.

Niome focused.

We must find a way for the benefit of Mork. If Merlik and Garkhktak are correct, then Mork is indeed in need of reinforcing power. Never am I wrong, but lately things are shown to me to prove me wrong! This is the first time I doubt myself. I doubt others . . . But why is it . . . ?

Through her excitement at hearing more, Niome lost her focus and began to lose some of the thoughts. She reined in her mind, steadying her breath and her heart rate.

. . . Who are they, and what are these creatures that they can transform themselves into dust and appear again? I knew of their existence before, but we knew so little. Now with more, I have even more questions. If my sarikh-pekamav *were so terrified of them, then indeed they are a threat to Mork.* The speaker growled in anger, yelling, *I shall not have it!*

Niome's eyes shot open. She knew the voice – and she knew when she'd first heard it.

Though dawn had not yet arrived, Niome hurried to the rooms of the other four and woke them, excited to announce her revelation. Vigh and Boreth were more alert, but Jimmy and Meysah trudged sleepily into Niome's room, yawning.

Niome turned to them. 'It's Mirauk.'

Meysah and Jimmy were suddenly awake, eyes as wide as their mouths were agape.

'What?!' said Meysah.

'The voice I hear – it's Mirauk! When he's thinking, or meditating. I just meditated, and I heard clear thoughts. Full sentences!'

'Are you certain?' asked Boreth.

'I doubt anyone else would say: "Never am I wrong!" or *my* this and *my* that or "I shall not have it!" When he shouted, I knew. It is Mirauk I hear, and he's doubting himself. We have the advantage.'

'How can you be sure that Mirauk can't hear you when you hear him?' inquired Vigh.

'Because if he did, he wouldn't be so afraid of the Kikies,' Niome said, smiling.

Meysah and Jimmy exchanged a smirk.

'He's afraid of the Kikies!' repeated Meysah. 'You think they can look him in the eyes and not be cursed?'

'Perhaps, or at least not as polcs are,' replied Niome.

'What did he say about the Kikies?' asked Jimmy.

Niome recounted what she heard of Mirauk's thoughts. 'This is refreshing, now that I've gained control over this ability, to be able to be in complete and utter silence and not hear anything.'

'Right,' said Vigh. 'You didn't want people thinking you were going crazy, hearing voices telling you mysterious things.'

'I hear other voices, too,' said Niome.

'More Morkans!' exclaimed Jimmy.

Niome smiled. 'No! Memories. It is similar to when I was Navë, as though memories with meaning are coming to mind. Like when I heard you, Meysah, shouting, "For the Freedom of Life!" Most often, what I remember and hear when I listen carefully is Tharguen's voice. "Promise me you'll never forget me." He said that to me once, after a nightmare. It was a premonition he had.'

Niome held out her hand. 'He thought Tweedle put this ring in his wood on purpose for Tharguen to find. He thought it a pleasant coincidence. Maybe Tweedle did do it. Regardless, this ring links me to the love of my life and allows me these memories while our mission keeps me away from him, and will for some time.'

'What do you mean by that?' asked Boreth, struck by a pang in his heart as his thoughts wandered to Clahria.

'There is still much to be done here before our task is done, before time to go home. The Tellens need us still.'

'Niome,' began Meysah, his tone serious, 'we've been here a long time now. It's *you* they need.'

'Maybe so, but it's not me alone they need. It's *us*. They need our power, the Star as an entity, the five of us.'

Boreth looked disappointed. 'I long to be with Clahria again. It is a shame we must linger here.'

'Well,' said Jimmy, 'at least Summer is nice here, too!'

'Oh, you,' said Meysah, nudging his friend. 'One of these days . . .'

'What? One of these days, what?! I'll one of these days *you* one of these days.' The Telorians chuckled.

'And you're certain you don't hear the voice anymore?' Boreth asked, concerned.

'Only in meditation.' Niome paused, brows furrowing. 'I sense something else, since my meditation, though I cannot fully grasp it. It is . . . farther away, elusive. Something or someone is not what they appear to be. But the time to learn of them is not anywhere near, in distance nor in time.'

'Then we're still safe,' Jimmy sighed with relief.

Niome spoke more with Stëinbøk in the coming days and aided the Tellens. When next she meditated, she perceived Mirauk's thoughts even more clearly, and no lingering voice remained afterwards.

Niome discovered that Mirauk was fretting over details he wished to share with his nephews. She also learnt that Merlik and Garkhktak had indeed been frightened of her in Dūnelor, and in awe. Mirauk was uncertain what Merlik's true thoughts were regarding Niome and her powers.

Kchalami approached Niome one day when he judged the time was right. At last, he would broach the matter he had waited all these years for, awaiting Niome's return, to bring up.

'Can I speak with you in private?' asked Kchalami.

Niome led Kchalami to the quiet garden. 'I have perceived through my magic that a calamity befell Firlan. Your father hinted at such when we spoke, mentioning an obscure attack.'

Niome sat down on the stone bench she used while meditating and Kchalami sat down beside her.

'Tell me everything that happened.'

'It occurred a few years after you'd been to Mork,' started Kchalami. 'The Morkans came to Firlan and we were prepared to fight them, but they didn't attack us. They shot a caltrop into the air, very high. It went past the trees and over the fortress walls. It exploded, and a fine mist fell from it.' Kchalami bowed his head. 'It poisoned us.'

'That's why your father had deep concern in his eyes while I was there,' said Niome. 'If this poison was made from a plant, then it's possible it was one that affected only polcs, and the fauna and flora remain unpoisoned.'

'That is our assessment as well. The magic of this caltrop was so great, the mist lingered for many days. We were all exposed to it.' Kchalami stared ahead. 'There's nothing left of it now. Anyone, like you, could visit Firlan and not breathe it in. We knew this, for the poison had a particular smell.' He turned his head to Niome. 'Did you smell anything unusual when you were in Firlan?'

'No. Nothing at all.'

'Then you are free of infection,' concluded Kchalami.

'Mirauk tried to eliminate you, but obviously you've since found a way to fight it.' Kchalami averted her gaze. 'Right? You've found a cure?'

'No. That is why I needed to tell you about it.'

'Why didn't you tell me when you came to Teloria?!' exclaimed Niome. 'I thought you wanted more knowledge on it, and that was all. I didn't realise no cure had been developed!'

'I was still in denial,' admitted Kchalami. 'Besides, you had enough worries, with Tharguen imprisoned in Dûnelor—'

'Kchalami, that doesn't matter. Just because there were untoward circumstances to deal with then doesn't make you or your family any less important than anyone else. I may have a lot on my mind, but it comes with being the Great Wizardess. If Firlan is in danger, then I can help at any time. You must tell me as soon as possible of such things!' She sighed, smiling at him in sympathy.

Kchalami smiled back tenderly. 'That is why you are so dear to me, Niome.'

Niome placed her hand on Kchalami's and squeezed gently. 'I will find a cure, I promise. This must be a slow-progressing poison. I'm certain once I find the name of the poison used, and with enough research, I can find an antidote to counter it.'

'That's not all,' said Kchalami. 'My father has many family secrets, spells that keep Firlan protected. To pass them on, he has to conduct what we call a meditation-bind.'

'I have done those with Maria. That's how bits and pieces of my memory returned.'

'Then you know how to do them?' Kchalami perked up. 'Because of the poison, my father has lost his ability to meditate. Perhaps you can read his mind and perform the meditation on me.'

'Wait. Firnamel can't meditate?'

'Some of us are losing other abilities. I believe the poison has affected our minds.'

'What about you?'

'We all have been affected – we know it – but many like me have not yet suffered symptoms.' Kchalami's eyes glistened. 'I'm frightened, Niome. I don't want my father dying until I know all the secrets. Normally, the King of Firlan passes them on when the receiver is ready. He told me I was going to be the next one to know them. Though, I am not ready yet, but . . . he's dying. We all are, slowly, and if nothing is done, all Firlanians will eventually wither away or destroy each other.

'Some of us have already turned against each other and needed some confinement to realise it stemmed from the curse, not their true thoughts. It has evidently been difficult for some, and many others like me do not know when the symptoms will hit or how it will affect us.'

'Now I understand why everyone in Firlan was so nervous when we fought the Morkan army that had been sent after Jimmy and Meysah,' said Niome. She placed her hand on Kchalami's shoulder, determination in her voice. 'Kchalami, I won't let this kill you. I *will* find the antidote.'

'Only you have the power to help my father meditate and to cure him and all other Firlanians. I don't intend on dying before fighting Mork during the final war.' Kchalami attempted a wan smile. 'I've tried searching for a healing herb, but we don't have complete records in Firlan.'

'You will not die before your time is up,' Niome asserted, repeating her reassurances. 'I'll find that cure. You just keep believing and fighting in the meantime.'

'Thank you.'

'Indeed, I have the lives of many in this world in my hands. Mirauk thinks it so simple. It is not, and he'll see that soon enough.' Niome sat straighter, speaking quickly. 'He's losing power. If he infected you all then – and now, on this first day of the sixth week of Summer, you are all still alive – it's because his poison is not as effective as it could have been many years ago. He needs poisons and phantoms and grand armies; he can't stand alone against millions of polcs. Without them, he risks being reduced to nothing. He knows if an army attacked him and did not care to die from his curse, there is a chance he could be slain. It will be a long fight between me and him, but well worth it in the end.'

Niome paused, taking a deep breath in. Kchalami was smiling in amusement.

'Sorry, I didn't mean to go off on a tangent. You just made me realise quite a few things, Kchalami. You've inspired me.'

'I'm glad of it, then,' said Kchalami. He sobered. 'But Niome, this poison surely comes from a rare kind of plant. If so, the cure will be just as rare. How will you find out what Mirauk used?'

Niome smirked. 'I have my ways.'

The conversation was left at that.

Afterwards, Kchalami contemplated what had been discussed. He observed his reflection in the mirror, almost as though waiting for something in his being, in his face – for something to change, for symptoms to appear. He stared long and hard, searching deep inside himself, trying to find the courage and faith he had once had long ago. He was afraid he'd find death sooner than he was ready for.

You used to have such ambition, such courage, he thought to himself. *What happened to change it all? You have no nightmares, no injuries or major scars. You cannot find any symptoms that indicate you are for certain infected. Mirauk is trying to poison your mind . . .*

He paused.

'That's it!' he shouted aloud. 'That's my symptom! My *mind* is being poisoned.'

He ran to find Niome and told her right away.

'I feel so much better just knowing what's been plaguing me,' sighed Kchalami. 'That would explain why I thought myself so much less a priority than others.'

'The poison,' said Niome, 'affects not one's mind, but their spirits. Your father's ability to meditate, your courage and faith, others' state of mind are confused . . . this is dirty magic. A very dark kind of magic. Few have ever experimented with it, and most who did – Morkans. To try to turn others to evil ways against their conscious free will . . . it's a very slow process, but if it works, Firlan will turn against Teloria.'

Niome shook her head. 'That is why the war against Mirauk is the war for the Freedom of Life. Freedom to think and feel our own way, not *his* way.' A thought occurred to Niome, and a smirk curled up the side of her mouth. 'Mirauk thinks he can infect people's minds and spirits, hm? What would happen if someone were to meddle with *his* mind?'

'I've inspired you again?' asked Kchalami.

Niome's eyes brightened. 'I have an excellent idea.'

'You must tell me.'

'Sorry. It's secret, only for the Star to know. But I think I can pull it off.'

Niome stood. 'Kchalami, there's no need for you to worry anymore. There was evil in the air, we all sensed it, and it's about to disappear.'

CHAPTER TWENTY-THREE:
Meditative Progress

Through further meditation, Niom discovered that Mirauk somehow knew specific things related to progress occurring in Teloria. She got the impression there was a spy in their midst.

Niome informed the other four of her conversation with Kchalami and what she had realised from their chat.

'Let me get this straight,' began Vigh, 'you wish to communicate to Mirauk telepathically through these meditations? That may be dangerous.' His concern was evident.

'Not if I do it while he's meditating,' explained Niome. 'I can have more control then, and he won't be able to communicate with me outside of these meditations, nor of his own accord.'

'I am uncertain this is a good idea,' voiced Boreth. 'You would be putting yourself in a vulnerable situation and walking a fine line between the will of good and taking Mirauk's free will away. Even if he is our enemy, I would hate to see you become tainted by the desire to control another.'

'I understand your concerns,' said Niome. 'I promise to maintain control over myself as well. As for my vulnerability, I am prepared to take that risk.'

'Prepared to sacrifice your own life?! Your own mental well-being?' demanded Boreth.

'Yes!' insisted Niome. 'Mirauk won't get to me. This is to save the lives of our friends. How else am I supposed to find out what he used?'

Boreth let out a slow breath through his nose.

'How will you know when Mirauk's meditating?' inquired Jimmy.

'Through meditation,' replied Niome.

'I don't agree with this at all,' murmured Boreth.

'I could've very well not told you anything of it and gone through with it without your knowing,' retorted Niome. 'I wanted you to know. We are a team, we are five, but sometimes we each have to make decisions on our own.'

'*I* think it's a good idea,' expressed Jimmy.

'I'm still going through with this,' Niome asserted, acknowledging Jimmy's support. 'No one's opinion will change my mind.'

'It's true, the lives of our friends are at stake,' admitted Vigh. 'And if the curse completes its progress before a cure is found, they will become our enemies . . .' Vigh gave Boreth a pointed stare. 'Against their free will,' he emphasised. 'I don't want to be forced to kill one who was once a friend.'

'But Niome, you're putting your *life* at risk!' insisted Boreth.

'When I face Mirauk in the final battle, I will be then, too.'

'The five of us have been putting our lives at risk since day one, Master,' Jimmy said pointedly.

'Jimmy's right,' Meysah chimed in. 'Boreth, you're a Master and a Lord – one who teaches how to remain *level-headed*.' He widened his eyes for further emphasis in support of his friend.

Boreth's gaze remained fixed on his pupil. 'Jimmy, perhaps you don't quite understand my concerns. If Niome does this, Mirauk might have access to *her* thoughts and everything she knows and can do. He might be able to enter her mind at will or poison her mind, for all we know.'

'He won't,' insisted Niome.

'Boreth, don't you trust her?' said Jimmy. 'It's Niome! The most powerful! Hello! Why can't you separate from your fears?'

'Jimmy, you're out of line!' spat Boreth.

Jimmy was not deterred. 'You're too proud to admit that you're afraid to lose Niome right after getting her back. I know you get like that when you fear for those you love. I love Niome as if she were my own sister, but I believe in her power.' Jimmy's tone became more reassuring. 'Boreth, it's not like she's putting herself in the centre of a battlefield alone against the enemy.'

'What did I say, Jimmy?' Boreth glared at the younger knight.

'He's right, Boreth,' said Vigh. 'You're overreacting!'

'I'm not overreacting! This is dangerous!'

'But he's right.' Vigh's tone was gentle. 'This is necessary.'

'A necessary evil?' Boreth asked through his teeth. He turned his gaze from Vigh back to Jimmy. 'And if I am your master, does that not mean you must know your place?'

Vigh and Meysah exchanged a glance, letting out a silent hoot as Jimmy pressed his lips into a thin line.

'Boreth,' said Niome, uncertain how to make him see the importance of this decision. 'I understand you're afraid to lose me again – that if this is the end of me, it is the end of us all, the end of the Five, and then Mirauk wins. You need to believe. I *need* you to believe in me. I'm doing this, and it will work.' She sighed. 'I don't know anymore why I spoke to you about it.'

'Because you respect us and would like to have our support,' answered Meysah. 'Because we're the Five.'

'For the Freedom of Life, eh?' said Niome, looking at her brother.

'I don't think this is the only solution, nor the best one,' insisted Boreth.

Jimmy threw his hands up in defeat. 'You discourage me.'

Boreth narrowed his eyes at Jimmy. 'Can I ask you to remain silent? . . . My pupil?'

'Yes, Master,' Jimmy muttered between his teeth.

'I have nothing more to say,' sighed Niome. 'I just think it's ridiculous for us to argue like this, after everything we've been through.'

'Everything we've been through is precisely the reason why I feel the way I do,' Boreth countered. He stood, starting for the door.

'Boreth! None of us will be harmed,' Niome insisted. 'We've been through the worst. From here, things are going to get better.'

'Get better?' said Boreth, voice low. 'You call a war getting bet—'

'Boreth,' Vigh warned. 'Take time to breathe, my friend. Think, how would Clahria feel about this? Feel the magic. Can you sense it?'

Hand on the ajar door, Boreth took a moment, bowing his head. 'I'm sorry. You're right . . . I worry. I'm terrified. This *could* be the end of us, the end of the Five. It's not that I fear for my life – I fear for the future I want to give Clahria, the happiness I have promised her.'

'Niome has this gift for a reason,' said Meysah. 'We need to let her use it. And we need to trust that she will use it wisely.'

Boreth took another moment before nodding, his eyes softening and meeting Niome's.

Vigh walked over to his friend and put his hand on Boreth's shoulder, squeezing gently, hoping to convey reassurance.

The Five parted ways. Boreth caught Jimmy's arm.

'Jimmy,' he began. 'I'm sorry I snapped at you.'

'That's all right, Master. I'm sorry I tried to jolt you. I just wanted to snap you out of whatever fear was gripping you.'

'Consuming me,' admitted Boreth.

'You teach me a lot,' Jimmy reminded him.

'You, too,' Boreth said with a wan smile, draping an arm over the polc's shoulder in a sideways hug. 'Good night, Jimmy.'

'Good night, Boreth.'

Niome reckoned the cure she would find would benefit all polcs. If Mirauk could create such a poison to attack Firlan, he could do so to attack anyone who stood against him.

Niome's meditation led to discovering that Kàtchah believed the Five invincible – not unlike they thought him undefeatable.

Mirauk wished to send twice as many armies to Dalvar. This could bode ill, for it could mean their secrets getting discovered, with that many more Morkans attacking to manage. If Teloria was to help Dalvar, the best scenario would be to send someone who knew how the Morkans worked and patrolled. That polc was Tharguen. He and his small army would be the boon the Dalvarans needed.

As for Bahvley, Niome needed him by her side once the Five returned home, and now more than ever.

Through the meditations, Elina's reassurances had also been proven. Mirauk didn't know more about the Pleessies than he should. He knew nothing of the Old

Grey Houses, nor of the Dalvaran secrets. He had not known that people dwelt in the Twisted Forest until his armies explored it.

An interesting phenomenon occurred when the phantom took Niome's memories: it lost much that it had gained from the Tellens and Firlanians whose blood it had taken. Though how the other phantoms were destroyed, the phantom retained, for that was its own experience. This phantom was indeed the very one who had gotten Bahvley. Its sole purpose had been to hunt for the Fairhaven blood – blood filled with magic Mirauk was intent on destroying.

Mirauk mused about the Kikies, wanting to explore the ocean to find their lands. He wished he had killed Bahvley when the polc had stood before him.

At least the Fairhavens exist now and not before Malgar was alive, Mirauk thought, *or worse, during my grandfather's reign. I will always be pleased with the choices I made before Malgar's death. My grandfather was a weak Morkan. I did well. It gives Mork an advantage, for we are stronger than we were before, strong enough for our enemies. I'm the strongest – no one can defeat me. I'm the strongest.*

Niome, however, knew she and the others were meant to exist now, not before. Mirauk's rivalry with Malgar puzzled her, yet it made her realise the importance of helping her brothers develop their magic to a higher proficiency so Bahvley and Meysah could execute spells if the need arose.

All these perceived thoughts were from Mirauk's musings, and for many weeks Niome meditated when she had the time and energy to put her full focus on Mirauk. Still, she did not know when Mirauk would meditate, and she required him to be in a meditative state to enact her plan.

Niome exchanged recipes for potions with the Tellens and shared many secrets of medicine lore. She taught them spells, unlocking many of their hidden proficiencies through practice.

For the rest of the Summer and well into the new year, Niome shared her wisdom, showing the Tellens how to become masters of their own craft and intuition.

Finally, she discovered Mirauk's sporadic meditation schedule – every six days – and prepared accordingly.

Meditating only every sixth day is not enough for someone who hopes to gain power over the world, Niome thought. Either Mirauk was getting cocky, or he was preparing something major that occupied the rest of his time. Niome hoped for the former.

Krystal and Elmezni found Meysah alone, sitting and pondering, a forlorn look on his face. They sidled up beside him, taking a seat.

'What's on your mind?' Krystal asked, prompting Meysah.

'Does it ever happen to you to sit and think?' Meysah asked curiously.

'Sometimes,' replied Elmezni. 'Why, are you feeling down?'

'It was just thinking of all that has happened in my life. Of Ihal.'

Elmezni and Krystal nodded knowingly.

'I'm certain she thinks of you just as much,' said Krystal.

'I wonder sometimes,' admitted Meysah. 'I was not yet mature or appreciative of her when we met. So much time has passed since then. I'll understand if she's chosen . . . someone else. And if she's waiting for me, you can be sure I'll know how to be grateful to her when I get home.'

'When you say "someone else," you mean Lóim, don't you?' deduced Elmezni. He nudged Meysah with his shoulder. 'I think you'll find that he respects you more than he lets on.'

Meysah perked up. 'He does?' He worked his jaw. 'You know, if I'm honest, I think I've grown quite fond of him. I would hate for a petty rivalry to stand between us.'

'I think he cares more than you know,' said Elmezni. 'He told me so.'

Meysah smiled. 'It's strange, the way I feel about him now, compared to before. He used to bully me, always with the verbal assaults.' He let out a chuckle. 'Once you get to know him, though, he's not so bad. He's changed – something changed him.'

At that, Meysah sobered. 'And I know he cares about and respects Ihal. I want her to choose to remain faithful to me, but if Lóim is fated to be with her . . .' Meysah shook his head, frowning. 'Never mind that thought. I am filled with a strange sense of jealousy.'

Krystal laughed, nudging Meysah with her shoulder. 'You've changed, too, though. Grown wiser. You almost look like Bahvley now. We can barely tell the difference between the two of you!'

Meysah let out a short laugh.

'You inspire us, you know,' said Elmezni. 'We want you to know we appreciate your friendship.' Elmezni and Krystal exchanged a glance. 'Should anything happen . . .' He hesitated.

'I know,' said Meysah. 'I appreciate you, too. And . . . I know about the poison. Niome will find a cure for it.'

Elmezni chewed his lip. 'We're frightened. It's been a while since we spoke of it with Kchalami, but we know it's eating away at him, too.'

Meysah wrapped an arm around each of them. 'No matter what happens, I'll never forget your friendship.'

'Even if we try to kill you?' muttered Krystal.

'As if you'd succeed,' Meysah boasted teasingly. Krystal hissed and the three of them laughed, shoving each other playfully.

Niome found Meysah and beckoned him with urgency. Shrugging, Meysah left the Firlanian siblings to follow his own.

Niome led Meysah to Vigh's room, where Boreth and Jimmy were waiting with the Lord.

'What's this about?' asked Meysah.

'I'm going to meditate now, and I'm going to communicate with Mirauk for the first time,' Niome announced.

'Are you nervous?' asked Jimmy.

'It's been almost eleven years since I saw or spoke to him last,' she answered. 'What do *you* think?'

'Yeah, your first encounter with him was rather . . . torturous, considering he, well, tortured you with his mind and all.'

'Niome,' began Boreth, 'if ever you feel – how should I say it? – that things are not going as planned, stop the meditation right away. Please be careful.'

'I will.'

Niome proceeded to the gardens and began her meditation. When she connected herself to Mirauk, she sensed him right away.

Mirauk started his meditation.

So much boggles my mind, he began.

You should try clearing it, suggested Niome through her thoughts.

Who's there? Mirauk demanded, his voice frantic.

No one is in the room with you, Mirauk.

I don't understand.

Isn't it funny how you hear a voice and automatically assume someone is in the room with you?

Now, I am no fool, Niome Fairhaven, but how are you doing this?!

Hello, Mirauk. Niome allowed herself a satisfied smile. *I'm glad you can sense me and recognise me. I must have left quite an impression on you when last we met. Or should I say, when you connected your mind to mine. Are you so surprised I'm still alive? I must admit, your phantom was rather persistent. Be that as it may, just as you could not, it couldn't contain all of what I know.*

So I'm told. Mirauk sighed gutturally. *If your purpose was to enrage me, consider yourself on the right path.*

I don't wish to upset you, Mirauk. Niome genuinely felt that. Her goal was to find out what poison he used, and that was it.

Then what do you want? he demanded.

Your cooperation. That is all.

I'm not telling you anything, Mirauk growled. *I'm terminating this communication.*

Niome fought to keep Mirauk in meditation. She was uncertain how she was able to do it, but with effort, she kept their minds linked. Mirauk fought hard against her.

Why can't I break this connection?! shouted Mirauk.

I don't want to have to do this either, Mirauk. But there are things I must know.

Over my frigid corpse. By kurssus, you won't! Mirauk seethed. *You can try to get me to divulge my secrets – you will fail. Good luck trying to communicate with me again.*

I will speak *with you again. You* know *I've grown more powerful, and the more obstacles you throw my way, the more strength I shall gain.*

Oh, how I loathe you, Niome, and all Fairhavens!

Mirauk fought his way out of the meditation bond. Too spent to hold him, Niome fell to the ground.

Derfbøk was helping her to her feet before her mind registered she had heard running footsteps in the garden.

'Where did you come from?' Niome asked, taking hold of the Tellen as he lifted her up.

'I was passing and saw you fall,' replied Derfbøk. His brows furrowed. 'Are you all right?'

'I'm relatively okay. I tried something that used up my strength.' Niome dusted herself off. 'The more I do it, the stronger I'll get.'

Derfbøk pointed behind him. 'Do you want me to get the other four?'

'I know where to find them.' Niome realised she felt a little weak. 'Can you help me there?'

'Of course.'

Derfbøk put one arm over Niome's shoulder and she did the same to him. Slowly, he helped her to Vigh's room. Niome felt like Elina looked when she had been ill with Mirauk's curse.

'She's drained,' explained Derfbøk, helping Niome sit on the bed once they reached the room.

Niome thanked her Tellen friend, who dismissed himself as Vigh offered Niome some water.

'What happened?' asked Boreth, his voice equal parts concern and scolding.

'It didn't go as well as I thought. Mirauk is very stubborn.'

'To be expected,' muttered Meysah.

'The more I do this, the stronger I'll get.'

'How many times do you think you'll have to taunt him before he responds in our favour?' asked Jimmy.

'I don't know,' replied Niome. 'Perhaps enough times to practice and get strong for the time I truly need this gift for.'

'Then you have no choice but to get stronger,' said Meysah.

'This kind of communication takes a lot of energy, especially when one is fighting to break the link and the other is fighting to keep it. I think next time, I'll have a big meal before,' laughed Niome. She rubbed her forehead. 'Mind battles.'

'And wait a while to digest,' suggested Meysah. 'You don't want cramps from working your body too much! Take it from the stomachache expert.'

The two siblings exchanged a warm smile.

Niome dropped her shoulders. 'He didn't even let me ask him about the poison mist.'

'He may next time,' said Vigh. 'If he understands that you'll leave him alone when he does, perhaps he'll cooperate.'

Niome finished the water.

'Feeling better?' asked Jimmy.

'Much!' replied Niome. 'I suppose for a first time, it went rather well. I didn't expect that much resistance on my part. And I certainly didn't anticipate it would last that long, though I had suspected my abilities were better now.'

'Well, if this is better,' began Meysah, 'it's going to be a celebration when we get home.'

'Well, it will be, even if it's difficult!' said Jimmy. 'People will be so happy that we're back, they'll *want* to celebrate.'

Meysah shot Jimmy a look. The others chuckled.

Niome let the week go by and prepared herself accordingly for her next session of mind battling with Mirauk.

That day, she installed herself comfortably. When she connected her mind to Mirauk, he was in meditation already.

Started early today? sent Niome.

Mirauk seethed Niome's name slowly and gutturally. *Niome.*

That's me. I have returned, as promised.

Mirauk hissed a tisk. *I already told you my answer.*

But you didn't let me tell you what it was I needed from you.

Fine. You want to waste my time, I'll waste yours.

Mirauk attempted to break the meditation bond. Niome kept him linked.

How do you do this?

That's my secret, Mirauk. I have many.

I see your pattern, Niome. I'm not stupid. You link yourself to my thoughts while I meditate. Well, you won't be able to anymore. I'll change my schedule, and you won't figure me out that easily. Goodbye!

Mirauk again tried to break the bond, but Niome was even more resistant. It was more of a struggle than the last time for both of them; Niome could hear Mirauk's straining breath, and she was breathing heavily as well.

The more you resist, the stronger I resist, asserted Niome.

What do you want from me?! demanded Mirauk.

Finally, progress – in Niome's opinion. She went straight to the point.

I want you to tell me what plant you made the poisonous mist from that you released over Firlan.

What, you think I'll tell you my secret potion recipe? Keep fantasising.

Tell me! Niome's tone was firm. *What did you make the poisonous mist from?*

I'll never tell you! growled Mirauk.

Mirauk pushed hard to break the bond. Niome resisted again. Sweat dripped from her brow and down her face, so strenuous were her efforts.

As time stretched on, long did Mirauk and Niome duel this way.

Mirauk at last relented.

Niome, he demanded, no longer actively resisting. *Release me.*

No!

Mirauk laughed mirthlessly. *You do not realise what you resemble through this ability of yours.*

Are you suggesting I am becoming like you? Niome asked, curious as to his train of thought.

I am suggesting there are gaps in recorded history that if you could decipher, you would fear this ability that you possess.

And yet you abstain from explaining further.

Mirauk sighed. *Perhaps someday we will be able to discuss it, but today is not that day. Now, I demand you to—*

No! Niome's response was quick and dry.

Please!

The tone gave Niome pause. *Are you begging me?*

I tire of this. Just do it!

Not until you tell me what I need to know!

I will not.

If you tell me, I will never bother you like this again, ever. I promise.

How can I trust you, Niome Fairhaven?

Because I'm not you!

Mirauk yelled in anger and fought against Niome again. This time, he succeeded in breaking the bond.

Niome opened her eyes and fell into Boreth's arms – he was crouched before her.

'You hung in there quite a bit,' he said.

'How long have you been here?' asked Niome.

'Almost as long as you've been meditating. I wanted to make sure all was okay. It was the least I could do, and this.' He held up a glass of water. Niome smiled and drank it all. 'I think someone was thirsty.'

Niome let out a laugh, wiping her sweaty brow. 'He's going to change his day of meditation, but I can listen in like I did before and find a way to connect to him again.'

'Did you ask him?' inquired Boreth.

'Yes. He didn't want to tell me.'

'He will eventually . . . I hope.'

'Once this is all over with, I won't have to fight him like this. I won't need to communicate with him any-more. It'll be a relief.'

'Will you still listen in?' asked Boreth, helping Niome to sit straighter.

'It is my duty now to listen in from time to time – for Teloria. It isn't for nothing that I have this gift. I don't want to do it all the time, but this ability came to me, and I intend to find out why. There's something great that I'm going to discover through this ability, something more than a plant, and I sure am going to find out what it is.'

Niome stretched out her arms, looking at her hands. '*Mirauk* gave me this gift. Some of the powers I have are due to what he put me through when I encountered him in Mork. Perhaps I should thank him,' she added with a wan smile.

Eager was she to speak again with her rival, for she was more eager to heal her friends. The Firlanians knew not of the meditation bond Niome was attempting with Mirauk, but trusted in her abilities to find their cure.

The Firlanians were perhaps Teloria's most faithful allies, and that was why Mirauk had targeted them thus.

'I would rather die than turn on my allies and friends,' Kchalami vowed to Niome. 'If ever the un-thinkable happens, do what you must.'

Instead, Niome assured him it would not come to that. That was *her* promise to him.

When Niome discovered Mirauk's new meditation schedule, she was ready for more telepathy duelling.

I'm back, once again, as promised. See, Mirauk, I keep my word.

How do you— He paused, sighing gutturally.

I told you I had grown in power.

I am uncertain whether I am more angered or impressed. Mirauk chuckled mirthlessly. *I'll change my schedule again.*

Mirauk immediately began to fight his way out of the bond. After a relentless mind battle, Niome let Mirauk go.

Don't think I won't return, Mirauk. I'll talk to you soon.

Now wait here, Niome Fairhaven. I have a few questions of my own.

Niome had already disconnected from Mirauk and was too exhausted to reconnect. Even so, she did not falter, as her strength had grown.

Mirauk now meditated at random, no longer holding any set schedule. A master of magic as he was, Niome knew he needed those meditations to grow in power, lest his age catch up to him, and through her diligent efforts, Niome found him once more.

Did you think you could get rid of me that easily? Niome chided him. *Did you think you could get rid of me at all?*

Mirauk didn't respond.

I just need you to answer that one question.

Still, he gave no response.

Niome sighed. *There's no point in giving me the silent treatment. It's childish. Nor is there any point pretending you're not there. You'll wait, then try to get out of the meditation, and I'll fight you – and we both know what the result of that will be.*

Pause.

Niome sighed, then droned on. *What discourages me is that you expect me to do things as you plan them. You wanted me to give you the Complement Book, you wanted me to give up Tharguen to you, you wanted me to lose my memory. I did do a few things for you – I gave you reason not to trust the Dûnelorians. I gave you information about Teloria. The least you could do is give me* one *piece of information.*

What I don't understand is how you can possibly find me!

Good morning! Niome enthused, genuinely happy to hear Mirauk's voice in her mind.

Why do you keep returning? Mirauk sounded exasperated.

Because I need you to tell me the name of the plant you used to create the poison mist that has infected the Firlanians.

Mirauk hissed. *What guarantee do I have that you are not going to send some of that same poison mist to Mork and infect Mork with it?*

I give you my word, Mirauk, that's not my purpose for it.

Do you swear it? Because I *swear, if you do send it to Mork, I will crush Teloria in an instant. I will send every demon and plague possible, even if that means losing . . . that part of the world.*

What do you mean? You have not destroyed Teloria like you say you can thus far.

If I destroy Teloria by poisons, it will make it uninhabitable for Morkans, but it will be worth it, for I'll have destroyed you. I've destroyed before, to the point of disintegrating one of my own islands. I swear to you, I'll do it again. I would rather not, for Teloria's soil has many minerals and metals that I want – poison is but a last resort if nothing else works. However . . . Mirauk paused after a downward inflection, and Niome's anxiety rose. *If you are lying to me and you send poisonous mist to Mork,*

I'm warning you now, I will not hesitate to slaughter your kingdom, and everyone will suffer a slow and painful death. So, I ask again: Do you swear it?

Niome swallowed hard. *I swear it upon Tharguen's life.*

There was a pause.

I suppose that was sincere. He chuckled sinisterly. *How easily you are fooled. I'm not telling you anything.*

But you said you would! Niome pleaded.

I lied.

I defy you, Mirauk!

Mirauk laughed hideously. *What is your secret for finding me?*

I have my ways, Niome disdained.

I believe it was merely pure chance. Let's see if you can impress me!

Niome was too upset to fight Mirauk, her hold on him weakened now.

The Wizardess was puzzled, though. Teloria's soil couldn't possibly be what Mirauk was avoiding destroying. There was something else there – Mirauk's tone and brief pause had indicated that much – but Niome's mind was too bogged down by emotions to contemplate the possibilities further.

'He is insidious!' she complained to herself.

By pure chance did Niome catch Mirauk meditating the following day. Yet Niome knew, deep down, this wasn't pure chance.

Niome spoke as though they were children. *Are you still upset with me, Mirauk? I'm not upset at you, at least not anymore. I just need you to tell me the name of the plant, and I'll leave you alone.* She paused. *I promise!*

Already? I can't get rid of you.

Tell me the name of the plant! Niome was firm.

Mirauk screamed his rage aloud, and it echoed throughout his tower – Niome perceived the echo through his mind. *And you'll leave me alone?*

I swear it upon Tharguen's life!

There was a brief pause. *Fine!* Canétal. *Now leave my mind!*

Thank you! Niome sighed her response, tears filling her eyes in relief.

Quickly, her excitement took over. She immediately released Mirauk from her hold and left to write down the name of the plant.

Niome prayed to the stars that Mirauk had told her the truth. Yet, when she began searching for known poisons, she found it not.

'What do you mean it's a nonexistent poison?' asked Stëinbøk when Niome returned from the Tellen library archives.

'It's not in the list of poisons,' said Niome. 'I need all your books on medicinal herbs and plants. Any herb used to an abusive amount can be deadly, even the ones most commonly used for the most common potions and poultices.'

'Of course, whatever you need for your research. Who told you about this plant?' inquired Stëinbøk.

'Mirauk.'

Stëinbøk gaped at Niome. 'When did you have time to speak to Mirauk?'

Niome briefly explained how she acquired this information. 'Now, I need to know all the properties about *Canétal* to know how to counter it with a plant that has the same properties.'

'I see.' Stëinbøk kept a scrutinizing gaze on Niome, though his smile showed amusement. 'Niome, you never cease to surprise me. If you want to know everything, I suggest you speak with Hanorlenk.'

Niome did just that.

'What can I do for you, Niome?' asked Hanorlenk.

'I need all the information you have on a rare herb called *Canétal.*'

Hanorlenk took the necessary books out, and together they read its properties.

'Rare, indeed, is this *Canétal,*' said Hanorlenk.

Niome grabbed her notebook, ready to transcribe the necessary information.

Canétal was described as a low-growing plant, fairly large with deep-blue flowers and bright-green leaves. In the flower centre, a tint of purple could be found.

'I've only seen one other deep-blue flower in my books, and it came from Mork – the Morkan dandelion.'

'If *Canétal* is medicinal, I must find a flower that could be poisonous,' said Niome. 'I must find its complete opposite. Something just as rare, perhaps.'

Canétal was said to be found at the very top of Darakön, between the 173rd day of the year and the 192nd.

"'It was discovered in the first generation of Kaulchèc History by a Kaulchèc Wizard named Canétal,'" read Hanorlenk. 'Hence the name of this medicinal herb.'

Hanorlenk continued reading, revealing this plant was not found anywhere else in the Great Ocean or Colama valleys, nor at any other time of year.

'Mirauk used this?' Hanorlenk let out a low whistle.

'He must've sent his bravest polcs to retrieve it,' said Niome. 'Morkans are afraid of Darakön. Whether Mirauk has replanted some to grow in Mork or not, he had to send polcs there in the first place.'

'He surely made a heavy dose. Listen to this: "Used in small amounts will cure headaches, will help with inspiration and boggled minds, for those who have trouble clearing their minds or with meditation. Good for concentration and memory, will help with sleep, focus, and will help with the development of mind abilities. But beware, *Canétal* oils must be extracted when this flower is in full bloom and taken once only, in a small dose diluted in water. Taken to excess or in large non-diluted quantities may cause opposite effects, such as drowsiness, inability to meditate or concentrate, discouragement, fear, and rage."' Hanorlenk looked up from the book. 'Is this what you were looking for?'

'Yes!' exclaimed Niome. 'I have everything written down here. I need to find a plant that has the same effects and same countereffects. A herb that has to be taken in the same way.'

'But of opposite appearance?' said Hanorlenk.

'Perhaps. A purple flower with hints of blue in its centre. I need all the information I can get on all the medicinal herbs that are relatively petite and of purple hues. Let's start with that.'

'Wait here, I'll return with me best selection.'

Moments later, Hanorlenk returned with a significant stack of books. 'There's more,' he said.

Several stacks later, he and Niome concluded that should be enough. The Tellen insisted the books remain in the archives, so Niome installed herself at a desk and got to work, poring over the books. Niome read about many plants, their appearances, their properties and countereffects. She jotted down all possible antidotes she could find.

When she wasn't researching rare flowers, Niome was teaching her class to the Tellens or meditating. Seldom now did she connect to Mirauk's thoughts. She did not want to fall into the trap of abusing her newfound ability.

At last, Niome found the cure she sought. Right away, she went to inform the other four.

'I found the match to the *Canétal* plant!' she announced proudly. 'It's called *Ligfulm*.'

'And is *Ligfulm* as rare?' inquired Vigh.

'Yes, but we are in luck, for we have access to it.'

'Is it really the opposite of the other?' asked Meysah.

'It is. When in full bloom, *Ligfulm* is violet and blue in its centre, difficult to spot, apparently. And it has dark-green leaves. *Ligfulm* and *Canétal* are the same size, though.'

'Interesting,' expressed Boreth, rubbing his chin. 'I used to sleep through my herbology classes. I never thought such information would be of such interest to me.' He chuckled.

Niome explained that this plant offered the same properties as the other, used for the same symptoms with similar dosage, yet its effects were opposite.

'Both plants are the same. Just as rare. Opposites in some ways, twinlike in others. And both are in full bloom during the same time of the year.'

'I thought everything about it was going to be the complete opposite,' said Vigh.

'When you're looking for the perfect match for something,' explained Niome, 'you want to look for something that has some properties that are the same, yet some that are different. Something that complements without being identical, so it can complete the other. Two things the same, yet different. And that doesn't just go for plants.'

'That goes for people, too,' Jimmy said wistfully.

'Thinking of Gahli?' asked Meysah.

'Uh . . .' Jimmy shook his head. 'Well, yes.'

'So, we'll have to wait until the end of Spring to go out and find it,' Niome concluded.

'And where do we find it?' asked Vigh.

'That's where we're in luck. It's been under our noses this whole time!' Niome beamed, bouncing back on her heels. 'It grows in the Twisted Forest.'

The others reacted with relief and excitement.

'Where in the forest is not mentioned, so we're going to have to search. That's where you'll be having fun, Boreth. There are many purple flowers, but of its distinct description, only *this one* looks exactly the way it does.'

'Oh, I'll find it. I'll crawl on all fours or even slither like a snake if I have to,' chuckled Boreth. 'It's a low-growing plant, right?'

'Yes.'

'And is it a weed?' inquired the Lord.

'A medicinal herb, just like *Canétal.*' Niome paused, smiling. 'I must inform Kchalami!'

'We'll tell Elmezni and Krystal,' volunteered Jimmy, pointing at himself and Meysah.

'We'll inform the Tellens,' said Vigh.

Thus, they all left to find their friends. Stëinbøk had already heard some of it from Hanorlenk. Word spread quickly of this good news, and the fortress began to stir.

Niome found Kchalami in a quiet corner of the gardens.

'At least I can still meditate,' he said when he saw Niome.

'And when you go home,' said Niome, 'so will your father.'

'Meditate?' said Kchalami, surprised. 'Niome . . . ?'

'I found the cure!'

'You did!' A wave of relief washed over Kchalami, and tears sparkled in his eyes. He passed a hand through his hair. 'I suppose hassling Mirauk telepathically had its benefits.'

'The best part of all is that the plant grows in the Twisted Forest.'

'Niome! This is great news!' Kchalami embraced her tightly. 'So we can get some right away?' he asked as he pulled away.

'We have to wait until they're in season, but that will come soon.' Niome smiled and placed her hand on Kchalami's, squeezing gently. 'I promised you I'd find the cure. I never gave up . . . for you.'

Kchalami sobered, averting his gaze before clasping Niome's hands in his. 'Niome, I'm very grateful towards you for this. I'm endlessly happy and relieved you are alive and returned. I'm overjoyed you found this cure . . .'

He peered deep into her eyes. 'You know you mean a lot to me, Niome, more than I can put into words. Tharguen is a lucky polc to have your love. And I am lucky to have your friendship.' He smiled. 'You will always have my affection.'

The Firlanians were impatient for Spring to arrive, for it meant the *Ligfulm* could be picked and brewed. Niome kept her word to Mirauk and seldom listened in on his thoughts. He had conveyed, during one such incursion, how he trusted Niome would be true to her promise regarding the *Canétal*, for she would not swear on Tharguen's life without meaning it.

On the ninetieth of Spring, equipped with straw baskets and shears, the Five stepped out to search for the *Ligfulm*.

'So others know about your meditation bond with Mirauk, but not that you can hear his thoughts?' inquired Vigh.

'That's correct,' replied Niome as the Five searched the underbrush. 'We don't want word of this ability to reach him.'

'Is it safe to talk about out here?' asked Boreth, glancing about warily, a hand coming to rest on his sword.

'It should be,' replied Niome.

Meysah bent down to gently cup a purple flower too pale to be their quarry. 'Do you know how to prepare this plant for ingestion?'

'They list the instructions in the books,' Niome confirmed.

'Ooh, they're so smart,' said Meysah, moving on to other flowers.

'And what exactly are we looking for?' asked Jimmy, looking at a series of hanging white flowers that rose in vines towards the canopy.

'Violet with a blue centre.' Niome took Jimmy's hand, guiding it towards the underbrush. 'It's low-growing, and the flower is the size of the palm of your hand.'

Jimmy made a face, looking from the canopy to the underbrush. 'And how many insects are we to encounter as we search?'

Meysah laughed, nudging his friend. After the group continued on for a while longer, the polc pointed at a large purple flower, grinning at his friend. 'Purple, not white.'

Smirking mockingly, Jimmy took Meysah's hand as Niome had his and guided it from the bush to the underbrush. 'Low-growing, not in a tree.'

'It's low-growing,' argued Meysah, 'from the trunk!'

'It's too small,' rebutted Jimmy.

'It's a lot bigger than the one *you* pointed at earlier!'

The two Lords laughed, with Vigh snorting in his throat.

The lads realised what their argument sounded like. Both suppressed their laughs before their chuckles won out.

The Five continued onward.

'Over here!' Boreth called out.

He crouched and took a stem in his hand, observing carefully. He cupped the flower.

'Palm of hand size,' he said to himself, though the others could hear. 'Violet, dark leaves. A centre too blue to be purple, yet too purple and matching to be a neutral blue.' He looked up at the others. 'I think this might be it.'

Niome crouched down and verified with her notes and the drawing she had copied.

'This is *Ligfulm*,' she confirmed. 'See how the petals have an indentation on the sides where they overlap with each other?'

'Shall I collect this one, then?' asked Boreth, readying his small shears.

'It is in full bloom.' Niome gave her answer by opening the basket up as Boreth cut the stem and placed the flower inside.

'What about this one?' asked Vigh.

'The centre colour cannot be seen,' said Meysah. 'You should be more observant, Master Vigh.'

'This, coming from the one who thought it grew out of a tree,' Vigh teased.

'Still,' said Niome, 'it isn't in full bloom yet.' She smiled at her former Master while Meysah's grin broadened at his sister taking his side.

The Five went along observing all of the *Ligfulm* flowers they could find and collecting those that were ready. As they moved through the forest, they wound up separating in different directions, always nearby, yet far enough to cover a wider range of the forest floor.

Rustling nearby drew Niome's attention. She took several steps into a tanglement of trees and bushes a little further along, and the rustling persisted. Niome followed until she came to a natural alcove created by low-hanging branches. The susurration echoed around it.

'Show yourself,' Niome commanded.

The sound of many swords unsheathing at once filled the space as a dozen Morkans surrounded Niome from all sides, stepping into the alcove. They stopped a few feet from her, standing on guard, the tips of their swords an arm's length away.

Niome calculated that if she were required to escape, she would have to use her magic to jump to the trees.

From behind the largest of the trees, stepping into the alcove, was one Morkan she recognised immediately. His face was stern, eyes boring intently into hers, and his long black hair fluttered in the warm wind.

Niome swallowed. 'Where is your brother? You do not usually travel alone.'

'This is not alone. I have my guards here.' The Duke paused. 'Garkhktak is waiting for me further down. This was something I needed to do . . . alone.'

'What was something you needed to do alone, Merlik?'

'See it for myself,' he replied, his gaze growing ever intense. 'I would have come straightaway upon learning of your survival, but obligations kept me. I hope you understand. I needed to see if you truly lived.' He paused.

'Rest assured, my guards won't harm you. They are merely ensuring you do not harm me.'

Merlik waved his hand and the Morkan standing directly in front of Niome stepped aside. Merlik stepped closer to Niome, now with no obstacles between them. His weapons were sheathed, his hands by his sides.

Merlik allowed himself a small smile. 'In case you're wondering, we have skills beyond any other for sneaking about. We've been waiting out here for you a good number of days now.'

'Why did you need to come here and see if I was truly alive?'

Merlik's smile widened.

'Wouldn't you just love to know!' he snickered. 'What's wrong, Niome? Do you not like the attention? I'm certain you're the type who enjoys being pursued.'

Merlik took another step closer and put a gloved finger on the side of her chin, pressing tentatively, his expression inscrutable. He then took a step back, signaling the other Morkans, who took a half step towards her to tighten the circle.

'My concerns are for the people of this forest,' Niome said harshly.

'I have not come to fight or attack anyone, only to investigate.' Merlik spread his arms out in surrender.

'Doesn't Mirauk trust his armies to report accurately?' Unsure if the Dukes had been informed of Mirauk's invaded meditations, she decided not to mention it.

'*I* don't trust,' replied Merlik. 'I wanted to see you. I needed to see that it was true.' His tone gave away an earnest emotion.

Niome and Merlik stared at each other for another moment.

'Why did you let me go? At the caves. You let me get away.'

Merlik's eyes never left hers. 'I knew you would get caught by the phantom, which was better than being captured and brought to Mork by us. So, I let the better course take action.'

'Sure it was,' Niome said, unconvinced. 'So, why are you being nice to me now?'

'Courteous. I am merely—'

'You fear me.' Niome took a step towards him, her voice almost a whisper. 'You fear me, and that is why you let me go, in fear of what I might have done to you. Same thing now – in fear of what I might do to you, you are being kind to me.'

'Oh, you have already done many things to me, Niome Fairhaven,' snickered Merlik, 'as you have done to my armies, to Mirauk, and to Mork, as your precious friends have done to my tunnels.'

'They were Kàtchah's tunnels.'

'Oh, no. He commanded them, but they were not his.'

'Anyone who fears me . . .' Niome began, taking another step towards Merlik, who stood his ground. Her voice faltered. 'Would not confront me like this,' she realised. Niome found herself uncomfortably close to Merlik.

She pushed her theory further. 'Your guards would have already bound my hands and immobilised me. But you fear me, do you not? So why have you come?'

'I learned the first time I met you that tying you up is of no use.'

'Still . . .' Confused by Merlik's behaviour, Niome started to doubt herself. 'I can see it in your eyes, your fear,' she insisted. She would not accept it could be anything but that. 'So, why have you come? Why have you risked—'

'To deliver this.'

Merlik produced an emblem from his satchel. It was the Sign of Twelve that Bahvley's team had carried when they went to Mork. The twelve-segmented leaf carved out of wood still had its authentic engravings on it.

'Mirauk sends it.'

'Mirauk?' Niome had not heard his thoughts on the matter. She felt certain she knew everything Mirauk had been planning, yet this took her by surprise.

'Yes. Give this to your King. I'm sure he'll appreciate it,' said Merlik, handing the icon to her. 'It belonged to the one whom we thought to be him.' Niome glanced down at it. 'Oh' – Merlik's wicked grin returned – 'don't forget to read the message we left on it.'

Niome flipped the leaf over. Newly engraved on its surface were the words: *Perhaps you fooled us then, but next time, it will be* you *we shall kill, for real and for good.* Signed: *Mirauk.*

'What kind of a sick joke *is* this? What is he playing at?'

Merlik smiled again. He held Niome's gaze a moment longer than was comfortable to her.

'I don't fear you, Niome.' He leaned forward, seething in her face. 'I *loathe* you . . . for the way you make me feel about you.'

Niome's breath caught in her throat, and her pulse quickened. The admission left her feeling bereft. Merlik's gaze never left hers.

Niome shook her head quickly. 'I cannot and do not feel for you what you feel for me, Merlik.' Niome reckoned if he were Telorian she might fancy him, for his features were handsome, yet the evil in his eyes made her chest clench.

Merlik narrowed his eyes, removing a glove. He grazed Niome's face with the back of his fingers. 'You are a peculiar one, Niome Fiarhaven. With my reputation, I could have any woman I desired, and yet you are the one to enchant me. So many grovel at my feet, vying for my attention, and yet you squander the opportunity to become the Lady of the Duke of Mork.'

Niome took a moment to steady her quickened breath and let her magic guide her as she met Merlik's gaze. Her eyes darted up to the canopy.

'You can come down from that tree, Garkhktak. You do not have a good shot from there. Besides, I will not attack your brother, nor his guards. You no longer need to pretend you are "elsewhere".'

Merlik scowled as Garkhktak jumped down to stand beside his brother. 'How did you know?' demanded Merlik, wonder and fear in his voice as his eyes searched hers.

'Tell Mirauk there will *be* no next time. He will not have a chance to kill Bahvley.'

'Then maybe he will have a chance to kill Tharguen!' Merlik declared wrathfully, closing the distance between them, his body flush with hers.

'Come, brother,' Garkhktak cautioned. 'We gave her Mirauk's message. Now let's go, before I am tempted to kill her.'

His jaw clenched, Merlik took a step back from Niome, staring at her for a moment more before he and his twin turned and began to walk away.

The Morkan guards retreated from their positions, sheathed their weapons, and followed the Dukes.

'Tell me why I should not kill you both right here and now!' Niome called, her anger winning out.

'Because,' snapped Merlik, spinning around and marching back as close as he had been before, his eyes peering deep into hers, 'if we do not return to Mork, Mirauk will come here himself and curse every single living soul in Teloria.' His breath was hot on Niome's face. 'I don't think you want to condemn your friends to death, now, do you?'

Niome said nothing.

'Consider yourself fortunate Mirauk wants you alive,' hissed Garkhtkak, glancing back. 'At least for now.'

'No,' said Merlik, making sure there was not an inch of space between them. 'Consider yourself fortunate that *I* want you alive.' He cupped her face. When he spoke again, it was through his teeth. 'I cannot put into words what it is you do to me, Niome Fairhaven. But it has protected you from Mirauk's wrath.'

Niome took that in. Internally, she allowed an ounce of gratitude towards Merlik, in that case.

'No matter what you do or say, it will never counter the love Tharguen and I have for each other,' Niome whispered in defiance.

She took a staggering step back. Merlik gripped her by the arm, pulling her back to him, and held her tight with his other arm wrapped around her. Niome reflexively turned her face away.

Merlik leaned closer and slowly brought his mouth to her ear. He whispered harshly, 'The love you have for Tharguen will die, just as *he* will, and you *will* be mine.'

Roughly, Merlik released her and took a step back. He stared at her a moment more as she stared back. It was not desperation in his eyes, Niome realised, but determination.

Then he turned and the host of Morkans departed, leaving Niome standing alone.

CHAPTER TWENTY-FIVE:
A Long-Awaited Farewell

$\mathcal{S}$afely back in the Fortress, the Telorians worked together with the Tellens to prepare and blend the flowers. They embarked again the following day to gather more while the first batch macerated. The final result was a clear solution that gleamed an indigo hue.

'I think I saw a potion like this in Drúgan's Great Rock,' Jimmy observed.

Niome found Kchalami, who seemed to be suffering most from the effects of the *Canétal*. He had offered to be the first to test the potency of the *Ligfulm* potion.

'I don't know how quickly or slowly it will work,' said Niome. 'But I want you to tell me everything. I suggest keeping a journal of the progress.'

'I will. I feel very excited about this,' Kchalami said before drinking the potion. 'Now what?'

'We wait and see.'

As the antidote took effect, drowsiness took over Kchalami. The Firlanian Prince slept long and deeply for the next several nights, feeling refreshed and rejuvenated upon awakening.

'Are you feeling lightheaded?' asked Vigh as he, Niome, Boreth, and Jimmy assessed his progress.

'No, normal. I can still meditate, too.'

'So we know we blended everything well,' said Jimmy.

'No side effects,' Niome said thoughtfully. 'That's good news. I would have hated to have miscalculated my dosage. I'm no expert like Drúgan, but I still pride myself in the knowledge I do have.'

'That, and it would have reflected poorly on the Great Wizardess,' teased Jimmy. Niome playfully slapped him on the arm.

'He does have a point,' chuckled the Firlanian Prince. 'It would have been counterproductive. Thankfully, our Great Wizardess friend is rather intuitive and *does* read all the instructions.'

'Unlike someone we know,' muttered Boreth.

'And he was given the title of Lord!' Jimmy muttered back.

Vigh snickered. Niome cleared her throat, bringing their attention back to her notes.

'Any improvements on your mind?' she asked.

'Yes, I believe,' replied Kchalami. 'Somewhat. Perhaps I am not entirely certain.'

'Well, that answers that question,' said Jimmy. 'Still doubtful of himself and uncertain.'

Kchalami conceded that was the case. Vigh assured him he would have more than enough antidote for everyone in Firlan.

'So, where's Meysah?' asked Kchalami.

'We don't know,' said Boreth. 'He was supposed to join us for a game of cards, but he's mightily late.'

'That's not like him, though,' observed Kchalami.

'We know,' Jimmy said with a shrug.

'Niome!' Nastafin shouted from the hall. She was accompanied by Elmezni, Krystal, and Lenarbøk as they all ran to the Telorians.

'What is it?' asked Vigh, concerned.

'It's Akchmassiel!' said Krystal. 'He needs the potion NOW! His mind is—'

'He thinks everyone is the enemy,' said Elmezni, overlapping with his sister, 'and he's cornered Meysah!'

'Meysah!' cried Niome.

'He's blaming him for what he's lived through here,' explained Nastafin, out of breath and frantic, 'with the phantoms, everything.'

'Where are they?' asked Vigh.

'Come!' called Lenarbøk.

They ran to a secluded wing of the fortress used primarily for storage and found Stëinbøk, Hunbøk, and Derfbøk already at the scene.

'And what would either of them be doing in the storage area?!' cried Niome upon seeing Akchmassiel pinning her brother to the wall, hand pressed against his chest, sword pointed at his heart.

'I was looking for more bottles!' cried Meysah.

'And I was looking for *him*!' seethed Akchmassiel.

Several jars and phials lay strewn about the floor, none of them broken, thankfully. Meysah still held one jar.

'We found several polcs in a brawl after the infection was known, but nothing like *this* ever occurred,' Kchalami whispered to the two Lords who stood beside him.

'Niome,' whispered Stëinbøk. 'I may be a King, but he won't listen to me. You need to take charge.'

'We have the potion ready,' Jimmy assured.

'Why were you looking for Meysah, Akchmassiel?' Niome asked gently.

'Because he and the rest of you caused this.'

'What did we cause?'

'Everything that has gone wrong in my life! Firlan was safe before the five of you arrived. You sent us out here to get attacked by phantoms. I nearly lost my life!' His shout resonated in the room. 'I still have a scar. You—'

'Akchmassiel!' shouted Kchalami with authority. 'Think of what you are saying. Does it make any sense to you?'

'Why would you harm a friend?' Niome pleaded. 'Mirauk has poisoned your mind. *He* has caused this.'

'Because my so-called *friends* have turned on me,' Akchmassiel seethed. 'They are no longer our allies!'

'Can't we grab ahold of him?' Elmezni whispered.

'You'll get hurt,' replied Vigh.

'This is exactly what Mirauk attacked Firlan for,' said Boreth. 'To turn them against Teloria. To steal them as allies of his own. Freedom of Life is not just a saying anymore – this proves the meaning of Bahvley's words.'

'Niome,' said Nastafin, 'I know of an ancient Tellen spell that could help.'

'Please,' replied Niome. 'I doubt any spells I know will work, not without me harming Akchmassiel.'

'It's a song, actually – a special tune you sing the person's name to. It soothes and calms. Perhaps it will reach his soul.'

'It's worth a try.'

Nastafin sang out in pretty, soft notes, 'Akch-ma-ssi-el!'

Instantly, Akchmassiel dropped his weapons and froze in surprise. Niome went to him and offered him the potion, which he accepted as though he knew he had to drink it. As in hypnosis, he downed the potion in one go. Akchmassiel faltered a step, then fell into Niome's arms, already asleep.

Kchalami stepped up beside her to take his friend and gently lowered him to the floor.

'I guess the more urgent the situation, the sleepier one gets, indeed,' said Jimmy.

'Are you okay?' Boreth asked Meysah.

'Fine, uh . . .' Meysah rubbed the back of his neck. 'He just appeared before me and started yelling and threatening me with his sword. I was worried if I sent a message through our magic or if I uttered a single word, he would render me lifeless. I knew it wasn't anything natural, I just wish I could have been more prepared to fight him off – I'm not even armed.'

'You're both going to be fine,' Niome reassured him. 'We have to give this potion to every Firlanian here. Kchalami, you'll have a lot to carry home, and so will we. The potion must be made from fresh flowers.'

Kchalami, who remained crouched beside Akchmassiel, nodded.

'I just hope nothing bad has happened at home!' voiced Krystal.

'This illness works in odd ways,' noted Vigh.

'If you wish to return home now and cure your father, you should,' Stëinbøk told Kchalami.

'I want to let Niome know of our progress and for us to heal here before we go,' answered Kchalami.

Elmezni retrieved Akchmassiel's sword while Derfbøk and Hunbøk picked up Akchmassiel and carried him to the infirmary.

Vigh took Kchalami aside. 'We must gather every Firlanian in the infirmary at once. We must avoid another incident.' He glanced at the others. 'Don't wait for us to leave. Go home as soon as possible and help Firnamel.'

'If that's what must be done,' said Kchalami. He sighed. 'I wish the Kikies were here.'

Vigh clapped his shoulder, smiling in sympathy. 'Me too.'

Niome walked with Nastafin as they collected the necessary stock of potions.

'That spell, the song spell – it is an old Kaulchèc spell that Elina spoke about. It has been lost for generations. How do you know it?'

'Me very great aunt, deceased now, taught it to me.'

'Then I believe that the few who knew it were part of your family and came to the Twisted Forest with your ancestors, for in Teloria, it has been forgotten.'

'That is possible,' replied Nastafin.

'Many scribes and Wizards have searched for it and never found it in any book. Only records *of* it exist, as well as its effects, but the spell itself has never been found. Somehow, it never made its way into the *Book of Enchantment*. Most spells that didn't,' Niome explained, her face sullen, 'have now been forgotten.'

'I have the book,' said Nastafin. 'I believe it may be the last of them. It may very well be the one brought here by me family. If you would like, I can teach you the spells.'

'I'll recopy them into my notes,' said Niome, smiling eagerly, 'and transcribe them for Teloria.'

Once their task was complete, Niome and Nastafin arrived at the infirmary where the the other four Telorians, along with Stëinbøk, Derfbøk, Hunbøk, and Lenarbøk, were already tending to the Firlanians.

'Akchmassiel seems to have been overcome by calmness,' Hunbøk informed them. 'When we brought him here, his body was still tense. I believe the medicine is working.'

'That is a relief,' sighed Kchalami. 'I would have hated for a good friend of mine to hurt another friend all because of Mirauk's poison.'

'Or worse,' said Meysah, 'turned evil, over to Mirauk's side. Then he would have been done for, and so would I.'

'How are *you* feeling?' Stëinbøk asked his Firlanian cousin.

'More optimistic,' replied Kchalami. 'I'm beginning to feel more like myself again.'

'Will this work even if no symptoms have yet shown?' asked Stëinbøk.

'The poison has been in them for several years,' said Niome. 'No apparent symptoms may have occurred in many, but they will feel a change in their being, and we will know the severity for each of them by how soon they fall into a healing sleep and how long they sleep as well.'

'Well, we're ready to receive the medicine,' said Saviel.

'Indeed,' said Laurelmi. 'It may be a darker period for Firlan, but soon enough, it will come to an end. And if this is our dark period, then our victorious one will be a great one, and all will have been worth the while.'

'You're quite optimistic about the situation,' observed Boreth.

'If anything's been affected, obviously it's not my ability to reason and find the good in things,' Laurelmi surmised.

As Niome gave them each their dose, some fell asleep quicker than they would have thought.

Kchalami looked on and said softly, just to himself: 'Sleep, my people, and let us heal together. We will conquer this brief part of the war.'

'And the greater part of the war as well,' asserted Niome. 'I have faith in Firlan. I have faith in you. And I have faith in King Firnamel, your father.'

'Thank you. I, too, have faith in us. But I have more faith in you.'

Niome took Kchalami's hand and squeezed gently. Words could not express what she wished to convey to her friend, but somehow Kchalami understood, and serenity replaced all doubt.

As the days passed, the Firlanians felt a change. They felt refreshed, revitalised.

Akchmassiel, who now seemed back to his normal self, approached Meysah.

'I feel ashamed of what I've done. How could I have been so blinded? What madness possessed me to err, to forget myself and act so aggressively towards you? You, who has helped me more than anyone else? I just hope you haven't lost your trust in me, for I was not angry at you.'

'I know,' Meysah soothed. 'I still trust you, Akchmassiel. You were ill, and it was time to cure you. I knew that it wasn't *you* yelling at me.'

'I'm too wise, though, to have let such a thing occur.'

'Don't blame yourself,' insisted Meysah. 'You had no control—'

'I should have!' shouted Akchmassiel, bringing a hand to his brow.

'But you lost control, and that is nobody's fault but Mirauk's.' Meysah placed his hands on his friend's arms. His voice was firm, but his eyes soft. 'You understand?'

'I suppose,' murmured Akchmassiel.

'Akchmassiel,' Meysah said gently, 'it's all right.'

'Thank you,' said Akchmassiel, nodding his appreciation.

More time passed, and the Firlanians continued to heal. Summer was past its peak and the Telorians, too, were ready to depart. They and Kchalami announced their mutual intentions to Stëinbøk on the second day of the ninth week of Summer.

'You will be greatly missed,' said Stëinbøk. 'Your presence is welcome anytime. Stay for a feast, and take your time in saying your farewells.'

'That, we can do,' replied Kchalami.

The five Telorians stood together in the hall awhile, taking in their surroundings, as though something about the fortress walls comforted them.

'I suppose this is it,' voiced Vigh. 'Our last days here in the Tellens' fortress, here in the Twisted Forest.'

'It's been a long time since I wanted to go home,' said Boreth. 'I'm going to miss the Tellens, though.'

'We all are,' added Niome.

'I wonder how Bahvley's doing,' said Meysah. 'How things are at home. I hope he's not lost hope from us being away for so long.' He slumped his shoulder, looking forlorn.

'He has Selemil and Henker,' said Niome. 'And there are other loyal Wizards in Teloria with whom I consult, and we advise each other with magical plans to protect Teloria. They do their part also. And I'm sure Nsarmön is contributing just as much as Gorthan would.'

'Bahvley has the Kikies with him, too,' added Boreth, offering Meysah a warm smile.

'It's worth it, to keep the hope going strong in the people's hearts,' said Jimmy, 'even if so many unanswered questions remain. And you know why?'

Meysah shrugged.

Jimmy beamed. 'Because it's worth fighting for and defending what you believe in – just because everything's worth it, for the Freedom of Life.'

'For the Freedom of Life,' the others repeated softly, looking up at the ceiling.

After a moment, a smile came to Meysah's lips. He let out a soft chuckle. 'We sound like we're reciting a ritual or a prayer.'

'Are we not?' asked Jimmy.

The others laughed.

'Okay, let's get out of here before the Tellens start thinking we're going mad,' said Jimmy. 'No, don't say it,' he added to Meysah as soon as the other opened his mouth.

The farewell feast was held on the fifth of the ninth of Summer. Many Tellens had come from the shelters in honour of their departing friends. The celebrations reminded both the Telorians and the Firlanians of the feast Firnamel had once held in honour of the Five.

There was a bounty of food laid out across the tables, including many delicacies for which the Telorians wanted the recipes.

As Stëinbøk stood, everyone's attention turned to him.

'Visitors came to our forest at our most dire time, visitors who asked to be friends and allies. These visitors are more than friends and allies – they are our cousins. It warms me heart. Dangers may have come to us, but so did the Firlanians, the Telorians, the Kikies, and the

Five. This is why, despite me past heartaches, today I feel blessed.'

Stëinbøk looked from each of the Telorians to each of the Firlanians. 'I would not trade this joy to erase the doom that befell on this forest. Dark times were near, and together we vanquished them. Through this alliance, through this friendship, through familial ties of millennia past, we gained courage and hope.' He smiled warmly. 'And much, much more.'

His eyes grew distant. 'I understand now that our paths were not meant to cross before. Now that they have, our loyalty will never falter. We honour you today and all that you have done for us.' His smile grew. 'I may be King, but Bahvley is *me* King. Together, we will fight against the evil forces of Mork. Together, we will regain the Freedom of Life.'

Stëinbøk lifted his glass of wine in a toast, and everyone cheered. Niome thanked him with kind words, while Boreth expressed how the Tellens had inspired him and helped him keep hope that Niome would return.

'All I have to say,' said Meysah, not-so-soberly, 'is that I've learned from you. I used to be afraid all the time. For the record, I have not had a weird stomachache in at least three years. Or if I did, I didn't notice! Your courage gave me courage.'

'With your help,' added Jimmy, who was no less tipsy than Meysah, 'we discovered more things about the Morkans. With your help, we got rid of perhaps those who were on the verge of becoming too powerful to get rid of the way we did. You took good care of us and tended to our needs. You gave us hope when we needed it, you gave us boldness in necessary times. In short, everything you say we gave you, you gave us.'

'Yes, and someone's going to need to take care of you fairly soon and ensure you start pacing yourself with your wine,' teased Boreth. Jimmy waved him away, chuckling.

'You taught us love,' Vigh said tenderly, his eyes landing on Nastafin. 'Mindful of the future, remembering our past, I learnt to forgive mistakes and forge new paths, focused on what lay before me now.'

A few of the others whistled at Vigh, who suppressed a bashful smile.

Elmezni and Krystal expressed their gratitude as well, a little teary-eyed.

'I want to stay as much as I want to go home,' Elmezni said. 'I know I am torn.'

'You are welcome back any time,' said Stëinbøk.

'Stëinbøk,' said Kchalami, rising. 'You and all Tellens are welcome in Firlan at any time, for any reason. You're welcome to stay as long as you like. We would love to show you our home. I would love to share my home and gardens and surrounding forests and delicacies with you, too. In fact,' he smiled, blinking back tears of his own, 'you *have* to come to Firlan! It's obligatory.'

'All right, we will,' chuckled Stëinbøk. He lifted his glass again. 'To our dear friends! To our cousins! To Firlan, to Teloria!' He named each and every one one of the Firlanians and Telorians. 'To the power of the Star, and most importantly, to the Freedom of Life.'

Everyone cheered again and the festivities lasted long into the night, with singing, dancing, and much more feasting.

Vigh sat with Nastafin, holding her hands in his.

'It feels like my time here has been too short to be leaving. Yet at the same time, it feels too long to believe I'm actually going back home.' He chuckled. 'I want to go home . . .' He sobered. 'But I am afraid to. I'm afraid to leave you here alone. I'm afraid that if I go, if I turn away, I'll look back and you'll be gone, and I'll have lost you, too.'

'Vigh,' said Nastafin, tenderly placing her hand on his face. 'I won't disappear. No one's going to kill me or take me away. I'll be here when you return, and I'll be visitin' you in Teloria before even then. Nothing is goin' to come between us. I'm not goin' to let it happen.'

'I don't know if you understand the fear I feel when I think of being separated from you,' expressed Vigh, his heart clenching. He turned his face away and muttered, 'Look at me, a grown polc in his middle years, and I feel fears greater than Meysah now that he can handle his.'

Nastafi gently turned Vigh's face back to look at her and leaned her forehead on his. 'You must trust that the stars will protect our love.'

That brought a smile to Vigh's lips before he pressed a gentle kiss to hers. 'I'll do my best not to worry about you, then.'

They each had an emotional attachment to the Twisted Forest. For Vigh, it was Nastafin and his love for her, newfound love after years of suppressing his need for it.

For Meysah, it was having been away from home so long, separated from the others. There was an uncertainty in his heart, a longing which he could not fully grasp. He feared what awaited them at home, good or ill.

Jimmy hated to have to leave his friends behind and wished they could all go to Teloria together.

Boreth worried about the magical ripples their travels would cause. He feared Mirauk would perceive their movement and attack Teloria. Boreth had lost so many he cared for because of Mirauk, his family all dead. The other four were his family now, as were many others. He would defend them with his life.

For Niome, it was the closeness to Zaccher Lake. Going home meant leaving that other home behind for a long time, if not for good. It meant facing the responsibilities that came with the powers she possessed for being the Great Wizardess of Teloria. It meant letting go of Navë completely. Part of Niome grieved that side of herself, yet she knew Navë would always live inside of her and make her even stronger.

Swords that had not been used in a long time were sharpened. Shields that had become dusty were cleaned. Bow strings were tightened and adjusted.

It felt to the Five as though they were going into battle, and they could not deny the excitement it brought, odd as it was, since they always wished battle would no longer be necessary when they were engaged in it.

As the Telorians got themselves ready, they heard the sweet sound of singing about them. Almost celestial, it was, and they did not know from where it came, but they could comprehend the words of the reverberating and resonating verses.

Fear has escaped us,
Faith has returned.
What we thought was forgotten,
Has been reestablished in our hearts.

One day, peace will reign!
Too long a time it has been!
Three decades gone since hope was lost!
For a new day will arise, now that
Five saviours have come to us.

Pursue our dreams, we must,
And for a trust well earned,
Give gratitude to friends well gotten,
For it's time to play our part.

One day, peace will reign!
Too long a time it has been!
Three decades past since hope was lost!
For a new day will soon arise, now that
Five saviours have come to us.

Niome smiled, realising. 'Listen,' she said. 'They're singing to us.'

'They're thanking us,' said Vigh.

'But who's singing?' asked Jimmy. 'It almost sounds like the music is coming from the walls.'

'Everyone,' said Niome, awed. 'It's all about the fortress, resonating to the skies and to the stars.'

Boreth leaned against the wall, closing his eyes to take in the melody. 'I'm moved.'

'Tomorrow is the day,' said Meysah, 'the day we leave for home. That is why they sing.'

The chanting kept on the whole night long, and it was still going when the Telorians and the Firlanians woke up early on the morning of Summer the sixty-sixth, the third of the tenth.

Ensuring their vials of antidote were equally distributed in their satchels and that their weapons were secured, the Five made their way downstairs, where the Firlanians and many of their Tellen friends were gathered.

'This reminds me of Firlan,' said Jimmy.

'Why?' asked Elmezni. 'Does their formation remind you of the way we saluted you?' Jimmy nodded in response.

'All that's missing,' said Krystal, 'is for them to bow to you.'

'We need to be in our Star formation, then,' said Jimmy.

'You are!' exclaimed Krystal. 'Take away us Firlanians and there's the Star.'

Jimmy looked about, wondering if they had once again instinctively stepped into formation.

The Tellen King took a step towards his friends. Stëinbøk first walked to Kchalami.

'I wish you a safe trip,' he said. 'And I wish that all goes well with the cure. Send our regards to your father. Let all other Firlanians know that the Tellens are there for them, always. The same blood runs through each and every one of our veins, and families look out for each other.'

Stëinbøk placed his hand on Kchalami's arm. 'Before he died, me father wished for past wounds to heal, that Tellen and Firlanian could break the silence after years of separation. His wish came true, and I am very grateful that he died knowin' it.'

'Your father was a good polc,' said Kchalami. 'We had but arrived, and he greeted us warmly. I'm glad to have known him, and I'm sure he watches over you and knows that what killed him has been destroyed. Though I knew him but a brief time, it was enough to know that he lives in you, Stëinbøk.'

Warmth radiating from their smiles, Stëinbøk and Kchalami embraced.

'You've brought a lot of hope back to the Twisted Forest,' said Stëinbøk, still in the embrace. Then he turned to all the other Firlanians. 'Bless Firlan!'

He walked to Niome. 'And bless Teloria,' he said softly. 'If Bahvley ever needs anything, he has only to ask and we shall answer his call.'

'Your friendship is more than enough, more than we expected,' said Niome. 'For with your friendship comes loyalty and trust, yours and ours, and the belief that together, we'll succeed. That together, we can make a difference.' She beamed at Stëinbøk. 'You rule your people well, for you don't *rule* – you guide them and aid them and make wise decisions. If you need anything, Teloria is there for you.'

'But you see, Niome,' said Stënbøk, 'it is *we* who are there for *you*. I may be King, but I am ever still your servant.' Stëinbøk knelt down on one knee. 'I bow to you, Niome Fairhaven, as I bowed to your brother, King Bahvley Fairhaven. I bow before the five of you, for you deserve at least that before you leave. We will ever continue to protect you.' He bowed his head.

The other Tellens bowed as well.

'Isn't this familiar,' said Meysah.

'You see?' said Kchalami. 'It really is in the blood, customs, manners. That is why I now bow, too.'

With a chuckle, Kchalami bowed, and the other Firlanians followed suit.

When everyone rose, Vigh embraced Nastafin tightly, afraid to let go.

'Master Vigh, it's okay,' Meysah soothed before giving them some privacy.

Vigh's eyes filled with tears. 'I love you. Don't you forget that.'

'I won't, I promise. I love you.'

They kissed. Vigh laughed through his tears. He had never been so emotional, never felt so strongly an emotion such as this, at least not for a long time.

Reluctantly, he backed away, hands lingering on hers until he was out of reach.

'Give your brother my regards,' Stëinbøk told Niome. 'And Tharguen, too. Tell his army . . .' He paused, eyes growing distant though he maintained a smile. 'Tell them I hope they are well.'

The gates opened for the departing guests, and their farewells were echoed before the travellers began their journey home.

Chapter Twenty-Six:
A Whirlwind of Magic

As the company of seventeen travellers stepped a little deeper into the forest, they realised that the singing still resonated. All across the forest had it spread. All the Tellens, to show their appreciation, joined in and sang cheerfully, voices ringing out. Where the travellers stood, it seemed as though the heavens were swelling softly with song. It was beautiful.

'They must've prepared this song long before we decided to leave,' Meysah surmised.

'It's a shame Clahria isn't here,' Boreth said wistfully. 'She would've loved to hear this. Perhaps even sing along with them.'

'And play her harp?' asked Jimmy. Boreth smiled fondly in answer.

'They do this so we know they all wish us to fare well,' concluded Kchalami.

Jimmy skipped ahead. 'Such a beautiful sound on such a beautiful day! Now this is what I imagine a perfect Summer's day to be.'

'It *is* encouraging to travel in such an atmosphere,' Vigh agreed.

'If only Bahvley and Tharguen were here with us,' said Meysah, catching up to Jimmy and dragging their Masters with him so they all skipped about playfully. The two Lords chuckled and joined in for a few paces.

Niome narrowed her eyes, slowing her pace as she looked about, distracted by something more obscure she could not yet sense.

Several paces behind the Five, the Firlanians trotted along merrily, unaware of Niome's sudden shift in mood.

'My sister's doing her thing again,' Meysah muttered to Jimmy. He sobered, growing concerned. 'Niome?'

Niome put up her hand for the others to quiet as she came to a stop. Vigh joined her.

'What is it? What do you sense?'

'I'm uncertain,' replied Niome. The Five grew worried as Niome continued to assess the air and the magic that had began to crackle within it. 'Evil,' she said in a very low, even tone.

'Where?' asked Boreth, placing a hand on his sword.

'That's the thing,' said Niome, 'it's not here yet. But it's around us somehow. I can feel it as though I were in a storm cloud filled with lightning.'

The Firlanians caught up to the Five. 'Everything all right?' asked Kchalami, concern in his voice.

Niome's face relaxed. 'Yes, for now.' She smiled. 'Appreciating the warmth.'

Kchalami accepted her answer, adding how the Kikies would very much enjoy this weather. The group then continued on.

Niome warned, her tone casual, 'There may be a cold draft in a while.' She eyed the other four, who wordlessly understood her meaning and the importance to feign ignorance.

That night, they retired at a shelter. They journeyed for five more days before reaching the edge of the forest where they made camp. The Firlanians chatted jovially with each other, whereas Niome set up a little further from the larger group.

Meysah looked worried, especially upon seeing Niome's solemn expression. He joined her, sitting down across from his sister, and whispered, 'How unsafe is it?'

'I'm unable to determine,' replied Niome. 'This is a different kind of sensation, different from any intuition or premonition I've felt before.'

'Do you think it's coming directly from Mirauk?' asked Meysah.

'Could be. Whatever it is, I sense it nearing, but it isn't upon us yet.'

'We'll have to be careful, then, and remain vigilant.' Meysah studied his sister. 'Why don't you meditate to find out?'

'You'll laugh at me, Meysah, but I'm almost afraid to meditate. I'm afraid to leave you without me conscious and aware for a certain amount of time.'

'I'm here for the others,' Meysah pointed out. 'If anything happens, if I sense anything, I'll bring you back from your meditative state. That's *if* I sense it.'

'If there *is* anything to sense, you'll be one of the first to do so,' confirmed Niome. 'You may even sense it before me.'

'Now you're giving me more credit than I deserve, Niome. Everyone knows no one could ever be as powerful as you.'

'Perhaps not completely, but by only a notch. There are only two who can come so close to my power.'

'Who?'

'You know who!' Niome raised her brows.

'Me? Bahvley?'

'That's right. And this is too obscure for me to put my finger on, so perhaps someone else's perspective – in this case yours – will be better able to determine the source. If Bahvley were here, he, too, would likely sense it.'

Meysah thought about that for a moment. 'I don't think I understand *entirely*, but I understand what you mean.'

Niome offered her brother an appreciative smile. 'That's why you both felt it when I was struck by the phantom. I am convinced that Bahvley felt exactly what you described when it happened.'

Meysah rubbed his chin in thought.

'To add to that,' continued Niome, 'the others who could have felt it but didn't are Jimmy, Boreth, and Vigh. This means it's the connection we have through our blood, through the magic that runs in our veins. It's something in the blood that only my brothers could sense.'

Niome pointed to her leg. 'My blood was being sucked out – my magic was seeping out. Both combined, only a bond by both blood and magic could sense it and be connected in a way no one else can be.' Niome smiled. 'I also know the day I remembered myself, you felt it, too, even before I sent out my message.'

'I did,' Meysah confirmed. 'I never mentioned it because I dismissed it, but you're right. I must've deemed it unimportant at the time.'

'Nothing is unimportant,' said Niome.

'All of a sudden, my part to play in this Star, my responsibilities, feel greater.'

'That's because they are.' Niome placed a hand on Meysah's knee. 'Be heartened. Your biggest part was to follow me to the Great Rock – you can accomplish the rest. You are much more powerful than you realise. You simply need to develop that side of you.'

'And what about Bahvley's responsibilities?'

'So are Bahvley's, though he may not realise it yet. Being King is not his only magical part to play. We five may form the Star, but Bahvley, Tharguen, Gorthan, Elina, Selemil, Henker, and perhaps others like Kchalami all form the wand in the centre of the Star.'

'Like the drawing on the gates of Firlan and the carvings on the floor of their entrance.' Meysah smirked with pride.

'Which are like the drawings of the visions of the prophets who saw a star and wand in the sky in their dreams,' completed Niome.

The two took a beat.

'So, are you going to meditate?' asked Meysah.

'Stay close to me. Look after the others.'

The two siblings shared a smile.

Meysah remained close as Niome drifted into meditation. He looked up at the cloudless sky and thought to himself, *Not today. Not yet. The air is too still.*

When Niome had finished, Meysah shared with her his magical musings.

'All I know is, Mirauk is planning something. You must trust your magic and intuition. I sense we may need counterspells.' Niome sighed, exasperated. 'Counterpotions, counterspells . . . does he ever learn?'

Meysah merely shrugged. The two settled for the night but slept warily.

The next day, they reached the Twisted Rapids. They were at a more narrow pass of the rapids where the water flow was slower and gentler with marshes around. The travellers took their time to carefully walk across the water, jumping from rock to rock before continuing, safe for now.

Two more days passed. Before long, they were in the fields closer to Teloria proper. The Sun shone brightly overhead.

'Now, this is a perfect end of Summer's day,' said Elmezni, nudging Jimmy.

The Telorian agreed. 'It's warm, yet cool – the Kikies would love this weather. No rain, no clouds.'

'A horse would come in handy,' Niome pointed out.

'Make that many horses,' chuckled Akchmassiel.

'I do miss Greyer,' admitted Meysah.

'We're quite grateful you wish to walk us to the gates of Teloria,' Boreth expressed to the Firlanians. 'It extends your trip.'

'But it's quite worth it,' said Laurelmi, 'to spend some extra time with the five of you. We know you'd do the same for us.'

Jimmy turned his face up towards the sky, eyes closed. He let out a content sigh. 'The weather truly is in our favour.' He looked at the others. 'Unlike a certain Winter we lived through.'

Meysah shook his head, his eyes darting from the sky to far ahead west. 'It isn't.'

'What! You disagree?!' exclaimed Jimmy, pointing up at the Sun as though he needed no further argument.

'It's the breeze,' said Meysah, his voice ever cautious.

'What breeze?' Vigh asked curiously. The two Lords exchanged a glance.

'It's cold,' said Meysah. He stopped and pointed at the copse of trees. 'There are trees nearby. We stop here and we wait.'

'Wait for what?' asked Elmezni, scowling.

'We wait for the evil to pass,' said Niome. 'I feel it, too, now.' Her eyes met her brother's. 'I told you you'd feel it first, because you are more attuned to that side.' She raised her voice. 'Make sure all your bags and weapons are well fastened.'

'And hold on tight to the trees!' shouted Meysah. He darted towards the trees.

'Meysah?' Kchalami ran to catch up and caught him by the arm. 'What's going on? The two of you are scaring me.'

'That's because we need to be scared,' said Meysah.

'I don't see why. In such—' Kchalami stopped.

In an instant, the sky darkened and a cold wind whipped up.

Kchalami clenched his jaw, eyes wide. 'Then again, why doubt your judgement?' He turned to his people and called out, 'To the trees!'

Terror filled the polcs' hearts as the wind began to whistle. Spirals and spirals of cloudy wind approached at great speed.

'A windstorm!' shouted Vigh.

The group reached the trees and held on as the gale's momentum increased. Several fastened themselves to the trunks for good measure.

'Can someone explain what just hit us?' cried Elmezni.

'It's Mirauk!' answered Niome, calling out to be heard over the din of the whistling wind. 'He's using the forces of the wind.'

The giant whirlwind approached closely before settling in one locus.

Niome turned to the tempest and roared out, 'Mirauk! Fire, wind. Will you attempt to flood us next?'

'Don't give him any ideas!' cried Jimmy. 'He doesn't need to be encouraged.'

'Hear me, Mirauk!' shouted Niome as she held onto her tree. 'Do you think you can stop us? What do you want? Mark my words, we will discover your new conspiracy concerning Teloria!'

'What do I want?' a voice boomed from the whirlwind. 'I want you five to die!'

In one chorus of ringing metal, every one of the Firlanians unsheathed whatever weapons they could as they held on.

'Weapons are no use against wind!' cried Meysah, almost as though asking a question.

'Is Mirauk here in person?' Krystal asked cautiously.

'No,' replied Niome. 'He is manipulating the wind. He must be in a meditative state, using all the magic he can muster. If we defeat him today, he will be weak and fatigued for a good long while.'

'So this is what we want, yes?' said Kchalami. 'For Mirauk to be weak and fatigued?'

Niome nodded.

'I told you that would be dangerous, Niome,' Boreth scolded, 'the meditation bond. Although he may have done this anyway.'

'You won't destroy us!' Vigh shouted in defiance at the gale. 'Go home!'

'Says one of the Lords who used *water* to destroy secret tunnels,' the voice in the whirlwind boomed. 'It seems I'm not the only one who uses the elements against my enemy. Why would I retreat now?'

'Fantastic,' Vigh muttered to Boreth, sarcasm in his voice, 'he has turned this into a contest.'

'The Star must burn out!' boomed Mirauk, his words reverberating with more intensity. The unnatural resonance grated on Niome's nerves.

'His voice is deeper than I remember it from Tower Fortress in Mork,' said Jimmy.

'That's because he's speaking through the wind,' said Niome. 'Yet his voice *has* grown harsh over the years. Even his thoughts were harsher than last when we met.'

'How *ever* are we going to get rid of him?!' said Meysah. 'He's not moving.'

'Then *I* shall move,' declared Niome.

'What?' protested Vigh. 'Niome, don't do anything stupid!'

'After everything he's put me through, I can swirl and spin in a whirlwind.'

Niome let go of the tree, allowing herself to be swept up by the wind.

'Niome! Don't!' the other four yelled out.

It was too late for her to hear them. The wind took her, and she was lost in the spinning clouds of dust.

'Why?!' yelled Kchalami, terror on his face. He looked to the Lords for answers. 'What madness drove her to do that?!'

Vigh and Boreth were at a loss.

'I know,' declared Meysah. 'Just wait.'

'Oh, certainly, we'll wait, because we can't exactly do anything else, can we?' complained Krystal.

'Trust me,' insisted Meysah. 'I'm her brother. I sense something.'

The group waited. When nothing happened, Meysah called out to the whirlwind.

'Mirauk! What is the purpose of this?'

Mirauk only laughed.

Resistance against the strong winds was weakening, and everyone's grip was loosening.

Now Meysah began to worry.

'What have you done to my sister, Mirauk?' cried Meysah, anger in his voice.

After another pause, a low rumble indicated Mirauk's laughter.

'Gone, dead,' laughed Mirauk. 'No more. Into oblivion!'

'No!' shrieked Kchalami, taking a step forward. 'That can't be. You'll pay, you selfish, unrighteous—' He let go of the tree.

'What are you doing?!' shouted Meysah, darting towards Kchalami. 'Don't be stupid!' He pulled the polc back as he grabbed hold of another tree. Kchalami took hold of the tree again.

'How did you do that, Meysah?' Jimmy called out. 'You dashed with the wind and it didn't pick you up!'

Meysah studied himself, realising what Jimmy was implying.

'Such strong magical will,' Vigh agreed.

'Whatever it was,' said Meysah, 'magic or no, I'm not trying it again.'

He held on to the same tree as Kchalami, one hand still gripping the Firlanian Prince.

Mirauk continued to laugh, more heartedly now.

'Lost in *oblivion*! Destroyed!'

Kchalami's eyes brimmed with tears as he turned his face away from the tempest.

Boreth scowled. 'Is it just me, or do his words sound like . . . *questions*?'

'Dead?' laughed Mirauk. 'Impossible!'

With a loud whistle, the whirlwind bent and Niome popped out from the high end. She landed heavily on the ground but was cushioned by her magic, her knees bent low and body bowed. She rose and stood tall. Her hair fell long and loose, copper highlights shimmering as it flew about wildly with the wind, yet she stood firmly, anchored like the strongest tree.

Niome placed her fists on her hips, calling out to Mirauk's whirlwind. 'That's right! I'm telling you, Mirauk, that's what you'll be before you know it. *Dead.* You might as well accept it. You can never destroy me.' She allowed herself a smirk. 'Yes, I'm feeling arrogant, I admit it. A little trait my friend Lóim helped me with.'

Meysah let out a chuckle, more from relief than anything else. Others watched in awe.

'If laughing is your way of dealing with it, then so be it,' Niome went on matter-of-factly. 'But you might as well face the truth.'

'But oblivion? When did you start being so funny, Niome Fairhaven? Nonetheless, perhaps I failed to destroy you now, but you will see.' Mirauk's laugh turned more sinister.

'I've seen a lot already,' Niome said slyly. 'It hasn't been very impressive, if I'm perfectly honest.'

'Your friends, they're not as strong as you. If I increase the wind's speed even just a little . . .'

'No! Do not touch my friends!' Niome bellowed protectively.

'Now, I've got *your* attention,' declared Mirauk.

'You won't be able to harm them, Mirauk,' cried Niome. 'Not as long as I'm alive, and I'll be alive a lot longer than you will.'

She narrowed her eyes. 'Now, tell me. What is it about Teloria that you want to stop us here? Something's there, isn't it? And if I am home, I might discover it, but with me gone, I can't do anything about it. You're hiding something from me, and your plans can only work if we don't make it home.' Niome pointed a finger at the whirlwind. 'Forget it. We *are* going home.'

'Perhaps you should rethink your attitude, Niome. Once I've finished with the wind here, there'll be nothing left of your friends for you to go home with.'

Mirauk broke into a spell, recited in Ancient Morkan.

Tekhnolkiv sadinwik!
Yiganar sadinwik!
Takereth alathekhes colsap!
Khlitaw kuyokhor pokhew,
Takereth rikhet sadinwikm,
Rofkuyokhor nokhw
Sutefakhok ethme!
Achnad bowolo ethme yakham!
Khikli ethme ala!
Enekhon alash ekhilvo kit lekhelt eth elghat!

Although Niome understood not a word from it, a sudden certainty came over her. She immediately knew the words she needed to pronounce.

'I knew this would involve a counterspell,' Niome added, glancing towards Meysah.

'You can close your eyes,' Meysah reassured her. 'I'm here to look after the others.'

Niome nodded. Turning back to the tempest, she closed her eyes and lifted her arms. She beautifully yet terrifyingly recited the verses, just as terrifying as it had been for Merlik and Garkhktak in the battle defending Dûnelor.

Reiůeh opfo ehelt teghil!
Siyessofor fo dolug!
Yoiratesd sieth liûvë dinalwë
*   taithos ileratesdep sehnitot tûrah sui,*
Tiserefad, tiskenirsah, tisi amërëi fûfap.
Dolûg snigerni sieth solûwor.
Liûvë lahlas revnë ferus shiripë tinsagati.

Niome opened her eyes. The whirlwind was still there – Mirauk was still reciting. Niome began again, louder and with more intensity. The tempest began to sway, but not of its own accord. The whirling slowed, the wind's force fading, until the chaos finally began to shrink.

'Why would you do this, Mirauk?' demanded Niome. 'You are not a polc of your word! I didn't send you any *Canétal!* I don't see why you would spring this on us.'

'I have my reasons!' replied Mirauk.

'What reasons?!' Niome demanded fiercely. 'I know you're hiding something or someone. You know that once I discover what it is, I will get back to you. But not in the way you think. Revenge is not how *I* go about things.'

'I'll see you, Niome,' began the Morkan Lord through gritted teeth. The rest, he roared out in anger: 'Sooner than you think!'

The tempest vanished, dying out to a mere puff of dust.

Letting out the breaths they'd been holding, everyone released their hold on the trees slowly, reluctant to test if the whirlwind was truly gone. The sky cleared up again; the air was still.

'What was *that* all about?!' asked Jimmy. "'I'll see you sooner than you think!'" he imitated. 'Does he think he'll see you tomorrow?'

'No,' replied Niome. 'He believes, I think, that he'll see us before the great war.'

'What does that mean?' inquired Kchalami, who quickly turned away to wipe his eyes, a little embarrassed.

'It means he's planning a trip,' Vigh deduced. 'He means to leave Mork. Am I correct?' Vigh looked to Niome for confirmation.

'Where to?' asked Boreth. 'He could go to Teloria like he went to Dalvar.'

'I don't know,' said Niome. 'What I do know is, he's still in Mork now, and he's not going anywhere soon. Not after using this amount of magic.'

'I hope you're right,' said Elmezni, still flustered.

'I hope so too,' Niome muttered under her breath.

Kchalami recomposed himself. 'So, what now? We continue on our way and hope we don't run into him again?'

'We continue on our way,' said Niome.

'What, that's it?' snapped Kchalami. 'Do you expect us to accept that answer? That's not good enough! We were nearly taken from this world by a tempest made of magic. We thought that thing had swallowed you whole!' Kchalami pointed to where Mirauk's storm had been. 'And he just said, before us all, he'll see you soon. What are we to expect?'

Eyes wide, Kchalami paused. He bowed his head, continuing more softly. 'I'm sorry, Niome. I'm afraid of what's to come.'

'We all are,' said Boreth. 'But we cannot allow it to get to us. It's the way of things . . . unfortunately.'

'I know,' Kchalami conceded. 'I'm just glad I have friends like you to remind me . . . and who care.'

'Whatever is to come,' said Niome, putting a hand on Kchalami's shoulder, 'you'll be protected. Mirauk is attempting to frighten us, attempting to discourage and upset us, because *he's* frightened. Perhaps he hopes to control us better if we're scared. I'm not going to let him find out, because I'm not going to let him scare me.'

'I understand,' said Kchalami.

As the group continued on, the mood lifted as quickly as the storm had earlier.

'I say,' began Boreth, 'let us sing, for soon, we'll be home! Home sweet, cosy home. And then, I can deliver that letter to Drúgan. But first, I think I'm going to sit down in my garden and smoke a good pipe.'

'I think I'll place in my bag for future travels, in order to never forget it again, the light-cube,' said Vigh. 'It would have come in handy on many occasions throughout the past years.'

'I'm going to play a good trick on Lóim, I think,' mused Meysah. He smiled, realising how eager he was to see him again.

'No, not me,' said Jimmy. 'I think I'm going to gather up all the courage I have and tell Gahli how I truly feel about her.'

'Because that takes more courage than fighting a Morkan?' Meysah teased. Jimmy only responded with a surreptitious look before both breathed out a small laugh.

'Well, I say, good for you,' said Elmezni.

'What about you, Niome? What are you going to do once you're home?' asked Krystal.

'Well, I think that goes without saying,' said Meysah. 'We all know where she's going to go.' He chuckled.

'Actually, I think I might make breakfast for Mom and Dad,' mused Niome. 'They bug me enough that I'm never home to help out.'

'Oh, and I suppose you're going to add how *I* should help Dad with the crops? Some boring fun.'

'Oh, there he goes again,' laughed Elmezni.

'No,' protested Niome.

'But you were thinking it! I know you were.'

'Maybe.'

'See!'

'It's not the same!' Niome insisted.

'Uh-huh, and if I wouldn't have said a word just now, you *would* have said it, and then added how it would be fair and I shouldn't be lazy or complain.'

'That's not true! I wasn't even thinking it, but now that you mention it, yeah!'

Meysah nudged his sister with his shoulder as the two continued bickering in more hushed tones.

'Funny how in most cases,' began Vigh, 'the younger one starts the arguments . . .'

'Hey!' shouted Meysah and Elmezni both. Krystal and Niome snickered, sharing a look.

'Sorry.' Vigh lifted his hands in surrender, suppressing a laugh.

Chapter Twenty-Seven:
The Return Home

'Look!' Boreth enthused after they'd been travelling for three more days. 'It's our home. It's Teloria!'

The group stopped to marvel in relief at their proximity to Teloria proper. In the distance, the wall and its towers could be seen.

'And the wall is still up – the world hasn't ended!' cried Jimmy, relieved to see his kingdom the way it was when they last left.

'Do you think they can see us from here?' inquired Vigh.

'Do you think they even know it's us?' asked Meysah.

'I'm sure that even if they don't see us or know who we are, they can sense your arrival,' said Kchalami. 'I'm certain everyone in Teloria can feel it within them that the Five have returned.'

'Not just those in Teloria,' said Niome. 'Everyone in Mork, too.'

'Come,' said Vigh. 'We'll never reach it if we just stand here in awe of our kingdom's wall!'

'And I thought I had missed Teloria when we were in Mork,' sighed Boreth.

'A prisoner will miss his cell while in Mork,' said Krystal. 'But it *has* been a very long time, and I myself miss Firlan.'

By the time the Sun was dipping beneath the horizon, they had reached the wall. They kept on with enthusiasm, resting when they needed it. A few days passed as they neared the Main Gate, finally arriving at the break of dawn.

Kchalami turned to Niome. 'I suppose this is good-bye. At least until the next time we have a chance to be together again.'

'I have a feeling it won't be too long till we meet once more,' said Niome.

'I hope not,' said Elmezni, smiling.

'Everyone in Firlan will be cured,' beamed Jimmy.

'You'll be able to keep tradition now,' said Niome. 'It will soon be your time, Kchalami. After all you've done for Firlan and for Teloria, you deserve at least that!'

'But Niome,' began Kchalami, 'although I am ever thankful to you and grateful for your encouraging words, I am saddened. If I learn all of Firlan's secrets from my father, I will be named King, and that will spell the nearing of the end of his life. He would leave us sooner than we want.'

'Your father is strong and young at heart,' Vigh reassured. 'I'm certain he has many years yet.'

'Perhaps, though he will pass eventually,' said Kchalami. 'That is everyone's doom.'

'Or fate, depending how you look at it,' said Boreth.

'At least I am comforted knowing that when he leaves me and the rest of Firlan, he shall be going on his own accord and not by some curse or poison.'

'There is an end to everyone's story,' said Niome. 'Yours is but beginning. With every end, a new beginning starts, and to have a new beginning, there must be an end somewhere.'

'I know once grief passes, there will be joy for the fate of Firlan. But only once Mirauk is destroyed.'

The Five embraced their friends. Niome bade the Firlanians to give her tidings to Meltissel, who had indeed not been meant to accompany her.

'You survived the phantom,' said Krystal, 'while he would have died. This was your fate. His was to stay.'

'Give our tidings to Bahvley and Tharguen as well,' said Kchalami, his hands lingering around Niome for a moment longer before he stepped back.

'Farewell,' replied Niome. 'Take care, and be well. Cure your folk and bless your land.'

'We will,' asserted Kchalami. 'It seems difficult to part with you, but we are eager to arrive home as well.' He unsheathed his sword and lifted it up. Softly, he said, 'For the Freedom of Life.'

Returning his sword to its sheath, he added, 'We shall meet again, five saviours of the mighty Star for whom we awaited so long. We will think of you every day, and twice a day when we look at the carvings on our floor. For they are carvings of hope, of a new beginning, Niome.' He paused and hugged Niome once more. 'Farewell.'

The Firlanians turned northwards, following the Main Road. As for the Telorians, they turned to the gates and took a moment of reflection.

'Home at last,' said Vigh.

'Even if we're going to have greater responsibilities now,' said Jimmy, 'it doesn't matter. It still means being home.'

'I know what you mean,' agreed Meysah.

As the Five entered their kingdom, Niome began assessing what needed to be done now that they were back home.

'We have to go see Bahvley. That's our first stop of the day. We've been away so long . . .' She paused. 'Five years! We've been away for *five* years. One of the reasons why I saw the number five in my visions, perhaps. It was five years ago today that we entered the secret tunnels beneath the Gord Plains.' Niome let out a laugh. 'Everything seems to work in fives with us.'

She started towards the gates.

'Let's hope we have a warmer welcome than last time,' muttered Jimmy.

'I hope you'll think twice next time you wish for a great adventure,' teased Boreth. 'We all wanted it. Five years later, though, I could use a break.'

'A hero never takes a break,' stated Vigh. 'Unfortunately.'

'Halt!' a voice called out as the Guard Captain approached them. 'Who passes here unauthorised? State your full names and . . .' The polc's brows shot up. 'By the stars! You're alive! You've returned! Welcome, welcome! Welcome back. Please, go as you wish.'

Chuckling, the Five acknowledged the Captain.

'Niome Fairhaven! The Five,' he laughed. 'You have no idea how happy I am. King Bahvley told us you had business keeping you at the Twisted Forest. Many doubted his words, and rumours made us fear the worst.'

'Things did happen to us, but nothing we couldn't handle,' said Meysah. Jimmy laughed.

'Well, that explains it. I was told to keep an eye out for you.'

Vigh and Boreth exchanged a glance and said together, 'Henker.'

The Captain called out for the gates to be opened, shouting out joyously, 'The Five have returned!' and the guards rejoiced as the Five walked through, waving to whom their presence gave renewed hope.

'How fast do you think word will spread of our return?' mused Vigh.

'Fairly quickly, judging by the chanting of our names,' replied Boreth. Jimmy's stomach gurgled.

'I could use a good brunch myself,' said Vigh.

'Well, then, you're just on time!'

The Five were met by Henker, who walked up the path with a wide grin on his face.

'Exactly at the time that I predicted.' He beckoned them to follow him. He continued as they walked, 'Selemil and I are in these parts of the city for business purposes. I'm certain your brother will be relieved you've returned. He and Tharguen have been arguing more and more. Determined to keep the faith in Teloria, but losing hope themselves. They even lied to me, although I already knew what would happen to you all.'

Henker turned to walk backwards a few steps. 'I am glad you all survived. I was confident you would, but I must admit, it is a relief to see that day arrive where I have confirmation of it' – he spread out his arms – 'in the flesh.'

Chuckling, he turned back to face the road ahead. 'I only wish Bahvley and Tharguen would have been less proud to open up. When you find them, you'll understand what I mean. You'll understand better than ever before your importance in this world.'

'I think I understood when I remembered,' said Niome. 'When Niome returned and Navë left.'

The Five ate with Henker and Selemil at a small inn. Henker was pleased he had foreseen most events, even if Tlúnëe had not. He surmised some events were foreseen by the dragons alone and no other prophet.

As they ate and spoke, in another part of the city argued Bahvley and Tharguen. Early that morning, Tharguen had gone to the Royal Halls.

'We cannot wait for them anymore! As far as we know, they could be dead.' His voice cracked at the thought. He clenched his jaw. 'We can't let too much time go by – we haven't got that time. Mork's power is growing. Mirauk's armies are increasing. The codes are changing, and the patrolling armies will spread. It will become nearly impossible for us to voyage anywhere for any purpose, let alone for any of our allies to come to our aid.'

'Then I may just have to double my archers on the wall. What else do you want me to do?!' protested Bahvley. 'Send armies out to intercept all of the Morkan armies?' He pinched the bridge of his brow. 'Caring for a kingdom is so complicated. Perhaps because it's taking care of so many lives.'

'What happened to your previous plans, Bahvley? The ones where you said Teloria would move one way, Firlan would be on that side of the Ortim River, and the Dalvarans would attack one side of Mork. You had everything figured out.'

'Plans change, Tharguen! I think you know that as well as I do!' Bahvley lowered his voice. 'I think we both learned that the first time we entered Mork.' He sighed, raising his voice again. 'You'd think fifty years away from Teloria would have taught us a lesson.'

'You don't have to shout that loud. Mirauk doesn't need to hear you.' Tharguen folded his arms.

'Sometimes I wish he could so that he'd know how angry I am.' Bahvley leaned forward. 'He took my sister and my brother away from me.'

'He took the one person I love away from me!' Tharguen mimicked the posture. 'You're not the only one to feel the way that you do.'

'At least the person you love didn't die in your arms!' cried Bahvley.

'It's better for someone to die in your arms than for someone to die while away, out of sight.' Tharguen's tone was compassionate. 'I know that they're still alive, though. I just do, even though I said they could be dead.'

'I know . . . I feel it too. But how do you explain what I felt that night, too long ago for me to remember exactly when? That strange, unexplainable anxiety, as if something terrible had happened to one of them! If one of them dies, the Star dies.'

'I don't know how you felt that. I can't even explain how that letter got to me, the one from the wind.'

The two fell silent.

'If you think about it, Bahvley, Mirauk took us away, too.'

'I know. I . . . I wish Phynd were here. I wonder what's taking him so long.'

'Maybe he's preparing more Kikies than necessary so that Mirauk, however he estimates their numbers, will have underestimated. I trust in Captain Phynd.'

A knock came at the office door.

'What?!' demanded Bahvley.

Dex entered.

'Excuse me, but there is something interesting in the air.'

'There always is,' sighed Bahvley.

'Let him talk,' said Tharguen. 'Dex knows some magic.'

'Well, I can't determine what, but the birds are stirring excitedly. Magic is approaching.'

'Is it good or evil?' asked Tharguen.

'I cannot tell,' replied Dex. 'I just thought I'd let you know.' The Doorward began out again.

'I'm sorry, Dex,' said Bahvley. 'Thank you.'

Dex nodded and left.

'That strange woman, the one who disappeared,' concluded Tharguen.

'If the birds are anxious, then whatever magic it is, it's close,' said Bahvley, 'very close. I just hope it's not another one of Mirauk's tricks . . . or hers.'

'It's been a while since I ate this well,' said Meysah contentedly, patting his belly.

'You make it sound like you haven't eaten a proper meal in the past five years,' Jimmy chided with a playful grin.

'You know what I mean. Since we left the Twisted Forest.'

'*I* know what you mean,' said Jimmy, 'but someone else might not.'

Selemil laughed. 'Grown polcs, still as playful as when they were children. It is refreshing to see.'

The Five stood.

'Well,' said Vigh, 'we hate to leave you, but duty calls at the Royal Halls.'

'Your impatience has decreased, Meysah,' Selemil joked. 'Your Master speaks of going before you do.'

'Oh, no, it hasn't. I may look calm on the outside, but I'm ready to try to *fly* to Bahvley's.'

After a few quick farewells, the Five made their way towards the Royal Halls.

'You think we'll bump into Lóim along the way?' inquired Jimmy.

'It seems to be a tradition now,' said Vigh.

Meysah felt that small surge of excitement at the thought. 'I certainly wouldn't mind this time.'

'Nor would I,' said Jimmy. 'He's become our friend, and we his. I think I appreciate him.'

'Appreciate,' Meysah repeated softly.

Niome turned to urge the others on. 'You're all so slow! We need to get there *today*!'

Grinning with eagerness, the Five hurried on. By evening, they had reached the Royal Halls. They noticed that many Telorians in the market and the square near the Halls were busy in their shops, focused on their tasks. Teloria was preparing.

When Dex opened the double doors to the Royal Halls, he exclaimed in relief, 'Bless the Stars! I'm practically gasping here. I felt your magic, but try to explain that to the two most stubborn polcs in Kaulchèc History.'

'Hello, Dex,' laughed Niome. 'It's good to see you, too. So Bahvley and Tharguen are discussing?'

'"Discussing" is not the word *I* would use. Arguing, more like. They've been at it all day. "We're not waiting for their return!" "But what are we really to do?" It's become redundant. I worry sometimes for their state of mind.'

'Can you take us to them?' Meysah asked the young Doorward.

'Oh, that I can.' Dex began to lead them to the Royal Office. 'They kicked me out before. They'll slam the door on me next.'

'Don't worry about that now,' Niome reassured.

'Niome.' Dex stopped and turned to her. 'They were starting to run out of probable stories to tell to explain your absence. People started worrying and suspecting. I'm the only one, aside from them, who knew what happened to you at the river. They didn't even tell Henker! And there was a strange woman, too.'

'It's as I suspected, then. Mirauk is hiding someone here. I believe there is a Morkan spy in Teloria. And she, this lady, might be it.'

'Indeed there is, but the Kikies have searched everywhere after Bahvley first did himself.' Dex bade the Five wait in the plush chairs of the lounge area. Walking through the corridor, he approached the office door again and pushed it ajar. 'Good news!' he announced.

'Out! Now!' shouted Bahvley, shutting the door.

Dex returned to the Five. 'Can you wait a while?'

'Just the other day, you were insisting that we wait a little longer,' argued Bahvley. 'I'm not the only one here who's changing his mind! So don't you dare tell me I keep contradicting myself.'

'But you're not listening to me—'

'By kurssus, I am! You're the one who's not listening to me!'

Tharguen raised his hands in defeat. 'We're never going to get anywhere arguing like this!'

Bahvley glared at Tharguen from where he stood behind his desk. 'You weren't always like this.'

'What?'

'You're lucky you're my friend, because as the *King*, I could do anything I wanted – but I listen to you because you're my friend and I respect you. Though sometimes it seems you've taken on some Morkan traits.'

'Thanks,' Tharguen replied with sarcasm in his voice. 'We're actually worse than Jimmy and Meysah. Should I remind you that before running into your army of Kikies, they actually had a fight and weren't talking to each other for days? *They* are lucky they weren't separated as we were. They could resolve their conflict then. We never did. You'd think fifty years in Kikiland would give you more . . . Kikiness, but you're just as closed-minded when you choose to be.'

'I beg your pardon!'

'Listen to me, Bahvley!' Tharguen slammed his hands down on the desk. 'And wake up. The Five may not come back. Face the truth!' He leaned towards Bahvley, glaring, before his expression turned sorrowful. He took a breath before continuing in a calmer tone.

'What if . . .' He paused for a beat. 'We were gone fifty years, unplanned but for the better, and it was meant to be and we survived. I was giving orders – you were with the happiest of folks. They thought we were dead! What if they're gone that long, too? We may think they're dead, but I know from experience that it may be in the stars and for their growth. So, it's our turn to keep faith in Teloria. Bahvley, put aside your worries—'

'Like you're one to talk—'

'And feel them!' Tharguen raised his voice to continue. 'Feel the Five. *You* can do that – you have a special connection with Niome, because you're her brother.'

'You, too, have a special connection because of your love,' stated Bahvley. He scowled, changing his tone abruptly. 'Wait, you think I'm closed-minded?' Tharguen rolled his eyes at him. 'How many times was I forced to change views or to adapt?' Tharguen sighed. 'I'm not the only polc in Teloria with a closed mind.'

'Oh, and I suppose I have a closed mind, too.'

'Yes!' exclaimed Bahvley. 'What exactly did you mean by "we never resolved" our conflict? We resolved it. We reconciled our grievances and apologised, so don't bring things back to that now. Don't rehash what's already been resolved.'

'But you're doing it again now!' insisted Tharguen with a plea in his tone. 'You only see things your way! You think that it's done one way and only that way! You wanted to go into Mork your way, and you didn't stop to think about other people's suggestions. The dangers that were going to come of it. You listened, but you disregarded them. Even Elina tried to warn you.'

'You too! You wanted to enter Mork your way! Perhaps we both think our way's the best, but don't put the blame on me for the deaths of our team.'

'That's not what I meant!' Tharguen seethed. 'I meant that you didn't want to understand how I was feeling! Do you understand?'

'Not quite.'

'I'm not trying to rehash – I know we did resolve this. So please, don't be like that again. Don't disregard me.'

'I'm not disregarding you!' cried Bahvley. 'So don't bring it back to then. And so what if I'm acting like a King?'

'Bahvley!'

'Tharguen!' Bahvley glared, discouraged. This conversation was going nowhere. He had to get out.

He went to the door and opened it, pausing. 'I need some air,' he said softly, then left the room.

Tharguen went after him, intercepting him just outside the office.

'Think of the people of this kingdom! Think of us and the Kikies and my team, Selemil, Henker – they need answers! They need the truth.'

'I am not telling them what truly happened,' insisted Bahvley, slamming the door. 'They don't need to know about this tragedy, or that their King has been lying to them for the past five years. And *we* don't need to encourage that old spy!'

Out in the hall, Dex and the Five heard Bahvley and Tharguen's argument as the two started down the corridor at a fast pace in the opposite direction of where the Five waited with Dex.

Instinctively, the Five rose and hurried towards their arguing friends.

'We can't wait anymore. That's all I was saying before!' insisted Tharguen. 'We can't let the enemy gain on us. We can't let the days go by and let time and worry eat us up inside. Look at what it's doing to *us*!' As he marched beside Bahvley, Tharguen gesticulated between them. 'There isn't any time left. We have to take action.'

'And what are we supposed to do now?!' shouted Bahvley, raising his hands in defeat.

'Attack Mork!'

Halting, Tharguen and Bahvley both froze.

A soft, gentle, soothing voice had spoken in a firm and inspiring tone.

For a heartbeat, Tharguen believed he was going mad, but when he looked at Bahvley, he realised he, too, had heard it.

They slowly turned – their heads first, then their whole bodies – to face the five Telorians, who stood in their Star formation.

'Niome!' both Tharguen and Bahvley exclaimed, but so surprised were they, barely any sound came out, their voices mere whispers.

'Or at least *prepare* to attack Mork,' continued Niome.

Bahvley and Tharguen stood frozen, dumbstruck.

'Is it you? Are you really here?' Tharguen's voice cracked.

'Of course,' said Jimmy. 'Flesh and blood, right here. See?' He pinched Meysah.

'Ouch!' complained Meysah, scowling.

'There's your proof. Why wouldn't it be us?'

Bahvley laughed through the fresh tears that ran down his cheeks. He brought a hand to his mouth, attempting to hold back the sob that escaped him.

Tharguen stood in stark shock. He stared at Niome before slowly moving towards her.

'So many times have I woken up at night, heard your voice, and seen you lying next to me, Niome. And gone to reach for you only to discover that it was an illusion.' He stopped before her, eyes wide and welling with tears.

Niome held out her hand. 'You can reach out to me now,' she said gently. 'I won't fade. I'm staying.'

Tharguen took Niome's hand, and a sob escaped him. With his thumb, he rubbed the ring Niome wore, the ring he had given her when he expressed wanting to bind their love in marriage.

'I never forgot you,' said Niome. 'Just like I promised.'

'Neither did I,' said Tharguen.

Tharguen pulled Niome to him and took her in his arms, holding her tightly. Her eyes began to water.

'I love you,' wept Tharguen as he held her.

Niome tightened their embrace. Their lips met for a fiery kiss filled with longing and relief, as though they had finally come up for air and felt their chests unclench as breath filled their lungs anew. They both gasped, equally unwilling to part.

The others averted their attention to give the two reunited lovers some privacy. Jimmy turned to the Lords, feeling it was the appropriate place to direct his attention.

Bahvley stood in a state of wonderment and joy. Meysah walked up to him and put his hand on his shoulder.

'You don't have to hide how you feel anymore,' Meysah said softly. 'You never were alone. I know you felt alone. Niome will teach you to use the power that's in you, as she's showing me. It's in our blood. We have part of it, whether we want it or not. And Bahvley, soon enough, we will regain the Freedom of Life.'

'Thank you,' whispered Bahvley as he pulled his brother into a warm embrace. His tears fell on Meysah's shoulder.

Hands interlaced, Tharguen and Niome rejoined the group.

Meysah pointed at them. 'Look, they've paused for air.'

Bahvley could not help but chuckle. The Telorian King took a step back and observed the Five.

'You look older, brother. Handsomer, like me.' He grinned. 'You don't know how much it means for you to be home.'

'You have no idea how much it means to be back,' claimed Meysah.

'So many times have I come so close to leaving,' admitted Bahvley, 'and letting Mirauk know what he did when he took you away from us with his cruel magic.'

The Five shifted awkwardly, glancing at each other.

'Actually,' began Vigh, breaking the silence, 'Mirauk didn't take us away. We chose to go where we went. It was to protect you and ourselves that we never told you.'

'I'm sorry it caused such grief, let alone a fight between us,' Niome added quickly, turning to Bahvley. 'I did see things through the Dukes' eyes, and I did want to tell you.'

'But the drought!' exclaimed Tharguen.

'Mirauk had nothing to do with that. He took advantage of it for the fire, but . . . I created that drought.' Niome downcast her eyes. 'I'm sorry we caused you so much sorrow.'

'It's okay,' said Bahvley, wrapping his arms around his sister.

'It was to protect ourselves from the phantoms, the blood-suckers that came after us. Those *sarikh-pekamav*, as Mirauk calls them' – Niome shivered – 'caused a lot of trouble, even if certain outcomes were meant to be.' She stepped back. 'I'm sure things could have happened a little differently.'

'I'm relieved we destroyed most of them,' expressed Tharguen.

'It was a fright to remember them, though,' Bahvley added.

'Yes, the Firlanians shared the story with us,' Vigh confirmed.

'I reckon the remaining phantom returned to its Lord in Mork,' mused Bahvley.

Niome winced. 'It didn't exactly forget who it was hunting.'

'It was the reason why we were away for so long,' said Jimmy. 'Partly.'

Tharguen leaned forward, taking on a defensive tone. 'Did it harm any of you?'

'Yes. Me,' Niome declared. Tharguen and Bahvley both gasped.

As briefly as could be managed, Niome explained what had happened and the abilities she had gained as a result.

'Mirauk is one confused polc right now,' she said as the group turned and strolled towards the sitting area around the hearth. 'By rights, I should have died. Instead, I present a stronger front against him, and he hates that. I instinctively protected some secrets that the phantom could not gain from me, and Mirauk hates that even more.'

'You were separated from the other four!' Tharguen was stupefied, his grip on her hand tightening pro-tectively. 'Then where *were* you?'

Niome explained where she had stayed and how she was well taken care of.

Bahvley, in turn, shared some of the goings-on in Teloria. 'You've been gone for . . .'

'Five years,' Niome said, overlapping with Bahvley as he said the same. 'We've been separated exactly that long.'

The group sat down on the plush chairs and couches, the conversation turning to the mysterious old woman.

'I'll send my army after her,' said Tharguen. 'I just need to know where she's hiding.'

'Leave that to us,' said Niome. 'Another mission awaits you.'

'What other mission?' asked Tharguen, confused.

'The one I must task you with,' answered Niome. 'Mirauk wants to double his patrolling armies.'

'I knew it!' Tharguen gave Bahvley a knowing look.

'He wants to spread them across the lands,' Niome continued. 'This will weaken Dalvar further and test Dûnelor's magic, as well as Firlan's.' She squeezed Tharguen's hand. 'You're the only one who knows how to get by them unnoticed, how to recognise their patterns, how to understand their language. I've considered sending Nsarmön, but the best candidate to deal with this, whether I like it or not, is you.'

Tharguen placed a hand on Niome's face. 'But I don't want to be separated from you again. I know you have to stay here.'

'Bahvley has to stay, too.'

'Why can't I assist Tharguen?' demanded Bahvley.

'We need you here to help prepare the attack against Mork,' explained Niome. 'Your kingdom needs you.'

'You don't have to leave yet,' Vigh reassured Tharguen.

'Yet I know I'll have to go soon if we *are* to help Dalvar,' conceded Tharguen. He sighed, passing a hand through his hair. 'It's true. I know everything that is Morkan, whether I like it or not. It was a part of me for so long. I'm the only one who can think like a Morkan and predict their next moves.' Resigned, he nodded. 'I will leave for Dalvar as soon as you wish me to, Niome.'

Niome leaned into him as Tharguen wrapped his arms around her more protectively.

'We're together now. That's what counts!' said Jimmy.

Everyone paused, but there was so much more to discuss.

'I'll have Dex ask—'

'The cook to prepare tea for everyone,' finished Dex as he marched to the group and clasped his hands behind his back. 'It's already done.' He hesitated. 'May I ask if I might join you as you continue to share your tale?'

Bahvley smiled warmly. 'Make sure to bring an extra cup of tea for yourself, Dex.'

'Where shall we begin?' asked Niome as tea and snacks were brought out for them.

Dex took a seat near Bahvley as the group relaxed into more casual conversation, now that they had covered the most vital and could launch into their personal anecdotes.

'Perhaps, my dear sister, you could begin with what you had refused to tell me in Dûnelor, despite me demanding it of you as the King of Teloria,' Bahvley requested, a playful glint in his eyes.

Filled with relief, the group shared their stories, musing how even when written in the prophecies, they still held the power to change the outcomes by their choices.

'There is still so much to do to prepare for the final battle in this war,' sighed Bahvley. 'It is overwhelming.'

'And you and Tharguen both are as important as us five,' confirmed Niome, 'in terms of magic. We Fairhavens especially hold a magical bond like no other. Both you and Meysah felt it when the phantom struck me – it is in our blood. I may be the middle child, where our family's magical bloodline is the most concentrated, but that does not mean magic cannot thrive in each of you the same way it does in me. That is why you survived the phantom as well, Bahvley.'

'I know.' Bahvley could feel the magic in him stirring. 'That is why I must remain in Teloria, while Tharguen's magic will serve him at Dalvar.'

'You see, you can sense Tharguen's magic, too, even if it's more subdued than it is in the rest of us. Ever wonder why Tharguen was never tempted by evil magic all those years he was in Mork?'

'Never did I wonder,' declared Tharguen. 'The answer was laid before me every single day. I was never tempted, though it had crossed my mind to use evil as a means to get out of Mork if I had no other choice. Instead, I used the evil of others to my advantage and utilised my Telorian traits to mine.'

'All that both of you have survived,' Niome went on, 'it's because of the magic that's in both of you. You have the strength to fight, to survive, and to grow. Anyone else, under the same circumstances the two of you were faced with, could have – and almost certainly would have – died.'

'So now that we realise our importance to the fate of Teloria . . .' began Bahvley.

'You must realise the things that are left to be done,' said Niome.

'It's not just fighting armies of Morkans and destroying the most powerful Morkans that will restore the Freedom of Life,' surmised Tharguen. 'It's not just defending the rest of polcs and helping them. It's not to rid the world of evil polcs completely.'

'It's to help others understand how important it is to let compassion reign in our hearts,' concluded Bahvley. 'Another reason why I must stay. To show courage, hope, belief, and love to the people of Teloria. Let us hope we are well prepared for what comes next.'

'I know I am,' declared Tharguen, shifting to kneel before Niome.

Meysah nudged Bahvley, grinning at the scene. He whispered, 'It's the moment we've all been waiting for.'

'Niome,' said Tharguen. 'I know I can ask you properly now. Before I go to Dalvar, while we are together, and while we can . . .' He paused, his eyes earnest. 'Will you marry me?'

'I will.' Niome beamed at Tharguen.

Tharguen leaned his forehead on Niome's, his grin as wide as hers. They kissed, laughing in joy with their dearest friends all the while.

Niome cupped Tharguen's face. 'In terms of magical things to come, are you ready for the future?'

'I believe the question is,' said Bahvley, 'is the future ready for us?'

TO BE CONTINUED

<u>THANK YOU SO MUCH FOR READING!</u>

*If you enjoyed this book,
please consider taking a few moments
to write a review on Amazon or Goodreads.
It would mean so much.*

*Thank you.
May the stars shine upon you!*

THE JOURNEY CONTINUES

*A mystery and spy keep Bahvley and the Five
in Teloria to strive to find this hidden menace.*

*Tharguen and his small army travel to Dalvar.
However, when Tharguen is captured
by the Dukes of Mork,
his death becomes imminent.*

<u>Map of the Great Ocean Valley</u>

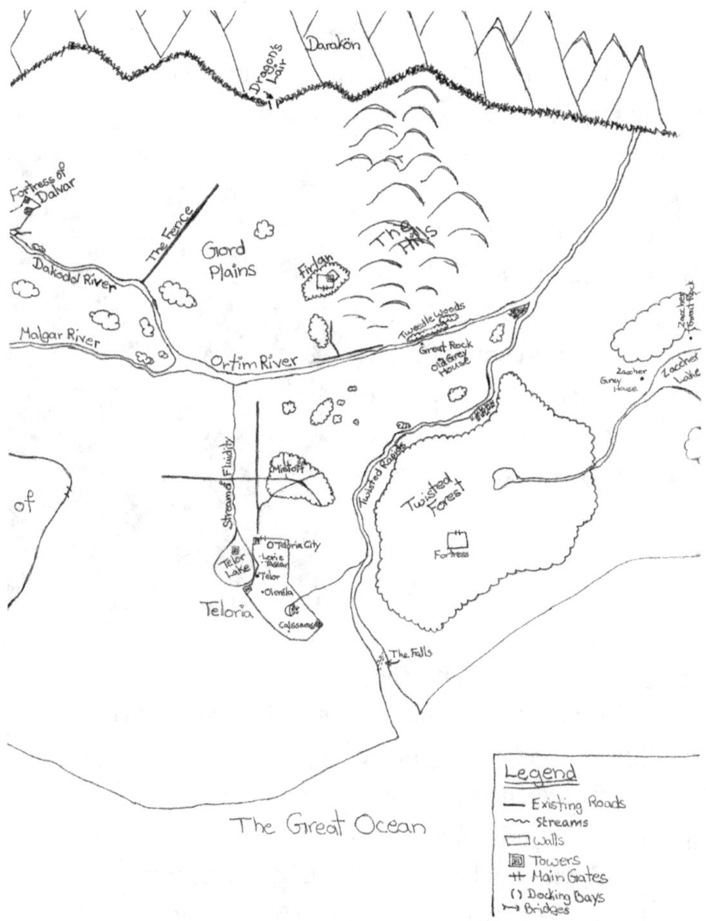

Darakön
Dragon's Lair
Fortress of Dalvar
The Fence
Giord Plains
Firlan
The Hills
Dakodal River
Malgar River
Ortim River
Tweedle Woods
Great Rock
Old Grey House
Zacher Forest Rock
Zacher Grey House
Zacchar Lake
Stream of Fluidity
Misthoff
Twisted Roads
Twisted Forest
Fortress
O Teloria City
Loris Tagar
Telor
Olenia
Telor Lake
Teloria
Calssanar
The Falls
of
The Great Ocean
Legend
Existing Roads
Streams
Walls
Towers
Main Gates
( ) Docking Bays
Bridges

About The Author

Celinka Serre is an indie writer and video producer working in freelance and sharing short stories of various genres, as well as anecdotes, on Medium. She believes in the freedom of creativity and always continues to pursue her dreams. Having begun *Stardust Destinies* at age 19, the novel series is but one of her many projects, being also a writer of fan-fiction, various indie film screenplays, and a few collaborations as well.

Wordpress Website and Blog:
>   https://binkyproductions.com/binkyinkwriting

Medium - Stardust Destinies Extras:
>   https://medium.com/stardust-destinies

Medium - Main Profile:
>   https://medium.com/@binkyinkwriting

Twitter: https://twitter.com/binkyinkwriting